N

E

W

S

Constantinople

N E A N S E A

Damascus

Acre

Jerusalem

Damietta

Cairo

RO DI DONATI

1250 A.D.

THE SARACEN BLADE

Other Novels by Frank Yerby

THE FOXES OF HARROW

THE VIXENS

THE GOLDEN HAWK

PRIDE'S CASTLE

FLOODTIDE

A WOMAN CALLED FANCY

A Novel by FRANK YERBY

THE SARACEN BLADE

Dial Press New York • 1952

Library of Congress Catalog Card Number: 52-5616

DESIGNED BY WILLIAM R. MEINHARDT

Printed in the United States of America
By The Haddon Craftsmen, Inc., Scranton, Pa.

*". . . . Dissemi: Qui con piu di mille giaccio:
Qua entro e lo secondo Federico. . . ."*

Dante
The Inferno
Canto X

". . . . He answer thus return'd: 'More than a thousand with me here are laid, within is Frederick, second of that name . . .' "

THE SARACEN BLADE

Prologue

Part 1 HELLEMARK

FROM WHERE THEY STOOD, they could see the castle. The clouds were behind it, and when the first light came up out of the Adriatic, it got into the clouds, making them luminous, so that they could see the towers and battlements still black, but separated a little from the blackness behind them. The light was very pale at first, but after a little it began to get color into it, and Hellemark, the castle, greyed out of the purple clouds, brightening minute by minute as they watched, until its stones were grey yellow and the sun was up.

"Come," Donati said.

Maria didn't move or answer him. He looked from her to her parents. They were very old, and very dirty. Yesterday that would have meant nothing to Donati, but today he was conscious of it, because this morning he had taken the second all over bath he had had in his whole life. After all, this was an occasion. Getting married was a thing a man usually did only once. And what he had to do this morning was even more important than the wedding itself, because unless the Baron approved of his choice, he wouldn't be able to get married at all.

He remembered what Baron Rudolph had said, and reddened to the ears at the thought of it.

"Before God!" the Baron had bellowed, "I'll not have the best armorer in the Empire ruined by some tavern wench! Fetch the strumpet before me, and then we'll see. . . ."

Such words to use of Maria. A little knot of muscle formed above his jaw, and jerked. Maria squeezed his hand a little.

"It's all right, Donati," she said; "I won't be afraid. . . ."

Donati took her arm and they started off up the steep path that led to the castle. The old ones came more slowly. Donati didn't know how old Maria's parents were, but he guessed they were both above forty. He must marry her soon, because they couldn't be expected to live many more years, and so fair a maid needed protection. . . . He'd once heard of a vassal on a neighboring fief who'd reached fifty years, but he didn't believe it. Only nobles and priests lived that long.

As they wound up the path that twisted back and forth between the holdings of Rudolph von Brandenburg, Baron Rogliano's serfs, Maria looked at Donati. She did it very quickly and shyly, with a birdlike movement of her head, so that he wouldn't see it. He was very fine, and Maria loved him very much. In the back part of her mind, she always thought of him as her knight. It was a daring way to think because peasant girls weren't supposed to have knights. But Donati didn't look like a peasant. In the first place, he was very big, towering head and shoulders over all the other men she knew; in the second, his skin was very white, and his hair was blond.

His mother had named him Donati. But Maria knew very well he should have been called Hugh, or Gautier, or Jean—or some other such Norman name. Because his father must have been a Norman knight; that was the only way to account for Donati's looks. Of course his mother had sinned grievously; but Maria was secretly glad of that sin—else she would have had to content herself with some black thatched, brown youth, squat, greasy, and smelling forever of sweat and cattle dung.

How fine Donati was! He had combed and plaited his long hair into braids which he wound around his head, and carefully parted and turfed his great beard, which always looked like it had sunlight tangled in it, into separate ringlets, and tied each ringlet with bright colored thread, after the fashion of the Normans. He had put on a good woolen suit, of rough blue cloth, and affixed copper earrings in his ears.

They weren't very far from the castle, but it was going to take them a long time to get there. Each villein held so little land from the Baron that he was unwilling to have any of it taken away to be used as a path. And none of the villein's holdings were in one place. Every morning all the serfs had to get up in pitch darkness, and start out, working one by one the little patches of earth that were scattered all over the great fief without rhyme or reason.

So the path had to wind between the holdings, and Donati and his Maria had to walk nearly five miles to reach the castle perched on a hill barely a mile away. It was hard going, especially for the old ones; but Donati was content. It gave him more time to gaze at Maria.

She was little and dark, and all her movements were quick, like a bird's. She had on a green bliaut, or blouse, embroidered with gold thread. The bliaut had a history. It had been given to her grandmother by Yvonne, the late Baroness of Rogliano, when Rogliano had been a Norman fief, before the Germans came. Donati guessed that there must be a barony somewhere in Italy that was held by an Italian; but offhand, he didn't know of any. He didn't think about it too much, anyway; it made precious little difference to a villein whether a fief was held by Italian, Norman or German; the kicks and cuffs he got daily remained the same—except, maybe, the Germans could kick harder, being bigger and stronger.

He moved closer to Maria, so that he could smell the wild flowers she had twined in her black hair. He could smell her, too. She smelled like the petals of roses. Donati knew why. Lucia, Maria's mother, had told him.

"Donati, the girl is daft! Every fortnight, and sometimes oftener, she bathes all over—in hot water, mind you—and with flower petals in it. When you wed, you must promise me to stop her—else she'll be too weakened to bear you fine sons . . ."

But, Donati reflected, it felt strangely fine to be clean. His skin tingled. He looked at the parents of his bride to be. Giovanni, the tanner of the fief, and Lucia his wife, had merely passed a damp rag over their faces in honor of the occasion. The clothing they wore, rough woolens that served them weekdays and sabbath alike, were all they owned. What color the loose tunics had been originally, neither of them remembered; now they were the color of the dirt with which they were filled, and crawling with vermin.

They were close to the castle now—so close that they could see the corpses of the three villeins, hanging from the battlements on gallows swung out over the moat. The Baron's foresters had caught them taking hares with nets in his wood, so he had hanged them. It had been a very cold and wet spring and none of the serfs had gotten enough to eat. So several of them had taken up poaching.

Donati looked up at the bodies swinging on the ends of the chains. He had known all three of them. They had been stout fellows, good companions. He looked at them now, turning slowly in the little breeze. They had been up there a fortnight, and the crows had been at them. They weren't pretty.

Maria buried her face against the rough cloth of his sleeve and shuddered. Donati felt the little knot of muscle on the side of his face jerking again, as it always did when something moved him. He had the feeling that something must be wrong with a world where a single mangy rabbit could cost the lives of three men. But he didn't know precisely what.

His brain didn't work that well, or that clearly. Every ounce of intelligence within him was concentrated in his hands. Baron Rudolph called them a gift from the Angels, for with them Donati could fashion wondrous things. No man in Italy, or both the Sicilies could make a finer shirt of chain mail than he; none could bring a helmet to that bluish sheen, or to that hardness that could turn the edge of any blade. For that reason, the Baron valued him, and was even kind to him in a rough fashion.

They moved on then, all four of them, walking a little quicker, and went across the drawbridge over the moat. The portcullis was up so they went under it even faster, glancing up at the sharp spikes on the bottom of it ready to impale any foeman when this iron-barred raised gate was let fall. Behind the portcullis, the oaken main gates were still closed, but the porter opened a smaller gate cut through one of the main gates itself, and let them in. The porter knew Donati well. All the vassals did.

Maria had never been inside the castle before. She was astonished that even after they had passed within the walls there were more gates and other walls and towers. But Baron Rogliano knew defensive warfare. With a hundred men at arms, he could hold Hellemark against twenty times that number, so cunningly was it built.

They had come by now into the bailey, that broad courtyard just outside the castle proper. Maria put her hands to her ears. There was so much noise! Pigs squealed, dogs barked, children screamed with laughter. In the long lines of stables hard by the wall, the Baron's horses stamped their shod feet and neighed. Children, a little less dirty than those Maria saw in her own village, played in the haystacks next to the stables, and beyond that the second armorer hammered the links for a shirt of mail while beside him the smith shoed my lady's palfrey.

Donati led her over to the smithy, and presented her to these two who served as his assistants. They snatched off their leather caps and bowed to her as though she were a lady, and stood at respectful attention while Donati showed her the vast quantities of swords, lance heads, crossbow bolts and helmets and shields that he had made for the Baron.

Clearly a personage of importance, this husband to be of hers. Maria shivered a little with joy at her good fortune. Now she would live within the bailey, perhaps even rise to serve the Gentle Baroness as a maidservant—which was an advancement over her former state beyond any dreams she had ever had.

They came out of the smithy and rejoined Lucia and Giovanni, and moved on, pausing once again at the mews to watch the chief falconer feed raw meat to the hawks, who screamed like all the fiends in hell. Then past the chapel—far more beautiful than the church in the village, with finer windows, stained in richer, deeper colors—until they came at last into the inner court where the Baron's living quarters were, and the great tower called the donjon, the final extremity of defense.

Donati walked up to the door of the palais, but there the assurance and the swagger that had been his in the bailey, deserted him. He knocked so faintly that Maria was sure that she could have made more noise herself.

It was much cleaner in the inner court, and the vassals here all wore the scarlet and gold livery of the Roglianos. But none of them seemed to treat Donati with the respect due his position. Maria pouted a little.

Giuliano, the Baron's provost came to the door. He stifled a yawn with the back of his hand; then he looked at Donati and started laughing.

"Well now, Donati!" he roared. "My God, but you're fine! What nice curly whiskers—with ribbons in them, too! What's that? My Lord Baron expects you? To be sure—and His Holiness, the Pope, as well, no doubt. Be off with you, you great oaf, before I take a stave to you!"

Donati stood his ground.

"No, good provost," he said in that curiously gentle bass voice of his, "I'm telling the truth. Go and ask him. He'll tell you he told me to come. . . ."

Giuliano stopped laughing and eyed Donati.

"Why?" he demanded. "Baron Rudolph doesn't send for anyone without a good reason. I'll have to know why, before I'll risk disturbing him at breakfast."

Donati took Maria by the arm and drew her forward.

"This is why," he said. "I'm only trying to get married. For God's sake, Giuliano, go and see—no harm can come of asking. . . ."

"Plenty of harm can come of asking Baron Rudolph anything whatsoever when he doesn't feel like being asked," Giuliano said drily, "up to and including a couple of broken ribs. You know that, Donati. All right, all right! I'll risk it. I'm sick of that silly, moonstruck expression on your stupid face. Besides he's in a good humor this morning . . . Wait here."

He came back after a moment and told them to come in. But there was still more waiting. From where they were they could hear the Baron in the dining room. He had a voice like a bull's. He was talking to the Baroness in German. Donati was glad of that. After several years of being cuffed and kicked because he didn't understand it, the meaning of the words had finally penetrated his thick skull. Now he understood it well, although he could never manage to speak more than six words of it at a time without sending the Teutonic knights off into gales of laughter.

Donati looked at Maria. No, it was clear that she understood not one word of that heavy tongue. That was good. For the Baron was telling his lady some jokes of so coarse a nature as to redden the ears of a stablekeeper. The Baroness laughed with evident enjoyment, then replied with a story that was worse than the one her lord had told her.

Donati stood there, blushing furiously.

Giuliano peeked through the doorway, and seeing that the gentlefolk had come by now to the sweetmeats, tiptoed in and whispered into the Baron's ear.

"Send them in!" Rudolph roared; "I must see the wench!"

Donati went in, then, leading Maria by one finger, which was a courtesy he had copied from the gentlefolk. The Baron's great boarhound got up from amid the rushes under the table where he and several other dogs had been gnawing the bones tossed them by the Baron after he had finished gnawing them himself. Donati noticed that the chamber stank. The rushes and reeds that covered the stone floor had not been changed in a year, and the animals had plentifully supplied them with fleas and other vermin. On a perch near the door, the Baron's gyrfalcon screamed, and his lady's sparrow hawk, and her parrots, brought her by a Saracen mountebank from the Southern coast of Sicily, didn't add to the aroma, splattering the floor beneath their perches with their droppings.

It was full daylight now but pine torches smeared with pitch, flared, sending up clouds of foul smelling smoke, for castles were built for defense, not for light and air.

Baron Rogliano gave one look at Maria, standing there with downcast gaze, and got to his feet. He lurched toward her, as usual much the worse for drink, and lifted her chin with one huge, greasy hand.

"By God!" he bellowed, "a pretty wench—eh, Brigarde? Look at her features, wife—by Saint Hildebrand, I'd swear she isn't baseborn!"

The Baroness shrugged.

"She's as dark as a Moor," she said tartly, "I'll wager her mother was more than a little friendly with a heathen Saracen."

Donati looked at Maria's mother. The old woman flushed a little under her tan, but the Baroness paid her no attention.

"My Lord tells me," she said to Donati, "that you want to get married. Now I know why my gelding has cast three shoes in a fortnight. Your mind was upon other things, eh, Donati?"

"Your pardon, gracious lady," Donati whispered.

"Oh, I forgive you," the Lady Brigarde laughed. "I don't think much of your choice, though. You'll never get sturdy sons from such a skinny wench. What will we do for smiths if your sons inherit her limbs instead of yours?"

"For heaven's sakes, Brigarde, stop plaguing the lad," the Baron said. "I like her looks. But marriage is a serious step; I'd better question her a bit. What's your name, child?"

"Maria," the girl whispered.

"Maria—a good name. I hope you bear it well, for it graced the Mother of Our Lord. Do you go often to hear mass sung?"

"Every Sabbath, and all feast days," Maria said, "and early masses, too, sometimes before going to the fields. . . ."

"Well spoken," the Baron growled. "And you make your confession to the good father on Friday, and partake often of Our Lord's Body and Blood?"

"Yes, my Lord," Maria said.

Rudolph leaned forward so that his heavy face was close to Maria's.

"You're still virgin?" he whispered, in that deep throated bull's bellow that served him for a whisper.

Maria stiffened, turned white.

"Yes, my Lord," she said; "though that my Lord needs ask it pains me to my heart."

"One never knows," the Baron growled. "These days all the young are headed straight for purgatory—and I include many gently born."

He glared at Maria's parents, standing mutely behind the young couple.

"The wench is telling the truth?" he roared at them.

"Yes, my Lord," they quavered.

"Very well," Baron Rudolph said. "I grant you two permission to wed. Let the ceremony take place in my chapel this coming Sabbath, with Father Antonio presiding. And I will honor you,

Donati, with my presence. For, by God's Own Blood, you've served me well!"

"Thank you, my Lord," Donati said; then he and Maria kissed the hand that the Baron extended to them. The Baron even went so far as to walk with them into the hall and bid them Godspeed, which was a courtesy usually reserved only for those of his own rank. But just before they were out of range of his big voice, he turned to Giuliano and said:

"A comely wench, eh, provost? I've a good mind to invoke my *ius primae noctis* . . ."[1]

Giuliano laughed.

"I'm afraid, my Lord, that Donati has scant means with which to redeem his bride," he said.

"Who cares for his coppers?" the Baron bellowed. "The girl's good looking. She has a nice face, and her figure's not bad either. I'll hold to the letter of the law, Giuliano."

Giuliano looked worried.

"It'll cause trouble, my Lord," he said. "No one in these parts has invoked the *ius* these last hundred years."

"I am Baron here!" Rudolph roared; "I shall invoke it!"

Maria looked at Donati.

"What on earth is he talking about?" she whispered.

"I don't know," Donati said; "but I don't like the sound of it. It's Latin, that I know. . . ." He twisted his face with concentration and repeated the words over and over again: *"Ius primae noctis, Ius primae noctis, Ius . . ."*

"Why do you keep saying it, Donati?" Maria said.

"So that I can fix it in mind. Then when I see Father Antonio, I will say it to him and he will tell me what it means. . . ."

"Then you'll come and tell me?" Maria begged.

"Of course, Little Bird," Donati said.

But it wasn't until the middle of the next day that he finally saw Padre Antonio crossing the bailey. He went up to the priest, cap in hand, and stood before him.

[1] For this and all other footnotes, see pages 393-406.

Father Antonio smiled up at this huge, childlike barbarian.

"Well, Donati?" he said, "I hear that you're taking Maria to wife. A good choice, my son. She's a sweet and gentle child. She'll be good for you . . ."

"Thank you, Father," Donati said. "Father. . . ."

"Yes, Donati?"

"What means—*Ius—Ius primae noctis*?"

Father Antonio stared.

"Say that again," he commanded.

Donati repeated the words. The Tuscan dialect he spoke every day was not too far from Latin, and Donati was Italian enough, despite his Northern bulk, and fair complexion, to have a flair for mimicry. So it was that he was able to repeat the words with proper accent.

"Who said that?" the old priest asked.

"My Lord, Baron Rudolph. It was about Maria, I know. He spoke to Giuliano about invoking this *ius* thing . . ."

Father Antonio paled under his tan.

"No, my son," he said to Donati, "your ears deceived you. My Lord could not have uttered this wickedness!"

"Good Father, I'm sure!" Donati insisted. "What does it mean?"

Father Antonio sighed.

"It grieves me to tell you, my son," Father Antonio said. "In our own good Tuscan, it means the right of the first night. It is an evil custom introduced by the Frankish knights, who called it the *droit du seigneur*—or right of the lord. By it, these gentle knights claim the right to require that any bride of their serfs be sent to her lord's bed on the night of her wedding, to be returned to her lawful spouse upon the next morning . . . It's a law more honored in the breach than in the observance. I have never known it to be invoked in Italy during my lifetime. Once or twice while I was a student at Paris, a French lord invoked it—but the French are half barbarians, anyhow. And even there the vassal was allowed to buy his bride's freedom from his lord's attentions for a small fine. . . ."

Donati's big hands clenched and unclenched. The cap between them stout leather though it was, was ripped from one end to the other.

"My lord doesn't want a fine," he whispered. "He said that Maria was good looking—that she had a good figure—that he meant to hold to the law!"

"I will speak to him," Father Antonio said, "though to what avail I cannot say. Beside our lord, Rudolph, Baron Rogliano, a mule is a creature of great tractability!"

"Yet," Donati said quietly, "a mule can be persuaded—with blows, good Father."

Father Antonio looked at Donati. As chief armorer, he had access to all the weapons in the castle.

"Leave it to me, Donati," he said. "I'll have no bloodshed. Think, man! The Baron is as big as you are, and trained to arms. He could cut you down while you're getting set to strike. And if even, which God forbid, you were to succeed in slaying him, his men at arms would hack you to bits before Maria's eyes . . ."

"Better that I be dead," Donati said sullenly, "than she be dishonored. . . ."

"You think your death would save her from ravishment?" Father Antonio groaned. "Ah, son, son—how little you know of this world! In such a case she would be passed from knight to man at arms and so on down the line until even the stableboys had enjoyed her. Come, let us go into the chapel where we cannot be overheard, and take council together . . . There is one road open to you, Donati—escape the fief. By the law, if you can remain away for a year and a day, you are free of your vows to your lord. . . ."

"But," Donati said, "the gates, the portcullis, the drawbridge—the crossbowmen in the towers, and the mounted men at arms. . . ."

"Will think merely that you ride forth upon your honeymoon, with the Baron's good blessing. You see, Donati, I've changed my mind, I'm not going to speak to him about this matter at all. Come. . . ."

Baron Rudolph, might have noticed, had he paid attention to such things, that Donati ate little, and drank not at all during the banquet in the bailey yard that the Baron had been good enough to give for his prized vassal. And a little later, during the afternoon, while everyone was intent upon the jugglers and acrobats, the sword swallowers and the fire eaters and the antics of the dancing bear, he was so filled with merriment that he failed to see the villein of the Abbey pass through the bailey and around behind the chapel, leading two fine riding mules as swift of foot as the average palfrey.

But the Baron was in much too good a humor to notice such minor things. His small blue eyes kept straying to Maria's slim form, as she sat beside Donati with downcast eyes. Truly a pretty wench. She would be fearful and perhaps even struggle. But Baron Rudolph was not lacking experience in such matters. He was sure that forever after she would be dissatisfied with her great dolt of a husband. He laughed aloud, thinking of it.

Toward nightfall they all trooped into the chapel and Father Antonio read the Sacrament. At the end, looking Baron Rudolph straight in the eye, he said in a great voice:

"Whom God hath joined together, let no man put asunder!"

Rudolph squirmed a little in his seat at the words. But the priest was speaking again:

"My liege," he said, addressing the Baron directly, "good Messires, and Gentle Dames, with our good Baron's permission, I crave half an hour with this newly united couple, in the rectory. They are both young, and but little trained. It is my custom, therefore, to give to such ones private council upon divers matters, that they avoid the sins and temptations of the flesh. Have I your permission, my Lord?"

The Baron frowned. All these delays. He was burning to enjoy the little black haired wench, still—

"Granted," he growled. "But half an hour—no more."

"Thank you, my Lord," Father Antonio said, and led Donati and Maria through a passage.

Forty-five minutes later, when Baron Rogliano burst into the rectory in a fury of rage he found Father Antonio alone, reading from an illuminated copy of the Holy Writ.

"You said half an hour!" Rudolph bellowed. "It has been much longer!"

Then for the first time, he realized fully that the priest was alone.

"Where are they?" he roared. "You've helped them escape, you knew . . ."

"I knew what, my Lord?" the priest said mildly.

"Never mind that! Where are they?"

"Gone, of course," Father Antonio said. "After all, I only asked my Lord for half an hour. And as you have said, my Lord, it is long past that. They are young, and in love, and crave privacy. Now that that love has been hallowed by the Church to the glory of God, and the bringing forth of Christians, I saw no need to detain them. My Lord had, of course, already granted them leave to go?"

"No," Rudolph howled; "I had not! You fool! You blind, interfering sanctimonious fool! Or—are you? If you had a hand in this flight, I'll . . ."

"I am a fool," Father Antonio said serenely. "Let's leave it at that, shall we, my Lord? For either I am a fool who misunderstands great wickedness in high places, or my Lord is in grave danger of excommunication and the loss of his immortal soul. I think my folly is sufficient grounds upon which to drop the whole matter. . . ."

"Drop it!" the Baron snorted. "Never!" Then he rushed from the rectory out into the bailey. A moment later the good priest could hear him roaring:

"To arms! To arms! Hans! Karl! Otto! Waldo! Heinrich! Come, after them! After them! They cannot have gone far afoot . . . What? Mules! Oh, that devil of a priest! I'll— Come on, you churls! After them!"

In the rectory Father Antonio bent his head.

"God grant they've had sufficient time," he whispered. Then: "Holy Mother, keep them safe—they're so young—so young. . . ."

As they reached the shelter of the first trees, Donati's ears were still burning from the farewells of the sentries. Poor Maria was almost weeping from shame. For the rough men at arms had wished them godspeed coupled with advice so exceedingly physical that it had been half a sin even to listen to it. Besides she was half out of her mind with fear. If they were captured now Donati would certainly be slain. As for her—she shut her mind against that part of it. That could not be borne even in thought.

Inside the forest, Donati turned the mules straight toward the brook and forced them to enter it. Then they splashed along it for some leagues, following every twist and turn. Father Antonio had been a nobleman's younger son before taking the cowl. He knew well the ways of hunters. . . .

"This way," Donati explained to his bride, "the hounds won't be able to pick up the scent. But there is one other thing we must do. At this next bend we must leave the stream, and wind through the hills beyond. Up there are many rocky trails where the hooves of the beasts will leave no prints, and once beyond the hills we will be in Ancona in the domain of Alessandro, Count Siniscola. Not even the Baron would dare pursue us there. . . ."

"But, good husband," Maria wept, "I'm afraid of heights! Why must we leave the stream? If the dogs cannot smell out our trail . . ."

"The men will see our tracks enter the stream," Donati said. "They will follow it, looking for the place we came out. But once in the hills we aren't even going to take the main trail. It's going to be hard riding, Little Bird; but you'll be safe. That's all that counts . . ."

"And you," Maria whispered. "That counts, too, good husband. I don't want to be safe—without you. . . ."

They lay flat on their stomachs on the high ridge, and looked over the edge. Below them, like a ribbon twisted through the grey hills, they could see the trail. They had heard the hounds for some time now, and each time the baying was louder.

About fifty feet below them was one curve of the trail, but they had left no tracks on it. They hadn't been on it at all. They had reached this height by picking their way over the rocks, urging the sure footed mules upward through little ravines that would have broken the legs of any horse. But it had taken a long time. Too long.

Because already they could see the little cloud of dust on the trail. It was the afternoon of the day after their escape, and they hadn't dreamed that Baron Rudolph would continue his pursuit so long. They, Maria remembered regretfully, hadn't been able to stop last night at all. She was a little curious about this business of being married. She was also curious about Donati. He was so strong, yet always so gentle; she wondered how it would have been if . . . But each time they'd tried to stop they'd heard the baying of the hounds.

They lay there very still, watching the cloud of dust winding upward around the hairpin turns until finally they could make out the individual men at arms, and recognize the Baron at their head. The hounds ran yapping at their heels. Then they were just beneath them, only fifty feet below at the very highest point of the trail, and Maria turned to Donati. He wasn't there.

She rolled over at once and then she saw him. He was only a yard away and he had his hands around the throat of a bull mastiff. The dog was thrashing about, his blunt claws raking the blood from Donati's big arms.

Maria didn't dare breathe. If one of Donati's fingers slipped so that the dog could get out one yelp, they were done. But Donati's fingers didn't slip. Marie saw the frantic paws slow, stiffen. Gently Donati lowered the great mastiff to the rock. His fingers relaxed ever so slowly. The mastiff didn't move.

Down below them the trail was empty. The Baron and his men had swept on past. Even the dust had settled.

Maria got up and started to the place, just below the slope of the rock on which they had lain, where they'd tied the mules. There was a little clump of rock pines there.

"No," Donati told her. "It's no more than an hour's ride to the borders of Ancona. If we ride now, we will only meet them coming back. Let's rest here until we hear them come back again—then we'll ride. . . ."

"As you will, good husband," Maria whispered.

But the Baron's men did not come back in an hour. Donati and Maria had time to eat of the good wheaten bread and cheese and drink the wine with which Father Antonio had thoughtfully provided them. They sat there in the shade of the umbrella pine and waited, and just before nightfall they heard the hoofbeats on the trail below. They ran to the ledge and looked down.

"God's Death!" the burly Markvald swore; "I wonder what happened to Kaisar, my good mastiff?"

"He encountered a shewolf, no doubt," one of the others laughed, "and ran off after her—like his master!"

"Silence!" the Baron roared. "Enough of this banter!"

He was, Donati could see, in a thoroughly ill humor. Then horsemen rounded the bend and dropped out of sight.

"Now," Donati said, "we can go, little bird. . . ."

"No!" Maria said.

Donati stared at her.

"But . . ." he began.

Maria came very close to him.

"It's nice here," she whispered. "The pine tree's like a roof, but not too much so—I—I can still see the stars through it. Can't you, my Donati?"

"I see them," Donati said foolishly, "but I don't understand you, Maria. We ought to . . ."

Maria stamped her little foot.

"No wonder they call you oaf!" she said, and whirled away from him.

"But Maria, little bird, I don't understand—Maria, speak to me . . . What have I done?"

She looked at him over one shoulder, and a smile curved the corners of her mouth up, so that the tears had to change their course around them.

"That, good husband," she murmured, "is the wrong question. What haven't you done? Oh, you great fool, have I a husband or a driver of mules?"

Then Donati made the first and last poetical speech of his entire life.

"You, my little bird," he whispered, "have a devoted slave."

When, at daybreak, they resumed their journey and reached, shortly thereafter, the little town of Rezzi in the Ancona March, Maria's eyes had caught some of the light from the stars that shone above the rock pine. And they never lost it—not for the rest of her life.

Prologue

Part 2 IESI

DONATI LOOKED UP at the banners flying against the blue sky, and then down again at all the people milling about in the square. It was the day after Christmas of the year 1194, but it wasn't cold. Donati was glad of that. If the weather had been bad, he and all the other people of the town of Iesi would have had to miss this brave spectacle.

He looked down at Maria and frowned. She was great with child and it was very near her time. It would have been much better had she remained at home in the snug little cottage that the Jew, Isaac, had given them. Donati worked for Isaac now; he was in charge of all the forges that made the lovely wrought iron work, and Isaac was even beginning to teach him how to work gold.

Donati had had the time to do some thinking in the year and a half since he and his wife had escaped from Hellemark. His brain worked very slowly and with much ponderous effort over the simplest thoughts, but it also worked very well. The end product of his efforts was usually clarity. One of the things he had decided was that Jew or not, Isaac ben Ibrahim was one of the kindest men who ever drew breath. The second thought over which he had been musing for some weeks now, was that since Isaac was kind and good and his assistant Abraham ben Yehuda, almost equally so, was it not possible that other Jews—perhaps even most Jews—were good people? People made up things very often. Couldn't they be mistaken about the ritual murder of Christian children at Passover feasts? Isaac celebrated Passover. And Isaac was certainly too tender hearted to kill a fly, let alone a child. . . .

He shook his head, thinking of it. Isaac had given him the two days before Christmas and the two days after, off from his labors. But nobody had had any thought that they were going to witness such an event as was about to begin. . . .

Donati and Maria and all the others had been there many hours. The market place was packed with people. No one said anything, they simply stood there, held back without much effort by the burly men at arms, and stared at the silken tent. There had been many wonders in this age of wonders, but certainly never before in history had the common people of any Italian village been privileged to witness an Empress brought to bed to deliver their future King. . . .

Now, suddenly, two midwives lifted the tent flap, attaching it to the poles, so that all the people could see inside. The Empress Constance sat fully dressed upon the obstetrical chair, with one midwife holding her upright while another knelt before, pressing with furious vigor upon her swollen abdomen.

My God, Donati thought, but she's old!

Donati did not know it, nor did many of the others, but it was the Empress' age that had occasioned them this brave show. Constance of Sicily was forty-two years of age. Already those in high places who had much to gain by sowing confusion, had cast doubts upon the legitimacy of the child. Such was the character of this daughter of the Norman King, Roger of Hautville, that even her detractors had known better than to attempt to spread the falsehood that the child had been sired by other than her royal husband, Henry VI of Hohenstaufen. No, the story that had gained currency and increased with every telling, was that a baseborn child was to be substituted in the royal chamber—that because of her years the whole story of the Empress' pregnancy was the purest fabrication. . . .

She sat there now, her brown hair plentifully streaked with white, her face lined and haggard, and allowed herself to be stared at by noble and serf alike, in the very extremity of childbirth.[1]

Donati felt Maria shudder. He hoped that it would not take a long time. It wasn't a good thing for her to see anyhow—with her own travail so close upon her.

But it did take a long time. Hours. Maria was giddy and sick, when the midwife suddenly thrust both her arms up beneath the Empress' full skirt, and drew them out again, with their tiny burden. Another of the midwives was quick with the knife and the gold thread; then the child was dangling upside down by his heels from the midwife's grimy hand, while she slapped, with utter disregard for his regal state, upon his tiny backside. The child uttered a thin wail. All the people cheered.

Donati cheered with the rest of them, then he felt Maria's nails digging through the rough cloth of his shirt.

"What ails you?" he growled.

"Oh, Donati!" she whispered, "I shouldn't have watched it! It was too terrible, and he's so little and bloody and horrible—and—and—and now, oh God, now—it's started with me, too!"

Donati bent down and picked her up as though she were weightless. He shoved his way through the crowd toward the tent of the Empress. At once all the men at arms sprang toward him; but seeing the girl in his arms they did not strike him.

"What ails you, good man?" the Sergeant demanded of him. "Is your wife sick?"

"No, Master Sergeant," Donati told him. "Only she, too, is brought to bed with child. I think the sight of the King's birth has hastened her labor. Please, Master, have the goodness to ask of the Empress' midwives whether one of them would come and help us?"

The Sergeant frowned. Then his face relaxed. He knew of the graciousness of the Empress. Such a thing as this was made to order to help her gain the goodwill of the people.

"Wait here, good man," he said. "I will ask the Empress."

He disappeared inside the tent, for the midwives had put the flap back down again. He was gone only a moment. When he returned, not one, but three of the Empress' midwives accompanied him. The great lady had kept only one to serve her on her return to the palace.

The people cheered wildly as the three wise women knelt around Maria to examine her. And when they announced that she was indeed in labor and must be carried home the miller offered his cart, but all the men and boys unhitched his mules and fought for the privilege of drawing it to Donati's humble cottage. Many hands helped in lifting Maria down from the cart and laying her gently upon the little bed.

Attracted by the commotion, Isaac entered the cottage. At once he gave a purse of gold to each of the midwives, begging them to be diligent and careful. Then something caught his eye.

The hands and arms of the chief midwife, the one who had delivered the Empress, were crusted over with dried blood. He sent for a maidservant and told her to bring a basin with hot water and cloths.

The midwife eyed them scornfully.

"This," she declared, "is royal blood—a most sovereign remedy for all ills. Out of here, you dog of a Jew, lest you contaminate the birth of a Christian!"

Then all the people started muttering against Isaac. Isaac sighed and went back to his counting room. He sat there for several hours, listening to Maria's screams. When finally, they ceased, he came back to the cottage, just in time to see Maria take the child in her arms, and stare at it.

It was a boy. But instead of being large and fair, like Donati, it was tiny and wizened, and darker than its mother. And its head was thickly covered with curly, black hair.

Maria looked at her son.

"Oh," she whispered, "he's ugly! I hate him! I hate him! Take him away from me, please . . ." Then she turned her face to the wall and started crying.

Three days later, she died of childbed fever. And the people of Iesi stoned the house of Isaac ben Ibrahim, saying that he had destroyed her with his black arts. So great was their fury that he was forced for a time to leave the city.

Poor Donati went almost mad of grief. Never thereafter was he quite the same.

So, on that same day of December Twenty-sixth, 1194, were Pietro, son of Donati, and Frederick II of Hohenstaufen, *stupor mundi et immutator mirabilis* the marvelous transformer and wonder of the world, born. The same day, in the same town, Iesi, in the wild Ancona March, under the same stars.

Which, of course, had its consequences.

Chapter One

THE BOY, PIETRO, came awake in a kind of a soft blaze. He lay there on the great Moorish couch with its damasked coverlets, and blinked his eyes. It was late—very late; he knew that. Ordinarily he would have gotten up in the first light of morning, and dressed himself reluctantly to await the good fathers who came to teach him his Latin and his Catechism. That was the part of his studies that he hated, although he was quite good at them. The Saracen masters who came in the afternoon to teach him Arabic, arithmetic, algebra, logic and rhetoric, he adored. He also was enchanted by his good Uncle Isaac's informal lessons in the lore of the Jews, with the result that his Arabic and his Hebrew were both much better than his Latin.

The good fathers were such stern and gloomy men. Besides he had to be shut up in a close little room with them, which on warm mornings was almost unendurable since they regarded the Saracen custom, to which both he and Isaac were addicted, of bathing the body daily and using perfumes, as sinful. They regarded so many things as sinful—hawking on a Sunday, pleasant words exchanged with a fair maid, a song. . . .

And they demanded that he believe so much arrant nonsense: Saints who walked with their severed heads in their hands; holy women who died in defense of their virginity—at thirteen in warm Sicily, Pietro was already aware that the loss of virginity was rather a pleasant process—men who gained sanctity by the scourging of their flesh. . . .

Pietro ran his hands over his slim, brown arms. He hadn't very much flesh and he certainly didn't propose to lacerate it for the good of his soul. He swung his naked legs down from his couch and began to pick up the garments that Abu, his Saracen slave, had laid out for him. As he drew on his red, skin-tight stockings, it came to him that his Moslem friends also believed a great quantity of arrant nonsense; but their nonsense at least was attractive. A paradise—where the fountains sprayed wine and a man had his fill forever of sweetmeats and delicacies, not to mention the beautiful maidens ready and joyously willing to attend to his other needs—had its advantages over the cold and dull Christian heaven where a soul was supposed to spend eternity singing praises to God. God, Pietro reflected, must get rather sick of being praised all the time.

He continued to dress slowly. Then it came to him why he had not been awakened. Today was Saturday, the Holy Day of the Jews. Yesterday, his Arabic masters had not come, since Friday was their Holy Day. And tomorrow he must get up before dawn to go to early mass, since tomorrow was the Christian Sabbath. Three Holy Days a week were too many, Pietro reflected. It amused him that grown men could not even agree upon which days were holy, much less in their interpretation of God.

He phrased these curious thoughts of his in a dialect of his own making, a mixture of Arabic and the Sicilian of the streets. But he could have, had he wanted to, formed them almost equally well in French or Provencal, the langue d'oïl, and the langue d'oc. Hugh and Pierre and Jean, the sons of the Norman knights whom he hunted with on every possible occasion, had by the simple method of chattering at him in their native tongues, inflicted them upon him. So, in the same fashion, had he attained a rapid and fluent Greek—from Demetrius, Arcadius, and Theodosius, sons of the elders and dignitaries of Palermo's Byzantinian community.

This was, of course, an achievement, even in Palermo—a city so polyglot that an ordinary beggar could ask alms in half the tongues of the Western World and ragged urchins unable to print their names could switch in mid-sentence from one language to another, and in the next breath commence a third. But Pietro was distinguished for his cleverness. All his friends—Norman,

Sicilian, Greek and Saracen—agreed upon that. It was, in a way, a fitting compensation for his small size and lack of great physical strength.

He walked over to the chaliced window and looked out. He was still only half dressed, but today there was no need to hurry. He had the whole day before him, to do with it what he willed. For his foster Uncle did not ask of him that he keep the Jewish fasts or ceremonies. Isaac had scrupulously kept to his promise to Donati to rear the boy as a Christian.

That, Pietro knew, was another good thing about Sicily. In Palermo no one gave a second thought to the strangeness of a Christian youth's being reared by a Jew. In parts of Italy and all over the rest of Europe, neither Isaac's wealth nor his skill would have saved him the indignity of having to wear a yellow emblem upon his garments; anywhere else the good goldsmith would have been cursed and reviled and beaten upon any pretext or no pretext at all, if, indeed, he escaped being murdered in one of the frequent massacres by which good Christians demonstrated their devotion to the meek and gentle Christ.

Just thinking about it made Pietro feel sick. He had a poor stomach for fighting or arms or bloodshed, and he loved his good Uncle—in fact he could not remember his father and mother at all. He had been three years old when Isaac had brought him to Palermo. He was now thirteen, and he had no recollection of any other life. . . .

He didn't even know very clearly why Isaac had done so—except that it was mixed up with his mother's death shortly after he had been born, and his father's being forced to enter the service of Alessandro, Count Siniscola, as armorer in chief—though why any man should have to enter another's service when he didn't want to was entirely beyond him.

He wandered away from the window and ate a handful of dates, washed down by a flagon of watered wine. That was as much as he usually ate, having an appetite like a bird's—which accounted for his slimness.

There were so many confusing things in the world. Like the people who spat on the ground when his good Uncle passed; like the good fathers who insisted that his Saracen friends were followers of Mahound—by which they presumably meant Muhammad, the false prophet, and should be put to death—and this in the name of the gentle Jesus who bade them love their enemies; like the Moslem emirs who insisted that the good fathers were Polytheists who made three gods of one and that Jesus was a minor prophet who preceded Muhammad. What was he then to believe? Theodosius, his friend, was the son of a Greek priest; but the good fathers were forbidden to marry. Giuseppe, son of one of the city prefects, composed lilting lyrics—at fourteen—to dark Lucrezia; while to his Moslem friends women existed only as vehicles to serve their pleasure. . . .

It was characteristic of Pietro that he puzzled his head with things like these while his friends thought of nothing but hawking, dancing and riding behind their hounds. It was a brave bright world that stretched out before him; and, at thirteen, he already had that most terrible of hungers: the hunger after understanding. It had not always been thus with him. His thirst after knowledge and that pride of intellect that the good father warned him was a mortal sin, began upon his twelfth birthday, when seeking to impress his Saracen friends, he had related the story of Elijah's ascent into heaven in a chariot of fire—a tale he had had of the good fathers only the day before. But when they countered with the story of Muhammad's ascent from the rock in Jerusalem, mounted upon a winged horse with a woman's face and a peacock's tail, both stories unaccountably lost something. . . .

And Pietro lost something, too, that day: the virginity of his intellect perhaps, the pristine purity of naïve faith. Already, at thirteen, he was half a heretic; and in his day there was only one answer to heresy—a heap of smoldering fagots about an iron stake. . . .

But he had been still too long now, and it was already past noon. He fairly flew into the rest of his clothing and ran down into the courtyard where the fountains played and date palms and banana trees shaded the walk. Here Abu, his Saracen slave, stood holding his palfrey in the shade of that wall over which the brilliant flowers spilled, as dark as the blood of the holy martyrs.

He stopped at the mews long enough to get Caesar, his great

falcon, then ran over to where Abu waited with Adaba, his palfrey, pausing long enough to wave to Isaac who sat by the dovecot on the roof, his thin body doubled up, waiting for the messenger pigeons to come in from Italy with news. . . .

It was a June day in the year twelve hundred and eight, and Isaac's heart warmed at the sight of his adopted son. Truly, Pietro was wondrously fair to look upon. He was as slim as a girl and even more graceful. His garments were the finest that Isaac's great wealth could buy for him. He wore a tight fitting skullcap of green velvet, embroidered with gold threads and seeded with pearls, with a golden pheasant's feather stuck in it. His hair, blacker than the sins of nobles, hung below his ears in a short bob. He had a single earring, a great pearl, in one ear and a gold chain about his neck, tight about the place where his silken *chainse*—a kind of undershirt designed to be seen and hence richly embroidered—showed above his *bliaut,* or over-tunic, of green brocade, rich with gold thread and seed pearls like his cap. His *bliaut* did not, like the tunics of most of his friends, fall to his knees, but was cut high above to show off his good legs clad in red, skin-tight stockings clasped with garters of jeweled gold. Nor did Pietro allow it to hang loose as the commonality did, but belted it like a young noble with a wide leathern belt, gold-buckled, and laced with many a curious design. On his feet were soft shoes of good kidskin, dyed green to match his tunic and cap.

Abu held the palfrey for him to mount, and Pietro gained the saddle in a single bound without touching the stirrups. That was a feat for Adaba was a noble beast, brought all the way from Arabia for the boy. He obeyed Pietro partly out of love, and partly from the knowledge that the boy could master all his tricks —a fact that Pietro had to remind him of right often because he had not been gentled out of all spirit like a European steed.

Isaac saw the boy canter toward the gate, and raised up to call to him. Then he thought the better of it. He would wait for one more message from Abraham in Iesi; if the news were no better tonight would be time enough to ride. . . .

Pietro rode out of the courtyard into Palermo, city of his heart. He was going nowhere in particular, except that he had a vague idea of loosing Caesar after waterfowl, late in the evening, in the marshes by the Oreto. He rode aimlessly, passing palaces, churches, mosques—down the broad streets past the king's palaces and parks, seeing the dome of the Greek Santa Maria, bluish in the distance, and near it the noble bulk of the Cathedral, with its monasteries and cloisters by its side. The streets were filled with people, black garbed monks, beturbaned Saracens, bearded Greek priests, Jewish merchants and money lenders, Negroes blacker than the bottom pit of Hades, tall Norman knights, dignified in hauberks and helmets, and the latest comers of all—the German knights of the Emperor Henry VI, son of that Frederick called Barbarossa because of the redness of his beard.

Pietro gave these Germans a wide birth. They were of formidable size, bigger even than the Normans and of most uncertain temper. All men of Sicily, who before they came, had been able to live in peace in their babel of tongues and races, permitting to each his customs and his ways of seeking God, hated them. Pietro shared that feeling. More than once he had felt the weight of their heavy hands.

There were, of course, Sicilians in that motley throng, gay and laughing, their very speech a song, their every other word a quip, a jibe, a gambol. And now and again, some great lady would be borne by on a litter carried by stalwart Saracen or Moorish slaves. Most of these great ladies were blonde by nature, or by art; for certainly no dark-haired maid ever earned even a passing line in the romances of the jongleurs. Confronted with the pale charms of the Norman maids with their long, yellow tresses and the tall Germanic dames, with hair now golden, now red as foxfire, the dark beauties of the Island were hard put to hold their places in society or their men. Pietro had seen them often sitting on the rooftops, exposing their long hair, filled with some concoction prepared for them by a Saracen or a Greek—for of all the leeches, these two were most cunning in pharmacology—their curls spread out to the sun to aid the bleaching, and trying vainly at the same time, to keep the sun's rays from their naturally golden skins. What messes of mare's milk and mashed beans they smeared upon their faces—succeeding only in giving themselves a greyish hue that was most unbecoming. And the red that henna gave their hair and the dirty gold caused by other drugs was ugly, too; especially when the roots showed dark with the new growth.

Still, Pietro watched them all with joy, young as he was; for in that time the worship of women was almost a religion. He longed for the day when he would wear a maiden's kerchief or her stocking upon his lance and thunder the list in her fair honor. It pleased him greatly to catch a glimpse of them through the curtains of the litter, cloaked in elegant mantles of silk enriched with gold embroidery, artfully veiled, odorous with sweet perfumes, their shoes worked in gold, their finger tips rosier and their eyebrows blacker than in nature.

Pietro loved Palermo. What a brave, bright city it was! Like a jewel fallen from Paradise, it lay there upon the curving shore encircled by the barren hills and guarded by Monte Pellegrino to the north, where the beautiful green gardens of the Conca d'Oro met the matchless blue of the bay. Around it and in it oranges and lemons scattered their fragrance to the breeze; palm trees shook their murmurous fronds; stone pines stood in lonely grandeur contemplating their own solitary shadows. The gardens were soft with the blossoms of fruit trees and flowering bushes; and, as the boy rode out beyond the suburbs, wild flowers filled the fields and almond trees bloomed white, and the green-silver of olive trees was everywhere. On the banks of the canals and brooks, Persian cane rustled. It was to these marshes that Pietro had come to try once more his good falcon, Caesar.

The jingle of the silver bells on his palfrey's trappings roused the marsh birds almost at once; this time they were not herons but fast flying ducks, shooting upward like bolts from a crossbow so that they were already black dots flying wedge-shaped before Pietro could unhood Caesar and fling him into the air. He mounted after them and arched out over the bay, turning them so that they came in over the land, but they hurtled over Pietro's head low and fast so that he could hear their wings thunder; then they were over the great woods that belonged to the King and there Pietro saw Caesar fold his wings and plummet downward like the vengeance of God.

But the falcon did not rise again, and Pietro swore maledictions that would have curled the tonsure of a monk. Then he rode into the woods to find his hawk. It was nearly dark when he succeeded, and then by sound rather than by sight. Caesar had driven his great talons so deeply into a fat mallard that he was imprisoned by them and the weight of the duck was too great for him to lift. Pietro laughed and got down. He bent to pick up the falcon, but there was a whistling noise through the leaves and a great boarspear stood quivering in the earth, inches from his outstretched hands.

The boy straightened, drawing his dagger from the sheath. No one came. Pietro stood very still. He looked down at the dagger in his hand. Such a small blade. And whoever had been able to throw a heavy boarspear with such force must be a giant of strength. The boy trembled. He was not cowardly; but he was rather a small boy for his age, and his strength was not great. He thought of springing into the saddle and running away, but he didn't do it. There was something shameful about running away from an attacker. Besides, in this thick brush Adaba could make little speed. Whoever had tried to kill him could put another lance or a crossbow bolt through his back with ease before he had gained two yards. . . .

So Pietro did the only thing possible under the circumstances. He pulled the boarspear loose and plunged through the underbrush with it. He was afraid. He was shaking all over. But he went forward. He did not yet know that this itself was a kind of courage.

He saw the other boy first, then the boar. The boy was about his own age and shorter than he, but much thicker and stronger. His hair was golden and his face well tanned, with no fear in it at all as he crouched there waiting, with only a poinard in his hand, for the most terrible of all beasts to come to him.

"Fool!" Pietro screamed at him. "What manner of ass are you to throw a boarspear?"

"He would not turn," the boy said calmly. " 'Twas the only way to stop him. Now toss it near me that I may kill him."

Then Pietro did a very foolhardy thing. Instead of throwing the spear to the strange boy, he picked up a branch and threw it so that it struck the boar hard on his shaggy flank. The beast whirled, and his fierce little eyes were coals of fire in the blackness of his head. Pietro saw him paw the earth just once, then he came running very low and very well, a thunderbolt shot by the god of death, a black, low mountain of a beast with curving tusks already reddened and the foam flying backward from his jaws as he came. Little Pietro crouched there, holding the boar-spear straight and level pointed at his breast, the blood beating a red torrent in his ears, muttering all the Ave Marias and Pater Nosters in the world, holding like that until the boar was upon him. The weight of the boar sent the boy over backward into the brush and the leaves flying, and the whole of the beast, swerving a little to the left, went past Pietro and the boarspear was torn from the boy's hands.

Pietro heard the boar squeal just once—an awful sound, high and wailing. Then the boy he had saved was picking him up and brushing the leaves and splintered branches from his good clothing.

"The boar?" Pietro whispered.

"A noble stroke," the boy grinned. "Dead. You pierced him from breast to withers. 'Twas bravely done! My thanks, vassal."

Pietro stiffened. He looked at this strange boy with his reddish-blond hair and sunburned skin, seeing his clothes poor and patched and that he wore no jewels. Yet, he had called Pietro "vassal."

"Vassal?" Pietro said. "Take back that word or I'll serve you equally with the boar!"

The boy's blue eyes held Pietro. They bored through the slim, bejeweled lad without wavering. Then he laughed. It was a good sound, deep and clear.

"I cannot take it back," he said, "since you are my vassal. All men of both the Sicilies are—saving the good prelates, of course, who are God's. . . ."

"Who are you?" Pietro said wonderingly.

"Frederick Second," the boy said, "by the Grace of God, King of Sicily. And you?"

Pietro dropped to his knees at once, snatching off his cap as he went.

"Oh, get up," Frederick said impatiently. "There's no need for that. Besides, I haven't rewarded you properly for saving my life. What are you called?"

"Pietro—Pietro of Apulia, and your servant, Sire."

"Good. When I become Emperor of the Romans I shall give you a Barony. Now, help me find my horse and come with me. . . ."

"You cannot," Pietro blurted. "You cannot give me a Barony, Sire—I—I am baseborn. . . ."

The King eyed Pietro sternly.

"I," he said flatly, "can give you a Dukedom, if it pleases me. But for this a Barony is enough, since you had only to toss me the spear and I could have done it myself. . . ."

That stung. Pietro was on the point of reminding the king that if he had not been there to pick up his weapon he would have been killed in any case, because the boar was between him and the place it struck. Then Pietro remembered that this stocky boy was, after all, king.

They went through the brush together, and Pietro freed the falcon.

"A noble bird," Frederick said.

"He is yours, Sire," Pietro said at once. This was courtesy, pure and simple; Pietro had no intention of giving away his prized falcon.

"Thank you," Frederick said, and transferred the hawk to his own wrist.

Pietro could have wept. But there was no helping it now. And Isaac would buy him another—though such another as Caesar existed nowhere in the world. Of that he was sure.

They retraced their steps, the king bearing Caesar proudly and stroking his feathers, and Pietro leading Adaba, his palfrey, and bearing the carcass of the duck. As for the boar, Pietro trusted that the king's retainers would take care of him.

They found Frederick's horse almost at once. To Pietro's surprise, it was no destrier, the noble warhorse of a knight, but a swaybacked palfrey, not even to be compared in the same breath with his own Arabian. Then, a little further, they came upon the king's hounds. They were scattered in a semicircle on the ground, all three of them dead. The boar had disembowelled them.

Frederick knelt beside them and wept. Pietro reflected that he would have done worse had he been in the king's place. If any boar had killed his great boarhound, Brutus, he would have beat the earth with his closed fists and howled.

Frederick dried his eyes and mounted and Pietro did the same. Then it came to him that he had not seen the slightest sign of the king's huntsmen. He asked Frederick about that. He shouldn't have, he realized almost at once; but it was plagued hard to remember that this thirteen year old boy in faded hunting green was King of the Two Sicilies.[1]

He laughed. Pietro didn't like the sound of it. It had an edge concealed in the merriment; a note of—bitterness, perhaps—Pietro didn't know.

"Do I have to instruct you, good Messer Pietro," Frederick said, "in all the details of my miserable life? Use four eyes! Which of us is dressed like a king—you or I?"

"I would gladly give you these clothes, Sire," Pietro said, "but I'm afraid they wouldn't fit you at all. . . ."

"True," Frederick sighed, "I'm much bigger than you. Besides, I haven't long to wait. Upon the twenty-sixth day of December of this year of Our Lord Twelve hundred and eight, I become of age. Then let my good guardian, the so very Holy Father, look to himself!"

Pietro was shocked. He was not yet so far gone in apostasy for such a thing not to trouble him. True enough, to his candid young eyes the brawling Christian knights, the slippery Venetian and Genoese traders and many another sample of Christendom compared but ill with the clean, dignified, scholarly gentlemen he knew among the Saracens. Certainly to call in a Christian leech, for example, was tantamount to committing suicide; while the Arabian physicians achieved many cures with their science and their art. The Saracens were commanded by their prophet to wash both hands and feet before entering a Mosque, while in Christian churches there were other smells beside the incense. But Pietro would never have dreamed of speaking of the Vicar of Christ in such a fashion. It bordered close upon blasphemy. His face must have shown how he felt, for Frederick looked at him.

"His Holiness," he said quietly, "received of my sainted mother thirty thousand tarens[2] a year for my care. It's no concern of yours, Pietro, but you will learn that Cope and Miter can cover villainy as well as any other dress."

"But, Sire," Pietro began.

Frederick lifted his hand. Boy that he was, the gesture was regal.

"Who delivered a third of my lands unto Walter of Brienne?" he said. "How came I to be tossed from Bishop Walter of Palear to Markward to William Capparone to Diepold of Schweinspeunt? Was that how the great Innocent III proposed to keep his word to my mother? I was elected to the headship of the Holy Roman Empire by all the Princes of Germany. Who opposed me, Pietro? Who wrote and declared that I was under age, unbaptized and promised only to the beggarly kingship of one half Sicily, adding 'Woe to the land whose King is a child!'?"[3]

"I didn't know these things, Sire," Pietro said lamely.

"No matter. Come, we'll have this fat duck done to a turn within the hour. I'm plagued hungry. That's another thing. What other king has ever had to gain his meat by the charity of his subjects?"

Pietro held his tongue. It seemed to him that every word he uttered only served to remind the king of the hardness of his lot. Pietro wasn't really unaware of these things, now that Frederick had mentioned it he remembered having heard it said more than once that the young king had lacked a guardian these last five years, and had played in the market with slave and Saracen and Moor. Pietro had even heard Isaac say that Frederick's chances of reaching manhood without being cut down by an assassin's dagger were slim indeed. He didn't like to think about that. He found that he liked this brave and sturdy boy very much indeed. In rags, unattended, yet a child, Frederick was still—a king.

They came just before nightfall to the palace. Though it had been built by Frederick's Norman grandfather, Roger II, the royal Frenchman had learned his lessons well from the genius of the Moors. To Pietro's eye it was the loveliest building in all Palermo.

The guard at the gate saluted them indifferently. Pietro could see Frederick's eyes blaze; but he restrained himself. Time enough later to teach this varlet who was king. But the burly Germans of his guard greeted him with some warmth, especially after he had told them that a great boar lay in the forest, ready to be fetched to the spit. Five of them rode out at once to bring in the beast that Pietro had slain.

"Poor devils," Frederick said. "They get enough of plain fare; but they hunger after flesh. So do I. But we'll turn this fowl over to Giullamo, who is not without skill in cookery, and then we'll dine. I'm unwilling to part with you, Pietro—you please me greatly."

"I'm honored, Sire," Pietro said.

The duck was good, but Pietro ate sparingly of it, despite the king's urging. Pietro knew hunger when he saw it. When the duck was gone, quicker than he would have dreamed possible, washed down by draughts of wine worse than that Isaac allotted to the slaves, the two boys sat back and stared into the fire. Pietro guessed that Frederick was planning how he would bear himself when he became king in fact as well as in name. At the moment, Pietro didn't give half a taren for his chances. The Saracens of the hills were in revolt against him. The Barons of the mainland and the Island openly defied him. He ruled, truly, only the palace in which the two of them sat.

Pietro wanted to take his leave. Isaac would be worried by now. But he dared not. It was the king's to command when he should go. They sat there without speaking for more than an hour. Pietro was beginning to believe that he was going to have to sit there all night, when a spurred knight, complete in chain mail was abruptly ushered into their presence.

"Sire," the man said, "I have news from Swabia. . . ."

Frederick studied his face.

"Ill news," he said. His voice was flat and very calm.

"Yes, Sire."

"Then tell it, man! Ill or good, it's all the same to me."

"Your uncle, the good king Philip has been slain," the knight whispered.

"By whom?" Frederick said. He might have been asking the time of day, by his tone.

"Otto of Wittelsbach," the knight said.

Frederick didn't answer. He turned his back and stared into the fire. He was a boy of thirteen, but Pietro saw him become a man then. The fireglow danced on Frederick's cheeks in that moment, long as death itself, that he stared at the burning logs. Then he turned.

"My thanks," he said. "Giovanni, my seneschal, will give you lodging and food. Leave us."

The knight bowed and clanked out. Pietro thought that the king had forgotten his presence, but Frederick turned to him at last.

"Do you know what this means, Pietro?" he said.

"No, Sire."

"I am the last of the Waiblings[4]—the last Hohenstaufen alive. Now I shall become Emperor! Now neither the Holy Father, nor the devil in hell, nor God himself shall prevent me! You may leave me now, Pietro—I must think about this thing alone. . . ."

Pietro felt cold as he walked toward the stables. Frederick had uttered his blasphemies so easily. Pietro was beginning to realize that there was something terrible about his king. He mounted, and rode homeward, thinking the thought that had not entered Frederick's mind. The last Hohenstaufen. One knife thrust and the Empire would become a Welf fief—forever. Then, suddenly, he doubted it. That devil boy would never be subdued so easily. Pietro was astonished to find suddenly in his own mind, the absolute conviction that Frederick would win.

When Pietro reached home, Isaac was waiting for him, his face dark with worry.

"What Saracen wench detained you this time?" he roared at the boy. "Tonight of all nights you could have returned early; but no—that was too much to expect! It's that wild Frankish blood of yours!"

"Have done with my blood," Pietro said tartly. "Good Isaac, I spent the day with the king."

Isaac stared at the boy. He pulled at his beard thoughtfully. But he knew Pietro spoke the truth. Then—in those days—the boy had not yet learned to lie.

"Bad," he said. "Take care that you are not murdered with him when it is noised abroad that Philip of Swabia has been slain. . . ."

"You know that already, good uncle?" Pietro said in astonishment. "Why I was with the king when the messenger came."

"A fit night for messengers," Isaac groaned. "We, too, have received one here."

Then Pietro saw that Isaac was not wearing the loose, flowing Saracen robes as was his custom. He was clad in European garb and there were spurs at his heels. Under his tunic Pietro caught the glint of chain mail, and his waist was belted. His thin, brown hand rested upon the hilt of a curved Saracen scimitar, and a dagger was thrust in his belt.

"Go arm yourself," he said curtly. "We ride this night for Messina. God grant that we reach it!"

"Why?" Pietro began, but Isaac thrust the boy from him with a shove that was far from gentle.

"Go!" he spat. "I'll explain as we ride!"

When Pietro came out into the courtyard, he saw that a guard of ten spearmen awaited them. Adaba was worn from the hunting, so he had to mount a great black stallion. Then they were off, pounding through the dark streets almost at a gallop, the torches the spearmen bore, to light their passage, spluttering in the wind.

Pietro stared at his adoptive Uncle as hard as he could in the darkness. This was an Isaac new to him. Always, before, he had been the very soul of gentleness; but tonight, for the first time, a new side to his character showed. Considered later, in after years, it was not strange to Pietro that Isaac could act with decision; hardly could he have held together his far-flung mercantile empire, consisting mainly of traffic in jewels and gold and in the products of his own skilled hands as well as those of his better artisans, had he not had both courage and dispatch. But this role of man of action was little to his liking, that Pietro knew. Isaac much preferred reading the Torah, or Maimonides' *Dalalat al-Ha'irin;*[5] "A Jewish merchant," he was fond of saying, "is a lost scholar. . . ."

Pietro had the feeling, now, that Isaac would use that curved blade with force, if need be; and the boy was suddenly proud of him. But he was consumed with curiosity. That they must ride so fast and so far meant that great events were shaping; still Isaac said no word.

They rode all night over the rugged hill country. Outside of Palermo, the torches were put out lest they attract bandits; and the horsemen picked their way cautiously through the darkness. Pietro caught up with Isaac.

"Good Uncle," he began, "why. . . ."

"Silence!" Isaac hissed; "would you bring down brigands upon us? I'll tell you in the morning. . . ."

They came into Messina early in the morning and rode down to the straits that separated the two Sicilies. Pietro was dog tired; his slender limbs were not up to that furious, nightlong ride. But beyond the fact that his face appeared taut and drawn, Isaac gave no sign of the fatigue he must have felt. Pietro sat there, reeling in the saddle, while Isaac dickered with the Genoese captain of the galley that lay at anchor in the harbor. Clearly their journey was not yet at an end; but by then Pietro was too tired to care.

Isaac wasted little time in haggling. He agreed to the second figure that the villainous Genoese named, which was hardly sensible practice for any competent merchant. But he seemed in great haste.

Immediately, Pietro's horse and Isaac's were led aboard but their spearmen turned back. Pietro watched them go with not a little fear. They were stout fellows all, capable of dealing hard blows in their masters' behalf. And Pietro was small for his age and had but little strength. He knew that only too well. Even his feat in killing the boar yesterday didn't help his state of mind; actually the animal had impaled himself upon the spear that the boy had held—and the whole business had been a piece of rank folly from which now, Pietro could take scant comfort. . . .

Isaac lay a gentle hand upon his shoulder.

"It is better thus, Pietro," he said. "What we must do is better done by diplomacy. . . ."

"What is it?" Pietro demanded crossly. "All night we have ridden, and now. . . ."

But before Isaac could answer, all other sounds were drowned out by the voice of the black-bearded captain, roaring orders at his crew. The hawsers were cast off and the oarsmen bent to their task. The galley slid out from the quay and headed into the open sea where the shore of Italy could be seen, pale blue and misty in the distance. Then the sailors swarmed up the single mast and the fat sail bellied out, decorated with the device of a dragon. Messina dropped behind and the white water flew beneath the prow.

Now at last it was quiet, and Isaac drew Pietro a little apart.

"I had," he said, "during your absence, last night, a message from Abraham ben Yehuda, keeper of my warehouses in Ancona. Know you the village of Rezzi, nigh onto Iesi where you were born?"

"Only what you have told me, good uncle," Pietro said. "I do not even remember Iesi, itself. . . ."

"True," Isaac sighed. "How could you? You were but a babe in arms when Donati entrusted you to my care. But no matter. Rezzi is a village of no importance, meaner even than Iesi. It's part of the fief of Alessandro, Count Siniscola, with whom in evil, not even Satan himself could compare. . . ."

Pietro waited. There was more to this, he knew.

"The chief of my warehouses in the Ancona," Isaac went on, "lies in Rezzi. The Count allows it to remain there because year by year he falls deeper into my debt. A debt, which, since I value my health, I have no hope of collecting. But the point is this, Pietro—Rezzi now lies under siege of Count Alessandro and his men at arms. . . ."

"Why?" Pietro demanded. "If it's his own fief, why should he besiege it? Another knight I could understand—like Baron Rudolph of Rogliano—they've always been enemies, didn't you say?—but certainly. . . ."

"Not so fast, my boy. No noble in all the land is crueler to his villeins than Count Alessandro; none extracts more côrvées of forced labor, or higher tithes. Count Siniscola has hanged more poor devils for poaching than any man in Italy; and his readiness with the whip or his own mailed fist is proverbial. You know that your own father is now a vassal of the Count?"

"Yes, but I've never understood that either. You told me that when my father fled Baron Rudolph of Rogliano's fief, to save my poor mother from being ravished, he stayed away a year and a day. That should have made him free. . . ."

"True," Isaac sighed, "but no man is free while such beasts as Alessandro are unchecked. He forced your father into his service to make arms for him for his war against Rudolph of Brandenburg, Baron Rogliano—your father's former master. You see, Pietro, Donati is the finest armorer in Italy, which Count Alessandro had sad reason to know well. . . ."

"Still," Pietro said, "I don't see. . . ."

"You will," Isaac said grimly. "Last year there was famine in the March. Round about Rezzi, men were burned for selling the flesh of infants for food. And Count Alessandro of Siniscola did nothing to help. Instead of alms, he gave redoubled blows. So finally, when the great rains rotted the seed this spring, the serfs revolted. They were led—by your father. . . ."

Pietro knew what that meant. Even in his brief life there had been peasant revolts in Sicily. And each of them had ended the same way—in death for the rebels dealt out with such fiendish cruelty and so slowly as to make them beg for death long before it came.

Pietro felt sick, just thinking of it; but he watched Isaac's face. Inside the goldsmith's keen brain was a plan; of that the boy was sure.

"I," Isaac said, "will dicker with Count Siniscola. I will advance him monies—monies enough to beggar all my mainland holdings—but no matter. You, my son, will slip into Rezzi—and compel that great oaf of a father of yours to accompany you into hiding at a place that Abraham will have set. After that, I will join you . . . if any of us is alive. . . ."

Pietro stood up.

"By God and His Blessed Mother," he swore, "I will not fail!"

Isaac smiled. Then Pietro remembered that he did not believe in Jesus or His Mother.

"So be it," Isaac said quietly.

Then the two of them sat watching the shore of Italy coming up out of the blue sea.

Chapter Two

PIETRO LEANED FORWARD in the saddle. God and His Mother! he thought, but I am weary . . . Surely there must be someone left alive who knows something of roadbuilding. The antique Romans did. But dear, merciful Saints—these!

It was late in June now, and very hot. The dust came up off the road in clouds. Now and again, Amir, the great black stallion, stumbled in the stone hard ruts that the cart wheels had cut during the rains of early spring. The dust got inside the boy's clothing. It went up his nostrils, into his hair. His brows and lashes were white with it. He felt dirty all over.

He looked at Isaac, lolling in the saddle with his eyes closed against the sun's glare. The good Jew was reduced almost to a skeleton by the journey. Yet he seemed to have within his thin frame a hidden reserve of strength. It was always Pietro who gave up first, not he.

Sleeping on the ground at night under their little tent didn't help, either. The hardness of the stones prevented rest. But they had no choice. The first time they had come to an inn Pietro had been overjoyed—especially when the innkeeper had greeted them unctuously with:

"Gentle Lords! Do me the honor to enter. Within we have the very best of comforts: painted rooms and soft beds packed high with white straw under soft feather mattresses! Here, good sires, you will fall asleep on pillows of violets after you have washed out your mouth and rinsed your hands with rose water!"

"A bath," Pietro whispered, "can that be arranged, too, Messer Innkeeper?"

The innkeeper stared at him in purest astonishment. His expression clearly showed that he thought the boy mad. But he recovered quickly.

"Assuredly, young prince! In a tub of marble, and fair maidens to massage your aching limbs if that be your noble pleasure—come!"

But Isaac stared at the innkeeper sternly.

"Out of our way, you lying varlet," he growled. "Fetch us a flagon each of your best wine, and look to the price because I've travelled these roads before."

The wine was sour and very bad, and the price was outrageous. Isaac gave the scoundrelly innkeeper one third of it and they rode on, with him running behind them screeching curses. He gave it up, finally, and turned back, having made a profit of three hundred per cent upon his villainous wine but still feeling cheated, so great was his greed.

Pietro was close to tears. He had wanted that bath. And feather mattresses! By God, his good uncle had never displayed such parsimoniousness before. . . .

Isaac grinned at him.

"Good Pietro," he said gently, "do not grieve. Had you stuck your nose inside his public room, the stench would have bowled you over. You'd have seen nothing but drunkards and gamesters, and a plentiful supply of the most ill-favored bawds that ever it was your misfortune to meet. As for his bed chambers, they contain four beds each, and sometimes six. You and I would have been forced not only to share the same bed, but perhaps to accommodate other travellers whose persons would have been anything but savory. As for resting, if the fleas and other vermin ever permitted you to fall asleep you'd have been promptly awakened by the noise of some roisterer enjoying the favors of his ancient, unwashed whore—if others of her sisters had not by then molested you beyond all patience by their attempts to gain similar employment of you . . . Yet, there are worse inns. . . ."

"Worse than that?" Pietro demanded.

"Yes. The really bad ones are sometimes a little fairer of aspect. But in them the wine is invariably drugged. And if the daughters of joy seem younger and better looking, they are also more skilled at cutting a purse. You awake from that type with a splitting headache, naked as the day you were born, stripped of your goods, your horses, your money and your clothes, and transported while you slept to some distant and barren spot—if they were sufficiently courteous to refrain from cutting your throat."

"Aren't there any good inns?" Pietro asked.

"None," Isaac said. "It's better to sleep in the open."

So sleep in the open they did, with their weapons close at hand. But by God's Own Good Grace, they escaped being attacked by robbers. They had entered the Ancona March by now, a land as different from the Island of Sicily as any that could be imagined. Much of it was salt marsh, with tall grasses blowing before the wind and rocky hillsides that rose starkly out of the blue curve of the Adriatic Sea. A hot wind swept over it, rustling the grasses, and the gulls hung above sea and land, crying. A stark land, with edges to it—none of that lush blending of outlines that the tropic vegetation of Sicily provided. A clean, hard land. Brutal, clearlined, sure. The ospreys hung over the white water and screamed, and the sound of them was like music, harsh, discordant—but the right music, the real, the fitting—part of this, part of the wildness of it.

But they had reached their journey's end now. They had come to the farm of a yeoman, who had Isaac to thank for his start in life. This man had been born of peasant parents but had come into the world so crooked that none of the nobles valued him enough to receive his homage. He had subsisted after the death of his parents by cutting fagots in the wood belonging to Baron Rogliano, a privilege he had paid for with monies borrowed from Isaac. After a number of years these marginal lands, formerly a source of warfare between the fiefs of Rogliano and Siniscola, had become so cut over, barren and obviously worthless, that neither of those haughty nobles troubled himself to defend them any longer. It was at this juncture that the hunchback, Paoli, at Isaac's suggestion, had ventured to buy two parcels of land—one from Count Alessandro, and the other from Baron Rudolph—the money again provided by Isaac, whose heart always melted at the sight of great misfortune. In Paoli's case, the misfortune was coupled with real intelligence for he followed eagerly and to the letter Isaac's instructions on farming his miserable five acres. Working almost around the clock, the hunchback sank a well at the intersection of two hillslopes and found, as Isaac had told him he would, a plentiful supply of water not far below the surface. Then, following a drawing that Isaac had made, he constructed a waterwheel[1] after the fashion of the ones Isaac had seen in Egypt. This lifted the water from the well and splashed it down a wood causeway lined with pitch from where it fanned out through irrigation ditches all over Paoli's acres.

In one season the land had blossomed out of all belief. In five years, Paoli had paid off his debt—except the debt of gratitude his simple heart would always bear Isaac. Paoli's waterwheel, however, caused him some trouble at first. It earned him the reputation of being in league with the devil and brought priestly inquisitors down upon his head. But the good monks of the Abbey were learned men and no mean scientists themselves; they studied his apparatus for twelve days, watching his mule creaking it around in an endless circle, and the silver water flashing out of the clap pots bound to the rim of the wheel. Then, instead of punishing Paoli, they went back to the Abbey and promptly produced vastly superior copies of it for use upon the Abbey's lands, thus doubling their own produce.

Paoli received a visit from the Abbot—and his special blessing—whereupon Paoli, who was no fool, swore homage to the princely churchman and gave his lands to the Abbey—receiving them back as a fief, thus effectively preventing both his great and rapacious neighbors from taking them away from him by force, as they most certainly would have done now that they had become valuable again.

Now, for many years, it had been Isaac's custom to visit Paoli briefly upon his journeys to Rezzi. Paoli was always overjoyed to see his benefactor both out of gratitude and because he dearly loved to ply Isaac with questions about the world beyond his little valley.

They rode through the gates past Paoli's stone wall, and Pietro straightened up in the saddle. He was too proud to let a stranger see his weakness, and the very hope of rest strengthened him. Paoli came running to greet them, looking for all the world like an overgrown bullfrog, his enormous, ugly face split with a grin. He held Isaac's stirrup for the goldsmith to descend, then quickly noting how weary the boy was, put out his great arms and lifted Pietro down as tenderly as though he were a baby.

"Oh, the poor little fellow!" he crooned. "Worn out, ain't he? We'll soon fix that. . . ."

Half an hour later, Pietro was fast asleep in a good bed. He slept the entire afternoon, evening and night, and woke late the next morning, feeling alive again.

During his sleep, Isaac had plied Paoli with questions about the state of the siege. The townspeople of Rezzi were holding out stubbornly. But Count Alessandro was pressing his attack, knowing that sooner or later starvation would bring them to terms. Isaac, too, took his rest that night, but rose early the next morning to reconnoiter the situation. When Pietro got up, his good Uncle was gone.

Pietro found then that Paoli's good wife, Gina—for even so ugly and misshapen a man had had no difficulty in getting married once it was noised abroad that he was possessed of considerable means—had washed his travel-stained garments and even unpacked his finer things from his saddle bags and hung them up to air and lose their wrinkles. So it was that Pietro was able to bathe and attire himself once more like a young prince.

He ate the good breakfast that Gina prepared for him. Gina was a handsome wench, fat and jolly, much younger than her husband. Having married Paoli for his wealth she found, to her great surprise, that he was so gentle and good—never in all their years together having even cuffed her once, a great rarity among the peasants to whom wifebeating served as a safety valve to let off their pent up animosities toward their oppressors—that she had come finally to love him, despite his ugliness. But they had not been blessed with children and Gina was starved for someone to mother. Pietro, with his delicate, almost girlish beauty, served her need admirably. Within half a day, he had come to love this jolly peasant woman with all his heart.

He walked all over the farm, after having attended to the weary horses—for Paoli had lent Isaac a fine riding mule to replace his completely blown mount. Paoli showed him his fine irrigation system and told him how Isaac had designed it and the great miracle of how it had won him the Abbot's favor.

They were in the midst of this discussion, when the winding of horns sounded loud from the neighboring woods. Paoli's face contorted with fear and grief.

"What ails you, Paoli?" Pietro demanded.

"It's those Roglianos," Paoli almost wept. "They're hunting again—and if the stag or boar chooses to cross my fields—why there goes half a year's labor. . . ."

Pietro knew of this—the most dearly held of all feudal rights. A noble could always trample the fields of a villein in pursuit of his prey. But legally, only the field of his own villein—while Paoli was the vassal of the Abbot.

"Can't you," he said, "complain to his Lordship, the Abbot?"

"Yes—but what good is it? The Abbot is not warlike—as some churchly princes are—and he does not like to risk war with either the Baron or the Count. He sends me grain to keep me from starvation when my crops are ruined, and bids me bear my lot with patience; but 'tis hard—plagued hard. . . ."

"Wait," Pietro said, and ran back to the house. When he came back he bore both his good Saracen scimitar—that curved, flexible blade whose steel was vastly superior to that of any Christian blade, having been forged at Moorish Toledo in Spain—and his arbalist.

He put his foot in the stirrup of the arbalist, and began to wind the bow into the cocked position with the two-handed winch.[2] It was hard work for a boy as slight as he, but finally he had the great crossbow cocked and dropped the short steel-tipped arrow, called a quarrel, into the slot. Then he stood there, waiting.

The olifants sounded again, louder now. Paoli wept openly—both for fear of his fields and for the life of the boy that Isaac had left in his charge. And now the great stag burst out of the forest and came plunging toward them, bleeding from several wounds, the hounds hot on his heels.

Then Pietro did a strange thing. Instead of waiting and using his arbalist to defy the young lords, as Paoli expected him to, he lifted the weapon, and sent the quarrel through the stag at close range. The great buck plunged just once and fell dead at their feet.

The huntsmen spilled out of the woods now, racing upon their palfreys. They were all young and there were girls among them, flushed and laughing. They came bounding over the low wall, and when they saw their hounds milling about where Pietro and Paoli stood they reined in their horses.

"There is your stag," Pietro said coldly. "Take him and go!"

The faces of the young lords twisted. There were three of them—heavy, blond lads, standing nearly six feet tall and ranging from eighteen down to fifteen years. With them were three girls, two of them obviously unrelated since they were dark-haired and swarthy, entirely Italian; but the youngest was as rosy blonde as her brothers.

"Who are you?" Hans, the eldest Rogliano spat, "who dares kill our deer?"

"Who are you?" Pietro countered, "who dares trample the lands of a vassal of the Abbot?"

Hans rode his palfrey forward, his hands already on his sword.

Pietro felt his knees begin to shake. Against this solid German knight he hadn't a chance and he knew it. But he couldn't run—not before these maids. I'm a fool, he thought despairingly, and put his hand on the hilt of the scimitar.

"Wait!" the soprano voice was as clear as a bell. "Stop, Hans! I won't have it!"

Hans turned toward his sister. She was a year younger than Pietro, and to his young, Sicilian bred eyes, as beautiful as an angel. Actually, she was not beautiful, having the square face of the Brandenburg house; but she was so pink and blonde that it would be many years before Pietro realized this simple fact.

"Look Iolanthe," Hans growled, "I won't have this base vassal. . . ."

"What base vassal?" Iolanthe said crisply. "When have you ever seen a serf that looked like this one, Hans? Look at his clothes, good brother—his jewels. I think he's very likely a prince. . . ."

Hans studied Pietro with some interest.

"Who are you?" he demanded.

"Pietro of Sicily," Pietro said proudly. Now they knew no more than before. Pietro didn't like to lie, but clearly this blonde angel approved of him. He knew what would happen if she discovered his lowly birth. There were times, he guessed, when it didn't hurt to lie. And if there ever were such a time. . . .

Iolanthe rode forward, between them.

"Help me down," she said to Pietro.

Pietro put up his arms and helped her down. Good God, but she was wondrous warm and soft!

"Are you a prince, good Messer Pietro?" she teased.

Pietro's tongue was frozen with astonishment. In Sicily, all the maids were more or less secluded after the Moslem fashion—except certain commercially available ones, and those few amiable girls of the streets who, wanting protection from father or elder brother, were also available out of the warmth and goodness of their gentle hearts. But these Northern girls with their great boldness were to astonish him for a good many years—until he learned how innocent that boldness was, how little it meant.

But he rallied quickly.

"No, gentle lady," he whispered.

"Are you a vassal?"

"Yes—but only of my liege lord, his majesty Frederick Second, King of Sicily." This was truth. Clever truth.

"You talk riddles," Iolanthe pouted. "Just who and what are you?"

"As I told you, my lady—I am Pietro of Sicily. As for my station I am a poor gentleman, owing homage to no suzerain save alone my king. But I would gladly become a vassal—even a serf—if it were granted unto me to serve—you, my lady . . ." Then Pietro bowed grandly and kissed her hand.

"Well I'll be damned!" said Hans, Mark and Wolfgang in the same breath.

"Perhaps," Iolanthe said, dazzling him with her clear grey eyes, "perhaps even that can be arranged. For by Our Lady, Messire

Pietro, you're a wondrously handsome lad. Now help me to mount again."

Pietro did so. His hands tingled, felt scalded.

"My brothers will never again trample the fields of this villein," Iolanthe said. "If they do, I'll tell my father, and he'll beat them. Come boys, have the sergeants pick up the stag, and let us ride . . ." She paused, and smiled at Pietro.

"Good Messer Pietro," she said, "if you are ever in the neighborhood of Hellemark, pay us a call. My father, the Baron, will be most happy to receive you. . . ."

"The devil you say," Hans growled. "Father won't receive any penniless mountebank no matter how well he dresses. . . ."

"Oh yes he will," Iolanthe laughed, "if *I* ask him to. You know that right well, good brother."

Then she waved gaily to Pietro, and turned her palfrey toward the woods. Pietro stood there without moving until even the sergeants bearing the stag had disappeared into the forest. Then he turned to the hunchback with a sigh.

"Would God that what she said were true," he said.

"Oh it is!" Paoli said. "Everyone hereabout knows that. Baron Rudolph fairly dotes on that daughter of his. She can wind him about her little finger with ease. All my thanks, good Messer Pietro, for saving my fields. But you have also done yourself a great service; you have just bought your entry into the ranks of nobility—for no one hereabouts save good Isaac and I know that Donati is your father, and believe me I'll keep my lip buttoned. I do dearly love to see a peasant's son rise in life. . . ."

"Thanks," Pietro said listlessly. He felt giddy and sick, not knowing what sickness held him. He was dimly aware, however, that the cure for it rode laughing through the forest.

Isaac returned late that evening, and what was in his face was not good to look upon.

He toyed with the food that Gina put before him, without half tasting it. When he spoke, it was to Paoli.

"Goodman Paoli," he sighed, "get me some rags of villeins' clothing, small enough to fit the boy. . . ."

Pietro stiffened.

"When do we ride?" he whispered.

"Tonight," Isaac said. "There is no time. I go to Roccablanca, Count Alessandro's castle, to give myself up as hostage until the gold arrives. But first I have arranged to get you into the town. It will be risky work."

"The count has agreed to spare them?" Pietro breathed.

"No. He has agreed to spare my warehouses and my vassals—who have taken no part in the rebellion—upon the payment of enough gold to ruin me. As for the others—it's death, Pietro. You must convince Donati that his only hope is to flee. I've already paved your way in—and the way of both of you out—with gold . . ."

Pietro didn't say anything. Half an hour later, they rode.

When they came in sight of the city, Pietro shook all over as with chill. It was flaming in twenty places. Count Alessandro had his engines all around the walls. Great counterweighted trenchbuts groaned as their winches were wound; then the ropes were cast off and the arms swung and the stones, weighing half a ton, soared over the walls and crashed into the houses, smashing roofs, barricades, men. Lighter ballista hurled smaller stones, and mangonels threw casts of Greek fire into the already flaming town. There were also catapults, huge mounted crossbows, shooting iron-tipped arrows greater than a knight's lance into the city.

Besides all this artillery, Count Alessandro had two great sows already at work at the walls. These were sheds, roofed with wood and green hide against the fire and stones that defenders dropped from the walls, with long battering rams swinging from ropes within them. Pietro could hear the very earth shudder as the rams kept up their incessant pounding. Sprawled across the moat lay an overturned *bellfroi,* in mute tribute to the valor of the defenders. Pietro looked at this wood- and hide-covered tower, mounted on wheels and having its own drawbridge. As it lay there on its side he saw where the count had made his mistake. His engineers had filled the moat with fascines—bundles of branches—but they hadn't done the job well. One of the wheels of the tower had dug in, tilting it dangerously. Then a party of the defenders had used a great beam as a lever to topple it over. They had boiled the crushed men-at-arms alive with great kettles of scalding water and molten pitch flung down upon them as they scrambled to escape the overturned *bellfroi*—greatly increasing Count Alessandro's fury.

A party of crossbowmen crept forward now, behind a mantelet, a great shield mounted on wheels. In spite of all the efforts of the townsmen, it got close and the arbalists started their deadly fire. Even from where he sat trembling upon his mule, Pietro could hear the quarrels whine, and the screams of the men picked from the walltop with deadly accuracy. Their own bolts, and the arrows from their puny three foot longbows, stuck harmlessly into the front of the movable shield.

While the defenders were thus occupied, another shed was hurried forward. This one was even longer, lower and sturdier than the sows and Pietro saw that it had no battering ram under it.

"A cat," Isaac explained. "They're going to try to tunnel through the walls."

Even as he spoke, the workmen protected by the heavy roof, attacked the wall with crowbars and pickaxes. But it was slow work. It would take days—even weeks perhaps.

"The age of scientific warfare," Isaac groaned. "In nothing have we greater skill than in the art of killing each other . . . Come!"

They rode in a great circle about Rezzi until they came to a quiet sector, guarded by the Count's men at arms to prevent the entry of food or supplies into the besieged town. Here were no engines, for lack of suitable targets. Isaac got down and began a whispered conversation with a sergeant. Then the man came back to where Pietro stood.

"Come, boy," he said gruffly. He rode rapidly, right up to the wall itself, exposing himself boldly, secure in the knowledge that the women and old men guarding this section with boiling pitch and rocks, would be able to do nothing until he was directly beneath them.

Five feet away from the wall, he brought out a white cloth and waved.

" 'Tis the son of Donati!" he bellowed. "Let him pass!"

Then with ease he hoisted the boy up until Pietro stood upon his shoulders, and rode up to the wall. By climbing gingerly into the saddle and standing there, he was able to boost the boy high up the wall. Then, after some debate, the old men let down a knotted rope.

Pietro caught it and they drew him up. Instantly he found twenty daggers, swords, butcher knives and scythe blades pointed at his chest. Then, seeing how small he was and that he bore no weapons, they stood back while an old hag thrust a torch into his face.

" 'Tis indeed our leader's son," she announced. "The boy is the very spit of Maria, his mother—I remember her well. Well, son, what news have you?"

"None," Pietro whispered. "Where is my father?"

"I'll take you to him," the old crone said.

She led the boy to that part of the walls under heaviest attack. Donati was there, commanding improvised mangonels. These had been made by cutting off the tops of green trees, splitting the trunks half way down, binding their bottoms with stout ropes to prevent them from splitting further, and then bending one split portion back with winches so that when released it struck the butt of a heavy lance perched atop the other part of the trunk, driving it with great force into the ranks of the besiegers.

Pietro stood there, staring at his father. Donati, at that moment, seemed to him half a god. He was the biggest man his son had ever seen, his wild, grey-streaked blond hair and beard flying, his great voice thundering commands everywhere at once; bleeding from a dozen minor wounds without appearing to notice it yet inspiring his men so that weary, already beaten, all of them wounded, some of them half dead, they fought on like demons.

"My father," Pietro whispered; "Good God, that from such a man came such a thing as I!"

They led Pietro up to him.

"Donati," the old woman said, "behold your son!"

Donati stared at the boy a long moment. Then suddenly, he dropped to his knees and crushed Pietro to him so hard that the boy's breath left his body. He could feel Donati's great frame shake, and the wiry whiskers almost smothered him as Donati covered his face with kisses. It wasn't pleasant. Donati's breath was compounded half of wine and half of garlic, and he smelled rankly of sweat and blood.

But Pietro couldn't help crying. It was all intensely moving, the love this great man bore him shining out of those flooded blue eyes, the big, fine emotion that shook that giant frame beyond speech.

"My son," Donati rumbled. "My son, my son, my son!"

Then he stood up suddenly, and lifted the boy for his men to see.

"Ye rats!" he roared. "Ye doomed, dirty, hopeless scum of earth! Ye sons of filth—behold—my son!"

And the men rocked the blazing heaven with their cheers.

Pietro knew it was hopeless then. Never would this man—this man—no other word, no finer word existed to describe him—leave these gallant street rats who for weeks now had held off the finest professional fighters in all Italy. It was too much to even ask him to. It was more than too much—it was shameful.

But he had to. He had promised Isaac. And his father deserved life. Besides, what other choice had he?

He had one all right. He knew that. It kept whispering inside of him. It shook him. Tore his insides to bloody, quivering fearful shreds. Stay with him, Pietro! Die with your father. With this great man, your father. It's not so hard to die—to die with honor is easy. . . .

Only—he couldn't. He was a coward through and through. He was a little boy, thirteen years old and all of life was before him and he didn't want to die. He was thirteen years of age and tomorrow he could ride away from here and call casually at Hellemark and be welcomed. At Hellemark. Where Iolanthe was. Where her grey eyes laughed. Her red mouth . . . Her softness . . . Her warmth.

"Oh, God!" he wept; "oh God, oh Jesus, I—" Then he screamed it out, spat out between his clenched teeth, babbled it, sobbed it, screeched it: "Father! You don't have to die you don't father Isaac has bribed them you can come with me now over the back wall and into the wood they will not stop you father come, oh God, oh Jesus, father!"

Donati put him down then. Slowly.

"Look at me, boy," Donati said.

Pietro's dark face came up.

"You're your mother's son," Donati said gently. "That's her softness talking—her love for me. She'd have put that love above all else too. Even above—honor. . . ."

Pietro shook all over with weeping.

"Don't cry, boy. But you're my son, too. And you won't shame me again, will you?"

"No, father," Pietro whispered.

"Good. Then go back to Isaac, and give him my thanks. His gold is lost—Count Satan will never give it back. I'm sorry about that. But give him my thanks. He meant well—as always. And Pietro *mio*—know this, I'm proud of you! You rode weaponless through that hell out there to try to save me. It was wrong but it was very brave. . . . Now kiss me, boy, and go!"

Pietro looked at him.

"No, father," he said.

Donati's big face was puzzled.

"Don't you want to kiss me?" he rumbled.

"Yes, father. Gladly. Only—I'm not going."

The big man stared at him. Then he lifted his eyes toward where the flames of the burning town bloodied the sky.

"Holy Mother," he whispered, "I thank thee for such a son." Then, with scarcely a pause, he lifted Pietro into his great arms and strode away from the walls, back through the crooked, tortuous streets, flame-lighted, flickering, thundering to the crash of the stones from the trenchbuts and the screams of the dying. He walked until he came to the wall that Pietro had mounted. He climbed upon it and lifted his big voice.

"Ye swine!" he bellowed. "Ye sons of serpents and things that crawl 'neath the earth. Ye bloody whoresons! Especially he that conducted this boy hither, come!"

There was a flickering of motion among the enemy troops. Then the big sergeant rode out, bearing his white cloth.

"Here!" Donati roared, when the man was beneath him, "catch!"

Then he threw the boy out and away from him. The sergeant

caught him neatly, and carried him back toward where the mule waited.

Pietro mounted and rode back to the villa of Paoli. And never for an instant over all that distance did he cease crying.

Three days later, Rezzi fell.

Pietro hid in the house of Paoli until he could stand it no longer. Then he rode toward Roccablanca, the castle of the Siniscolas, to beg a word with Isaac. When he was close, he saw Isaac.

The good Jew was hanging from one of the parapets. Naked. Upside down. His belly was ripped open, so that his entrails dangled. Other things had been done to him too. Unspeakable things.

Pietro slumped forward on the neck of his great stallion Amir. He could neither see nor speak, but he clung to the destrier's coarse mane. And the wise beast whirled and ran away from there, down a long row of oaks. The wind revived the boy. He straightened. Then he saw that the trees bore strange fruit. From each of them, for leagues in the distance, men were hanging. Count Alessandro had had his vengeance.

Pietro didn't faint. He didn't even weep. He was beyond that now. Inside him the songs of Palermo died, the sunlight that had entered him through ten happy years turned black. His youth died. Some part of his beauty. What was left was very simple. It could be summed up in a word. One word.

Murder.

He rode until he came to the tree upon which they had hanged Donati, his father, after having of him certain other prolonged and devilish pleasures. Then he knelt down and tried to pray. He couldn't. Murder leaves no room for prayer.

He stayed there a long time, trying. He was still there when he heard that clear voice, recognized at once, well remembered, crying:

"Oh father, how ghastly, what an unspeakable beast Count Alessandro is! You must fight him, father! You must! You must!"

Pietro got to his feet.

"When you do, my lord," he said quietly, "please accept my services."

"Pietro!" Iolanthe said.

Baron Rudolph stared at the boy, half with recognition. There was something plaguedly familiar about this youth, clad so magnificently in black velvet edged with marten fur and resplendent with jewels.

"Who are you?" the Baron rumbled.

"Pietro," the boy said. "Son of that Donati—who hangs—there. . . ."

They followed his pointing finger. Iolanthe shuddered and covered her eyes.

"No wonder I thought I knew you!" Rudolph roared; "thy mother was. . . ."

"Maria, whom my lord has cause to remember," Pietro said.

"Of course, of course! I was a fool to—"

"This is hardly the place to discuss it, my lord," Pietro said. "Nor the time."

"You're right," the Baron said. "Where do you live, Pietro?"

"I have no home," Pietro said. "My father and my guardian have both been slain."

"Then what the devil do you propose to do?" Rudolph roared. But Iolanthe whirled upon her father.

"What do you propose to do, father?" she cried. "That's the question, isn't it? The poor boy has had his father and his guardian murdered in a single night, and you ask him what he's going to do?"

"But . . ." Rudolph spluttered.

"I'll tell you what you're going to do," Iolanthe said. "You're going to take him home with us before Count Siniscola kills him, too! And you're going to keep him, and. . . ."

Baron Rudolph lifted a heavy hand.

"I can't make a serf of this boy, Io," he said. "From the looks of him he's been gently nurtured despite his birth. . . ."

"I can serve my lord," Pietro said in that tone of his that under the circumstances was so dreadful in its calm, "as scribe, keeper of records, chamberlain—what my lord wills. I know Latin and Greek and French, and divers other tongues. I write a fair hand. I am good with figures. . . ."

Baron Rogliano stared at him. All these accomplishments were beyond him.

"Good," he said, "I'll—"

"You'll do nothing of the kind!" Iolanthe wept. "He's going to be Hans' esquire. And when the time comes, you're going to knight him yourself, father."

"But, Io," the Baron protested, "the boy's baseborn. . . ."

"So is many another great Lord!" Iolanthe said. "I don't care. He's going to be a knight. My knight!" Then she swung down from the saddle and kissed Pietro, before her father's astonished eyes, full upon the mouth. "There!" she said. "Now come with us!"

Pietro mounted. In the saddle, he turned and looked at the thing that had been his father.

"I'll send men to cut him down, and Father Antonio to give him Christian burial," Baron Rudolph growled. In his way, Rudolph of Brandenburg was a kindly man. Then he looked at the boy, riding so slim and straight in the saddle. "God's eyes!" he swore. "That lad would make a knight—at that!"

Chapter Three

IOLANTHE CAME INTO the hallway where Pietro slept just outside of Hans' door. She stood there a moment, looking at him. Then she knelt down beside him and kissed him, very gently, on the mouth.

Pietro stirred. Groaned. He threw out one arm so that Iolanthe had to move quickly to avoid being struck by it. But he didn't open his eyes.

The girl knelt there, looking at him. Then she put out her hand and let it rest on his bare shoulder. She let it stay there a long moment, feeling the hard sinew under her palm before she shook him.

Pietro sat up at once. He caught at the coverlet, and drew it up around him.

"For God's Love, Io!" he said.

Like everyone else in those days, Pietro slept entirely nude.

"Don't be silly," Io whispered; "I didn't come here to look at you. Besides, I know how you look. . . ."

Pietro blushed bright scarlet. That, he reflected unhappily, was quite true. On several occasions when he had come back dogtired and smelling of sweat from practicing at arms, Io had come into his chamber as he was indulging in his Sicilian custom of taking complete baths. She had even scrubbed his back for him. Only she had done it so innocently. Like a sister. That had vexed Pietro. He was ashamed of the reason why it had vexed him. But he didn't want Io for a sister. That was the last way on earth he wanted her.

Except that she wasn't always sisterly—thank God. Except that there had been times when. . . .

"Come on," she snapped at him. "Get up, you lout!"

"Why?" Pietro said. "It's very early and—"

"I know it's early. Thank the blessed saints for that. If we ride like the devil we may be in time—"

"In time for what?" Pietro said.

"To prevent Mark and Wolfgang from getting themselves killed, the fools! Oh, why didn't they have sense enough to keep Andrea from leading them into this!"

"Io," Pietro said wearily, "in the first place, you're talking riddles; in the second, I can't possibly get up with you standing there. . . ."

"I'll turn my back," Io said. "No, I'll go down into the bailey and get the horses saddled. You join me there. As for the riddle—Andrea of Siniscola has been quarrelling for months with his cousin Ricardo over that pale little Elaine. She's our cousin—on her mother's side. On her father's, she's a Siniscola, too, though she doesn't look like them. . . ."

"More riddles," Pietro groaned.

"That's right, you don't know Elaine, do you? No matter. Andrea and Ricardo are rivals for her hand. Now that everybody knows that Ricardo is getting the best of him, Andrea has decided to attack Ricardo at Rocca d'Aquilino. And Mark and Wolfgang, my precious, thick headed brothers are going along. So, naturally, I have to stop it."

"You?" Pietro whispered. "How can you stop it? Why don't you just tell your father and let him—"

"And take a chance on his being killed in the bargain? No, thank you, Pietro. I'm going to stop it—without anyone's help. Not even yours. I only want you along for company. Men are much too stupid to handle a matter like this. Now hurry. I'll be waiting. . . ."

Pietro waited until the whisper of her velvet slippers turned the corner, then he got up from his pallet. It was early in September of the year 1211, but already the air had a bite to it. Pietro slapped his arms against his naked sides to restore the circulation. But that didn't do much good, so he put on his linen underdrawers, and his long woolen stockings, and gratefully dropped his pelisson over his head. To his great vexation, his pelisson was not edged with fur. That luxury was reserved for the gently born.

Over the pelisson, he put his long *bliaut,* which was of good enough stuff, but rather plain. Pietro ruefully remembered the finery of the garments he had now outgrown, and the jewels that Iolanthe kept for him in a chest, since he was no longer allowed to wear them.

He could hear Hans snoring in his good bed. Ordinarily in another hour or so, he would have been obliged to enter Hans' chamber and awaken him. But, from what Io had said, this was no ordinary day.

This business of having to wake Hans up and dress him was actually no humiliation. Baron Rudolph's sons—Io's brothers, Mark and Wolfgang—had to do the same thing for Count Alessandro of Siniscola and his sons. As a squire, even a Duke's son was expected to be a servant. At court, great nobles vied to carry the spiced boar's head before the king. . . .

His own position, at Hellemark, was a curious one. He served Hans as squire, to the scandal of all the Baron's noble vassals. But he had absolutely no hope of being knighted—not ever. True enough, the sons of peasants had sometimes been knighted in the past; but that invariably happened upon the field of battle when the baseborn lad performed some feat of signal heroism. For even so powerful a Baron as Rudolph to willfully knight the son of his former armorer was to bring his own nobility into question.

Today, at nearby Rocca d'Aquilino, there was going to be fighting. But he and Io were going to ride forth in secret, and even if the world later discovered what had happened, Pietro, who knew himself, realized how slight his chance of being knighted for heroism in battle was. By dint of much practice, he had acquired remarkable skill in arms, which served him not at all. What good was it to be able to hit the exact center of your opponent's shield ten times out of ten in a practice joust, when you lacked the strength to even dent it? Every time he jousted with Hans, he was tumbled unceremoniously out of the saddle. Yet he was actually a much more skillful fighter than Hans. But Hans stood six feet two inches tall and weighed one hundred ninety pounds. Pietro, at sixteen, was a bare five foot eight, and weighed one hundred thirty. That is, he was half an inch taller than Iolanthe, and five pounds heavier. . . .

Even Mark and Wolfgang, Hans' younger brothers, were both much bigger than he. Every time he thought of them, living now among the Siniscolas at Roccablanca, Pietro felt sick. In a word, the fact that Rudolph of Brandenburg, Baron Rogliano, had sent his younger sons to Roccablanca for their nurture as squires expressed exactly Pietro's chances of doing anything whatsoever about the murder of his father and his good uncle, Isaac. Count Alessandro of Siniscola and Baron Rudolph hunted together these days, and kissed each other when they met. There was even talk of a closer alliance—of a marriage between Enzio, Alessandro's thirty year old eldest son and Iolanthe. . . .

"God, thou son of Saint Mary!" Pietro swore aloud, thinking of it.

Inside his chamber, Hans groaned in his sleep. Pietro froze, listening. There was no other sound, so he let his breath out slowly. Hans was a heavy sleeper. But in this, as in several other matters, Pietro's position had improved. No longer did Hans send him sprawling with a well directed kick. Strangely enough, a kind of rough camaraderie had grown up between them; because, by slow degrees, Pietro had earned Hans' respect.

That had been hard. Pietro remembered the first day he'd tried jousting against the target shield. It was mounted on a post with a swinging weight on the other end. The beam was attached to the top of the post with a pivot. So, if you didn't hit the target dead center with the point of the lance, the weight swung around and fetched you a mighty buffet. Enough in the case of one so light as Pietro to knock you out of the saddle. Twelve times Pietro had tried it, and twelve times the weight had knocked him over the pommel of his saddle into the dust. Hans had been doubled over in the saddle, speechless with laughter. Even Iolanthe laughed until the tears ran down her face. On the thirteenth try, with his own tears streaking the grime on his face, Pietro hit the shield in the center.

That night he got up from his pallet and went out to the stables. He hung a stolen lantern over the shield. The next morning there wasn't a place on his body he could bear to touch with his own fingers; but he could hit the shield's center six times out of ten. Every night he practiced until his body grew hard as whipcord. The next time, two weeks later, that Hans proposed a trial, Pietro scored not a single miss.

Later, further to test him, Hans gave him a stallion colt to break. But Pietro had a way with horses. He clung to the rangy young beast tighter than a burr, defying all the animal's efforts to unseat him. And Hans laid a hand on his shoulder and growled: "Well done, Pietro!"

He held his own at hunting, and the master falconer spoke to him with marked respect. At hawking, Pietro could outdo anyone at Hellemark, including Messire Ruffio, himself an impoverished knight.

But he needed both hands to raise the sword that Hans swung with a flick of his wrist. If unseated while in mail, it took him forever to get to his feet, while Hans could leap into the saddle fully armed without touching the stirrups. . . .

True enough, Father Antonio employed his services often in the copying of manuscripts. True, he wrote all the Baron's letters in fair and courtly Latin, and aided Messire Giovanni, the Seneschal, in keeping records. True, in many such details, he was so valuable to the upkeep of Hellemark that he was sure of a home there forever; but when had a fair hand and a knowledge of divers tongues been accounted knightly accomplishments? Many of the greatest lords in the land couldn't read their own names in Gothic script. . . .

He was so lost in his own thoughts that he didn't hear Iolanthe until she was almost upon him.

"For God's Love, Pietro," she whispered. "What's keeping you? We must ride now!"

"I'm ready," Pietro said.

In the bailey, they mounted and started the long ride to Rocca d'Aquilino.

Riding along beside her over the some twenty miles that separated the castles of Hellemark and Rocca d'Aquilino, Pietro stared at Iolanthe quite openly. With admiration. Respect. Tenderness. Love—and great sadness.

The sun came up over the mountains. He could see her now. Her young face was serene, composed and without fear.

While I, Pietro thought miserably, am shaking in my boots for fear of what lies before us. . . . Is it perhaps true that there is a difference between men—that the gently born have a certain extra something? A command of themselves, maybe, a happy freedom from fear?

He didn't know. What he did know was that Io was lovely. It wasn't a delicate loveliness. Rather she had the glowing health and high coloring of a maid who had spent much time in the open air, riding beneath the sun. Already, in the three years that he had known her, Pietro understood many things about Io. And all of these things filled him with awe.

She is so gay, he mused. Full of laughter. She has a flippant tongue, but that is a surface thing, like the foam upon deep waters. And the depths within her are bottomless. Baron Rudolph is the Suzerain of Rogliano, but she runs it. She's but fifteen years old and yet she commands all things that matter at Hellemark like a woman grown—no, not even that—like a man. A very gentle man of delicacy and breeding and wisdom and great kindness. . . . I, he thought sadly, put to such a test would have been destroyed by it. . . .

Io turned in the saddle and looked at him.

"Why are you looking at me like that, Pietro?" she said.

"Because," Pietro began, and hesitated. Then he blurted it out—the thing he had wanted so long to say: "Because you're lovely," he said. "And because I love you. . . ."

She reined in the little white palfrey until their knees touched. Then she leaned over and put out her arms to him.

He kissed her. It wasn't the first time. He had kissed her many times. The first time—at her command. She liked being kissed by him. He knew that.

But this time, it was different.

She leaned against his shoulder and her face was very white.

Then the color came flooding back into it. She opened her eyes.

"Do that again," she whispered. "Like that."

"Do what again," Pietro got out, "like what?"

Her lips moved slowly, brushing his ear.

"Like that. Make my toes curl again. It's the first time you ever did that. It's very interesting."

"God, Thou Son of Saint Mary!" Pietro swore.

"Don't swear. It is. You've kissed me before, and I've always liked it. It always makes me feel warm and soft—and sort of—sort of sleepy. . . ."

"And this time it didn't?"

"No. I don't feel sleepy at all. Not the least bit. Stop wasting time, Pietro—kiss me."

He did. A long time, and very thoroughly.

She tore free of him.

"No," she said, staring at him. "Don't. Not any more."

"Why not?"

"Because—because I've found out something."

"What?" Pietro said.

"I won't tell you. Oh, yes—I will. I—I've always wondered why women permitted men their bodies—in the way that resulted in a child. Now I know. You just taught me. . . ."

"I?" Pietro said wonderingly.

"Yes—you. It always seemed strange to me—and rather disgusting. I've seen the animals and my brothers told me that people did much the same sort of thing. That made me feel sick. But I don't feel that way any more. You know, Pietro—it's like a storm in the summertime. Everything is quiet, and the air is very still—almost oppressive. Then there's a thunderclap. And lightning splits the sky apart. Then torrents—roaring so loud you can't hear your own heart. . . ."

"It," Pietro whispered, "was like that—with you?"

"Yes. Inside me—the thunderclap. And the lightnings. And the torrents. Still the torrents. They keep on pounding—and—I—I cannot hear my heart. . . ."

Pietro looked at her and his face twisted. He had the shameful conviction that he was going to cry.

She stared at him.

"What ails you?" she said.

"I," he said sadly, "have always felt like that—from the first. But it's no good, Io—"

"Why not?" she said clearly.

"Because we cannot. You—you're like a star. And I'm a mole grubbing beneath the earth. That far apart. I cannot even raise my head to look at you. . . ."

"Pietro," Io said.

"Yes?" he whispered; "yes, Io?"

"I love you, too. Really love you. And all the difference in our stations and all the other foolishness that men dreamed up to make themselves feel important and better than other men aren't going to make any difference. . . ."

"But they will, Io," Pietro half wept. "Ah, but they will!"

"No, they won't. I won't let them. I always knew that when I finally did fall in love it would be forever. It is forever, my Pietro—for always. I'm going to be your wife. And if—they—my father and people like him, prevent that—I'll be your mistress. I'd rather be your wife and live with you and have your sons. But if I can't, I'll be the other and take what crumbs of your love I may have and never be ashamed. . . ."

"Crumbs!" Pietro cried. "Good God!"

"Amen to that," Iolanthe said. "Come, we still have far to ride. . . ."

It was late in the evening when they got to Rocca d'Aquilino. Andrea and Mark and Wolfgang and the knights of Siniscola that Andrea had commanded in the absence of his father were already before the walls.

The crossbowmen were shooting down at them. They were firing back with mounted bows and small catapults, and were already hammering away at the walls with a ram.

"Wait here," Iolanthe said.

Pietro sat very still, watching her. He didn't know what she was going to do, but he didn't like it. Even not knowing, he didn't like it. He was afraid.

Io clapped spurs to her white palfrey and galloped out. In half a second, she was going to ride between them. Into that cloud of arrows.

"Io!" he screamed. Then he was pounding after her.

She heard him coming, and turned in her saddle.

"Go back!" she cried. "You'll spoil it all!"

The arrows darkened the sun. The crossbow quarrels whistled.

Pietro came on. He wasn't afraid any more. He wasn't thinking about himself. He was outside himself. His heart, his breath, his life rode before him on a white palfrey.

There were three feathered bolts through his cloak and he didn't know it. He didn't know anything, see anything but those red blonde braids flying out proudly, like plumes.

She was waving something now. Something white. The whistling of the arrows stopped. The thud of the ram.

"Sire Ricardo!" she called out, clearly; "I bid you cover me with your fire. Slay any man that rides out to seize me—even my brothers!"

Pietro came up to her.

"Io!" he got out, "Io, for God's love!"

"Save this man, who came with me!" Io called out quickly. Then, to Pietro: "Oh, you fool—you sweet and tender fool!"

He could see the tall figure of Ricardo of Siniscola standing upon the walls.

"You are covered, my Lady Io," Ricardo laughed.

"Good!" Io called. "Andrea, thou stupid beast—think you to win love by force of arms? And brothers mine, what can you do here except die in this unworthy cause? Go back! Call back your knights and ride!"

"And if we do not?" Wolfgang called.

"I shall deliver myself up to my Lord Ricardo to be held as hostage, until our father and Count Alessandro return from Sicily. Then will my messenger and mine own lips acquaint him with your murderous folly. Now upon the honor of our sainted mother, I bid you—go!"

Pietro sat there, staring at her. She had them. She had them because she was right. That was one thing. But the other was greater and more terrible. This fifteen year old girl could vanquish these hundred odd knights because she was prepared quite simply to die to enforce what she believed.

That was it. That was the thing in Iolanthe that had always

awed him. Frightened him. She was a child. A gentle lovely child—and a woman at the same time. A real woman.

A lady. A very proud and great and fearless lady, sitting there like a queen.

I, Pietro wept inside his heart, shall never be worthy of her—never. . . .

Then Andrea of Siniscola rode out a little from the others.

"You win, this time, Fair Cousin Ricardo," he called. "Though there is small honor in hiding behind a woman's skirts! But there will be other times—and I shall have Elaine yet!"

They could see Ricardo stiffen.

"Sire Ricardo," Io called, "give no heed to the mouthings of this braggart! My cousin Elaine bids me tell you that she would not have him were he the last man alive! Now you, Andrea, you half-fledged knight be off or I'll have my father deal with you—and yours!"

They made, after that, a small show of defiance. Then the older knights compelled them to break ranks and ride. These knights of Siniscola had had from the first, misgivings about this stripling-led expedition upon which they had embarked.

After they had gone, Ricardo of Siniscola came down and invited Io and Pietro into the castle. He was taller than Count Alessandro's family and fairer. He was also very handsome, with a smooth and kindly face.

"My thanks, Cousin Io," he laughed; "God's Eyes! Were I not promised to Elaine I could fall too much in love with you!"

"But you are promised," Io said smoothly; "now, by God's Gentle Mother, give us food—for we are starving. . . ."

After they had eaten they rode forth again, though Ricardo begged them to stay.

"We left without Hans' leave," Iolanthe explained. "And I fear me that it will take much talk to make him keep his hands off Pietro here. My brother is not noted for his trusting mind. . . ."

"Then I will send my sergeant with you with a note to him. I wouldn't want the boy harmed because of me," Ricardo said.

It was a good thing that he did. Hans was furious, when they arrived early that next morning. But with proof of their truthfulness in his hands there was nothing he could do. He stood there staring at Pietro for a long time after Io had gone.

"You've polished my mail?"[1] he said at last.

"Yes, my Lord," Pietro said.

"And your own? We'll be needing them, you know. . . ."

Pietro stared at him. All Italy was upside down, since Otto of Brunswick the gigantic Welf, had invaded the Tuscan patrimonium in the autumn of 1210, almost exactly a year ago.[2] At the moment, Otto was in the province of Calabria in mainland Sicily, the very toe of the Italian boot, making ready to cross over into the Island. And Frederick, the sixteen year old—Pietro paused, groping for a word—certainly not king any longer—then the phrase *regulus non rex* suggested itself. Strange how Latin adapted itself to the formation of unpleasant thoughts. Frederick, my friend, he thought proudly, ruler, not king—but only for a time—is reduced to attempted bribery with money he does not possess, and to keeping a swift galley near the fort of Castellmare in the harbor of Palermo, ready to flee to Africa.

He cleared his throat so that Hans would notice neither the nervous huskiness, nor the tremble.

"We ride to war, then?" he whispered.

"No! Whatever gave you such an idea, Pietro? You know father's a firm Waibling? He's still mooning over the idea that some miracle will save young Frederick. . . ."

"He's right," Pietro said.

"Ha!" Hans snorted. "Otto has all Italy and most of Sicily already. He lacks only the Island. All Frederick's barons have revolted. The Saracens have invited Otto to take over—and the Spanish knights he was depending upon to put down the barons, his only reason for marrying that old woman, died of the plague within a month after they landed.[3] Father's old, and soft in the head. What makes you so sure that royal ragamuffin will win out?"

"I know Frederick," Pietro said.

"You know Frederick?" Hans laughed. "Now I'll tell one!"

"But I do," Pietro said quietly. "I hunted boars with him in Sicily."

Hans stared at him.

"Look, Pietro, I've never known you to lie; but when you tell me that a blacksmith's son went hunting with the king. . . ."

"No one in Sicily knew I was a blacksmith's son. You saw how I dressed when I came here."

"That's true," Hans mused. "We thought you were a prince. Tell me, what's he like?"

"Short, thickset, blond. Very strong and exceedingly handsome. Prouder than Lucifer himself. To beat him, they'll have to kill him."

"They might do that, too," Hans said.

"But if we're not going to war. . ."

"Look, Pietro, Count Alessandro has declared for the Welf. You want us besieged here in Hellemark?"

"No," Pietro said.

"I thought not. Now about the armor. You and I are riding to Roccablanca. . . ."

"No!"

"I forgot, that business about your father, eh? Good Pietro, forget it. Even Father Antonio had trouble about that. He was called before the Bishop and made to do penance for giving your old man Christian burial. The Bishop held that any man who revolted against his liege lord had broken vows sworn before God and upon Holy Relics—and hence in effect had revolted against God. It took some persuasion on Father Antonio's part to convince him it wouldn't be a good idea to exhume your father's body and pronounce anathema on it. . . ."

"Very well," Pietro said quietly, "for what reason do we go to Roccablanca?"

"To hunt, of course. Tomorrow Count Alessandro's knighting Anweiler, heir to the Duchy of Spoleto, and. . . ."

"You mean heir to the County of Acerra, don't you?" Pietro said drily.

"Pietro you're the limit! All right. Anweiler's father was Count of Acerra; but the Emperor made him Duke of Spoleto. When are you going to learn to acknowledge facts?"

"When I'm convinced they're accomplished. Diepold of Schweinspeunt, Count Acerra, is a common traitor and should be hanged. Spoleto is one of the Papal States—ceded to His Holiness by Otto, himself. How can Otto now make a Duchy of it and give it to that thief?"

"You speak of noblemen, remember," Hans growled.

"I know. That always excuses villainy, doesn't it? My father fought for liberty, and for bread, so that made him a felon to be tortured and hanged. Diepold and the rest of the Apulian barons, including Count Alessandro are nobles. This makes their treachery —which has as its excuse only their own lust for power—smell of rosewater and other fair savors. . . ."

"Pietro, I'm warning you!"

"You mean to strike me, Hans? Go ahead. It would be fitting. The Apulian barons band together to rob a youth of my own years. Great and powerful nobles against a tattered, ragamuffin king. Well, why don't you strike? It would display your bravery beautifully for you to vanquish so huge and powerful a churl as me, especially in defense of that same Count Siniscola who murdered your own good uncle Liepold, took Rocca Acerra from your father, besieged you here in Hellemark for so long that the confinement and poor food cost your own mother, the gentle lady Brigarde, her life. . . ."

"My mother died in childbirth!" Hans roared; "Pietro, by God. . . ."

"Your mother bore you, and Mark and Wolfgang, great infants weighing many pounds, and lived and was healthy. Why should she die of being brought to bed of your fair sister, who was small and delicate and should have been the least trouble of all?"

"You know, Pietro," Hans said grimly, "I wasn't going to strike you; but now, by God, I think I will!"

"You," Iolanthe called through the doorway, "will do nothing of the kind, Hans!"

"Io, for God's sake!" Hans began.

"Do not swear, good brother. I won't have you striking poor Pietro. In the first place, he's half your size. In the second he's only told you the exact and blessed truth. . . ."

"And in the third," Hans roared, "you're a mite too fond of him to suit me, sister mine!"

"True," Iolanthe sighed. "I am, in fact, most fond. He's a very pretty lad, Hans."

"His father was a villein!"

"I did not say I was fond of his father," Iolanthe said tartly. "All I'm saying, Sir Hans, my most unknightly brother, is that if father persists in considering this folly of marrying me to that blackbearded beast Enzio, I shall submit, dutifully. But I shall take Pietro along to sing me those pretty Sicilian songs, and twang the lute and console me in the absence of my husband!"

"Io!" Hans roared.

"My lady jests, of course," Pietro said smoothly. "It is not good to so provoke my lord. I am sorry for my hot words, Sir Hans. But I'm afraid I still don't understand what connection the knighting of young Anweiler has with us, here. . . ."

"They're knighting Mark and Wolfgang along with him," Hans said gruffly. He was still looking at his sister. "Io, if I thought. . . ."

"If you thought what?" Iolanthe demanded.

No, Pietro thought miserably—no. I have been kissed by that red mouth until my blood ran fire, Hans. I have had my back scrubbed by that fair hand while taking a complete bath. I have been visited upon my pallet outside your door, you lout, by this angel clad only in a pelisse of finest silk[4]—but what you're thinking, no. By Our Lady, Count Alessandro could learn the refinement and subtlety of cruelty from Io!

"Never mind," Hans growled. Hans was as brave as a lion in the saddle. But in certain other matters, he was a coward. Even his dull brain was able to comprehend the folly of pushing this matter too far. If what he suspected were true, he would have to kill Pietro, whom he was fond of, upon whom he depended in many ways, and whose death would solve nothing. One might clear the stain upon a sister's honor by killing a great knight in her behalf; but if one slew merely a villein, the stain not only persisted, but deepened. Actually, without knowing it, Iolanthe had made Pietro's life completely safe at her brother's hands. To kill his squire would be to make public admission that his sister had stooped to unbelievable baseness; for while the nobles of thirteenth century Italy could forgive folly, never for an instant would they countenance the crossing of the hard drawn lines of birth and privilege. . . .

"All right," Iolanthe said, smiling. "We have quarrelled too much, haven't we? I'll join you at Roccablanca tomorrow. It'll be wondrously diverting—especially since I can amuse myself by tormenting that balding fool. So much hair upon his chin, and so little upon his head![5] And inside that head such a twisted mass of villainy that I can always confuse him utterly, merely by telling him the truth. . . ."

"Father should give you to some true German knight," Hans said. "Even a Norman wouldn't be half bad. But these Italians! They're half Moors,[6] anyhow. . . ."

"I'll get your armor, my lord," Pietro said.

When he came back with the hauberks and helmets, Iolanthe was gone. Pietro was glad of that. He had troubles enough without her there to put Hans into an ill humor.

At the sight of his armor, Hans became cheerful. Castle politics irked him. But put him in the saddle with his good sword in his hand—that was another matter. As far as Hans was concerned, Providence could have arranged things far better than it had—so that a true knight could spend his life dashing over the fields in the hunt, making glorious war upon his enemies and dallying at love. . . .

And eating. A good banquet was almost as much fun as a tournament. Hans did not include drinking in his list of pleasures. He had not yet acquired his father's slavish addiction to wine. . . .

Half an hour later, after an almost sinfully brief mass, and a breakfast of a few pieces of hard bread washed down with watered wine, they rode away from Hellemark. Hans was in complete armor, helmet, hauberk and shield, with his good sword, Heilhand, at his side. His hauberk, made of many little rings of annealed steel, fell to his knees and covered his arms with long sleeves. Under it he had stockings also of the same chain mail, and his spurs were of silver.

Pietro's armor was not so fine, but it was good and serviceable. He rode bareheaded, and had neither sword nor shield nor lance—as these were knightly weapons, not permitted a mere squire. Only if—by some miracle—he became a knight, would he be able to protect his head with a helmet, and give hard blows with sword or lance. Of course he was required to practice with these weapons daily; but in the hunt or in actual battle he had to attend his master almost unarmed.

Pietro carried a boarspear, a weapon which even baseborn huntsmen were allowed to use, and a light crossbow of the kind usually used in fowling—much less powerful than the great arbalist, but permitting a certain rapidity of fire, since he could cock it with his hands—its wooden bow requiring no winch. He was skilled at the use of this little toy of a weapon, but he was more than a little ashamed of it. Knights despised archers. "The first bowman," they said, "was a coward who feared to come to grips with his foe. . . ."

To his disgust, Pietro saw that they were not going to enter Roccablanca after all. The huntsmen had already assembled outside the castle. From their numbers, Pietro saw at once that this was a serious business: they were not hunting today just to amuse themselves.

Tomorrow was going to be a great fete. Count Alessandro would have to feed more than a thousand people. Every piece of game that they could bring down, from mere rabbits up to great stags would be actually needed. The master forester was taking no chances: he had brought in some hundreds of stout villeins from the fields and armed them with staves to beat the brush and drive the animals before them.

They killed many animals. Hans and all the others were delighted. But the stags, racing ahead of the packs, terrified by the thrashing staves of the villeins, reminded Pietro of something—he didn't know exactly at first; but afterwards it came to him: the villagers of Rezzi. The boars and stags and hares and netted birds hadn't a chance. There was no skill to their taking—only overpowering force. He had that feeling again that he had had before: that life was neither good nor pleasant nor worth the living. You started out in blood and stench with the echoes of your mother's dying screams inside of you somewhere so that unrecognized, unremembered, they were there a part of you; then afterwards you were the hunted, always the hunted, running with that tiredness inside of you that was part of death itself, the knowing always in the end that the running was no good because you'd be pulled down—by the big ones, the strong ones, the ones whose world would crash about their heads if they permitted you, the small, the wily, the different, to go on living. Or they worried you to death in small and ugly ways: by telling you what seat you might take at a table, by the epithets with which they addressed you, by forbidding you to wear fur or bear a sword or take to wife a girl of different station. Small ways and ugly, but they killed something inside of you—your pride of manhood perhaps your belief in yourself until you became the beast-thing that they were and lit candles and rang bells and ran weeping and howling to prostrate yourself before the unknown and unknowable because you had to have something to cling to against the onrushing dark even if it were only the gibbering ghosts of other men's fears labelled god or saint or holy spirit. . . .

Which was far afield from the hunt. But all his life Pietro had known a world that killed the Isaacs because they were both intelligent and different, and the Donatis because they were really noble and proud and brave and freedom meant something to them.

Somebody had to turn on the pack. Somebody had finally to do it right and skillfully, until this world where everybody alive was somebody else's man was replaced by one where a man could be his own man—unless he chose to be God's, and that, too, finally a choice so that he needn't even be God's, could reject if he had the bigness in him even God and face the dark alone and uncowed. . . .

That will I do, Pietro vowed, I'll turn on the hunters. I'll smash their beaters, overturn their horses, drown them in their own blood. . . .

"For God's sake, Pietro!" Hans roared at him. "Watch what you're doing!"

Pietro turned his palfrey aside just in time.

"Sorry, Sir Hans," he said.

"You'll never learn anything," Hans groaned. "Always woolgathering. It's unmanly. If I didn't know that you can ride and shoot, I'd swear you were half a maid. . . ."

The Siniscolas had come up to them now, and sat on their horses studying Pietro curiously.

"This is your squire?" Ippolito, the next in years after Enzio asked.

"Yes," Hans said shortly.

The Siniscolas didn't say anything. They just sat there looking at Pietro, all of them, Ippolito and Ludovico, and Andrea, and Enzio. He felt surrounded, crushed. Those four faces, all the same face, replicas one of the other, different, of course, but more alike than different. They reflected their father, Count Alessandro, like mirrors set at slightly different angles. Pietro didn't like what he saw. Pride was a part of a man, a proper part, but not such pride as the Siniscolas had. In them it was changed somehow into something else: into—Pietro groped for the meaning—into a cold and towering contempt for everyone and everything else alive. They had something else, too—a well mastered force that was as direct as it was terrible. A force that lacked humor or pity.

They were big men, as broad across the shoulders as Hans himself, thickset, powerful but short. You didn't notice that while they were in the saddle. Only when they were afoot could you see that their legs were roped with muscle, knotted, thick as tree trunks, but lacking in length so that not one of them was as tall as Pietro himself, and Pietro was not much above average height.

"I," Ludovico said finally, "have heard it said that your squire was the son of that churl, Donati, who revolted against my father. But I see now that the rumor was groundless. . . ."

Hans stared at him.

"What makes you so sure it's groundless, Ludovico?" he said.

"Donati," Ludovico said simply, "was a man. Come. We'll have to ride like the devil to make Roccablanca by nightfall. . . ."

Pietro saw the dust spurts fly up from under the horses' hooves; but after that he didn't see anything. The trees, the hills, the pleasant valley, the blue sky itself swam before him in a scalding haze, and the veins at his temples beat hammerstrokes. He was sick all over, inside and out, deathsick with that kind of fury that can only be healed by killing, that held in, corrodes a man's guts until they are weaker than water and the heart itself fails within him. But he rode after them, seeing Enzio's broad back just ahead of him so that his knuckles tightened about the shaft of the boarspear. One thrust. Push down against the stirrups until you are erect in the saddle. Let the blade lance out. . . .

Iolanthe would be free then. From Enzio. But there would still be Ippolito and Ludovico and Andrea; and Count Alessandro's great desire to consolidate the two fiefs would remain unchanged. Any of his sons would serve. Enzio and Ippolito were widowers—the whole countryside swore that the Siniscolas always starved and beat and tortured their wives to death—and Ludovico and Andrea were still unmarried.

All right. Kill Enzio. That would pay for Donati. But what would pay for poor Isaac, put to death by slow inches over God knew how many hours of agony? And what would pay for himself, for young Pietro, living now, breathing air, able to see Iolanthe's grey eyes light with a smile? They, the others, even Hans, would hack him to pieces so fast that . . .

No. Hans might do that. A Brandenburg of Rogliano might. But not a Siniscola. They'd take wounds to capture him alive. For the man who killed a son of Count Alessandro, death would be measured out over days so that in the end, he'd grovel in the dirt beseeching them to finish him.

Pietro had a sudden romantic picture of himself under torture, standing proud in his chains, refusing even to whimper. But at the same time his imagination conjured up the details of those tortures and his stomach turned over. He knew with miserable and abject certainty what actually would happen in such a case. They would need only to show him the implements and he would start screeching and begging and groveling before them—even before the irons were heated or the knout . . .

They came up to Roccablanca at dusk. From the chimney of the cookhouse in the bailey, the smoke was rising in great clouds. In addition to this, fires blazed all over the bailey yard, in the garden, even in the tilt yard; and sweating varlets stood by awaiting the huntsmen. For such a mob as Count Alessandro expected tomorrow, the cooking must go on all night and all the next day. Maids from the village were already busy with great pasties, and the Count had brought a master cook all the way from Rome to make the huge cakes and elaborate pastries. Now, as the huntsmen came in bearing the boars and stags slung on poles, they were surrounded by butchers. Almost before Pietro could dismount, the beasts were deprived of their skins and hustled to the spits.

In the cookhouse they could hear the master cook swearing at the horde of youths that served him. Tomorrow would be one brave feast. Just thinking about it made Pietro hungry.

Inside the castle, he held the basin for Hans to wash, and then stood behind his chair at supper. The supper was simple—mostly pork of every variety, from suckling pigs roasted whole to great sausages and black puddings, with a fowl or two on the side. At first Pietro was acutely conscious that he had eaten nothing all day; but then Count Alessandro came into the dining hall and Pietro forgot his hunger.

Alessandro of Siniscola was taller than any of his sons, and far better looking. In a day when nearly every knight was shaved daily by his squire, Alessandro wore a neat beard, trimmed to a point as sharp as a spear's. Enzio, aping his father, also wore a beard; but his did not approach the groomed perfection of the Count's.

Pietro reckoned that the nobleman must be over fifty years of age, but it didn't show. Count Siniscola had few strands of grey in his hair and beard. He was as straight as a poplar and proud of bearing, though much slimmer and less well muscled than his sons. Pietro guessed that their heavy, barrel-shaped bodies must have come from their mother's side.

But the thing that intrigued him most was Alessandro's face. The Count was by long odds the handsomest man present, if Pietro, himself, and one or two other of the youngest squires were excluded. Yet his face, for all its beauty, had nothing attractive about it. It was utterly, completely, contemptuously cold. So, Pietro thought, a subtle artist might paint the face of Mephistopheles himself. Then he remembered what the peasantry hereabouts called Alessandro. Count Satan. It was wondrously fitting.

During the supper, Pietro noted that Baron Rudolph, who sat at the Count's right hand and shared his cup and his trencher, was most cordial toward his host. They talked together in confidential whispers, passing the great cup back and forth between them. Rudolph attacked the roast pig manfully with his dagger, but Alessandro ate daintily, hardly greasing his lips and barely soiling his fingers. His manners were exquisite. Under other circumstances Pietro might have admired him; but now the sight of the two of them together afflicted him with a misery almost too great to be borne. God's Eyes! Were they speaking now of Io? Were they settling the terms of the contract by which she was to be given to that squat, black bearded beast?

But watching Baron Rogliano and Count Siniscola conferring together, Pietro reached a state of desperation greater than his rage at the brothers Siniscola that afternoon. Had he been armed he would have killed Count Alessandro with no thought of his own fate.

But he was not armed and after a moment his native good sense reasserted itself. To assume the worst before it happened was folly. His head ached so. The jugglers who performed before the great table, looked queer to him. Their outlines were not quite distinct. And the songs of the jongleurs, one of whom was actually a troubador from Languedoc, made little sense. Everyone talked at once, laughed, sang and threw coppers to the beggars who upon this gala day were allowed to invade the castle itself. The noise beat upon Pietro's ears. A slow sickness curled upward from the pit of his belly. He felt faint.

At that moment, mercifully, Count Alessandro stood up, indicating that the banquet was at an end. The guests formed a line behind him and left the hall. Now all the other squires dived upon the huge amount of almost untouched meats that were left upon the table. Except Pietro. A moment before he had been starving; but now he couldn't eat. He followed the guests out into the great hall where the Lady Beatrice, mother of Anweiler, heir to the Duchy of Spoleto or the County of Acerra, depending upon the onlookers' political preferences, had laid out his first knightly garments for public inspection. Iolanthe had done the same for her brothers.

Seeing her now, standing proudly beside the table—where lay the spotless white shirts, the costly robes of ermine, the chain mail plated with silver, the polished helmets, the shields embellished with the families' coats of arms, the great swords with jeweled hilts, bearing each a Saint's relic embedded in the ball of the hilt to give them virtue, the golden spurs—Pietro felt his sickness leaving him.

God and His Mother, he thought, there is no one alive lovelier than she! Then, as if to confirm his thought, he swept his gaze over the ladies assembled to admire these brave vestments. He looked from face to face almost mockingly. But he had slowly the disturbing feeling, that something was amiss—that in passing he had seen a lady's face strangely different from the others. It was a feeling, no more. He looked at the ladies again, becoming conscious as he did so that he had not really looked at them before—not with his eyes. Among them now, he saw several that only his prejudiced taste would have placed below Iolanthe in beauty. He looked on, frowning a little. Then he stopped. Stared.

"God, thou Son of Saint Mary!" he swore under his breath.

The girl—for she was no more than that—younger than Iolanthe by perhaps a year—returned his gaze. Her blue eyes held his brown ones. Pietro looked at her, then at Iolanthe, then back at this young girl. Her hair was so pale gold as to be almost silver. Her eyes were clear blue. Her skin was as white as the petals of certain flowers, except that now it was getting pinker by the second under his gaze. This is wickedness, Pietro thought, disloyalty . . . My lady is fairer than . . . But he saw now, for the first time, the heavy Rogliano jaw in Iolanthe's face. He saw her freshness, her youth, her glowing health—and knew sadly, that these things were not really beauty. Not now. Not when he saw beauty's self clothed in flesh and breathing air.

He caught the sleeve of a stout burgher, standing in the throng.

"In God's name, Messire," he breathed; "who is that lady?"

He didn't even need to point, so intense was his gaze.

"The Lady Elaine," the burgher said, "of Siniscola . . ."

"Of Siniscola?" Pietro said. "She!"

"It's certain, good squire," the burgher said, "that you are a stranger to these parts. The house of Siniscola has several branches. That lady is a daughter of my lord, Count Alessandro's late brother. . . ."

"But all the Siniscolas are dark, and. . . ."

"True, but the lady Hilda, mother of that fair maid, was a Saxon princess. The girl's her image. . . ."

"I see," Pietro said. But he was aware then that Iolanthe was looking at him, frowning. Even from where she stood his preoccupation had been evident. But he had to glance once more at the Lady Elaine. As he did so, she tilted her nose skyward, and deliberately turned her back.

Pietro dropped his gaze. His face felt hot as fire. Had he really been as obvious as all that?

The guests crowded about the table, admiring the garments. Then Anweiler and Mark and Wolfgang presented themselves to the Count and begged his leave to depart. The Count granted it and the boys, together with their squires, left the room. Pietro knew what lay before them. They must now take a ceremonial bath with which they cleansed the body and at the same time, symbolically, removed the stain of sin from their souls. After that, they and their squires to be, for the lads who attend them do not truly become squires until their masters are knighted, must go to the church in the village. There, before an altar upon which their arms and armor have been placed, they must keep a nightlong vigil, with meditation and prayer and many vows of rectitude in their future conduct as knights. In the morning, they will hear mass sung and then return to the castle for the ceremony of being knighted. Pietro envied them with all his heart and soul.

He was, for the first time, glad of the custom of going to bed early. He was tired to the marrow of his bones. Besides, he needed to do some serious thinking. Lying in the darkness, listening to the snores of the other squires, all of them sodden with much wine, Pietro tried to do something about the confusion inside his head.

He loved Iolanthe. Of that there was no doubt. But the maid a man loved was supposed to be, in his eyes, the fairest of all maids. And Io wasn't. Elaine of Siniscola was beautiful—so beautiful that looking at her hurt. He had the feeling that if he ever got to know her better the way he now felt about Io would stand some danger of revision. Still Io loved him and that other maid had turned her back upon him in bitter scorn.

Then Pietro laughed aloud, thrusting his hand against his mouth to stifle the sound of it. He had remembered suddenly that he was Pietro son of Donati, a villein. His relationship to either of the two maids existed in the realm of pure speculation.

Even to Io, he told himself bitterly, I am a toy—no more. . . .

Then he felt soft hands grope against his face in the darkness. He caught at their wrists but one of them tore free and swept across his face in a slap that echoed through the dark hall. Pietro stiffened; but all the other squires snored on.

"That," Iolanthe hissed, "was for making sheep's eyes at that little Elaine!"

"Io!" Pietro whispered, "for God's sake! This isn't Hellemark—Somebody might waken and . . ."

"Coward," Iolanthe said.

"Io—"

"Oh, shut up, and kiss me. You haven't, you know—not for the longest time. . . ."

Pietro drew her down beside him. He could see her face dimly—now that his eyes had become accustomed to the darkness—slanted a little so that their mouths would fit. He bent down to her, and touched her mouth ever so gently; but she swept her hands up behind his head and locked them and clung to him grinding her mouth against his so that he felt bruised, her mouth, and the whole warm length of her, silken clad, so that he was scalded breast and thigh, shaken terrified kindled deathlost uncaring thinking for this I will be killed and at the same time that it was worth the dying, and boldly he freed his hands from about her waist and pushing aside her one garment caressed her bare flesh roughly almost brutally as though she were a peasant girl. Then she rolled her mouth away from his and he felt the wet of tears upon her face, and tasted their salt at the same time.

He turned her loose.

"Io," he whispered, "I'm sorry. . . ."

She raised up, so that her long, reddish blonde hair trailed down about his face like a veil.

"Don't be," she said almost calmly. "Not for that. I liked it. You're all man, Pietro—for all your girlish looks. I would let you—do what you liked, if I didn't think these swine would awaken. That's not why I cried. . . ."

"Why did you?" Pietro murmured.

"Father has agreed to wed me to Enzio. He hasn't told me yet.

He's afraid to. But one of the servants overheard the talk. They—plan to announce it tomorrow—after the tourney. . . ."

"The sweet blue eyes of God!" Pietro swore.

"Pietro," Iolanthe whispered. . . .

"Yes, Io?"

"Remember the story you told me of how your father and mother fled Hellemark?"

"Yes, but Io—"

"But, nothing! Tomorrow night, after the tourney, everybody will be dead tired. And drunk. Everybody but us. I will not touch wine—nor must you. . . ."

"What about the porter at the drawbridge and the portcullis?"

"You have seen where the lists were placed for this tourney?" Iolanthe said.

"Yes. They're outside the walls. But I have to attend Hans, and. . . ."

"After you attend him. He won't ride but once—at the most twice. While he's watching the others, you ride away. Wait for me at the house of Paoli, the hunchback—where we met, remember. . . ."

"But how will you . . . ?"

"I will grow faint at the sight of blood. My maids will lead me toward the castle, but I'll never reach it. I'll have a good palfrey waiting by the woodcutter's hut. . . ."

"They'll miss us," Pietro said. "They'll come after us and . . ."

"We'll get away. . . ."

"And if we don't?" Pietro said.

The red blonde hair curled about his face. Her breath rustled against his bare throat.

"That depends upon you," she whispered. "At least we can get far enough away to . . ."

"To what?" Pietro demanded.

"To see that Enzio of Siniscola takes no virgin to wife," Iolanthe said and sprang to her feet.

"Io!" Pietro called, and leaped up forgetting his nakedness. She backed away from him.

"Is that not worth the risk, my Pietro?" she whispered.

"God, yes!" Pietro got out. "But, Io . . ."

"Until tomorrow, Pietro," she said, and turning, ran down the long hall, skipping over the sleeping squires.

Whatever need he had had for sleep was gone now. He went over the whole thing in his mind. Even being captured. Even the tortures. It was folly and worse and he knew it. But his mouth still hurt, and his whole body smelled of perfume—of the scent that she used. His oversensitive nerves remembered physically the feel of her moving against him so that he tingled still from mouth to toetip, and the ache in his loins was as real as death. More real. He would die. His chances for escaping the Siniscolas were not one in ten thousand he knew. But first—that. God and His Sacred Mother—that, the beard of the Prophet Muhammad the wrath of Jehovah the Thunderer hell and its fires—that. . . .

He would not be captured. He'd fight until they had to kill him. Or he'd die by his own hand. After having known that glory, he couldn't dishonor himself because of the weakness of his flesh. . . .

He got up suddenly from his pallet and went into the room where the arms of the guests were piled. He took his little Saracen poinard and strapped it against his left thigh where it would be concealed by his *bliaut*. It was sharper than a razor. When at last he lay helpless upon the earth, he'd reach and bring it up to the place an inch above his left ear, then in and downward quickly so that the great vein whose bleeding could not be stopped by the most cunning leech on earth would be severed. Before they got him half way to the castle he would be dead.

But as he stepped out into the hall, he heard voices. One of them, he recognized at once. Only Count Alessandro could speak the lilting Tuscan with that precision.

"You lie!" the Count spat.

"Good My Lord, no," the man whispered. "Would God that I did. It's true, your Grace. The Welf has fled!"

"But why? Why, man, why? He had all of Italy in his fist. He had only to reach out his hand to take the boy. . . ."

"Otto, My Lord," the strange knight said, "was not distinguished for cleverness. He proved that when he broke his agreements with the Pope. After His Holiness had crowned him, he proceeded to do what Innocent feared most—join Sicily with the Empire; but my Lord knows that. . . ."

"Ha!" Count Siniscola said. "What did that matter? Where are the Pope's legions? Who stood to defeat Otto of Brunswick—with all Italy at his feet?"

"His own stupidity, my Lord—or rather the Pope's cleverness. His Holiness hated like the devil to swing over to the house of Hohenstaufen; but what choice had he? And as my Lord says, he had no legions. But he has spies and agents, and provocateurs—and the ear of Philip Augustus—King of France. . . ."

"Good God!"

"Amen. A letter to His Royal Majesty of France. A note to the princely bishops of Germany. A plea here. A threat of excommunication there—and the very princes who elevated Otto to the headship of the Empire repudiated him—especially after King Philip let it be known that France would view allegiance to the Welf most unkindly. . . ."

"Still Otto had his armies and a *fait accompli*; he had only to seize young Frederick and . . ."

"True. But strange knights turned up with the news that all Germany is in revolt, which I doubt. But the Emperor believes it. He's marching back across the Alps. . . ."

"And young Frederick?"

"Is by now in Rome, or nearing it. He too is for Germany, to stage a new election. With Philip supporting him—and Pope Innocent gone over to him, he'll win hands down. . . ."

There was a long silence. Then Alessandro spoke again.

"Say nothing of this," he whispered. "It is important to me that certain of my guests do not learn of it until after tomorrow. There is a matter of some importance to me, a betrothal—that would certainly be affected by it. . . ."

"As my Lord wills. . . ."

"And, Lorenzo . . ."

"Yes, my Lord?"

"It's conceivable that Diepold of Schweinspeunt would be well—in a generous frame of mind if an accident occurred to young Frederick upon his journey—as would other nobles whom I could think of. . . ."

"I quite understand, my liege," Lorenzo said.

"Good. Everything must go as planned tomorrow. But if certain knights would like to ride with you, I'll raise no objections. . . ."

Pietro heard their footsteps retreating down the long hall. Slowly he went back to his own pallet. This put quite another face upon things. All he had to do now was to see that news of the sudden change in Frederick's fortunes reached Baron Rudolph's ears. He'd never betroth Io to Enzio then. In fact, if Frederick became Emperor anyone having connections with the Welf cause through marriage or otherwise would be in actual danger. . . .

But if he told the Baron, the flight would be unnecessary. He would have to wait some years before he could assure himself of elevation under the king whose life he had saved. By then the Baron might have arranged another marriage for Iolanthe . . . And if they did not flee, that unthinkable unnameable reward Io had promised him would be forfeit. . . .

And his life would be saved. To die for dear delights was one thing when the alternative to that death was unbearable. But the alternative had become vague now. Hope entered in. . . .

He got up and dressed himself. He tiptoed down the hall toward the chamber assigned to noble guests. Then he stopped. Shrank against a pillar.

Two knights stood before the door with unsheathed swords in their hands. No message would reach Baron Rogliano that night.

Tomorrow then. Tomorrow in the press of the crowd come to see the tourney, he'd . . .

But when the ceremony started early in the morning, Pietro hadn't the slightest chance to get near Baron Rudolph. He stood behind Hans, watching miserably as the Baron stopped before Count Alessandro. The Count was alone upon a platform covered with fine Saracen carpets, while in front of him Baron Rudolph, Count Diepold, and two other nobles Pietro didn't know, stood waiting.

Count Alessandro's armor was gilded, and he looked finer than any king.

The three young candidates for knighthood stepped forward. Count Acerra, Diepold—who once served for a time as guardian to Frederick, himself—kissed his son, then kneeling down, placed the golden spurs upon Anweiler's heels. Then Baron Rudolph and one of the other nobles, an uncle of young Anweiler's, Pietro guessed, pulled the silver plated hauberk of chain mail over his head, and adjusted his cape, and last of all placed a jeweled helmet upon his head. Then the last sponsor placed a mighty sword in his hand, telling him to use it worthily.

Anweiler stepped upon the platform.

"Bow your head!" Count Alessandro roared at him. "The blow!" Then he brought his mailed fist crashing down upon the young man's head so hard that Anweiler was sent reeling. But a moment later, the count embraced the new knight and bade him "serve God, honor all knights, protect all ladies, and remember your lineage. . . ."

Mark and Wolfgang went through the same ceremony, though their armor was not quite so fine. Then all the new knights ran toward their waiting warhorses and sprang into the saddle fully armed, weighed down as they were with heavy steel, without touching the stirrups. To have failed this test would have disgraced them from the outset.

And I, Pietro groaned, can scarcely walk in armor!

All the people cheered. The young knights put the horses through their paces and fought a mock combat, using, however, blunted weapons and dealing light blows. They'd need their strength for the tourney in the afternoon.

All day Alessandro did not leave Baron Rudolph's side. Pietro was wild with despair. Finally, as he buckled Hans into his armor, Pietro told him. Hans could go boldly to his father with the news—especially since Count Alessandro didn't know the younger Rogliano knew it.

But Hans only stared at Pietro coldly.

"In God's name, Sir Hans!" Pietro said, "Aren't you going to tell him?"

"Why?" Hans said.

"Why?" Pietro almost wept; "Hans, can't you see?"

"No, I can't," Hans said. "Frederick now has a chance of becoming Emperor; but we've never openly taken sides. Otto or Frederick, it makes little difference to us, Pietro. Why should I rush off to father with this news?"

"Because your father has agreed to give Iolanthe to Enzio! Your father really doesn't want to—you nor your brothers don't like it, and I. . . ."

Hans looked at him.

"It's no concern of yours, Pietro," he said. "All right, I'll tell him—after the tourney. . . ."

"But Hans—!"

"It'll keep. Why get the old man upset? In any case he won't announce the betrothal until the banquet tonight—so there's no hurry. I know what you're thinking: it'll do us no good to be allied to avowed Welf supporters in case young Frederick does get the crown. Still there's no use stirring up trouble until the last minute; you see that, Pietro . . . Now get me my lances. . . ."

Hans was right, in a way. The longer any unpleasantness between the Siniscolas and the Roglianos could be postponed, the better. There must be time to point out to Count Alessandro, as delicately as possible, that great nobles though they were, they were after all Italian—and with the confusion and strife that had torn the Empire apart in some danger of being ended, it wouldn't be a good idea to offend good German knights, even though of lesser rank. Frederick, after all, was a Hohenstaufen—of high German lineage; if he won, or if Otto of Brunswick won, the results would be the same: the tightening of the Teutonic hold upon Italy. Italian nobles stood to gain only by continued confusion—by a struggle so exhausting and inconclusive that the hold of the German princes would be weakened to the vanishing point. . . .

But Pietro was consumed with impatience. It wasn't a good thing to know that his future rested now in other hands. Powerful, indifferent hands—which could open and set him free, or clamp into fists, crushing out his life.

All the people were thronging toward the lists, now. They made a brave, bright show under the blue sky. The lower orders crushed forward against the outer palisades, but the gentry mounted the high lodges, shaded with tentlike canopies of brightly colored silks, floored with carpets, and having the finest of tapestries slung over their rails. Above them on lance staves, the banners of the noble houses fluttered against the sky. And in them—

Ah, God! What a profusion of silks, and broidered *bliauts*! What ropes of pearls, and nets of cunning gold thread cradling soft golden and brown and midnight hair.

Pietro could hear their silvery laughter, see the play of sunlight upon bare arms and throats, the white teeth flashing in smiles as this or another favorite pranced by, a bit of lace, or a stocking tied to his lance in token of their favor. That, God willing, and young Frederick escaping all the perils still in store for him, Pietro might still attain. But now he must sit bareheaded and unarmed upon his palfrey, searching for Io's face in all that throng, and not daring even to hope, pushing the memory of last night out of his mind, trying not to recall the sweet delirium, the perilous nearness he had come to. . . .

He couldn't find her. He kept looking from face to face up there in the lodges, the song of the jongleurs reduced to beedrone in his ears, the blare of the warhorns unheard, the shouting, the challenges, the babble of excited voices . . . Even when he did find a face he recognized, it was not hers. He tried to tear away his gaze; tried not to shape that name with lip and tonguetip; but it was no good. Elaine. Elaine of Siniscola—a creature from another world, so far beyond his reach that he might as well have coveted one of God's own angels.

After last night, he had forgotten her. But seeing her now, clad all in white silk, simple and plain among the displays of marten and ermine and vair, of sendel and samite, of gold thread and pearls, he was troubled once more by the duality of his own nature: prepared last night to die to gain Iolanthe for an hour—and looking this morning with hopeless longing upon Elaine. . . .

He was aware at last that Elaine was looking at him, studying his dark face curiously, with a little frightened look in her eyes. He laughed aloud.

"I wonder," he murmured, "when I'll be able to see what *you* are really like. . . ."

The trumpets blared. Turning, Pietro saw the six marshals,

led, of course by Count Alessandro with Baron Rudolph next in line. They marched down the lists on foot, clad in *bliauts* that dazzled the eye with their colors. Behind them came the heralds blasting the very heavens apart with their horns, and the pursuivants who must assist and encourage the knights with brave cries reminding them of their lineage and the glories of their fathers. Then the varlets and sergeants who must keep order, clear the lists of broken lances, bring new ones, and lift fallen knights. . . .

In this, Pietro would have to take part as Hans' squire. He sat there watching nervously, as Count Alessandro raised the white baton.

"Bring on the Jousters!" the Count roared.

Again the blare of trumpets. Then four heralds in black and gold and scarlet, spangled with gilt so that Pietro's eyes hurt from the glare of their splendor, and behind them came a mounted mountebank, counterfeiting a knight, tossing a steady stream of swords and razor sharp daggers into the air and catching them as they fell always by the hilt, with his bare hands whirling them up again so fast that it seemed that he spun silver hoops of light through the sunwashed air.

Now the knights.

Two by two on powerful chargers. Battle scarred, powerful—all except the new ones, looking piteously young and helpless against that throng of burly villeins in armor. Suddenly all the knights began to sing. The thunder of male voices rose up to heaven, and above them the bright pennants flying, and the sunlight glinting on steel and, in the lodges, upon silk and gold and pearl and fair flesh and the women sang too now, their voices high and clear and sweet and the horses danced, curvetting under their masters' hands as they passed some maid fairer than the rest; and the maids standing now, modesty forgotten, shrieked with excitement as they hurled down kerchiefs, girdles, stockings, hair ribbons to the knight of their choice under the approving eyes of their sires. . . .

God's eyes! Pietro thought. It's not hard to be mad!

It had begun now. The first two pursuivants came forward and announced the initial contestants, each of them boasting his lord's bravery and lineage to the skies, while insulting that of his opponent in the next breath. Then these base born varlets turned back and the squires led their masters to the opposite ends of the lists.

Pietro could feel his blood stir. It was, he told himself savage foolish barbaric but he loved it. His mind might be two hundred years ahead of his time but his blood was Norman blood and Sicilian blood filled with mad excitements and sweet unreason.

"In the name of God and Saint Michael, do battle!" the marshal thundered.

Pietro saw the damp earth spurt from under the hooves of the destriers. These were big horses of French and Belgian breed, barrel-bodied, elephantine, heavy. Even where he sat upon his light palfrey, he could feel the earth quivering from the down-thrust of their mighty feet, but he couldn't hear them. From the lodges, from the palisades, from every part of the list a screaming mass of humanity battered the eardrums into deafness with one long rolling thunderous cry.

But when they hit, he heard them. The lances splintered with a sound that tore through his quivering flesh. The big horses went back on their haunches spewing clods bigger than a man's fist into the air, but both knights held. Then the sergeants brought new lances, and the two raced down the lists again, their shields scarred now, dented. But this time one of them caught only the edge of his opponent's shield, while the other struck home deadcenter, squarely lifting the green clad knight out of the saddle over the haunches of his charger and sprawling him senseless in the dust. . . .

There were more such jousts. Then, Pietro heard the pursuivants bawling the name "Rogliano," and he rode over to Hans a little way off, and led him into the list, sitting there beside him waiting feeling in his own all too sensitive flesh the unbelievable shock of steel-tipped lance splintering against a stout shield, his body being thrust back hard against the high saddle, until every bone within rattled. . . .

The trumpet blared again. Hans was off. Pietro couldn't look. He turned away his face and saw for the first time, Iolanthe's face, drained of all color, directly above him in a lodge, her lips moving as in prayer.

The marshals tried always to match the contestants equally. But Hans was a quarrelsome lad. And he'd given offense to Sire Laurent, a Norman knight bigger than he and scarred all over from years of jousting and war. When Pietro looked back again it was all over. Sire Laurent had knocked Hans, horse and all, flat into the sands, without even splintering his lance in the process.

Pietro spurred his palfrey to the aid of his master. But Hans leaped free from his floundering steed, and came upright waving his great sword and shrieking curses.

"Dear God!" Pietro wept; "he's earned his death!"

Sire Laurent had every right, under the rules, to ride the defiant young knight down. But Sire Laurent, for all his gruff exterior, was not lacking in chivalry. Besides, no honor resided in taking this advantage. He dismounted at once, and advanced upon Hans, swinging a sword so great that Pietro would have needed the aid of a stout winch to even lift it.

Pietro heard Io's despairing cry:

"Stop them, good Marshal! Someone stop it—Pietro, please. . . ."

Then the clash of steel upon steel ended all other sounds. Pietro forgot to breathe. Hans bore himself bravely. For ten minutes the two big men hacked and hammered each other, until pieces of their chain mail hung down in tatters and the ground all around them was bloody. The lodges screamed with pure delight.

Pietro saw it happen. He tried to turn his head, to shut his eyes; but he could not; he watched in terrible fascination as Sire Laurent's big blade lifted, the hilt clasped in two hands, and smashed down cutting through Hans' shield like so much butter, denting his helmet across his head so that he pitched forward upon his face and lay without moving at Sire Laurent's feet.

Io's shriek tore his heart in half. He raced to Hans' side. A dozen other hands lifted the young knight up, and they bore him to the lodge where the leech waited . . . Baron Rudolph was already there when they reached it, and Io and Count Alessandro and all the young Siniscolas. Pietro worked at the armor, stripping it off, tearing at the helmet straps.

Hans was breathing easily, quietly. He had a long welt across his head that swelled amazingly; but even without touching it Pietro could see his skull was not broken. As for his other wounds, they were slight, thanks to his good armor.

Sire Laurent arrived, looking worried.

"Your pardon, good Lords," he said. "I meant not to deal such a stroke—but the lad pressed me so hard that I forgot his years. . . ."

"He'll live," the leech announced gravely. "But he must be bedded for a week and bled to equalize his humors. . . ."

"Bled!" Io snapped; "you fool—he's lost blood enough!"

"The gentle lady does not comprehend the danger," the leech began.

"Oh, shut up!" Io said. "You men take him into the castle!"

Count Alessandro turned sternly to Sire Laurent.

"It seems to me that your zeal was excessive," he said; "but I leave the matter up to the discretion of the gentle Baron here—the boy's father. . . ."

"I crave no ransom," Sire Laurent said quickly. As victor, he was entitled to keep Hans' horse and arms until the Baron ransomed them back, even to take Hans as his prisoner.

Rudolph put out his hand.

"A brave fight, Sire Laurent," he said. "Since the boy is not badly hurt, I bear you no grudge. . . ."

Sire Laurent took the extended hand and kissed it.

"Thank you, My Lord," he said.

So ended the matter. Pietro was relieved. But he was inside the castle with Io and a few others, helping to bathe and dress Hans' wounds before it came to him that Hans' folly was more dangerous to him than to the great oaf who lay unconscious upon the canopied bed.

There was no chance now of his telling Rudolph that Otto, the Welf, had fled. There was no reason on earth for the Baron not to announce the engagement of Io to Enzio that very night. Try as he would, Pietro could think of no other course but the plan that Iolanthe had suggested. The plan was suicide, but before dying he'd. . . .

And I laughed at other men's madness! he thought bitterly.

He could send a note by a servant. But Baron Rudolph couldn't read. He could give a villein a verbal message—which Count Alessandro would laugh to scorn with conviction and authority. He could approach the Baron himself—and die for his pains at the hands of the Siniscolas without . . .

"The sweet blue eyes of God!" he swore.

"Pietro," Iolanthe whispered.

"Yes, Io?" Pietro's voice was a croak.

"He'll come to himself within an hour. There is nothing much wrong with him. Don't you see, Pietro, darling Pietro, this makes it all ever so much easier!"

"Yes," Pietro half wept.

"Go!" she urged him. "Ride to the hunchback's. Wait there. I'll join you within an hour . . ."

Pietro stood up. Looked at her. In the dusk she was something to look at something very special so that the illusion was upon him his bitter clarity of the afternoon forgotten lost his fear forgotten death taken into account reckoned with balanced against the curve of red mouth and warmth of white flesh against sweetsoft warmclinging length of limb ghostwhite last night in the darkness branding him along all his frame with the fire of the blood and the aching tumescence of all such imaginative ones as he. . . .

He turned and ran down the hall and out into the bailey. At the armory he paused long enough to purloin a helmet and shield and lance and sword. He stood there looking at these weapons, wondering how the devil he was going to get them out of the gates, when it came to him that no one would on this special day question them in the slightest. All the guards would assume that he was bringing them out at the request of Mark or Wolfgang, especially if he bore them idly in his hands.

He mounted a fresh palfrey, the swiftest and best he could find, and rode boldly through the gates and over the drawbridge and away from the castle passing through all the throngs about the tourney without having so much as one head turned in his direction.

At Paoli's the two long hours of waiting did things to his nerves that would last him the rest of his life. Then he saw Io's snow white palfrey, the worst color of horseflesh on earth for a fugitive to choose, racing over the valley toward the little farm. He mounted and went out to meet her.

"Have they . . . ?" he whispered.

"No!" she laughed. "The tourney will last until nightfall and father will be so drunken that the banquet will be half over before I am missed. Come Pietro, mio—ride!"

He looked at her with great admiration seeing the flush on her face, the reckless laughter in her eyes, and cursed himself in his heart for being neither romantic enough nor brave enough nor fool enough to forget that he was going to die because of this, nor yet passionate enough to count it really worth the dying.

They rode upward into the hills, riding half the night until Pietro was beginning to hope that perhaps they could, by riding the night long, get far enough away so that they could not be overtaken, when Io pulled up the snowy palfrey.

"Pietro," she whispered.

"Io," he groaned; "for God's love, Io—if we ride on there's a chance a small chance but still a chance. . . ."

"Pietro," she said.

There were poplar trees there, like black spears thrusting the darkness. And a stream, washed silver with moonlight. Even nightingales. A stage setting for this. Lovely—perfect. Too lovely, too perfect. Pietro hated it with all his heart.

He'd have chosen the barren hills, the outthrust of granite and the sweep of sand for the place of his dying. A place he could leave without regret but not this. This place of low stars and silver water and a big moon. This perfect place, where even the rushes were soft and fragrant.

He put up his arms and helped her down.

He was nervous and frightened and sad and it wasn't good. He felt like crying.

He climbed clumsily to his feet, and she got up too and came up to him and doubled both her fists and hammered at his chest, until he caught at her wrists, but she got her right hand free and slapped him across the face right and left and right again, until he caught her to him pinning her arms down against her sides, and she sobbing against him cursing him for a coward and a weakling and a fool and he holding her like that until she stopped struggling suddenly and arched her head back a little and found his mouth and clung, throwing her weight backward against his encircling arms so that they went down again.

It was lovely this time. Perfect.

He thought dreamily about getting up, dressing, riding on. But it didn't seem to matter any more. Io lay in the crook of his arm and the moonlight spilled over her. She was asleep, but she didn't stay asleep long. In a very little while she stirred.

"Pietro," she said.

Then it was morning, and she was helping him buckle the straps to his helmet when Mark and Wolfgang came riding over the crest of the hill and sat there looking at them. Just the two of them—not the Siniscolas.

Pietro knew at once why they had schemed to ride out alone. No man of another family must witness this.

He mounted, feeling his bones like water inside his legs, the tiredness down in him deeper than death, the fear curling out of his middle like a sickness.

He met their charge and sent Wolfgang reeling out of the saddle, but Mark unhorsed him with contemptuous ease and the both of them came at him with their swords unsheathed and death in their faces.

After five minutes it was all a blur. The whole world was filled with the clang of blades and he was hurt, bad hurt, blood dripping down his arms, so tired that he was unable almost to lift his sword; then Wolfgang brought his sword down across his shield splitting it, the blade landing high on his shoulder, cutting through the links of the mail into his flesh so that his right arm was useless and he couldn't lift his sword.

He shifted it to his left hand.

"Take Io and ride," Mark said contemptuously; "I'll finish him."

Mark moved in, taking all the time in the world about it, while Io pounded at Wolfgang who sat upon the horse holding her, and Pietro waited with the deathsickness already in him, proud at the last that he had not even the temptation to beg for mercy. He tried to get the sword up with his left hand. He couldn't. It was too heavy.

Mark came on. Pietro shut his eyes.

Then he opened them, hearing unbelievably the thunder of great hooves and seeing with wondering eyes the young knight pounding down the slope his lance leveled shouting:

"Varlets! Cowards and whoresons—two against one, and him but a child!"

Then the lance hit Mark's shield. Mark went down flat and came up crawling, and the young knight dismounted, drawing his sword; but Mark was up and racing for his horse, and Wolfgang clapped spurs to his mount and the two of them pounded up the slope and over the rise.

The young knight started after them. Then he looked back in time to see Pietro bending forward ever so slowly until the earth came up and met him and the poplars and the pleasant river and the nightingales' song and the night that was now a memory drowned in the roaring in his ears, went out in redfire and blood into the dark.

The young knight turned back, got down, lifted Pietro's head. The brown eyes came open.

"Who are you?" Pietro whispered.

"Gautier of Montrose," the young knight said. "Lie still!"

Pietro could feel the big hands, roughened, yet gentle, working at his mail. He had the feeling that presently he was going to remember something—some loss, some sorrow. But now it was good to lie there and rest. He felt the cool of water and damp cloths upon his wounds. He didn't feel so sick any more. Just tired. He closed his eyes. Slept.

"Poor devil," Gautier said. "I wonder who he is. . . ."

Chapter Four

IT RAINED all that fall and into the winter. Pietro and Gautier stayed in one of those monasteries which afforded hospitality to travelers. The weather was very bad and the leech that Gautier got for Pietro insisted upon bleeding him every week. It was almost Christmas time before Pietro was strong enough to ride.

They had put hot irons to his serious wounds so he wouldn't get gangrene. When he had seen the irons heating he had fainted. But the swoon hadn't been deep enough, and he had the shameful memory of Gautier's big hands holding him down, and the strong face looking down at him with tears in the blue eyes.

"Courage, Pietro," Gautier had said.

But he hadn't had courage. He had screamed. Terribly. Afterward his throat was raw from the screaming and he couldn't talk above a whisper. He was ashamed of his behavior, but Gautier didn't seem to mind. He treated Pietro like a son. A well loved son. Yet the difference in their ages was scarcely two years.

Afterwards, when he had really begun to mend—when Gautier had sent away the leech and the bleedings had stopped—they talked. Gautier was an only son; the heir to the barony of Montrose, near Paris. His father, Baron Henri, still lived; but his mother was dead. He had one sister, called Antoinette. He was very fond of her and spoke of her often. Toinette, he called her.

Pietro listened and said nothing. Gautier was a sound sleeper, so he didn't hear Pietro crying in the night.

It was very quiet in the monastery, because the monks had taken a vow of silence. They were allowed to talk to their guests, but not to each other. All during the early part of the winter, wayfarers stopped at the monastery. They brought news of the happenings in the places they had come from.

The German princes had elected Frederick of Hohenstaufen Holy Roman Emperor. But Frederick tarried in Sicily with Constance, his wife, awaiting the birth of their child. Some about him were opposed to his acceptance. His queen was. They feared he'd never reach Germany alive. They had a point there. Much of Italy and half of Germany were still of uncertain mind regarding him.

Pietro didn't care much any more. He hoped that Frederick would become Emperor, for Frederick's own sake. But what happened to Pietro di Donati didn't matter. He ate almost nothing. He was very thin and so weak he tottered when he walked. . . .

In the middle of November, 1211, a whole group of travelers rode into the courtyard. They were soaked to the skin but they were merry. They hadn't come from so great a distance that the rain had had much effect upon the wine they had drunk. The monks gave them dry clothing and ushered them into the hall where Pietro and Gautier sat before the table. Pietro didn't even look up. He kept on picking at his food.

Gautier talked with them in Latin. He could manage a few words of Tuscan; but most of the travelers spoke the Sicilian dialect. Fortunately for him a man could travel all over Western Europe in the thirteenth century on the strength of the crabbed priestly Latin—much declined, of course, from the language of Cicero and Virgil.

"You are very gay, Messires," he said; "you come from a fete?"

"Aye, and a brave one!" a stout nobleman laughed. "On yesternight Iolanthe, daughter of the gentle Baron Rudolph of Rogliano was wed to Count Alessandro of Siniscola's princely son. . . ."

Pietro pushed away his trencher. He got up very slowly. Looking at him, Gautier saw that the way he walked was curious. His steps were jerky, badly controlled. He looked like a puppet swung upon hidden wires. But it was his face that caused Gautier to excuse himself and go after him. His face was very bad to look at.

Pietro got to the doorway. Even out into the hall. But no further. In the hall, before Gautier could put out his arms to him, he loosened all over at once, becoming suddenly boneless, and went down as though someone had brought a mace down upon his head.

In the next three days, Gautier heard his story. All of it. By bits and snatches. Pieced together out of Pietro's ravings. Through it the name Io, Io, Io ran like a refrain.

It wasn't good to listen to. When it was over, when at last Pietro sank into a deep sleep, beginning in spite of himself to mend, Gautier of Montrose swore a great oath:

"By the holy blood of the martyrs," he swore. "By the passion of Our Lord; by the spotless virginity of His Sainted Mother, I will never leave this poor lad until he has attained knighthood and peace of soul. . . ."

For Gautier of Montrose was a true knight—one of the few who redeemed by their honor the blood and lust and terror of the age they lived in.

Sitting by Pietro's bed, he talked to the boy gravely, quietly.

"There are other maids," he said, "as fair. Maybe even fairer. That Iolanthe was lost to you was doubtless the will of God. Your father is at peace. That good Jew also—for God is of infinite mercy and can forgive those not of His fold if their hearts are pure. But Pietro, what's past is gone. There will be many brave tomorrows for you. . . ."

Pietro shook his head from side to side on the pillow.

"No," he said.

Gautier studied him.

"Have you ever thought, Pietro, that we were put into this world in order to accomplish certain things? To do certain duties which are not our wills, but God's?"

"No," Pietro whispered. "I had not thought of that. . . ."

"It's true. For instance, you have never asked why I am in Italy. . . ."

"It was your place to tell me, good my lord," Pietro said; "not mine to ask. . . ."

"Then I'll tell you. I was sent by my King to spend a certain time at your court."

"You have a message?" Pietro said.

"No. I am only to say that King Frederick should assume his role without fear—that His Majesty of France will back him to the hilt."

Pietro looked at Gautier.

"I've delayed you," he said.

"And will delay me, until you have strength to ride."

"No," Pietro said. "You must leave me—you must ride. . . ."

"Not without you," Gautier said.

That night Pietro made up his mind to get better. He was very thin, and on his chest and arms and right shoulder the scars were still red and ugly and peeling. The hurt inside him didn't have a scar. It would bleed forever. He half sensed that had he won Io, he wouldn't have been happy with her. He suspected that love usually eroded away by the wear and tear of years, by the daily seeing of the small irksome things in the beloved that distance and unattainability hide, that the goddess at one's side sweats—say—grows fat and dull, becomes a woman like many another, invites a stifled yawn of boredom—or irritates a man into active dislike.

But he was Sicilian enough and romantic enough to deify his lost love. To make daily, hourly sacrifice to it. To magnify it into unbearable pain—until the imagined became real. There was never in the flesh such a paragon as the Iolanthe Pietro dreamed of. And there never would be. But Pietro was not quite seventeen years old. And many a man twice his age has been no wiser.

The week before Christmas they started the long ride toward Sicily. There was snow in the highlands and Pietro suffered cruelly. A little further up the mainroad had been blocked by an avalanche.

They had to turn back then, toward the sea. Down the only road they could reach the Adriatic on—the one that passed a scant half mile away from Roccablanca.

Pietro didn't like to think about that. He hoped no one from the castle would see them. Though, for that matter, little danger existed in their being seen by anyone from Roccablanca. Only if the road had passed by Hellemark would he have been in danger. For only Mark and Wolfgang knew what had happened, and they, being knighted now, had doubtless returned to Hellemark.

Io probably believed him dead. From the crest of that little hill she had seen him fall. It was better so. She could bear her lot more easily if she believed that. Knowing he lived, hope might enter in. And there were no grounds for hope. No grounds at all.

Out of the hills the snow was sparse. There was rain in it. They rode bent forward, trying to shield their faces from the rain. But they couldn't. It was like a million needles. Ice tipped. Their breath and that of their mounts rose up in heavy clouds.

That was how they saw the others. By the fogpuffs of their half frozen breaths.

Pietro reined in at once. But Gautier kept plodding on toward the party of horsemen that were riding slowly toward Roccablanca. Gautier wasn't afraid. He rode in peace, secure in the knowledge of his own strength.

But Pietro sat there, shaking. God's Eyes! he thought, it might be. . . .

Then he saw that this party rode toward Roccablanca, not away from it. Guests coming for the Christmas feasts. From them, at least, he had nothing to fear. He clapped spurs to his beast and caught up with Gautier.

Five minutes later they met the party.

Pietro turned the bridle and lurched forward. He had to grip the high pommel to keep from falling.

Io and Enzio. Behind them Ricardo and Elaine and a heavy, blonde woman who he guessed at once must be Elaine's mother. Other people whom he didn't know. Sergeants, men at arms, knights.

But—Io.

God and His Angels—Io.

She was wrapped all in fine furs. Her face was white. And still. Her grey eyes were death. And hell. When she looked at him, he could see something in them screaming.

Oh God, he thought, Oh Jesus Son of Mary, and Thou Oh gentle Mother of God. . . .

Gautier bowed to them gravely.

"Why," Ricardo said suddenly, "it's the young squire who aided Io in saving my neck from that brother of yours, Enzio!"

"So," Enzio growled, indifferently.

"How do you fare, young sir?" Ricardo said pleasantly, and put out his hand to Pietro.

Elaine's voice cut through the air like a blade.

"Ricardo," she said crisply, "touch the hand of that villainous young swine and our engagement ends today."

Ricardo turned to her wonderingly.

"Why, my love?" he said.

"He is a serf and the son of a villein. But beyond that, there are people present who comprehend the extent of his villainy."

She looked then, straight at Iolanthe.

The grey eyes changed. There was fire in them now.

"Yes," Io whispered. "Two of us understand this—villainy—I think you called it? Only two. Thou, my fair cousin and I. What puzzles me is that you take it so much to heart, since his only contact with you concerns his aid to me in ending the strife between Ricardo and Andrea. And the other—villainy—touches you not at all. . . ."

"Still," Elaine snapped, "it was villainy!"

"Yes," Io said. "Would God there were much more such in this world."

Elaine stared at her cousin.

"I think," she said quietly, "that this sin was perhaps not his alone. . . ."

"No," Io whispered. "Almost none of it was. But, sweet my cousin, why does it affect you thus? Is it that you, too, see that he is fair? Women are never really concerned with the sins of others. And when they seem to be—scratch the surface and you will find envy that the sin was not their own!"

"Io!" Elaine said.

"I don't like this line of talk, Io," Enzio growled. "If I thought. . . ."

"But you don't," Io smiled. "You never think, do you, my good husband? You dare not. For if you permitted yourself that luxury you could only despise yourself as I despise you!"

"Io, please," Ricardo said gently. "There is a stranger present.

A knight, too, by his bearing. Young Sir, forgive our pointless bickering. We are of the House of Siniscola. And you?"

"Gautier, son of Henri, Baron Montrose—of France, my Lords and Ladies."

"What do you do so far from home?" Ricardo asked.

"I travel to the Court of the Emperor Frederick—on the service of my King."

"And this—boy," Elaine asked suddenly, pointing at Pietro with her whip, "travels with you?"

"Yes, My Lady," Gautier said. "He has joined my service as my squire."

"I see," Elaine said.

She was wrapped all in marten fur. Above it, her blue eyes were like ice.

But she is lovely, Pietro thought miserably. God and all the Saints but she is lovely!

"With my good cousin's permission," Ricardo was saying, "would My Lord of Montrose care to break his journey for the holidays? It's a most inclement season, and you, My Lord, have far to go. . . ."

"Might I suggest," Elaine said tartly, "that I and my gentle mother can only approve of this invitation if it does not include Sire Gautier's squire. There are reasons why he cannot be permitted to enter your castle, Enzio—reasons which you must not ask me to tell you, for I will not. Suffice it to say that reasons exist. I, Enzio, could never bring myself to sleep under the same roof that covers him—though he is only a baseborn churl. I—I should feel—unclean. . . ."

Enzio snorted. "There is something amiss here. And by heaven, I'll. . . ."

"What," Io said quietly, "will you do, my Lord? Since the death of your gentle mother, I am mistress of Roccablanca. Sire Gautier, you are welcome, believe me—you and your squire. If my fair cousin objects so to his presence, I am sorry. It's a long ride back to Rocca d'Aquilino . . ."

Gautier smiled. He had long since gotten the drift of the controversy.

"Nay, gentle Lady," he said. "My business is pressing. I cannot tarry. Besides, I am very fond of Pietro, who is like a brother to me. I don't want him subjected further to anyone's displeasure. When we return to France, my father and I are going to further his cause—to see, God willing, that he reach the station in life that he so richly deserves. . . ."

"And what station is that?" Elaine demanded.

"Knighthood, my Lady," Gautier said quietly. "For he merits it more than many more fortunately born—certainly one who could earn such great ill will on the part of one so highly placed as yourself, is a man of considerable force. Besides," and Gautier smiled full into her eyes, "I agree with the Lady Iolanthe. There is a difference between villainy—and love. Adieu, Mesdames. Adieu, Seigneurs—go with God!"

Watching them riding away, Pietro's heart was torn with pain. She loves me still, he thought. Io loves me still. And that is a bad thing, a very bad thing, the worst. . . .

But, as he turned his palfrey's head toward the sea, he thought suddenly of Elaine.

Dear God, he mused, why does she hate me so?

"The cloaks of those who stoned Saint Stephen," Gautier said, half to himself. "That's it . . . It must be that."

"I—I don't follow you, my Lord," Pietro said.

"Saul—Saul of Tarsus," Gautier said, "before he became our Saint Paul, held the cloaks of the murderers who martyred Saint Stephen. He was very bitter against the Christians; but afterwards he became one and suffered in his turn. People whose hearts turn rebelliously in directions they fear and cannot understand are always bitter—against the very objects of their yearning. You see?"

"You mean that Elaine . . . ?"

"If Elaine is that maid of the blue eyes and silvery blonde hair and of such loveliness that even her hatred cannot distort it—yes. She is very proud, and aghast and astonished at the fact that the human heart is so unruly. That it can love a villein's son—say. . . ."

"My God!" Pietro whispered.

"I think that your Io told her—confided in her, which was a mistake. A mistake only because Elaine has—although she hates it and fights against it—this feeling for you. She is not very intelligent, this Elaine. You've chosen the better one. Your Io is something—something rare. . . ."

"Much good that does me," Pietro said.

"I know. Come, we'll take ship at Gaeta." Three days later, they did.

As the galley crawled toward Palermo, the warm winds blew up from the coast of Sicily. Pietro's thin nostrils flared at the smell of them. He became very talkative suddenly—almost gay. He tried to tell Gautier how it was in Sicily, but he couldn't. The things he said, the words he used didn't have the same meaning to the two of them. He was confronted again with proof of how maddeningly complete is man's isolation in his world. Language, the means of communication was a barrier. He had the depressing feeling that people unlike in spirit can never reach one another truly: *oc* and *oïl* and *si* might all mean yes; but never precisely the same kind of yes nor even to the same degree.

He looked at Gautier, sitting there so quietly in the galley. He doubted if the fair young Norman had ever been guilty of a prank in all his life. Gautier was all seriousness and Pietro envied him. The Frenchman's mind was very simple and uncomplicated and peaceful. He'd go through life guided by rules that were very rigid and explained everything. Except that, actually, to a mind like Pietro's, the rules explained nothing and were sanctioned by a whole system of belief that was a mass of contradictions at best, and utter nonsense at worst—wicked nonsense at that.

Gautier stood up, suddenly. He let his hand drop on Pietro's shoulder and pointed with the other.

"Sicily?" He said.

Pietro looked at the blue hills coming up out of the sunlit sea.

"Yes," he whispered. "It's Sicily. . . ."

They landed near Castellmare, and Pietro looked around him at the city he had not seen in almost four years. It hadn't changed. He felt like singing. Like crying. Like—he didn't know what. The sky was the same, the same color, unlike any other sky anywhere, lovelier, nearer, warmer. And the brilliant flowers still spilled over gate and wall and palms nodded in the seabreeze and the domes of church and cathedral and mosque were still blue with distance. People laughed here still. Sang. Great dames went by in their litters and all the streets were bright with the colors that the people wore. There was the babble of tongues: Greek and Arabic. Sicilian and Provencal. Tuscan and French. Latin. German.

"A lovely land," Gautier said gravely.

"Yes," Pietro said.

They rode at once to the palace, but had some difficulty gaining entrance. Reluctantly Gautier showed the sentry a parchment bearing the oriflamme of the King of France.

Inside the palace, Frederick himself came at once to greet them, which surprised Gautier greatly, but Pietro not at all.

Frederick hadn't changed much. He was a little taller, and a good bit wider; but the width, Pietro could see, was all muscle —not fat. The sun of Sicily had burnt him a reddish brown, like mahogany, at the same time bleaching his blond hair to an even lighter shade. The contrast was startling. And those level blue eyes of his gazed at them with that curious way they had of never seeming to blink, absolutely steady, so that they seemed to be looking into a man, through him, exploring his mind and heart. All of Frederick the Second's life, people were to cross themselves as he looked at them.

"We give you greetings, Messieurs," he said in French, having in that moment correctly sized Gautier up as being Norman. "To what strange circumstance do we owe the pleasure of a visit from knights come from so far afield?"

Pietro noted that imperial plural. "We," Frederick had said. The clothes he had on would have disgraced a mule driver; but that towering pride had abated not one jot. There was reason for it now. Frederick of Hohenstaufen had every chance of coming into his own.

"I," Gautier said quietly, "bring you greetings, Sire, from His Royal Majesty of the House of Capet, Philip, styled Augustus, King of France."

Frederick's smile flashed in his tanned face.

"And rightly styled, too," he said. "No greater monarch graces Christendom than His Majesty of France—God save him!"

"Amen," Gautier said.

"You have a message for me, then?" Frederick said.

"Only that it is His Majesty's wish that you pursue that which is your own, Sire—in the secure knowledge that every honest knight of France, Burgundy, and Languedoc will spring to arms in your defense, Sire—should any enemy of yours threaten to harm you. . . ."

Frederick raised both clenched fists toward heaven.

"God, Thou Son of Mary!" he roared. "Thou art still with me!"

"Amen," Gautier said again. "And with Your Majesty's permission, my King has freed me for a time from all services to His Royal Person. I ask no greater honor than to be allowed to ride North with you, Sire. . . ."

"Granted!" Frederick laughed. "I would shower great rewards upon you—upon both of you—if I had them to give—" He paused, looking at Pietro once more, keenly.

"You," he said suddenly, in the Sicilian dialect, "are not of France. Moreover. . . ."

"Moreover," Pietro smiled, and knelt before the King, "you have known me in the past, as you were about to say, Sire. In this very room, Your Majesty and I consumed a duck, slain for us by that good falcon Caesar, which Your Majesty honored me by accepting from my hand. . . ."

Frederick gripped both Pietro's shoulders, and raised him to his feet. Then he kissed him hard on both cheeks.

"Pietro!" he said, "Pietro di Donati—I have wondered much what became of you!"

"I," Pietro said boldly, "have been spying out a barony—which you promised me, my King. . . ."

He laughed as he spoke, but Frederick's face was grave.

"So I did," he said. "And Frederick keeps his promises, with God's help. This little one," he said to Gautier, "once saved my life from a boar. But that hawk you gave me, Pietro, alone is worth a barony. I've been trying to mate him in order to preserve his royal blood. Come, Messieurs—let us eat and be merry, for truly this is a great day. . . ."

At the table he spoke of many things—of his battles with the Barons, of his plans for a model state, here in Sicily when the fate of the Empire should have been settled.

"As for your barony, my Pietro," he said, "I fear it must wait my return from Germany. Then many a noble who sneered at the Apulian Boy, as they called me, will have cause to regret his sneers. I have lived with treachery gentlemen, until I have sickened of it. There will be many new nobles in this land, I shall care not if their fathers were blacksmiths or cobblers as long as they serve me well. . . ."

Pietro looked at him.

"Sire," he said, "how did you know of my birth? I never told you anything about my father . . ."

"A King," Frederick said, "even such an impoverished one as I, has many eyes and ears. When you did not return to me, I made investigations. Fortunately for you, your enemies are also —mine."

Pietro studied the King's face, his brown eyes intense.

"The fief of Siniscola," he whispered, "is fair and pleasant land, my King. . . ."

Frederick clapped his hand down upon Pietro's right shoulder so hard that the tender scar tissue there smarted under the impact.

"Truly have I need of you, Pietro!" he laughed. "A mind as devious as yours would be of great service to me. The thought's a good one. I'll bear it in mind. . . ."

Gautier looked at Pietro wonderingly.

"Good Pietro," he said, "I think it seemly that I release you from your vows and my service. Had I known how high your connections were, I would never have suggested that you become my squire. . . ."

"I don't want to be released," Pietro said quickly. "All I want, Monseigneur, is a chance to win knighthood in France, perhaps. There, my Lord, since no man except you knows of my lineage, I could be knighted without reflecting discredit upon my suzerain. . . ."

"I could knight you," Frederick growled; "and by heaven I will!"

Pietro frowned.

"Please, Sire," he said, "I have no wish to offend you; but why perform an act now that you'll have to do over again after you return from Germany? Men still dispute your right to be Emperor. How much more would they dispute my humble claim to knighthood, if conferred by you now? As Emperor you will shine like the moon and the sun; and any knights made by you will then reflect your glory. But that will require years of waiting, and I am impatient. Forgive me, My King, for these harsh truths; but they are, after all, truths. . . ."

"Well spoken," Frederick said. "I would not value you half so much were you not an honest man, Pietro. The two of you will rest here with me until I am ready to ride. Another month must pass, I fear. For it was only this past week of February that my Queen was delivered of my son and heir . . ."

Both Gautier and Pietro at once stood up and bowed to the King.

"In the name of my King, may I offer you the felicitations of all France?" Gautier said.

"And I my own?" Pietro echoed.

"Thank you, gentlemen," Frederick said. "I fear me I have been negligent in this matter. Only His Holiness has been notified of Henry's birth. . . ."

Gautier stared at him.

"Then, Sire," he said, "I would suggest that you dispatch a messenger at once to the King of France. His majesty supported you, knowing that you were the last Hohenstaufen alive. Do you not see how greatly it strengthens your position that you now have issue? It is much easier to establish a dynasty than the rule of one man."

"You're right," Frederick said, and walked over to the mantel to strike a brazen gong. When the servant appeared, the King bade him bring ink and parchment and quills and a scribe. Pietro cleared his throat.

"Your majesty has no need of the scribe, if he will do me the honor of allowing me to serve in that capacity. . . ."

"It must be Latinized," Frederick said. "Of course I can dictate in Latin, but I have no great surety of grammar. . . ."

"Trust me, Sire," Pietro said. "The language will not shame you. . . ."

A few minutes later, he was bent over the parchment, the goosequill moving rapidly, neatly in the minuscule Gothic script, pausing now and again to amend the King's errors of construction and even to phrase an expression differently, giving it a more courtly turn.

He finished shortly after Frederick had ceased speaking, and poured the sand out of the sand box over the parchment to dry it. After some minutes he let the grains run back into the box and proffered the letter to the King.

Frederick read it, frowning.

"God's death!" he swore. "I have found me a Latin secretary for the Kingdom!"

He showed the letter to Gautier. Like most of the sons of the serious Norman barons, Gautier had been well schooled. He read it through and looked up at Pietro with awe.

"Are you sure that you would not prefer an Abbey?" he said. "So fair a clerk as you would go far in the Church. . . ."[1]

"Remember how you chanced to save my life?" Pietro smiled. "I fear I am too much of this world and of the flesh. . . ."

"True!" Gautier laughed.

"This I have not heard," Frederick said. "In what mischief were you engaged this time, Pietro?"

"Abduction," Gautier said. "The daughter of a great baron, no less. But from the way the maid fought her brothers who had come to rescue her from this vile churl, she didn't find the idea altogether displeasing, it seemed to me. . . ."

"The maid came willingly?" Frederick asked.

"Yes, Sire," Pietro said. "In fact, she joined me after I had fled the castle."

"I don't doubt it. You're a very pretty lad, Pietro—though a bit worn and thin at the moment. Then I'll see that she's returned to you, though you must wed her truly before the altar of God. . . ."

"She," Pietro said, "has already been given in marriage by her father since November last. . . ."

"Too bad," Frederick said gravely. "For unless this marriage lies within the forbidden degrees of kinship[2] there is nothing I can do about it. On the subject of marriage, His Holiness is a most stubborn man, as—" and Frederick smiled at Gautier, "your King has cause to remember . . ."

Gautier flushed. The subject of good Queen Ingeborg and her cruel treatment by the King of France[3] was not a happy subject with any Frenchman.

The wine, better now than the bitter brew that Pietro remembered, had warmed Frederick's blood. He strode to and fro gesticulating with his eloquent hands, talking.

"Look you," he said to Gautier, "I have no quarrel with nobility as such. Without good nobles, a kingdom cannot exist. But mind you, I say *good* nobles. Look at the state of the world today. The Moslem Sultans have better government than the Kings of Christendom. And why? Because their lands are not parcelled among powerful barons who dare dispute the King himself! When I am Emperor, I shall teach all Europe a lesson. . . .

"What is the root of the matter? Castles! A baron should have no right to keep a fortress and armed retainers. Armed men should serve the state—the only fighting force should be that of the King, called into service to defend the borders of the kingdom against foreigners. Enough of this crazy patchwork of tiny kingdoms within kingdoms—for by God's eyes that's what our counties, dukedoms, and baronies are today. They mint money, raise armed men, levy taxes—all of which rights should be the King's and his alone!"

Gautier stared at him wonderingly. But Pietro caught his drift. It was a revolutionary doctrine that Frederick II preached that day: the expansion of society from insular clans—eternally warring, plunging the land into bloodshed and anarchy—into nations, secure and serene in their sovereignty. A noble dream for that year 1212—and for many a year thereafter until the evils of nationalism should outweigh the good. . . .

"But, Sire," Gautier protested. "What need would you have then of nobles?"

"To captain my forces in the field. To sit as my privy council. To write and review my laws. To serve me—as Latin secretary, for instance. . . ."

"But if they have not castles . . ." Gautier said.

"God's eyes, Sir Gautier, they shall have houses—great houses, fair and pleasant with many windows to let in the light and air! They won't need fortresses for defense, since warfare among them will not be permitted. . . ."

"Suppose," Pietro said, "some among them persist in the old ways, Sire. Barons dearly love their petty wars. . . ."

Frederick brought down his fist upon the table so hard that all the flagons jumped.

"I shall crush them!" he said.

"A court nobility," Pietro mused, "dependent upon the King. Yet helping him, advising him. Loyal. Passing laws that benefit the whole land. Arranging things so that no peasant can starve in Napoli while Palermo has grain. . . ."

"Yes! You're clever, Pietro. You see my intent precisely. And more. I shall establish a university. A secular university—not for the training of mumbling priests to betray my people into folly with mystifying Latin and the bones of robbers cut down from the gibbet and labelled those of Saints—but for the training of lawyers and men of science. I shall collect scholars from the world over—men who can make rain to save the crops in a drought, and medicines to heal the sick, without magic or other vanity. . . ."

Gautier's face was a study. Clearly he considered this blasphemy.

"I am not overly clever, Sire," he said, shaking his head, "yet it seems to me that this course is fraught with many dangers. If barons cannot go to war, their very boredom would put mischief in their heads. . . ."

"Boredom? At my court? Never, Sir Gautier. I shall collect there the finest poets and singers of all Europe—the greatest scholars of the world, be they Jew or Saracen. My nobles will listen to sweet singers and join me in the hunt and hear promulgated propositions of such weight that just thinking them out will occupy their minds for a summer. They will watch Saracen dancing girls of such beauty that their senses will reel at the sight, and jugglers and magicians; and inspect my menagerie of curious beasts brought from all parts of the world. . . ."

"And they will hear mass said occasionally?" Gautier said severely.

"Yes," Frederick said shortly.

Pietro smiled. He knew how little Frederick cared for religious things. No man not born in Sicily could truly understand that feeling. Of course there were village atheists[4] all over Europe. With men of analytical bent many of the gloomier doctrines of the church sat but ill; but Sicily was the hotbed of thirteenth century freethinking and that was the fault of the Saracens.

Two hundred years and more in advance of their European contemporaries, many another follower of Muhammad, since the astronomer-poet Omar[5] had penned his lovely but completely skeptical *Rubaiyat* little more than an hundred years ago, had traveled from religious zeal to doubt on the high road of science. Pietro had read Omar's verses in Arabic translation from the Persian. At home, in Egypt and Morocco and Turkey and Persia, the scholars who had taught Pietro as a child would not have dared to express their doubts for fear of a fanatically orthodox group of amirs. But in Palermo, far from home and the control of the Khalifate they doubted with caustic eloquence all things from the authenticity of the camel driver's call to the very existence of God.

Frederick, too, had had such teachers. But Frederick was King, was becoming Emperor. What Frederick believed or disbelieved would shape the course of empire. What Pietro di Donati did not believe must be guarded well in the twisted recesses of his devious mind, lest it earn him a terrible death.

And Isaac had compounded the error by letting him read from the scriptures himself. The pagan superstitions ingrained into Christianity by men not ready for its message were bad enough; but nothing could reconcile for Pietro the cruelties committed in the name of Him who taught turning the other cheek to a blow and travelling the second unrequired mile. In the name of so gentle, sweet a Lord, all over Europe pyres flamed and living men screamed within them. . . .

It was not good to think like that. Ponder too long over such subjects and a man became mad. Pietro caught the king's eye.

"Sire," he said, "we would both be greatly honored if you would permit us to see the royal babe. . . ."

"Of course," Frederick said. "The crown prince begins to look almost human—come. . . ."

They followed Frederick down a series of long, winding corridors until they reached the women's quarters. Pietro saw Gautier start at the king's casual mention of the name of this part of the palace.

In France, there were no women's quarters as such. Nor, for that matter in any other European state save alone Sicily and Spain. But in many ways those two countries were Saracen to the core. In the rest of the western world there might be courts of love; the cult of the Virgin might conquer men's hearts; knights might vow eternal service to some fair dame, worshipping her from afar as though she were a goddess; but not in Sicily. There women remained secluded and alone—the toys and servants, creatures and slaves of their lords. . . .

A number of veiled Saracen slave girls bowed low at Frederick's entrance. He waved them away from him with a gesture of such regal contempt that Pietro swore under his breath. God's Eyes! he thought; they are, after all, human beings. . . .

Then they were in the Queen's bed chamber. Constance of Aragon lay in the vast canopied bed with the infant in the crook of her arm. Pietro and Gautier tiptoed near and bent to look at him. Pietro straightened, groping for fair words to praise the child's beauty. That was difficult, for Prince Henry, one week old, looked like any other week old infant on the face of earth: he was tiny and wizened and bald, and most exceedingly ugly.

"A noble son, Sire," he said at last. "Worthy of his father. . . ."

"You're a poor liar, Pietro," Frederick retorted. "The brat's as ugly as the image of sin; but no matter. Time will mend his looks."

The Queen stared at them with great dark eyes. She was more than thirty years old and she looked every day of it. Yet she had been lovely once. Pietro could see that. When her eyes strayed to the face of her boyish husband they were full of—of—

Pietro studied her face, watched the expression about her eyes. Of love, he completed his fragmentary thought, of longing, of hopelessness—even of terror.

He looked quickly from the Queen to Frederick, and he understood at last. He had been brooding, tormenting himself over Io's loveless marriage. But there were worse things. This was. Io would have, at least, the curious solace of hating her husband. But this proud Spanish princess had no solace. She had come to love Frederick of Hohenstaufen, which was a very bad thing for reasons that Pietro was beginning to formulate slowly—very slowly because even to shape them in his mind required the formation of a new language.

Frederick was so—complete. That was it. He was all man and his own man not needing the advice or comfort or even the presence of man or priest or god or devil. Least of all of woman. This tired, faded, exquisite woman must sense that. Frederick would come to her bed, upon occasion, for the purpose of begetting sons—after having consulted astrologers and other seers to see if the time were propitious. Beyond that she wouldn't exist for him. He'd have no real need for her, not even for the satisfaction of a quite momentary carnal appetite. A slave girl for that, would do as well. No—better—being less restrained, and having greater joy of it.

Pietro stared at his king as though he had never seen him before. He knew now that Frederick II was a terrible man—as terrible in his way as was His Holiness, Innocent III. And the battle that must presently break out between them would rock Christendom to its foundations. For in this boy king, Pope Innocent, whose pride of office exceeded that which had caused God to cast Lucifer from heaven, had met his match. Innocent demanded that the kings of Christendom kiss his feet, hold the stirrups of his gorgeously decorated palfrey for him to dismount, submit in all things to his authority; he laid interdicts upon the churches of all France, excommunicated princes when it pleased him. He had prevented Frederick's accession to the emperorship in the first place, crowned Otto in his stead, deposed Otto with a flick of goosequill when Otto betrayed him, and supported Frederick now at the price of vows that would beggar Sicily and wreck the king to keep.

But Frederick's pride was greater, and more terrible. He was a man in the grip of an idea, and upon the altar of that idea he'd sacrifice friend as readily as foe, moving from betrayal to betrayal without fear or scruple, knowing himself above the laws of men or even those attributed by priests to God. But he'd never betray the idea. For it he would die, counting it worth any man's pain and blood and tears—even his own.

And, Pietro realized suddenly, he was right. The destruction of feudalism, the creation of sovereign nations affording peace and security to all classes of citizens—who died for that would by generations unborn be called blessed.

Frederick stood there, chatting pleasantly with his Queen in Spanish.

"Her Majesty," Frederick said suddenly, "welcomes you right gladly. She regrets that she has not your tongue that she might converse with you, herself."

Gautier bowed, and said in Latin:

"Your Majesty, I bring you greetings from His Majesty of France. . . ."

Poor Constance was but little schooled. She understood the Latin of her catechism and breviary, and the responses to the mass, but little more. Yet, since all the western tongues were children of the Roman speech, she had little difficulty comprehending Gautier's meaning. She clutched at Frederick's sleeve.

"Sire!" she whispered. "Perhaps this is the French knight for whom the message came a month ago. . . ."

Frederick whirled and faced Gautier.

"Of Montrose! Of course, of course! Your pardon, Sir Gautier—but in my joy at the intelligence you brought me, I forgot a matter touching you personally . . ." He clapped his hands together and one of the Arab girls came toward him. He commanded her in her own language, rolling its harsh gutturals like thunder, and she flew off while Gautier stared after her in utter mystification.

"The King," Pietro said in a low tone, "commanded her to bring you a certain letter. . . ."

As low as he spoke, Frederick heard him.

"How the devil did you know that, Pietro?" he demanded.

Pietro smiled.

"In the name of the merciful and compassionate God," he recited, rolling the gutturals off his own tongue in music and in thunder, "O thou who art enwrapped! rise by night except a little—the half, or deduct therefrom a little, or add thereto, and chant the Qur'an chanting! Verily we will cast on thee a heavy speech!"[6]

"God's eyes!" Frederick swore. "Is there no end to your cleverness?"

"Yes, Sire," Pietro said sadly. "I am possessed often of both djinns and demons and in the presence of a fair maid lose both sense and speech. . . ."

"That I'll believe." The King laughed. "Ah, Sir Gautier, here is your letter."

Gautier took the parchment and started to break the seals. Then he paused.

"With your permission, Sire?" he said.

"Of course. Don't stand on ceremony, Sir Gautier."

Gautier opened the letter and read it. Pietro saw his face pale as he came to the middle of it. He put a hand against the bedpost as if to steady himself. At long last he finished it and looked up.

"Ill news?" the King inquired.

"The worst," Gautier groaned. "Sire, I must beg you to release me from my promise to accompany you on your journey. It is most necessary that I return to France at once. . . ."

"Why?" Frederick demanded.

Gautier hesitated.

"I—I have an uncle, Your Majesty—who holds a fief in Languedoc. He is a pious man and good, and a wondrous scholar. Like many another such, Sire, he has gone over to the Albigensians. . . ."

"Fallen into heresy, eh?" Frederick said. "That's bad. . . ."

"My father prays that I come back and save him from his folly. My uncle loves me greatly, Sire—he'll listen to me. . . ."

"To save a soul for the church is a worthy cause," Frederick said gravely. "You have my permission to go. . . ."

"And Pietro?" Gautier said. "I have sworn a solemn oath to see that he achieves knighthood. . . ."

Frederick frowned.

"I had thought of keeping the little one here with me. But

no matter. He will be of more use to me after I come back from Germany than now. Take him, if you will. . . ."

The queen had been listening to this exchange. She had caught much of it, and now she spoke rapidly in her native tongue.

Frederick translated.

"Her majesty says," he interpreted, "that if you go to Languedoc seek out the good monk Dominic and beg him to include her in his prayers. . . ."[7]

"The Spanish monk?" Gautier said. "Truly, all France has heard much of him."

"The same," Frederick said. "But tell me, how do you propose to journey north?"

"By sea," Gautier said quietly. "I have ridden the length of Italy, Sire, and know how its mountains would delay us. And there is need for haste."

"You're right," the King said. "In the harbor there are many swift galleys. I'd advise you to take a Genoese galley, as Genoa is loyal to us, and the Pisans are not to be trusted. They sail daily from Castellmare. There should be more than one leaving for France upon the first morning tide. If you like, I'll send a man to engage passage for you tonight. . . ."

Gautier gave a purse heavy with tarens to the King's man, who returned within the hour with the news that passage had been booked for Gautier and Pietro and their mounts.

That being settled, they sat in the great hall with the King until very late. Pietro's lids felt as though they had sand under them. Once or twice he nodded. But Gautier seemed to have no need of sleep. He sat there with his face tight and drawn with misery. As for Frederick, the boundless energy of his seventeen years, the vaulting sweep of his ambition, the restless questing of a mind of almost dazzling brilliance, cancelled the body's mundane need for rest. It was almost morning before he checked the flood of his speech long enough to notice that Pietro was asleep in the high backed chair.

"Poor little one," he said. "Take him up to bed, Sir Gautier. . . ."

Gautier gathered Pietro's slight frame in his big arms and took him to the chamber that Frederick's manservant pointed out to them. Not even while Gautier, aided by the manservant, stripped him of his clothing, did Pietro open an eye.

Gautier lay down beside Pietro, but he did not sleep. He couldn't.

"Toinette," he muttered. "Dear little sister—how could you. . . ."

Frederick himself and a small retinue of German knights accompanied them to the harbor. He kissed Gautier with grave courtesy and Pietro with real affection.

"Return to Sicily, Pietro," he said, "for great honors await you here. . . ."

"My thanks, Sire," Pietro whispered. "And may God guard you upon the journey that you must take."

Frederick stared at him.

"Your tone amazes me, Pietro," he said. "Has it not been evidenced that I am the chosen of God? Was not my delivery from the Welf at the last possible instant a miracle? And what of my elevation to Emperor when all hope was gone?"

"You are right, Sire," Pietro said. "Still, out of the love I bear you, I beg you, go with care. . . ."

"You're as tender as a maid, Pietro!" Frederick laughed. "Still, I return your warning. You—both of you—take care upon your own voyage."

Then he kissed them both again, and they went aboard to the blare of the king's own trumpeter.

The Captain greeted them with great diffidence. It wasn't every day that passengers boarded his galley accompanied by the king.

"I hope you will be comfortable, Messires," he said; "it's a long voyage to Genoa, and. . . ."

"Genoa!" Gautier roared. "We sail for France!"

"By way of Genoa, My Lord," the Captain said anxiously. "It is most urgent that I report to my superiors and deliver certain goods. . . ."

Gautier's hand went to his belt and came up with a purse so heavy that the Captain's eyes bulged at the sight of it.

"To France, good Captain," he said. "Any landfall west of the Rhone—in the Golfe du Lion will suit me. . . ."

"My Lord's arguments are overwhelming. We sail for France."

It was, Pietro reflected, good to be silent for a while. All the things that Frederick had told them—pouring eloquently from his lips without regard to sequence or order—needed to be sorted out, rearranged. A man couldn't clearly understand an entirely new conception of society until he had had time to ponder over it. To Pietro, thinking was one of life's dearest delights. But today, his explorations in the fair kingdom of his own intellect led him far afield: if ultimately kings and princes commanded nations and made war only on other nations, might not the time come when nations themselves became but fiefs under a super government that included the whole world? But what king would be powerful enough to control such an immense territory?

He labored over that one for half a day, while the galley crawled over the sparkling sea. Then he remembered something—something he had read with great difficulty because it was written in ancient Greek, a language that not even Isaac knew, and that he had had to acquire himself with some help from the Greek Patriarch, whose son had been his friend. In ancient Greece, and in early Rome there had not been kingdoms but republics. Republics! The very word was wine to Pietro. Venice was a republic. And if her Doge was in reality an autocrat more powerful than most kings, he was none the less elected by the nobles and upper class citizens. . . .

His world state, then, must be a republic. And her doge must be elected by assemblies of all the people—not nobles and rich merchants only, so that the interests of—of blacksmiths say, tanners, peasant farmers would be equally served.

The idea delighted him. Then, he thought, wars will end and there will be no more famine or pestilence and every child will have access to knowledge. . . .

He hugged his thin knees and rocked back and forth in pure delight, thinking of it. Then he caught sight of Gautier's face.

"Don't be troubled, My Lord," he said. "We'll save your gentle uncle. . . ."

"My uncle!" Gautier spat. "I loved him once, but now I care not. To have put poor Toinette in such hideous danger!"

"Toinette?" Pietro said wonderingly. "But you said to the king. . . ."

"I know! I know! But there are some things that are not for the ears of strangers, be they regal or not!"

"It wasn't my intention to pry, Sire Gautier," Pietro said quickly.

"You're not a stranger," Gautier said mildly, "and I shall need your aid. The truth of the matter, good Pietro, is that Toinette has disappeared . . ."

Pietro thought instantly of Io.

"Had she a—a lover?" he asked.

"No. Antoinette is very religious. For years father and I have had to almost forceably dissuade her against entering a convent. No, it's the fault of my Uncle Roget. . . ."

"How?" Pietro said.

"By going over to those accursed heretics! You see, the news reached Montrose while father was away. Count Forêtbrun our suzerain had some petty quarrel or another to settle with the Duke of Burgundy. Naturally, as Count Forêtbrun's most important vassal, father had to ride to his wars—especially since I was away on this business of the king's. . . ."

"I think you see now," Pietro said, "the advantages of the kind of state that King Frederick proposes. . . ."

"No more of your Sicilian riddles, Pietro! My poor head aches enough now."

"I'm sorry. Then your sister was alone at Montrose?"

"Except for Hugue, our seneschal. Father writes that Hugue had difficulty persuading Toinette from joining that wild band of young vagabonds who followed that idiot shepherd boy, Stephen. . . ."

"Stephen?" Pietro said; "I didn't know of him. I heard of Nicholas, the German youth who preached a crusade of children —one of the sailors who brought us to Sicily told me that when he left Genoa they were beginning to descend upon that city by thousands. . . ."

"Stephen, the shepherd, had the same idea. Father writes that he claims God spoke directly to him while he was tending his sheep. Our king told him to go back to his muttons; but thousands of children have followed him. They are for Marseilles. Stephen has promised them that the sea will divide so that they can march across to the Holy Land dryshod. . . ."

Pietro threw back his head and roared with laughter.

Gautier frowned.

"Such laughter is unseemly, Pietro," he said. "So must doubters among the children of Israel have laughed when Moses promised to lead them thus to deliverance through the Red Sea. . . ."

"I'm sorry, sir," he said. "You're right. It was ill of me to laugh. . . ."

"Anyhow," Gautier said, "Hugue dissuaded her. Then came this message from Uncle Roget telling of his decision to leave the church. You'd have to know Toinette, Pietro, to know how such news must have affected her. Hugue didn't think. The childish crusaders were gone so he relaxed his guard. The very next night, Toinette disappeared. . . ."

"Yet," Pietro said, "the whole thing to me appears to be quite simple: we need only to ride to the castle of your uncle and. . . ."

"Pietro, Pietro—my uncle is Baron Roget of Saint Marcel!"

"So?"

"Saint Marcel, my uncomprehending one, is in the middle of Languedoc—now under siege by the crusaders sent by His Holiness—and led by Simon de Montfort, the most terrible knight alive!"

"Good God!" Pietro whispered.

"They have slain tens of thousands of the Albigensians, and still the war goes on. I—I must confess I have sympathy for these heretics; they are simple men, and good. Their minds have been led astray. On visits to St. Marcel I met many of them—and I like them all. . . ."

"Yet Pope Innocent, whom men say is a kindly man despite his sternness, had them put to the sword?"

"His Holiness was grossly provoked. Yet the source of the provocation was not the true Albigensians, but the Pope had no way of knowing that. In Languedoc, the church was rich, and the nobles poor. Many of them professed the heresy as an excuse to seize church lands. They become bad heretics, as they had been bad Catholics; goodness was never in them. They believe the new faith they profess as little as they believed the old. But the things they did were terrible: Roger II, Viscount of Beziers, sacked the abbey, threw the Bishop of Albi into prison and set a heretic over him as guard. At Allet, Viscount Roger disapproved of the monks' choice of an abbot, so he burned the monastery, jailed the abbot, and when the poor man presently died, he placed his corpse in the pulpit and had a mock mass said! Thereupon he forced the monks at sword's point to choose a worldly libertine as their abbot. . . .

"And Count Foix, Raymond Roger, did even more terrible things: He drove the abbot and the monks from Pamiers; fed his horses from oats placed upon the altar; had his men at arms grind grain with the arms and legs of crucifixes as pestles, and used the image of Our Blessed Lord upon the cross as a target for crossbow practice! And Raymond of Toulouse has burned some twenty churches and variously maltreated the monks of Moissac . . ."

"I see," Pietro said sadly.

"The poor heretics themselves had little or nothing to do with these crimes committed in their name. It's true they hate the church; but they try to convert Catholics into their way of thinking by their way of life, which is nearly blameless, and sometimes by ridicule—but never by force. Why they refuse even to slay an animal!"

"What are they like?" Pietro asked.

"Odd—yet devout in their way. They have many names for their faith, so that no man knows the true one: For instance they call themselves Cathari, meaning pure—that's Greek, I think; others call them Bulgari, because the heresy is supposed to have begun in Bulgaria; and throughout Languedoc, they're known as Albigenses, Albigeois, Albigensians, because at first most of them were located in and around the town of Albi. . . ."

"But," Pietro said, "aside from having many names, what's so odd about them?"

"Their faith itself. They believe that Satan created the universe instead of God. All matter to them is evil—even the True

Cross, and the consecrated Host of the Holy Eucharist! They don't believe the bread becomes Our Lord's Body, nor the wine, His Blood. They deny all sacraments, they refuse to venerate the Holy Images of the Saints; they will not hear mass; they laugh at the Trinity, and worst of all—they reject absolutely the Virginity of Our Lady!"

"Now," Pietro said, "I understand why His Holiness preached a crusade against them. . . ."

"Yet," Gautier said, "this wicked theology produces men whose lives put the best of ours to shame. It puzzles me, Pietro—I confess I don't understand it. They really love their enemies—thousands of them died in 1209 by refusing to lift the sword in their own defense. They care for the sick and poor most tenderly; they hang no man, neither for thievery, rapine, nor murder—instead they kneel about him and pray to God to make him repent the evil of his ways. . . .

"They hold all sexual congress to be evil, even in marriage. The *credentes,* that is believers, the laymen of their faith, try to grow in faith until they can become like the *perfecti,* their priesthood—celibates and vegetarians, enjoying neither carnal lusts, nor the flesh of animals, because to them to kill anything living is wrong. . . ."

"You are most learned in their ways," Pietro said.

"I lived for three years at Saint Marcel, among them," Gautier said. "I left because my reason and my faith were beginning to totter. They don't believe in hell or purgatory. At death, an evil man's spirit returns in the body of a base animal, which is why they refuse to slay beasts. When they are dying, their priests give them a kind of Extreme Unction that they call *consolamenteum*; if they are so unfortunate as to survive, they believe they risk new impurity and the loss of their souls since the *consolamenteum* cannot be given twice. So they invented the *endura*—a patient who is recovering can refuse food and thus pass into paradise; but he cannot slay himself by force. If he has not the will to die thus, he can request the *perfecti* to smother him with his pillows which avoids their proscription against drawing blood. . . ."[8]

"Mad!" Pietro said.

"Clearly. But such a calm, sweet madness. They have such peaceful faces, Pietro. They care not for wealth, and chide our priesthood and our churches for their splendor. Our Lord Jesus, they say, had no place to lay His Head; yet His Holiness lives in a palace. Our Lord was penniless—rendering unto Caesar the only coin He ever held in His Hands, whence then the gorgeous cope and miter, the services of silver and gold, the brave broidered vestments? Whence our fine churches, carved, gilded, adorned, gleaming with alabaster and crystal and stained glass—when Our Lord had only the blue sky over His Head, and entered the Temple only to scourge the moneychangers therefrom? I had to cease listening to such things, Pietro, for in my heart I had no answers. They were wrong; they must be wrong! But I could not discover the place of their wrongness—except in their denial of relics and other sacred things . . . So I left Languedoc and took service under my king. . . ."

"Is there nothing that can be done against them, except to kill them?" Pietro whispered. "They don't seem to deserve death—explanation, reconversion would be better, I think. . . ."

"Only the good Spanish monk, Dominic, and his new order, the Dominicans have done a little with them, and then only by adopting their ways. Father Dominic himself, took the vow of poverty with the Pope's full approval, and by being more austere than the heretics succeeded in winning a few back to the Church. But only a few. I was at Montpellier when he met the three legates that the Pope sent to him: they came as papal legates always do, with dozens of retainers, the finest of robes, dazzling in their splendor. . . .

"I stood not a yard from him, Pietro, when he rebuked them. I have his words by rote, so thunderous were they: 'It is not by the display of power and pomp,' he roared at them, 'nor by cavalcades of retainers and rich palfreys, nor by gorgeous apparel, that the heretics win proselytes; it is by zealous preaching, by apostolic humility, by austerity, by holiness!'[9]

"And they knelt before him, Pietro, and took off their shoes!"

"You," Pietro said, "are half a heretic, yourself, my lord. . . ."

"Sometimes I am," Gautier admitted gravely. "But then I know within my heart that true faith does not require reason for its defense—that it is above reason, and beyond it—so that we must bear, believe and accept all things, being like the sparrows of the air in the sight of God. . . ."

"Amen," Pietro said; but he was troubled still; for to him reason and God were much the same things, and the speech he said amen to, the height of blasphemy. . . .

They inched day by day over the shining sea. From Palermo to the coast of France was many leagues. More than three weeks passed before their galley slid between Corsica and Sardinia; another two before the dim shores rimming the Golfe du Lion rose blue before them. They landed at the seacoast village of Séte, between Beziers and Montpellier. And there they were greeted with the news that Simon de Montfort and his younger brother Guy, but lately returned from the Holy Land, had already crossed the Tarn and were bearing down upon Castres, a village hard by Saint Marcel.

Gautier answered the unspoken question in Pietro's eyes.

"We must join them," he said, "and take part in the attack. Moreover, we must distinguish ourselves, the better to gain the confidence of the leaders. For, when Saint Marcel falls, as it must, I want to be able to trade upon whatever esteem I have gained to beg clemency for Uncle Roget—and Toinette. . . ."

"Toinette?" Pietro said; "but she is no heretic!"

Gautier looked at him, then turned away his face.

"At Beziers, in 1209," he whispered. "All were slain—and a third of the city at least were as good Catholics as might be found anywhere in France. . . ."

"Good God!" Pietro breathed.

"The men at arms asked of Arnaud, the papal legate, whether Catholics should be spared. But Arnaud feared that the heretics would claim devotion. He said—" Gautier stopped, his face like stone. "Good God, Pietro! I have not thought about this in years—I have not wanted to think about it. . . ."

"What did he say?" Pietro asked.

" 'Kill them all, for God knows His own!' "[10]

Pietro sat there upon the palfrey staring at his friend. He didn't say anything. He sat there, looking.

"Don't look at me like that!" Gautier burst out; "I didn't give that order!"

"Did you," Pietro said, "obey it?"

"No. In 1209 I was too young for knighthood. My Uncle Roget took part. They forced him, upon pain of excommunication, to join against people he had known all his life—who had been his friends. . . ."

Pietro wanted to say something. He wanted to make it easier for Gautier. But he couldn't. This was beyond words.

And Gautier went on talking. He didn't want to; but a kind of compulsion was upon him. He wasn't talking to Pietro. He was ridding himself of the horror that had dwelt within him from the time he had seen Roget of Saint Marcel last. You couldn't really live with things like this. They did something to you. Even his voice changed—took upon itself the accents of the South, became subtly the voice of his Uncle Roget that night at Montrose when he had told them. Quiet like that. With death in it. Things uglier than death. . . .

"It was July twenty-second, 1209, that they entered the city. They put the populace to the sword. All the people of Beziers—men, women, children. They took babes from the arms of mothers and tossed them into the air and caught them upon the points of their swords as they fell. They took toddlers by the feet and swung them against the walls so that the blood. . . ."

"Gautier," Pietro whispered. "By God's love, no more!"

Gautier wasn't looking at him. His eyes stared back into the past and his voice was Roget's voice, speaking.

"Some of the people—Catholics, I think, for the heretics had not won all the people of Beziers—took refuge in the church. The crusaders followed them there. In the church itself, Pietro—before the altar of God, they killed them. All of them. After that they burned the city. This was done by Count Raymond of Toulouse, a friend of the heretics, after having been excommunicated, done penance and been scourged, to demonstrate his loyalty to the church. Then he led the crusaders against Carcassonne. . . ."

Pietro straightened in the saddle.

"And His Holiness?" he said. "What said he to all this?"

"He was shocked and hurt by the overzealousness of his crusaders. He rebuked them sternly; but they paid no attention. . . ."

"Did he," Pietro demanded, "excommunicate any of them? Condemn any?"

"No," Gautier said miserably.

Pietro looked into the eyes of his friend.

"I have taken vows to serve you, My Lord," he said; "but I will slay no man because he does not believe what I believe. In such a case I would rather imperil my soul with the breaking of my vows, than to burden it with—murder."

Gautier put out his hand and let it rest upon Pietro's shoulder.

"You are my squire, Pietro," he said; "yet, contrary to custom, I have always permitted you to bear weapons. Now, before we enter battle, I shall conform again to custom—you shall ride without helmet and bearing no blade. . . ."

"Thank you, My Lord," Pietro said.

They had not many days' ride to reach Castres. But when they reached it, the battle was already over. They rode into the camp of the two de Montforts, and were seized at once by the sentries.

When they stood before Simon de Montfort, he questioned them sternly. It was fortunate for them that Gautier's tongue was the purest *Langue d'oïl*; his accent without a trace of Provencal speech. As for Pietro, his status as a squire absolved him from serious consideration.

"Of Montrose near Paris, eh?" Simon said. "Then you must be related to Baron Henri. . . ."

"I am his son," Gautier said.

"Good! I know your father well, Sir Gautier. A brave man and devout. Still, it's passing strange that you come from the South. Perhaps you can explain that?"

"I return from a mission to Sicily," Gautier said, "I bore messages from His Majesty to the Emperor Frederick II. Here are my credentials, My Lord."

Simon scanned them. Then he looked at Pietro.

"And this lad? You will vouch for him—that he is no heretic, I mean?"

"A Sicilian, My Lord, from the Emperor's court—lent to my service by Frederick, himself. . . ."

"Give him back his arms," Simon said to the sentries. Then: "Perhaps, Sir Gautier, you would care to join us?"

"Gladly, My Lord," Gautier said.

"Very well, I shall assign you and your squire to the corps of Sir Guy, my brother, who will lead the attack upon Saint Marcel—tomorrow. But first, you will have the pleasure of witnessing the examination of certain heretics captured at Castres. . . ."

Pietro's face greyed under its tan. Gautier saw his expression change.

"Please, My Lord," he said. "We have ridden far and are very tired. . . ."

"Or very sympathetic toward heretics, Sir Gautier—which? In the army of Our Lord, we know not fatigue; and the screams of the traitors against our faith are as music to our ears. Well, Sir Gautier?"

"We will witness the examinations, My Lord," Gautier said.

"Spoken like your father's true son," Simon said. "Come. . . ."

The examinations, Pietro found to his great relief, did not last long, nor did they include torture. More than a hundred prisoners were questioned. In the end, Guy de Montfort used a device that the crusaders had found infallible: he brought forth a herd of sheep which were to be slaughtered to feed the army, and placed knives in the hands of the suspected heretics. Since to kill an animal violated the basic tenet of their faith, this test easily separated the heretics from the believers.

Or the brave men from the cowards, Pietro thought bitterly.

Eighty out of the captives—a good majority—refused to strike the bleating animals. For the other twenty-five or so, there was one other test—to confess to a priest, and partake of the Host and the Wine. But, having committed the great betrayal, the former heretics among the twenty-five were resigned to this lesser one. But for the eighty—there was only death.

Pietro saw soldiers coming forward, bundles of fagots upon their shoulders. Others drove the stakes into the ground—eight rows of ten each separated by a little space. Then groups of them dragged the condemned men to the stakes and bound them with chains of iron.

Pietro found quite suddenly that he had to sit down. He wondered how long he was going to be able to keep from fainting. Then it came to him that to faint would almost certainly be interpreted by Simon as evidence of sympathy toward the Albigensians, that he might well, as the result of this churning sickness in his middle, presently find himself bound beside them with the first wisps of smoke curling about his head, straining his ears for the sound of crackling flame. . . .

Yet, stern as he was, Simon de Montfort was not without some vestiges of mercy. He stood up and announced to the condemned men, that even now, if they would repent of their errors they would be freed from the stake, made to do heavy penance and received once more into the household of the faithful.

Pietro searched the silent faces one by one.

Not one spoke.

Simon de Montfort nodded.

The soldiers came forward with the torches.

At the end of the row, a robed Priest opened his book and began to chant.

Then a black robed heretic, one of the *perfecti*, lifted up his voice. It was a good voice, deep and very calm.

"My brothers," the *perfectus* said, "in the Name of God, the Merciful, in the Name of the Lord Jesus, Who slew never, Who always saved—I grant unto you the *consolamenteum*!"

There were little tongues of fire about their feet.[11]

The smoke rose straight up, unstirred by any wind.

They died very well. They didn't scream any more than was absolutely necessary.

And Pietro didn't faint. He wanted to, but he couldn't. He could smell them. It would have been a mercy to have been able to faint. A blessing. But he didn't. He just vomited until his insides were raw and empty and retched with the terrible spasms of emptiness, until Gautier took him by the hand and led him away.

At once Simon de Montfort blocked their path.

"You vouched for this boy, remember," he growled.

Without answering him, Gautier stretched out his left hand and pulled aside the neck of Pietro's *chainse*. Around his throat was a little chain. On the chain was a crucifix of silver. Io had given it to him. Which was now the only reason he wore it.

But the Cathari denounced all images. They would die before they'd wear a crucifix.

"I see," Simon muttered. "Still, it's strange that. . . ."

"What's strange, My Lord," Gautier said, "that a gently nurtured boy, untrained to arms, lacks the stomach of a soldier?"

"Perhaps that you took such a one as your squire, Sir Gautier," Simon said.

"I saved his life, and found thereafter that he was orphaned and alone in the world. When I reached knighthood, I swore to defend all such. Besides, there is in French and Latin and every other language I've heard of a word called—mercy. What language do you speak, My Lord of Montfort?"

Simon met Gautier's gaze.

"The language of—justice!" he thundered, "which is often ill served by this mercy you speak of. But no matter. Just remember that I shall be watching you, Sir Gautier. . . ."

Then he turned on his heel and strode away from them.

The next day, they attacked Saint Marcel.

The heretics fought like demons. Since the fall of Beziers they had learnt the folly of nonresistance. On the very first day of the battle, Gautier ended the Montforts' doubt of him forever.

Both of the Montforts had nerves of steel. Often they were a hundred yards beyond the nearest of their men, in the thick of battle. That first day, Gautier saw Guy completely surrounded and hard pressed. Gautier loved to fight. In the press of battle he could forget that he found no real fault in these heretics, that he rather liked them. He stood up in his stirrups, and his big voice boomed out:

"For God and Montrose!" Then he charged.

His lance flashed by Guy de Montfort and caught the heretical knight full center on his shield. The lighter Southern horse went over backward so hard its back was broken. Gautier's lance shattered into a thousand pieces in his hands. His sword came out, the blade catching the sunlight. He stood up in the saddle, releasing the reins and using two hands on the hilt, smashing the smaller men of Languedoc down across their helms, striking right and down, left and down, and each time he struck the foeman went down upon the hoof-torn earth and lay there.

Still for all his strength there were too many of them. It came to Pietro suddenly that Gautier could not get out of that circle of steel, that he would die there, and he found himself suddenly leaning forward upon the neck of his palfrey, flying, not away from the battle but toward it.

Weaponless. Bareheaded. Inside him a great and terrible joy sang, bubbled along his blood, beat with the hoofthunder: "I'm not afraid I'm not afraid I'm not afraid!"

His light palfrey crashed into the flank of a Languedoc warhorse, and went down; but the blow had turned the Southern knight aside so that his lance missed Gautier's back, and the young Norman had time to turn and smash the Provencal's helmet into a jagged mass about his cloven skull. Pietro lay on the ground, rolling in the mud, trying to escape the frantic hooves; seeing Simon de Montfort coming down the field like the thunder of God, and the knights of Languedoc giving way before him, and the three of them together, Guy and Gautier and Simon charging after them, three of them charging more than twenty until they had caught up with them and cut down six more between them, the rest of them flying panic stricken toward the gates of Saint Marcel.

Then Gautier was galloping back, followed by the others, pulling up his destrier until the great beast reared, throwing himself from the saddle and gathering Pietro up in his arms.

"Put me down," Pietro said. "I'm all right. . . ."

Gautier kissed him fondly.

"Now we are quits, Pietro," he said, "for this day you have saved me."

Guy and Simon dismounted beside them.

Simon put out his mailed hand.

"For my brother's life, Sir Gautier," he said, emotion shaking his voice; "there exists no way to thank you. But know you that we stand eternally in your debt. . . ."

"There is more, Simon," Guy said, "that needs to be said. I demand of you, brother, that here and now you apologize to Sir Gautier for doubting either his honor, or his faith!"

"Which I do freely," Simon said.

"There was room for your doubts," Gautier said. "Come, Pietro, up behind me. We'll get you a new mount. That one, I fear, is done. . . ."

Simon looked at Pietro and laughed.

"The lad recovered his stomach quickly enough when *you* were in danger, Sir Gautier," he said. "God's blood! Never have I seen the like—charging like all the hounds of hell without even a willow wand in his hands. We must see that he gets the training he needs. . . ."

Thereafter, during the rest of the siege, Pietro exercised daily with arms. He was careful not to show too much skill. And nightly he prayed for the soul of the knight whom he had caused to be slain in saving Gautier's life.

But the knights of Languedoc, many of them devout Catholics resisting invasion of their home rather than heretics defending a new faith, were brave men and good soldiers. And supplies were running low in the army of the Crusaders. Finally they gave it up and retreated across the Tarn.

Gautier was sick with worry. He had feared meeting his uncle in battle. Now he was afraid that he'd never see Toinette again. Simon promised to renew the attack as soon as reinforcements and supplies arrived from the north. They bivouacked just north of the river.

They had been there just one week when Baron Henri of Montrose rode into camp.

After the greetings had been said, and the de Montforts had been loud in their praise of Gautier's bravery, Gautier took his father aside. Pietro went with them by Gautier's own request.

"It was no good, Father," Gautier said. "I haven't even seen Uncle Roget; as for Toinette. . . ."

"She," Baron Henri said, "isn't there. . . ."

"Not there! In the name of God, Father. . . ."

"I was wrong, my son," the Baron said heavily; "you see, Toinette never saw my brother's letter."

"But you wrote that Hugue said—"

"I know. Hugue sent the letter in to her by a maid servant. Toinette told the girl, 'I go about God's business,' and put the letter down upon the bed, with the seals unbroken. . . ."

"Then how," Gautier demanded, "did Hugue know its contents?"

"When he found it, the seals were broken. It seemed that Jeanne feared she'd be punished for her part in the matter; she thought for some queer reason that it would be better for her if we believed that Toinette left because of that letter instead of despite it. . . ."

"How came you to discover these things, Father?" Gautier whispered.

"I grieved to Hugue over your fate, saying that I feared you might be slain by now—here before Saint Marcel, trying to save your sister. Jeanne who was standing by, burst into tears. Hugue tried to quiet her, and she confessed. . . ."

"Then where is Toinette?"

"In Marseilles, by now," Pietro broke in, "or beyond it—where else, My Lord?"

"God's Death!" Gautier whispered. "That fool of a shepherd and his children's crusade!"

"The boy's right, Gautier," Baron Henri said.

Gautier stood up.

"Then," he said, "we must go to My Lord, Simon de Montfort, and beg permission of him to leave. I fear we'll even have to tell him why . . . but there's no helping that, now. . . ."

Gautier was right. He did have to tell Simon his reasons. The commander was extremely unwilling to lose so valiant a knight. But Gautier swore on the fingerbone of Saint Aliquis, which he bore embedded in the great silver ball atop his sword hilt, that he would return to join the siege. Thereupon, reluctantly, Simon gave them leave to go.

The country through which they rode was beautiful. They wound upward through the passes of the Montagne Noire range which ran southward in an unbroken line until they connected with the Pyrenees. It was very lovely in the mountains. At times their pass was more than three thousand feet high and the green valleys and the silver ribbons of the rivers lay below them in the sun. But the mountains delayed them sadly. It took them two days to cover the short distance from Saint Marcel to Lodeve.

For Gautier's sake, Pietro was sorry for the delay. Yet the slow winding climb through the black mountains pleased him. It was good to get away from the murderous faith of Simon de Montfort. Pietro didn't like killing people. Especially not such people as even their enemies admitted were generally good and led clean lives.

The cool air blew down the slopes and fanned his black hair. He thought about this business of killing. Then it came to him that if he had had a sword in his hand that day that Gautier was endangered, he would have killed too. But not gladly. In the world he lived in, you almost had to kill to stay alive. Even abbots went to war against their feudal neighbors. Pietro reasoned that it was not so wrong to kill a man if it had to be done for good reasons; but it was wrong to glory in murder. He leaned forward in the saddle thinking of it. So many knights did. Battle was their life. And this new thing that had so lately come into the world—this joy in killing a man as slowly as possible in the worst ways you could think of so that his dying was debased, robbed of dignity, and his corpse reduced to burned and shredded meat, so that the Image of God in him was no longer visible, that, Pietro knew, somehow, was a kind of a sickness in the souls of the men who did such things.

He would kill—yes. If the chance ever came, he'd strike down the Count of Siniscola and his sons. The men who'd tortured Isaac and Donati, who had taken away his beloved Io could not go their murderous ways unpunished; but to torture those who dealt in torture was to become one with them. . . .

Strange that now even the Church of God was beginning to sanction such things against her enemies. Were the prelates blind? Couldn't they see that no matter how high and noble the ends for which they fought, they'd be dirtied by the means used to attain them? That was the dangerous thing. If, little by little, the Church had surrendered the pure and lofty religion of Jesus to a neopaganism in which He was almost excluded, or so changed as to be unrecognizable—she had managed somehow to keep afloat.

But murder, no. The vicars of God could not sink to the methods of the sons of men. When you sent a man screaming out of this world, with the flesh blistering and popping and shredding away from his bones, his brains broiling within the caldron of his skull, you killed more than that man. You destroyed the one agency upon earth that had been above those things, that could only exist by staying above them. . . .

He wouldn't think about it any more. It was very cool and quiet here. At times they were above the clouds so that all the world was veiled in mist below them. The hooves of Baron Henri's and Gautier's palfreys, and the big warhorses they led, ready for instant battle, made a muffled clopping on the trail.

Pietro began to feel almost peaceful. Perhaps, when the time came that he could go back to Sicily all the broken strands of his life could be mended. Enzio of Siniscola was twice Iolanthe's age. Perhaps death would come to him—by natural causes, or at the hands of his enemies before Pietro arrived. Io would be a widow, then—a young widow, and. . . .

But a curious feeling of revulsion possessed him. What that black bearded beast had laid hands upon was inevitably—soiled. He remembered with almost physical vividness how it had been that night; but his curiously morbid mind persisted in cancelling out of memory his own lean and delighted body, fading it abruptly out of those soft white arms and substituting the squat and brutal form of Enzio instead. He tried to shake the picture but it lingered. It was as if he stood from some point of vantage near at hand and watched the actual, physical act of his betrayal.

For in this vision, Io's face never changed. There was no loathing there—no look of hopeless compliance even; but—sweet, blue eyes of God!—only eager appetite, swift passion, as fiercetender as he remembered, and for Enzio, not for him!

I'm mad, he thought, mad . . . Io hates him and. . . .

By now there might be a child. That was the other thing. Compounded of beast and angel. From the hot jetting of another's loins the child that should have been his. Ugly, malformed. Hateful, misshapen.

Quite suddenly he wanted Enzio to live. For if he died, Io would come to Pietro, bringing with her the son or sons whose very existence would be a daily, hourly reminder of that which was not to be remembered or borne. . . .

They made the journey from Lodeve to Nimes in one day's time, passing the great aqueduct built centuries ago by the

Romans. Weeds choked the causeways now through which the sweet waters had run.

From Nimes to Arles, another day. But from Arles to Aix, nearly two, for all the roads were choked. With children. Forlorn, ragged children, turning homeward once more, their young faces bleak with misery.

Baron Henri and Gautier peered into the faces of every young girl they passed, even those—all too many, Merciful God—whose young bodies were already beginning to swell with the fruits of unhallowed love. But each time, Pietro noted, they turned away, the expressions on their faces half relief, half fear.

Finally, at Pietro's suggestion, they stopped a group of the ragged, half starved children for questioning.

"Stephen lied, My Lords," one of them said wearily. "The sea did not part for us. But two shipowners offered us passage to the Holy Land free of charge. Seven ships they filled with our companions—but since we were twenty thousand and more, they could not take us all. . . ."

The youth paused, looking at them.

"We were sorry at being left behind. But now, it appears that we were the lucky ones: Of the seven ships, two went down off Sardinia—and not one soul was saved. The other five made Egypt and Tunisia—where those beasts of seamen sold our companions to the Infidels as slaves!"

"Know you anything of a maid," Gautier said, "with hair of brown but little darker than old honey—and brown eyes, too—very soft and tender . . . ?"

The youth who had served as spokesman looked at Gautier.

"My Lord," he said tiredly, "I know six thousand such maids. By now she is either drowned off Sardinia, or sold to some evil Saracen for his delight, or—or you shall meet her on this road."

Baron Henri eyed him sternly.

"That wasn't what you were going to say," he growled. "Why did you break off in midsentence and change your words?"

"Because—what good is it to lie?—Some hundreds of the maids among us were carried off a few at a time nightly in Marseilles by brigands who sold them into a worse bondage than to any Saracen." His face twisted into a bitter smile. "It seems that those gentlemen of Marseilles who, because of age or ill looks, must purchase—certain commodities—have grown tired of the used and shoddy goods offered for their amusement. The maids among us were young and fresh and mostly—virgin. I'm sorry, My Lords, but you asked me. . . ."

"Give him a purse, Gautier," Baron Henri said, "to speed his journey. . . ."

Gautier did so.

"Thank you, My Lords!" the boy said; then: "Come all you beggars—tonight at least we shall eat well!"

Neither Baron Henri nor Gautier nor Pietro spoke for a long time after they moved on. Then Gautier burst out:

"If we do not meet her upon this road, Father, I pray God she is dead!"

Baron Henri shook his head.

"No, Son," he said gently. "You know as well as I that Toinette had no sinfulness in her. A better, more devout maid never drew breath. If she has met this terrible fate, it will in no wise be her fault. We must find her if we can, and if we do, Gautier—no word of reproach, I charge you—not one word!"

I see now, Pietro thought, from whence came such a knight as Gautier. . . .

"You trouble yourselves too quickly, My Lords," he said to them. "We shall presently meet your fair Antoinette upon this road—have no fear. . . ."

But they didn't.

They came down into Marseilles in the morning. Without stopping to rest or seeking lodgings, they rode down to the waterfront and began to make their inquiries. Their quite futile inquiries—knowing them to be so.

It was, Pietro reflected, a tribute both to the human capacity for maintaining hope in the face of disaster, and to the love they bore Antoinette that they made their slow and diligent round of questionings: asking of ships departed and sunk and describing a maid to seafarers who could not conceivably have cause to remember one among so many. . . .

Thus the day was spent, and the night fell over that city depraved beyond human imagining—the abode of villains since the days of Julius Caesar. They sat upon a quay, peering through the darkness at each other. Each of them waiting for the other to say what must be said.

Pietro cleared his throat.

"My Lords," he said quietly, "the recovery of the lady Antoinette is what concerns us here, isn't it? Then—we cannot neglect the one other avenue open to us. You can give her up, if you will; you can assume that she lies now beneath the sea, or—God forbid—has become the slave of some Saracen Emir or Shaikh.[12] But in your heart of hearts you'll always wonder. I think that neither of you would know a quiet night again as long as the possibility existed that you had left her in the hands of men whose bestiality would put any infidel to shame. . . ."

Gautier groaned aloud.

"You're right, boy," Baron Henri sighed. "But how in this hell of human wickedness are we to find her? There must be God knows how many houses of ill fame in Marseilles. . . ."

"Simple," Pietro said. "We will pose as clients of these establishments, and demand of the proprietors that they show us their —wares. . . ."

"But," the Baron protested, "a man of my years!"

"And I," Gautier roared, "have never entered such a place in all my life!"

"God bless you for that, my son," Baron Henri said.

Pietro shrugged.

"Your pride, good My Lords, or the fair lady Antoinette—which?" he said. "I can assure you that white hairs are no strangers to such places—quite the contrary since the favors of the fair come more dearly to the aged. As for you, Sir Gautier, the old hags that run such houses will greet a man as handsome and obviously as rich as you most kindly. . . ."

"Pietro," Gautier said to his father, "was born a thousand years old."

"We'll have to separate, of course," Baron Henri said, "or else it will take three times as long. . . ."

"Twice," Pietro corrected him. "I'll have to go with one of you. I wouldn't know the Lady Antoinette if I were to see her."

"God's death, Pietro," Gautier swore. "I told you how she looks!"

"You gave me a description, Sir Gautier," Pietro said, "that reflected only your great love for your sister. How many maids with honey brown hair and brown eyes do you think there are in Marseilles? I'd wager you that half the young women of this town look like that to some degree. Has she some birthmark—some blemish? A mole—a scar?"

"No," Gautier said. "I see your point, Pietro. Father, would you like for Pietro to come with you? He's very good with arms in spite of his size, and if there were trouble. . . ."

"I could handle it," Baron Henri said. "Take your squire, Gautier. It would shame me to my soul to enter such a place accompanied by a youth young enough to be my son. . . ."

"And it would make them suspicious in the bargain," Pietro said. "Well, My Lords—shall we go?"

They got to their feet slowly.

The drunken sailorman that Pietro asked knew all right.

"God's death!" he laughed. "A house of joy? Take your choice, My Lords—rap upon the door of any house upon any street leading away from the waterfront. Even the ones that are not, will readily become such at the sight of so fine and gentle Milords . . . Now, by your looks, I'll warrant that ye'll not mind the price of a flagon for old Jean. . . ."

Old Jean got his flagon.

They separated, Gautier and Pietro taking one street; Baron Henri another. The two young men stopped before a door a little way up the street. There was a sign above the door, and under the sign a red lantern swung in the breeze.

"Le chat gris," the sign said. "The gray cat."

Gautier stood under the sign, his face working. He put up his hand to knock, then brought it down again.

"Well?" Pietro said.

Gautier knocked.

A window in the door opened, and a woman looked out. An old woman with a face grown old in sin. Pietro could see her eyes light at the sight of their rich dress.

"Enter, My Lords!" she cackled, and threw the door open wide.

It was dark in the place. Dim lighted. It stank. Of wine. Of male sweat. Of woman's flesh.

"A sup of wine for Milords," the old harridan purred, "before they proceed to other pleasures?"

"Don't drink it!" Pietro said sharply.

"I keep an honest house," the woman said. "Pierre—a flagon!"

Pierre was something out of a nightmare. Even looking at him, Pietro didn't believe him.

The ancient hag took the stone flagon out of his grimy hands. She poured herself a glass. Drank it down.

"Now," she said, "if My Lords would care to join me, the wine is gratis. This is not a wineshop. We traffic in other matters. . . ."

Pietro took a glass. The wine was unbelievably bad. One sip was enough. He put the glass down.

"You would like to see the girls?" the woman said.

"Yes," Gautier growled.

"Pierre!" the woman bawled.

He led them out. There were twenty of them. All sizes, ages, shapes, colors—from blondes from the far north to black women from Africa. They had on chainses of thin silk, as transparent as glass.

But Pietro didn't look at their bodies. It was their faces that held him. Their eyes.

He glanced at Gautier. The young Norman stood like stone.

The eyes of the older ones. Calm. Filled with such a coldly ferocious contempt for the entire race of man that Pietro quailed before them.

The eyes of some of the younger ones. Two or three perhaps. Hot and seeking. The born prostitutes. The ones for whom this had been inevitable since they reached puberty. Easy. Assured. Studying Gautier boldly. Speculatively.

Pietro passed over them. It was among the rest that they must seek. Among these new ones, these young, fresh ones—whose eyes were terrible.

Black with terror. Looking beyond death and hell.

Why, Pietro thought, they're dead! Living, they are dead. . . .

There was something else. Something other than terror. It wasn't there all the time. He only saw it when these new ones glanced involuntarily at their own bodies. He tried to puzzle out what it was. He made a game of it, trying to read their eyes each time they looked down at themselves.

Hatred? But that was to be expected. Except this hatred was different—but how, in what manner was it different?

Then he saw. It was directed against themselves.

They, Pietro shaped the thought slowly, building it up in his mind like massive blocks of granite, feel dirtied to a degree and an extent that I can only guess at. To the tenuous fibers of their souls with such layers of filth that they shall never be clean again . . . But—Dear Mother of God—why do they hate themselves?

He struggled with the thought. The men—so many men that their faces blur in the minds of these pitiful ones. So that they become meaningless and no longer an object for hatred. But the hatred stays. Cankers—festers. Until they turn it inward against the fine young bodies they were cursed with. Until the smooth and lovely flesh that has made them the objects of desire becomes more loathsome to them than the skin of lepers. . . .

And upon that misdirected hatred pile Pelion on Ossa—hopelessness upon hate, reasoning that if such things can be done to them, if nightly they must submit to practices for which there are no words in any language spoken by man, they must be beyond the reach even of—God.

It was bad even to look at them. To see a young maid, fair to look upon, who hated her own supple young body with a hatred beyond belief, except that it was there and seeing it you believed it, did something to you.

I, Pietro thought, shall never look at a girl again with the same single minded happiness as before. . . .

"Well, My Lords?" the woman said.

Gautier snorted.

"None of them pleases me," he said.

"Nor me," Pietro added quickly.

The hag stared at them.

"Perhaps—one of the black ones?" she said. "My clients find them novel—and wondrously diverting. . . ."

"God's Eyes!" Gautier roared. "Let us out of here!"

Out in the street, he leaned against a wall and shook his fair head.

"Pietro, Pietro," he groaned. "What manner of beast is man?"

Pietro shrugged.

"We must try others, My Lord," he said. "Many others. . . ."

In the morning they came back to the quay. Baron Henri sat there, holding his head with his hands. They sank down beside him. Nobody said anything. There was nothing to be said.

They found lodging in the city. That night they tried again. And the next. So many nights finally, that they lost track of them.

It was Pietro who brought it to an end finally. He pointed to a girl in the center, younger than the others and quaking with terror.

"I," he said, "will take that one."

Gautier stared at him.

"She's a peasant," Pietro whispered, "and certainly one of the lost children. She's going to be surprised that I want only talk of her. It's a chance. . . ."

"I'll wait," Gautier said loudly.

In the little cubby hole the girl shrank against the wall, watching him with the eyes of a trapped animal.

Pietro took a purse from his belt.

"Listen," he whispered, "I want nothing of you—except information. A—a girl I know, was kidnapped into one of these places. She was a follower of Stephen's Crusade. . . ."

"Like me," the girl whispered. "Was she your sweetheart?"

"Yes," Pietro lied. It would help to say that, and he knew it.

"What was her name?" the girl said.

"Antoinette—Antoinette of Montrose. Surely you remember her? She was very pretty—with brown hair like old honey and brown eyes. . . ."

The girl's eyes were blank.

"No, My Lord," she said sadly.

God, Pietro thought, again nothing. . . .

"Don't go!" the girl implored. "If you go too soon, they'll think you didn't like me and they'll beat me!"

Pietro sat down on the edge of the little bed.

"Try to think," he begged. "Perhaps you may have seen someone like that—you may know. . . ."

The girl's eyes brightened suddenly.

"I—I don't know your Antoinette, My Lord," she said; "but that last night—the night I was taken—there was a big raid. Many girls were taken. Only a few were brought here. The rest were taken to Le Boeuf Noir—the largest house in the city, where many fine gentlemen go. . . ."

Pietro gave her the purse. The girl counted the money in the darkness by the feel of the coins.

"Enough to buy my freedom—oh, God bless you, My Lord!"

She ran over to him to kiss him, but suddenly she drew back.

"What's the matter?" Pietro said.

"I—I have a sickness," she wept. "But now I shall be well. I'll pray to Our Lady. I'll pray for you, too—My Lord . . ."

"Thanks," Pietro said. "Is it all right if I go now?"

"Yes—and bless you, My Lord . . ."

Pietro slipped out into the corridor.

"How was she?" the mistress of the establishment asked with what passed for a smile.

"Wonderful," Pietro said.

He caught Gautier by the arm.

"The Black Bull!" he whispered. "She may be there!"

She was.

She stood on the raised platform before them, and her hands made futile little gestures to cover her nakedness. Pietro couldn't look at her. He knew her at once by the shame in her face. All the others were beyond that. He did the only decent thing he could do. He turned his back upon Gautier and his sister and stood like that, waiting.

Gautier climbed upon the platform and covered her with his cloak.

"This one, My Lord?" the old beldame cackled. "Truly you've chosen well. She's new—almost virgin, and. . . ."

She didn't say anything more. She sat on the floor, holding her head and screeching. It was the first time in his life that Pietro had struck a woman. His whole hand tingled. It was a wondrously satisfactory feeling.

But it wasn't smart. He saw that at once. At her first shriek two unbelievably dirty brutes came pounding through the door, cudgels in their hands.

Pietro saw that Gautier had lifted Antoinette into his arms. He wouldn't be able to even draw his sword. But Pietro had it again, that new thing that had caused him to thunder into battle weaponless to save Gautier's life. Except that now it was compounded with rage. Cold, merciless rage—completely murderous.

He ducked between Gautier and the hairy brutes, drawing his curved, Saracen poinard as he came. He was up on the balls of his feet, leaning forward, his body balanced, waiting.

"Finish off the little squirt," one of the brutes growled. "He's got a knife. . . ."

They came at him. Pietro saw the clubs go up together; but when they came down, he wasn't there. He sidestepped like a dancer and thrust out, putting all his weight behind the blow, feeling, with something like ecstasy, the blade going in through cloth and flesh; then jerking it out and the hot wetness jetting over his hand and arm, and he spinning out and away from the other's cudgel and slashing with the edge of the blade sharp enough to be used for shaving down across the face of the remaining churl so that it opened in a red line from ear to lip corner, the flesh gaping like a grotesque new mouth and the big brute dropping his oaken cudgel and sitting down upon the floor beside his already dead companion and screaming. Like a woman.

"Let's get out of here," Gautier said.

No one followed them. They got all the way back to their lodging before it hit Pietro.

He'd killed a man.

And he didn't care. He opened his mouth automatically to say: "God have mercy upon his soul . . ."; then he closed it again without saying anything. Upon such a soul, even God could have no mercy. For men who lived by the traffic in the flesh of the innocent, hell, for the first time seemed justified to Pietro.

He felt good. There was something to be learned from this encounter. Against those big ones, he had pitted his quickness and his skill, and he had won. It came to him then that he had always been beaten by the big ones in the past because he had been foolish enough to fight their way. He wouldn't any more. From now on, he would make his own rules.

Jousting on horseback against a man who weighed two hundred pounds to his one hundred thirty was foolhardy. And since that man was armored, too, it wouldn't matter how quick he was. But there must be a way—

He looked out of the window at the palfreys tied to the rail. He looked at them a long time, without really seeing them.

Poor Gautier, he thought, this is beyond him. Anything else he could fight, but—

Then he saw their mounts. A knight was armored. But his horse wasn't. The legs of a horse could be broken. His belly could be pierced. And when he went down, his master would be stretched dazed or unconscious upon the ground. That a little one could do—a quick one. It was unknightly. It was dirty fighting. But who in his short life had given him a fair chance?

He'd killed. He could do it. And Enzio of Siniscola, and his brothers, and his father, were yet alive.

He heard the sounds in the next room. Someone was crying. He listened. Poor little thing, he thought, you have enough to weep over—God knows. . . .

But it wasn't Antoinette who cried. The sounds were deep throated. Rasping, fought against, choked—ugly. Gautier. Mother of God, why should he cry now?

He went into the room. Gautier knelt with his head pillowed upon his sister's knees. Pietro could see his big body shake.

He looked at the girl. She wasn't crying. She was beyond tears.

He studied her face. She was quite pretty. Not beautiful, but definitely pretty. Her face, Pietro realized with an odd sense of shock, had once been sweet to look upon.

Now, he thought, now it is a horror.

He couldn't place why it was. It was unmarred, the features regular, clean lined. And though the brown eyes were sunken, and circled with great blue shadows, Antoinette of Montrose was pretty still.

Then he had it. Like the others, he thought, just like the others.

Dead eyes. Dull, lackluster. Never still. Shifting from one corner of the room to the other as if they were waiting for—

For the unspeakable. And—without surprise.

With acceptance. With a hatred turned in upon itself, a transferral to her own person of the loathing she must have felt for those who abused her.

She, Pietro realized, is cursing God for having given her those slender limbs and sweet upcurve of breast. The desirable has become the hated. Now, she might mutilate herself—or even choose death.

Pietro let his hand rest upon Gautier's shoulder.

"Don't cry," he said. "The time for crying is past. Now we must all see that life will be sweet for your sister. . . ."

"Sweet!" Gautier got out. "Dear God!"

Antoinette's eyes rested upon Pietro's face.

"I, Monsieur," she said, her voice flat, calm, curiously controlled, "am with child. I don't know with any degree of certainty who its father is. Gautier is crying because we have to tell my father—when he comes. . . ."

Pietro felt sick.

"Why do you tell me this?" he got out.

"Because you are my brother's squire. You will live with us. How could we conceal such a thing from you? Besides, you seem kind." She looked away from him. "Strange—a little while past I would have died before saying such a thing. Now I can say anything—anything at all, and it doesn't matter. . . ."

Her pale hand strayed over Gautier's hair, stroking gently.

"Perhaps I shall die, Gautier," she said in that same flat, expressionless voice. "Women do die in childbirth. Then you'll be rid of me, and no one need know that you had a whore for a sister."

"Toinette!"

"It's true," Antoinette said. "Why shouldn't I say it?"

"Because, My Lady," Pietro said, "what was done to you is in no way your fault. And because you wound your gentle brother by speaking so grossly. . . ."

She looked at him, tilting her head on one side to study his face.

"You are kind," she said, "but you aren't wise. What is done to us is always our fault, for in the end, nothing can be done to us that we won't permit."

Pietro was getting a little angry with her now. He felt sorry for her, but she annoyed him.

"You're small and delicate," he said. "How could you have prevented it?"

"I could have died," she said simply. "The first time was no sin, because I didn't know what they were going to do. But afterwards I knew. I chose to submit to save my life. Some of the other girls didn't; they died. . . ."

"I see," Pietro whispered.

"Where the sin lies? No you don't, Monsieur Pietro. God does not require of us that we save our lives. Life is neither that precious nor that important. He asks of us that we cleave to goodness, that we never bow to evil. So many people are born into the world, good Pietro—Our Heavenly Father has no lack of subjects. It mattered not in the least whether I went on living. But that I betrayed Him—that I accepted great evil as the price for my small life was sin—unpardonable sin. . . ."

"You're wrong," Pietro said. "But this is no time to discuss it. As soon as your father returns, we must begin our journey to Montrose. . . ."

Baron Henri did not return until morning. His face was grey with worry and fear.

"Father," Gautier said, "we've found her."

Pietro pushed the low chair forward just in time. Then he turned away his face. The joy in the old man's face was not to be borne—especially when it was going to be replaced so soon.

"Where is she?" Baron Henri whispered.

"In there—" Gautier pointed. "Sleeping, I think. . . ."

But she was not asleep. And when her father knelt beside her, crushing her in his arms, she whipped her head about, avoiding his kisses.

"No, Father," she said, "no, no, no!"

Baron Henri stared at her.

"You don't want me to kiss you, Toinette?" he said.

"No, Father."

"But, Toinette, before. . . ."

"Before, I was your daughter. Perhaps in small ways unworthy of your love. But in small ways only, my father. Not in great ones." She looked past him out the door. "Not in such great ones. Such terribly great ones."

Baron Henri didn't move. He just sat there, looking at her.

"Give me your hand, Father," Antoinette said. "No, no—don't take off your glove. . . ."

Wonderingly the Baron lifted the big hand that had dealt blows and scattered largesse, and done honorably always in the sight of God.

Antoinette kissed it.

"There," she said, "I have kissed you, Father—and your fair flesh has not been soiled. . . ."

"Soiled?" her father thundered. "By you?"

"Yes. By me. By the thing I have become."

Then she turned her face to the wall and started to cry.

Pietro had heard many people cry. But not like that. Not ever like that.

Gautier took his father by the arm and led him from the room.

"Gautier, by God's love—" Baron Henri began.

"She is with child, Father," Gautier said. "We found her at the Sign of the Black Bull. She was carried off by force and ravished. But she blames herself—as you see. . . ."

The Baron's powerful fingers closed over his son's arm.

"You say—you say there'll be a child?"

"Yes, Father."

"Dear God!" Baron Henri whispered.

Pietro knew what he was thinking. The House of Montrose would be forever disgraced. By the time they got back to Paris, even if they succeeded in finding a petty noble willing, for a price, to marry Antoinette, it would be too late. Great barons' daughters have to have public weddings. And every disappointed old crone able to count upon the fingers of her two hands would be able to reckon the dates to their dishonor.

It was very still in the room. Through the doorway they could hear Antoinette crying.

Pietro sighed. I could do it, he thought, that is—if they will permit me to . . . They are both men of station and of pride and they will both reckon the cost. Against this great evil they will weigh the other and who can say which they will count the greater? Public disgrace for Antoinette—for themselves, against the secret shame of knowing her wed to a man of villein blood. . . .

Still I could do this thing. For Gautier. For my friend who so often has dealt with me nobly. For this great hearted old man who deserves better of life. For—for myself.

He stopped. For himself. This small and ugly thought that had come unbidden. This thought that abruptly cheapened the nobility of his gesture, made mockery of his proposed sacrifice. . . .

I could take unto myself this soiled and tarnished maid, carrying within her the seed of God knows what ill-formed and brutish lout, accept, indeed, as my own whatever revolting little monster might result therefrom . . . But it is one thing to do this out of the love I bear my friend, out of gratitude for his many kindnesses, while to perform what ought to be an act of simple charity cognizant all the while of the possibilities that exist therein for furthering the vaulting sweep of mine own ambitions is quite another. . . .

No. I cannot. What a man does is ever less important than why he does it. I cannot buy my patents of nobility at such a price. I cannot use the disaster of my friends as the opening wedge into that world in which I propose to move. . . .

Gautier put down his head and cried suddenly. That was bad.

Pietro looked at him.

What good is there in this world, he mused, that is unmixed with evil? And what are all my fine scruples now, more than the sin of pride? I would not do this for myself, and for this pride of mine. For what I call mine honor, I deny them what is after all their only chance . . . Again in the silence he heard Antoinette crying.

Pietro sighed.

"My Lords," he said, "there is a way out. . . ."

They looked at him, both of them.

"The Lady Antoinette cannot be above a month with child. If she were married now in this city. . . ."

"But," Gautier said, "we know no one here."

Pietro bent his head. His voice was very low.

"You know—me, My Lords."

Gautier stared at him.

"Good God!" he got out.

"Consider the matter," Pietro said. "It's true I was baseborn—the son of a serf. But I was reared like a lord. And who in France knows anything of my birth? In Sicily, as Sir Gautier knows, my connections are indeed high, extending even to the Emperor, himself. And they have promise of becoming higher. . . ."

"That's true," Gautier said, hope in his voice. "Consider, Father. Pietro, here, is an old friend of the Emperor Frederick. I saw how fondly he was greeted at court in Palermo. He speaks and writes Latin better than any clerk, Arabic like a Saracen, Greek, French, Provencal, God knows how many tongues . . . His manners are gentle, better, indeed than ours. But you must have noticed that. . . ."

"I have noticed it," Baron Henri said. "The boy is good looking besides, and devoted to your service. Still, it involves a deception. . . ."

"God will forgive such a deception, my Father!" Gautier growled. "Would you then, rather than practice such a small deceit, return to Montrose and have every envious dame for miles around point the finger of scorn at Toinette? Or could she not return after a most romantic elopement, with her husband, a fair and pleasant Italian knight, whom she had met at Languedoc while sojourning with my uncle?"

Pietro had to laugh.

"You should have been a trouvere," he said, "so well do you spin romances."

"Well, Father?" Gautier said.

"Agreed," Baron Henri said tiredly. "We can give them Petit Mur, and with Toinette's dowry, they should be able to manage right well. The rest, young sir, is up to you."

"Trust me, My Lords."

"Then it's all settled," Gautier said happily. "You, Father, don't know Pietro as I do. He's been a fine companion and a staunch friend. For the once I saved his life, he's saved mine twice—once at Saint Marcel, and again last night with only a dagger against two great churls with cudgels. Pietro, I'm glad it's ended thus. It will be good to have so fine a brother. . . ."

"But," Antoinette said from the doorway, "It's not all settled, Gautier." They turned and looked at her.

"I know it's the custom that maids be given offhand with no thought to their wishes. I—I know I have no right, now, to any wish. But you promised me, Father, that I'd never be given in marriage against my will. . . ."

"So I did," Baron Henri said, "but Toinette. . . ."

"Listen, all of you. The sin is mine—and I have no wish to escape my just punishment. Good Pietro, I thank you for your kind offer. But you see, I don't love you. That will surprise you, I know. You're wondrously fair . . . handsomer perhaps than any man I've ever seen. . . ."

"Toinette—" Gautier groaned.

"Please, dear brother. M'sieur Pietro is also good and generous and very brave. I saw him fight alone against those two. How then can you ask him to take to wife such soiled and shoddy goods? To save my honor? But that is already lost. To give a name to my child? Named or nameless will he be in truth any less bastard?"

This one, Pietro thought, is as difficult as any prickly pear. . . .

"Fair Antoinette," he said, deliberately putting sternness into his voice, "you have talked about your sin—your punishment. All right. But what of your father and your brother and the love you bear them? What right have you to inflict upon them either sin or punishment, knowing them guiltless of all but a certain laxity in your behalf—fruit of too much love for you?"

Antoinette looked at him wonderingly.

"You can bear the punishment that you seem to be seeking. But in bearing it remember that every new fledged knight will sneer at the House of Montrose—that no guests will come to make merry in your father's hall, that his declining years must be spent in sorrow and loneliness, because of you!

"And Gautier—he'll have to fight daily to avenge the insults without number that will be his lot, brother of a sister shamed. All the worse because she was not really shamed, but simply pigheaded, stubborn and of most unseemly pride!"

"I—I have no pride, M'sieur," Antoinette whispered.

"Haven't you? It seems to me you take pride in this evil thing that has happened to you—against your will and without your cooperation. You persist in magnifying it into sin—what was a tragedy and sin against you. Go on, play the martyr. But the holy martyrs died in humble faith, out of the love of God, not by dramatizing themselves into heroines! You say you do not love me. That doesn't matter. Perhaps, if you tried, you could come to—as I will humbly and diligently try to learn to love a maid who left her good home and doting father to follow a mad shepherd across the wide sea, thinking to subdue with hymns brave men and warriors who love God as much as we though they call Him by another name. . . ."

"Bravo!" Gautier cried.

"That," Pietro said tiredly, "was your sin. That and nothing more. As for the rest, I have forgotten it. Not even the child will remind me. I shall try to bring him up as my own son—to love God, honor the saints, and obey his elders. Now, my lady, I'll have nothing more to say. . . ."

Antoinette looked at her father.

"Is it true, Father?" she whispered. "Will people scorn you and Gautier—because of me?"

"Yes," Baron Henri said.

Antoinette came out of the doorway. She walked over to Pietro and put out her hand.

"Then I will marry you, My Lord," she said to him, "and pray God I cause you no further sorrow. . . ."

They were married in the chapel of the Cathedral. Immediately thereafter they left the city. They reached Aix by nightfall and found lodgings there.

When Pietro saw that Gautier had engaged two chambers—one for his father and himself—one for Pietro and his bride, he was troubled. He did not love this strange maid. He'd much rather have commenced this business of being married later—much later.

Out of consideration for her, he blew out the candles and undressed in the dark. He lay there, waiting. He waited a long time.

He was very tired, and finally he fell asleep. He woke up later, far later, realizing that Antoinette still had not come to bed.

Slowly he got up, wrapping his cloak around him. He found a candle. Lit it.

Antoinette was huddled in the great chair, crying in her sleep. He put out his hand and touched her shoulder. She leaped as though she had been touched with a hot iron, and opened her mouth to scream. Then she closed it.

"Don't touch me!" she begged. "Please, Pietro—please!"

"I have no intentions of touching you," Pietro said coldly. "Go to bed. I'll take the chair. You'll have need of this rest—tomorrow. . . ."

Sitting in the big chair, he could hear her crying. He felt very lonely and sad and helpless. He was angry with himself, but he knew what he had done was right and honorable.

"Pietro," Antoinette called.

"Yes, my lady?"

"Come here."

Pietro went over to the bed, and stood there beside it.

"Lie—lie down beside me. . . ."

Pietro sank down.

"Now take me in your arms, but nothing more—good Pietro! By God's mercy, nothing more. . . ."

He put his arms around her. She was shaking. Her body was as cold as ice. He could hear her teeth chatter.

"You see now, how it is with me?" she wept. "Not because of you, Pietro—they—the others—did this . . . When Gautier, my own brother, kissed me, I sickened. I—I cannot bear my father's embraces! You see, Pietro? It's a sickness in me—you must have patience . . . Perhaps after the child. . . ."

Pietro put up his hand and stroked her soft hair.

"Go to sleep," he whispered, "my little one—my little lost one—sleep. . . ."

So on a summer's eve in the year 1212, with the almond tree outside his window catching the silver of a big moon, did Pietro di Donati spend his first wedded night.

And many another night thereafter.

Chapter Five

THE CASTLE AT MONTROSE was old fashioned. That is, its great keep or donjon was built of massive stones set in the form of a square. It towered high over the walls whose battlements and gate towers were also square. Square towers, Pietro knew, weren't too good. Ever since the returning Crusaders had seen the great Kraks of the Infidels, they had copied their round towers in their own castles. Round towers were much better. It was practically impossible to strike them a solid blow with a ram, since their curving sides made the ordinarily crushing stroke glance off.

I, he thought, would hate to have to defend this one.

He looked at his wife. She was directing her maids in all the thousand and one preparations that had to be made for this feast. They had been back at Montrose for a week now, and Antoinette looked rested. Some of the color had come back to her cheeks. It was nice to look at her, as long as you didn't see her eyes.

If, Pietro thought, she ever gets over this—this horror inside her, she'll make me a fine wife. She's really very good and very gentle, and pretty besides. . . .

He gazed at her. It's going to take a long time, though. Maybe the child will cure it. It'll be little and helpless, and will turn her thoughts outward—perhaps. And perhaps not. It may serve only to remind her. . . .

Every one of them dreaded this feast. But it had to be given. As soon as possible, too. All the neighboring gentlefolk had to be invited and told officially of the marriage. Between them, Pietro and Gautier were going to find occasion to place its date much earlier than it had really occurred. Casually—in the general conversation. Without too much emphasis, but with enough to make it stick.

Pietro had furnished them with a likely story—which, conceivably could be true—in part. During his last sojourn at Paoli's farm, Gina had told him many stories of Donati's youth and young manhood, including the widely held belief among the villeins that Donati had been actually the son of the good Baron Orri of Grostete, as Hellemark had been called before Rudolph of Brandenburg wrested it from the Norman knight by force of arms. Therefore to say that Pietro was the sole survivor of a noble house fallen upon evil days did not stretch the truth entirely out of shape. . . .

Thinking about it, Pietro smiled. His thoroughly ironical mind saw at once that it was far more likely that his father had been sired by some Norman sergeant or man-at-arms than by the Baron himself. Great Barons had too many amusements close at hand to concern themselves overmuch with peasant girls. But since he, himself, had no proof one way or the other, the story had to stand or fall on its own merits.

He saw Toinette take the precious tapestries, which were only hung out of a closet upon great occasions. They represented the deeds of a half legendary ancestor—a Baron Louis, who had fought with Charlemagne, and died with Roland, defending the pass. Toinette had woven some of them herself displaying a rare skill. And this was a great occasion, for on it depended whether or not they could live at peace at Petit Mur, the small castle some leagues away. . . .

The debate over this fete had raged half the preceding week. Baron Henri and Gautier wanted to make a brave spectacle of it, to invite as many people as possible. Antoinette wanted a small gathering—or no gathering at all. Pietro had been forced at last to enter the controversy, throwing the weight of his opinion with his new father and brother-in-law.

"Don't you see, dear Toinette," he had said, gently enough, "that we have to awe them into silence? When the child comes so soon, there will be talk; but by this fete we will have created at least a reasonable doubt in the minds of the more charitable. . . ."

"As you will, My Lords," Antoinette said dutifully, but her face was frozen.

She had ceased being so difficult. She was, it seemed to Pietro, growing resigned to her lot, especially since he had not insisted upon his husbandly rights.

He didn't feel noble about that. The truth of the matter was he felt little desire for his bride. His entirely oversensitive temperament rebelled at the thought of having relations with a woman who was with child, no matter how desirable she might ordinarily have been. On top of that there was a curious kind of pride: love for Pietro was always a shared experience—he had none of that excess of masculine lust that demanded satisfaction at any price. One look at the frozen terror in Antoinette's face, and any momentary desire he might have had died before it was half born.

Pietro wandered about the bailey, watching the womenfolk lay the great tables. The tablecloths were very fine, and the napkins were set in massive silver rings. At each place a knife and a spoon[1] had been placed, and between each a silver drinking cup, made in the form of a lion, a dragon, or a bird, so that they could be shared by each two guests. A cake of fine white flour, suitably iced and decorated was placed before each chair, and a silver porringer was shared by each two guests in the same fashion as the drinking cups.

Varlets were setting up the dais with its canopy under which Baron Henri would sit, with a few high ranking nobles at his side. In the cook house the fires roared, preparing the meats, for Baron Henri had sent his foresters out for game the very day they had arrived.

There wasn't anything for Pietro to do. He was still strange to the castle, and Gautier and the Baron and Toinette had the matter well in hand. So Pietro went back inside and sought out the sewing woman who was making his suit for the occasion. It had to be very fine, and on this score Pietro could teach the simpler northern nobles a thing or two.

He had drawn the design for her upon parchment, because

as a trained scribe, he could also draw wonderfully well. When she saw it, the seamstress dropped her needle and clapped her hands with delight. It was based upon the clothing he had worn in his youth and combined Oriental opulence with Sicilian taste. Nothing about this suit of his was radically new—except its total effect. The tunic was cut short and belted, the pantaloons were skin tight, and joined the hose so imperceptibly that they seemed to be one garment, except that they differed in color. His pelisson, edged with fur about the bottom, was short too, but little longer than the *bliaut* or tunic. In a day when men's garments were long and flowing, Pietro was displaying a scandalous amount of leg.

He had selected a dark, rich red for the basic color, which went wonderfully well with his swarthy complexion. His stockings were black silk with bright red stripes winding spirally up the leg. The fur that edged his red silk pelisson was black marten, and the *bliaut* was a rusty orange-red, lighter in color than the pelisson or the pantaloons. Pietro knew well the effect of sticking to shades of one basic color. The whole suit was red and black, with red predominating.

He cursed the fact that he'd have to wear a cape, hot as it was. A cape, fur-edged, samite lined, was the very declaration of gentle blood. His shoes were red velvet, embroidered with fine black thread like his *bliaut* and cape. On the cape, in the midst of little black rosettes, he had had the seamstress sew his rubies, so that not even the colors of his jewels would clash with the general scheme.

Despite all his misfortunes, Pietro was far from penniless. When he had left Sicily with Isaac, he brought with him all the jewels he owned at Isaac's suggestion, as the good goldsmith had anticipated that they'd need them to pawn, if Count Siniscola demanded too high a ransom for Donati's life. Iolanthe had kept them for him. And being as practical as she was romantic, she had brought them to Pietro when she'd fled Hellemark.

Pietro was glad of that. It made him all but independent of the charity of his wife's family. He'd sold some of the lesser ones the day after their arrival, and even after having bought the fabulously rich stuffs for his suit, he still had a good many gold coins in his purse. . . .

The seamstress had finished the suit. Pietro thanked her gravely, and gave her a silver coin—more money than she'd ever seen in her life.

"My thanks, goodwife," he said. "You've done well."

Then he took the suit and the tight fitting skullcap, embroidered like the suit with rubies, though, because he hadn't that many, these and the ones on his shoes were of glass—bought secretly and thoughtfully in the village some days before.

He had just laid the suit out on the canopied bed when Antoinette came into the room. She stopped in the doorway and stared at the suit.

"Why, Pietro," she whispered, "it—it's lovely . . . Put it on, please."

"Isn't it too early to dress?" Pietro said.

"No, some of the lesser guests are already arriving. But, anyway, I'd love to see you in that. . . ."

Pietro dressed himself, while Toinette sat on the edge of the bed watching him with grave eyes.

"You know, Pietro," she said, "you look just like a prince."

"Thank you," Pietro laughed, and bent to kiss her. But she turned her face away quickly.

"Sorry," Pietro said.

"Don't be," Toinette whispered. "I'll get over that. You're so good, and so patient. I want to get over it. I wish I did love you. I pray every night to the Virgin to make me love you. I should be very proud to have a husband so fine and so very handsome. Tonight all the girls hereabouts will envy me with all their hearts. . . ."

"Not so fine," Pietro said bitterly. "A penniless lout, who has scant chance of ever becoming a knight. . . ."

"Father will knight you—or induce Count Forêtbrun to do so."

"No," Pietro said, "not like that. Don't you see, Toinette, it's a thing I've got to win. I don't want it handed to me because of an accident of fate. I want to win it fairly by brave deeds. . . ."

"Most knights don't win knighthood by brave deeds," Toinette pointed out. "They're knighted first and ride out afterwards to do battle. Many of them never do anything brave. Much more often they plunder and kill and do all sorts of evil things. Besides, you've already done your brave deed. You saved my brother's life—and mine. And afterwards you did what was braver still, and much, much kinder—you took to wife a girl no longer a maid, carrying within her the child of God knows what ugly brute—out of loyalty to my brother, and out of pity—for me. . . ."

Pietro thought she was going to cry again, so he said quickly: "Better dress, little one—we must go down soon."

The maids came in and dressed her while he waited. When they had finished, she was fair enough to suit anybody. One of the older maids pinched both her cheeks hard to give them color, and then Pietro took her by one finger and led her down the stairs.

All over the bailey, the gay chatter died. The silence started out in waves, moving out from where they stood, until one by one all the guests had become aware of them, and turned to stare quite boldly upon the stranger.

Pietro's face felt hot. But he carried his head high as he marched toward the dais, leading his bride. Toinette looked down at her feet and would not raise her eyes.

A ripple of whispers broke out behind them.

"By God's blood, whoever he is—she hasn't gone beneath her!"

"They say he's a natural son of the Emperor Frederick—"

"Don't be silly, Frederick is no older than that, himself. . . ."

"By the fingerbone of Saint Aliquis, I'm going to have my tailor make me such clothes as those! I've never seen anything quite so fine. . . ."

"Strange though. She disappeared from Montrose God knows how long ago. Baron Henri was away when she left, I have that on good authority. And when they brought her back, she had this boy with her. For all you know, he may be no more than a jongleur or other such wandering vagabond. . . ."

"Vagabond! In those clothes?"

"How do you know who paid for them?"

"I know this—Montrose is not rich enough to afford those rubies. And another thing, stones of that size cannot be purchased in either France or Languedoc. . . ."

The impression then, Pietro thought, is favorable. With some dissent. If, God willing, we carry it off. . . .

The trumpets rocked his eardrums, ending the whispers. All the guests crowded forward at once toward the long oaken tables set under tents of bravely colored silk. At the entrance, two handsome varlets stood, one holding a silver jug filled with water and a small basin, while the other was supplied with a great length of bright toweling. Each guest as he entered, put out his hands and the first servitor poured water over them while the second dried them dexterously.

This done, the Lord Bishop took his place at the head of the long table, while Baron Henri stood two places to his left. Ordinarily, the gentle Baron would have sat next to the Bishop, but today, with rare courtesy, the seats of honor were reserved for Pietro and his bride. Still further to the right, in the secular place of honor, the stately Count of Forêtbrun—whose name never ceased to puzzle his vassals since his forests, God knew, were green enough—stood.

Each guest was guided to his place by an army of servitors, many of them young nobles, glad to do honor to their liege, Baron Henri. They stood behind their chairs until Auguste, Bishop of Montrose, had said a powerful Latin Grace, and followed it with a lesser one in Roman, as those who spoke it insisted upon labelling the Langue d'oïl. Its resemblance to the tongue of the Romans was now but slight, as anyone could tell by merely listening to the two prayers. But human pride cares little for technicalities.

Then they all sat down. There was silence. Then cymbals clashed and the trumpets brayed again, and Sire Hugue, the seneschal, appeared in brave livery waving a white wand like a field marshal leading a train of servants which stretched all the way across the bailey to the cook house. Each servant had a huge platter of some succulent viand upon his shoulder. All the guests cheered as a haunch of venison was set upon the table.

The Baron's head carver displayed real skill, slicing huge slices, holding the meat in the prescribed fashion with two fingers and a thumb, while all the time the flute players played runs and trills. The cup bearers scurried about pouring the wine into the drinking cups that stood between each two guests, while the squires and young knights sworn to the Baron's service performed the function of courtesy by taking the meats from the hands of the villein servitors and serving it themselves—for nobles, from noble hands, the phrase went. . . .

Pietro couldn't eat. The sight of so much food took what little appetite he had. He sipped his wine, passing the goblet back and forth between Toinette and himself. She wasn't eating either. All the noble dames smiled approvingly, taking this as evidence of the power of love. . . .

Besides that mighty haunch there was also for the first course, boar's head larded with herb sauce, beef, mutton, legs of pork, roasted rabbit, and pastry tarts.

The guests tackled all this with gusto. No one talked. Two low clowns of minstrels performed before the table, climbing a pole balanced on the forehead of a third, juggling apples on the points of daggers, eating fire. . . .

But by the time they had reduced the meats to broken scraps the guests were in a mood for talk. So between the first and second courses, Pietro's ordeal began.

"My Lord Baron," Bishop Auguste thundered—which was his usual tone of voice since he was somewhat deaf—"We know little of your new son-in-law. He seems a fine and knightly lad. But who is he? Who are his antecedents?"

This was shouted across the space occupied by Pietro and Antoinette.

Pietro felt his wife stiffen. He took her hand.

"Courage, Love," he whispered.

Baron Henri met the challenge.

"You know, of course, My Lord, the House of Grostete—and Baron Orri who left these parts many years ago?"

"Of course," the Bishop bellowed. "This lad is related?"

"A grandson—though on the distaff side. His father's family were a line of proud Italian barons—the Roglianos. . . ."

God rest my soul! Pietro thought. If Hans or Mark or Wolfgang could hear that!

"I'm glad he has French blood," the Bishop said. "No offense meant to our Italian friends, of course. . . ."

"And none taken, my Lord," Pietro said quietly.

"Heh, what's that?" the Bishop roared, cupping his ear.

"I said I'm glad too," Pietro shouted.

The good Bishop drank his wine.

"No irregularity, Baron," he demanded, "in this match? I heard it was an elopement. . . ."

"You heard rightly. My daughter met young Messire Pietro in Languedoc, whither he had fled, since his family, being stout supporters of Emperor Frederick, had been put to the sword by the Welfs. They were wed by none other than your own good friend, my Lord—Clement, Bishop of Marseilles—in the Cathedral . . ."

This was a masterstroke, Pietro knew. To mention the very name of the officiating priest was to lull suspicion. Everyone knew that Baron Montrose would not have dared be so specific on this point, if an irregularity existed. The great Bishops were frequent correspondents—even visitors in one another's synods. Auguste knew now just whom to ask, if doubt still existed in his mind. But that the Baron had given him this information, tended to remove the doubt.

The guests hacked themselves new trenchers from the great loaves placed before them[2] throwing the old, now well soaked with the juices of the meats, to the dogs beneath the table. Even here, Pietro saw that distinctions of class were drawn. The nobles had platters of silver beneath their trenchers of bread; lesser gentry—landless knights and such, had pewter platters; while the wealthy burghers—actually of the villein class, some of them indeed the sons of serfs, grown with the widespread growth of commerce in these late years into men of considerable importance—had only the tablecloth on which to cut their meats.

"No irregularity then," Bishop Auguste growled. "Still it seems strange . . ."

"What seems strange, my Lord?" Gautier said calmly, though he raised his voice to make sure that the good Bishop heard him. "My sister was united in holy wedlock with a man of gentle blood—though, admittedly, his fortunes could stand some mending. My father and I could find nothing to quarrel with in that.

And now that Frederick of Hohenstaufen has, with the help of our own great King, been elevated over the Welf. . . ."

He did not finish the sentence, for at that moment the viols and flutes sounded, and Sire Hugue came in with the swan, spread out as though it were alive and swimming, its beak gilt, its body silvered, resting on a mass of blue tinted pastry to represent the water, and little banners all about it. That culinary masterpiece occupied the company for some time; and after it, the royal peacock served in his own magnificent feathers.

The guests had eaten and drunk so much by now that they were in a mood to approve of everything—even this unknown and suspect Italian who had carried off so fair a prize.

He held Toinette's cold hand, without being entirely aware that he still held it. His mind followed a curious pattern, having nothing to do with the fete or the noise about him or the wine. The hilarity had reached a new height now, because Baron Henri had caused to be brought in that favorite novelty of the time: a huge pastry baked in a tub. Pietro, who had never seen one before, found it mysterious but all the other revelers looked at it with eyes that shone with delight and anticipation. Baron Henri stood up, flourishing a dagger. Then with one deft motion he ripped the top crust open, and a host of small birds flew out.

My God! Pietro thought. What will they think of next?

The answer to that one was easy, and with a little thought, he could have guessed it himself: the nobles, who kept their prized hawks even in their bedchambers, quickly unhooded the falcons and sent them after the small birds.

Hawking had always delighted Pietro; but now, curiously, it didn't. Watching the great falcons arching upward above the helpless birds then plummeting downward for all the world like projectiles, he thought about the talons tearing and the old wounds in his own body ached.

The little ones. The little helpless ones, and above them the gyrfalcons mounting—like death. Like destiny.

The small birds had no more chance than he had had against Mark and Wolfgang. Than Donati and Isaac had had against the knights of Siniscola. Than Toinette had had against her ravishers. . . .

Little birds. People were all little birds, playthings of fate, fools of destiny. They plunged blindly through life and things happened to them—without rhyme or reason—and in heaven God laughed.

Pietro wanted most of all now to escape, to be alone, to put his thoughts in order. But he knew how slight the chance for that would be.

Already the viols, the flutes, the oboes, the trumpets and the lutes were sounding, and the couples were joining hands for the dancing. He didn't know these French dances, so he kept still and watched them for a while. He would have been quite content to watch them all evening, but a tall blonde maid broke out of the dancers and caught his hand.

"Oh, come on, Sire Pietro!" she begged. "Come, dance with your lady—and then with me!"

Pietro got up and danced "Drop the Ring" with Toinette; and after that he danced the "Dance of the Chaplet" with the tall blonde, which proved an agreeable surprise, because at the end each knight was supposed to kiss his partner on the cheek. Whether by accident or design Pietro never knew, but Yvette—for already he knew her name—turned her face so that his kiss landed full upon her mouth. She laughed gaily.

Pietro threw a quick glance over his shoulder to see if Toinette were watching. She was. That troubled him. He didn't mean to hurt her. Especially not in such childish fashion.

Thereafter he avoided the fair Yvette, and danced an intricate galliard with his bride. Each time he advanced toward her, and bowed, he searched her face for some sign of displeasure. There was none.

Why, he thought bitterly, she doesn't care! If this night I left the castle with Yvette and returned only on the morrow, she wouldn't care. . . .

That hurt. His life had made Pietro a man grown and more; but where his heart was concerned, he showed his seventeen years. So he danced the next set—a violent tourdion—with Yvette.

In the midst of it, while they were whirling violently with linked arms, she whispered:

"Would God I had seen you first, Sire Pietro!"

Pietro smiled.

"The last is better than the first, fair Yvette," he said, and bowing, went back to his seat beside his bride.

While the lesser folk were being entertained by a dancing bear, some jugglers and three dancers who performed most grossly, the great Norman trouvere, Maître Raymond, accompanied by a harp player of real skill, entertained the nobles, chanting the sonorous lines of the Chanson de Troye, making the ladies weep as he described the fate of Queen Hecuba, and the wanderings of Sire Ulysses, and the faithfulness of Dame Penelope. . . .

Many of the villeins were asleep on the grass by the time that Maître Raymond finished his chanson. Some of the nobles, too, were a little worse for wear. Seeing this, Baron Henri brought the festivities to a close, offering his hospitality to as many as cared to avail themselves of it.

Pietro was most happy to take Antoinette by the finger and lead her upstairs to their chamber. But on the way Gautier stopped them.

"We've won!" he whispered. "I have ten invitations to noble houses hereabouts, each with the request to bring you along, good Pietro. Some of the dames are mightily taken with you—so my sister, you'd better look to him. . . ."

Antoinette shrugged.

"At the moment," she said, "all I can look forward to—is sleep."

"Go to sleep then," and Gautier laughed. "You'll have to get up early in the morning anyhow in order to see me off. . . ."

"Off?" Antoinette whispered. "Where are you going, Gautier?"

"Back to Saint Marcel," Gautier sighed. "I promised my Lord, Simon de Montfort—and besides—there still remains the matter of Uncle Roget. . . ."

Pietro looked at him.

"I go with you," he said.

"Look, Pietro, a man just wed does not fly off to the wars. . . ."

"Gautier, listen," Pietro said; "I took vows to serve you. I mean to keep them. Besides, Toinette needs time to herself—this business of being married takes a little getting used to. . . ."

Gautier stared at his sister.

"I see," he said quietly. "Toinette, is it your wish that he go?"

"Oh, yes," Antoinette said quickly. Then she realized how ill that sounded. "If—if he wants to . . ." she added lamely.

"I want to," Pietro said.

"I see," Gautier said again. "Be ready in the morning, Pietro." Then he turned and left them.

They went on up the stairs.

Pietro and Gautier rode away from Montrose in the morning. They didn't talk to each other. The matter that occupied both their thoughts was too delicate for discussion, even between such close friends.

To the wars, Pietro thought, yes to the wars, to hell itself is infinitely better than staying. She accepts even the service I have done her reluctantly and me not at all. It wouldn't be good to stay. I'm not of such stuff as saints are made of and ultimately the time would come when I should begin to desire her. Or thwarted there, turn to some other maid. . . .

The image of Yvette rose unbidden in his mind. That was another thing too. If to flee from such dangerous temptation was cowardice, it was at least wise cowardice. The castle of Geoffroi, Count de Harvengt, whose wife Yvette was, was too close at hand. And the Count was nearing sixty, while Yvette had yet to see her eighteenth year. . . .

Of the long and weary journey from Montrose down into the lovely country of Languedoc, little need be said. Both Pietro and Gautier knew the need for haste and drove their mounts cruelly. As it was, only the valor of the Count of Foix and the other brave defenders of Saint Marcel permitted them sufficient time to reach that city before it fell.

They rode into the camp of Simon de Montfort before the walls of the city while the nightly operations were at their height. The trenchbuts, the catapults, the mangonels, and the mounted bows were casting an endless stream of missiles into the town. It was burning. Pietro saw a corps of engineers firing one earthen pot of Greek fire after another into the city. Each time they struck, new flames arose.

Simon greeted Gautier warmly.

"You've come in time, my Lord," he said. "Tomorrow we'll

take them by storm. In fact, I'm about to send them a little message of encouragement now. . . ."

As he spoke, a vile stench assailed their nostrils.

What the devil? Pietro thought.

"On top of yonder building they've built a cistern to catch the rain," Simon told them. "We've cut them off from all other sources of water. But the lucky scoundrels have had rain in God's plenty. So they've water for a good long time. I mean to change that . . . Come!"

The stench was stronger now.

As he followed Simon de Montfort, Pietro felt sick. Every step made the smell worse. Then he saw it.

A dead horse. Long dead.

The soldiers had wound down the greatest of the trenchbuts, capable of casting a stone weighing half a ton. But in the place of the stone they had put the horse. The so very dead horse.

The square cistern was outlined by the flames. They could see it very clearly.

"The honor is yours, my Lord," William, Archbishop of Paris, who served as chief of the Engineers, said.

Simon roared with laugher.

With one deft movement he cast off the ropes that held the casting sling of the trenchbut down, counterbalancing the enormous stone that weighted the other end. The beam creaked. Groaned. Then it whipped upward in a long arc. The horse left the sling. Soared over the wall. They saw the water rise in bloody wings before the dancing flames.

"Well, aimed, my churchly Lord!" Simon bellowed.

It was. William, Bishop though he was, was one fine engineer.

"Now, if you with the mangonels will keep up a shower of small stones," William said grimly, "so that they won't be able to fish that carcass out, by morning that water will be beyond human consumption. Now, let us go—I have need of rest. . . ."

Simon, Guy, Archbishop William,[3] several other leaders and Gautier went back to the campfire. Pietro went with them.

He looked at the prelate with the great iron mace swinging from his belt. Good God, how many evasions were there in this life! The law forbade a priest from "smiting with the edge of the sword." But since it said nothing concerning the delicate matter of knocking his brains out with a mace—a short staff with a chain on the end, and to that chain attached a smooth round ball of solid iron—such martial Bishops as William felt quite free to thus strike down the enemies of the Lord.

Pietro had a bellyful. He remembered again that a man always had a choice of what he'd submit to, so he spoke out boldly to the Archbishop.

"Your Grace," he said, "I find myself puzzled. . . ."

"How so, young squire?" William rumbled.

To Pietro's astonishment, his face viewed thus closely, was not unkindly.

"By our faith," Pietro said, "we are taught to deal mercifully with our enemies . . ." He was conscious all the time that Simon's eyes were upon him, hard as steel. "But it's plagued hard to reconcile such mercy with throwing the rotted carcass of a beast into their drinking water!"

"Pietro!" Gautier warned.

"Leave the boy alone," William thundered. "He has the makings of a clever disputant—which, by my troth, I do dearly love. And you my Lord Simon, a difference of opinion is not necessarily heresy. The boy's to speak freely, do you hear!"

"As you will, my Lord," Simon said. But his voice was surly.

"Look you, Messire—"

"Pietro. Pietro di Donati," Pietro supplied.

"Italian, eh? They're usually subtle devils. Now about my horse. That was the very embodiment of mercy."

"How so, my Lord?" Pietro asked wonderingly.

"Every day that this siege lasts, souls within that city pass unshriven to their dooms. If my horse can quicken their surrender by one day, I will have saved many souls. You see, my son, they don't have to die for their heresy. The choice is up to them. They can repent even at the stake, and after suitable punishments, God will receive them again. . . ."

"But, my Lord," Pietro said, "if a man does not really repent, but only pretends to—out of fear . . . ?"

"God will know the difference," William said serenely. "They but postpone their taste of hellfire."

"I have heard it said," Pietro put in, "that their faith, strange as it is, produces many good and kindly men. . . ."

"True," William said. "But goodness is not enough, young squire! A man must also believe. There were good men among the pagans. The Sultan Saladin was a wonderfully good man. I think sometimes that God must have a gentler hell for such as they—without torments say, and chance even to come to the true faith after death. . . ."

He paused looking into the fire. Then he gave to Pietro the first answer that any of the Crusade had proposed in defense of their mission which made sense.

"Look you," he said quietly. "It's not their goodness I fight—but their error and the spread of it. God's Church, in the hands of men, has made its mistakes and committed sins—though I see my Lord Simon would gladly burn me for saying so. But I am God's representative here. Yet, good Sires, so has every kingdom upon earth—every secular government—made errors—far more grievous, sins many times greater than any the Church unhappily and unwittingly has been party to. Yet no man proposes to do away with the government of kings!

"These heretics, though their lives may be blameless—which I doubt—set up nothing to take the place of what they would destroy—God's castle of defense against human violence, the sinking of society into chaos, and the iniquity of kings!

"We have our unworthy priests, our luxurious abbots—younger sons usually of great lords who placed them in the church to rid themselves of them—but the world has its bad kings, and its wicked nobles, yet no man does more than grumble against them. Yet these people would pull down the institution that has preserved learning, saved the poor, shown mercy even upon Jew[4] and Saracen, checked the lusts of the rich and powerful, taken care of widows and orphans—the only institution upon God's green earth that works ceaselessly for good.

"And what propose they in its place? A system that forbids parenthood and counsels suicide. A system that destroys the incentives to sober industry by idolizing poverty; that would cast down the sacrament of marriage and leave the relationships of the sexes to bodily lust, and the rearing of children to purest chance!

"Good Messire Pietro—Catharism is a mess of nonsense, poisoning the simple minds of the people. Against it, we do well to fight!"

"Thank you, my Lord," Pietro said. "You have cleared my mind. But if only we could fight without cruelty—and kill, when killing becomes necessary, without slow bodily torments. I don't believe God requires that. When we do it, my Lord—we become like those who scourged Our Blessed Savior, pressed a crown of thorns upon His Head, and pierced His Sacred Side."

"You," Simon said, "should have been a maid. Sire Gautier, you'll never make a knight of him."

"If," Pietro said, "becoming a knight means becoming a butcher—I'll remain a squire, and gladly, my Lord!"

"Look to him, Gautier!" Simon roared. "Sometimes he provokes me too much!"

"Hang your provocations," William said mildly. "The boy's right. I'm for bed. We'll need our strength in the morning. . . ."

Pietro found it hard to sleep. All night the thudding of the battering rams against the walls kept up, and the long creaking and the far off crashing of the casting engines. He thought about the people who were dying. It wasn't a good thing to think about. Infants. The aged. Women. Warriors. Priests. The stones from the engines did not discriminate.

It took them all day, but this time there was no stopping them. The Albigensians were too tired, too weak, too starved; and by night a raging thirst consumed them. But that was not what did it. Being human, there were many among them, who knowing their lives would be spared if they repented of their heresy, were ready to exchange their faith for their lives. The urge to cling to life was strong and most men didn't die very readily for an abstraction, for an idea, a belief.

But their leaders would not hear of it. Some of them, like the Count Foix, had committed too many crimes to permit them to surrender themselves into certain death by torture. So at nightfall, they made one last sally in force.

And Simon de Montfort, that very hammer of God, crushed them. But not without losses. Great losses, terrible losses.

In the press of battle, Pietro lost sight of Gautier. After it was over he searched for him. And what he saw during that search, he never forgot as long as he lived. The crusaders were maddened by their losses. Those heretics who expected mercy upon repenting their errors were disappointed. The crusaders spared no one.

Pietro looked all over the battlefield for Gautier. Each time he came to a mound of dead horses and men, sometimes twenty or more in one heap, he stopped and tore into it with his hands, dragging men out from under their mounts. Some of them were still living and groaned as he pulled at them.

It was hard work. Especially since he couldn't see very well. It was getting dark and the tears that flooded his eyes didn't help either. Nor the intermittent spasms of vomiting.

I'll never get used to it, he thought, never. . . .

Not the battle. He didn't mean that. In the noise and heat of action he could forget his fear. He was even beginning to enjoy fighting. But now every time one of the crusaders in the name of God rode by dragging a knight of Languedoc tied by his heels, living, to the tail of the horse, Pietro retched again.

Or when the hammers thudded against the nails they were driving through the hands and feet of the ones they were crucifying upside down on the olive trees.

And the screams.

They had made a huge fire in the middle of the battlefield. Every few minutes the French knights would come up to it by twos and threes, dragging a man of Saint Marcel between them. They swung the captives back and forth by their legs and shoulders. Then they threw them into the fire.

In the city it was worse. Everywhere, tall knights pulled the skirts of women up over their heads; and two or three of them were holding each woman down while the lines formed, waiting their turn.

Everywhere. In the houses. On the doorsteps. In the middle of the street. In the cathedral itself, before the altar of God.

Pietro thought about Toinette.

I will not, he swore, before God the Most High upon the honor of my mother not from this hour forth will I take part in it.

Children, some of them. Years before puberty. Old women, white-haired and weeping.

I must find Gautier, Pietro wept. I must—Toinette will never forgive me if. . . .

He was surprised suddenly, to find how important that was.

Nobody paid any attention to him. They were all too busy with their various pleasures.

He left the burning city and came out into the countryside, past the wells choked with bodies. Past the bonfires become pyres of living men. Past the hayricks burning. The farmhouses. The villeins' daughters running screaming before groups of laughing, drunken men.[5]

It was his sickness with it all that forced him to ride on until he was far out, beyond the sound of it and the sight and the smells. He rode into the barnyard of a small farm, and got down. The farm was deserted, the owner having prudently fled with his family. Pietro was glad of that. He didn't want to face these people. Not mounted and bearing arms.

He went over to the well and looked down. It was clear. Nobody had thrown refuse or the bodies of animals or of men into it. He drew up the wooden bucket and drank. The water was cool and sweet.

He took the bucket and started toward his palfrey. It was very hot and the animal was foam-flecked and suffering. But when he was close, it neighed shrilly.

From behind the barn another horse answered it. Pietro put the bucket down, carefully. He drew his sword and walked very slowly around the side of the barn, and when he was all the way around he saw it.

A great destrier, bearing trappings he knew so well. Gautier's.

Pietro put up his sword. Then he ran around to the door of the barn, and pushed it open. Gautier was there all right. He was sitting on a pile of straw looking down at the body of a man. Then Pietro saw that the man wasn't dead.

He came up to Gautier and looked down. He didn't have to ask. The wounded man was Baron Roget of Saint Marcel. His resemblance to both Baron Henri and Gautier was striking. He was talking to Gautier in a low voice.

He was also bleeding to death.

Pietro came closer. He bent down and examined Roget's

wounds. If they were attended to now—at once—there was a chance. Bandages would stop that bleeding and if he escaped infection he would live. Yet Gautier made no move.

It came to Pietro that his young master had been there for some time, perhaps even hours. Yet he had done nothing. He was deliberately letting his uncle die.

A faith that breeds such cruelty, Pietro began within his mind, but then he stopped. Gautier was not one of the murderously faithful, whose certainty excluded mercy. Pietro knew he had his doubts; that indeed he more than half sympathized with the heretics. Then why in the name of heaven—?

"Who is this?" Roget croaked.

"Pietro, of whom I told you," Gautier sighed. "Uncle Roget—please!"

"The boy who married Toinette, eh? A fair lad, Gautier—and a gallant one, from all you've told me. . . ."

"Uncle Roget, in God's name!"

"In God's name, Gautier? But you've seen what was done today in God's name."

"I shall never lose my shame at having had even a small part in it," Gautier whispered. "Still. . . ."

Roget put up his hand and patted Gautier's arm.

"What is there about the world we live in, boy," he whispered, "that I should want to linger? Besides, it is a tenet of my faith that once we receive the final rites, the *consolamenteum*, we risk loss of our souls if we recover. I did not deal myself these wounds—this is not suicide, my nephew. I merely will not interfere with what has happened. . . ."

"The *endura*?" Pietro asked.

"Yes, yes," Roget said with surprising strength, "the *endura*. Who taught you our beliefs?"

"Gautier," Pietro said.

"Good," Roget whispered. "You will both live to see them triumph. . . ."

"What makes you so sure of that, Sire Roget?" Pietro asked. Not in mockery, or even in insensitivity; but because his mind was like that. The hunger after knowledge was the strongest hunger he possessed.

"The things I've seen. The things I've learned. Listen—in 1202 I took the Cross. I embarked the following year upon a crusade against Egypt. You know what happened. Those villainous Venetians, who love gold above God diverted it into an attack upon—"

He stopped, his face contorted with pain.

"Uncle Roget!" Gautier cried.

"No—matter," Roget whispered. "It will pass. What was I saying?"

"That the Venetians diverted the attack," Pietro said. There was in his mind now, the beginning of an idea. Talking would tire Roget faster. When he was unconscious, Pietro could bandage his wounds. Gautier, apparently, had promised not to; but Pietro hadn't promised anything.

"Yes. They diverted the attack upon Constantinople. From the infidels upon Christians. They had a profitable trade with Egypt, and secret treaties—but no matter. Deluded like the rest, I took part in what I thought was—a—a rightful attempt to put the deposed king back on his throne. . . ."

"Uncle Roget," Gautier begged. "You must not talk! You'll tire and. . . ."

"I must talk, Gautier. It's my last chance. I have things to say. Important things. I had then a high conception of knighthood. I had absolute faith in the religion into which I was born. When I left Constantinople, I had neither. . . ."

He paused, looking off into space, his eyes fierce.

"They burned a mosque in the city, and the worshippers in it. The fire laid waste three miles. The Venetians stole the best of everything—gems, slaves, statues, great works of art—know you the four bronze horses that gallop so beautifully above the Piazza di San Marco in Venice? The Venetians stole them from Constantinople. But the other crusaders were not far behind. They knew not the value of art, but they knew gold when they saw it, and silver, even when used to decorate God's altars. Perhaps they felt it no sin to desecrate the churches of schismatics. . . ."

Gautier made no attempt to halt him now.

"They quartered their steeds in the beautiful Santa Sophia—the loveliest church of Christendom. They made fires with manuscripts stolen from the libraries—campfires—my sons, with the pages of Sophocles! Helmets and chain mail were polished with Euripides' immortal words . . . You know, Gautier, how I love knowledge. When a Greek captive told me our noble French and Venetian and Flemish knights had destroyed the only complete works in existence of these giants, I wept. . . .

"I had—had always revered our religious sisterhoods. My sister, your aunt, is Mother Superior of the Nunnery of Saint Giles—but that you know . . . Yet our knights took perverse delight in singling out the Greek sisterhoods for rapine, divesting them of their chaste and sacred garments in the very streets. . . ."

"No wonder you lost your belief in knighthood," Pietro said. "But, Sire Roget, Pope Innocent specifically forbade any such attack upon Byzantium. . . ."

"That I know . . . But when our leaders threw to him the subtle sop of reuniting the Eastern Church with Rome—a reunion in name only, since the Greek Prelates fled and continued their church elsewhere—he removed the ban from us, sent us his legates and his blessing! For an orgy of pillage, murder and rape, we received from His Holiness finally, a mild chiding. . . ."[6]

Gautier looked at his uncle sternly.

"Uncle Roget," he said, "if it is your wish to make Albigensians of us, I must warn you that you waste your breath. The sins of men are not God's sins; and great office does not exclude error. Yet the religion we were born in is the only true one; through it alone does God speak!"

Roget smiled at him.

"I envy you," he whispered. "I sometimes wonder if God ever has spoken to man—or even if there is a God at all. . . ."

"Uncle Roget!"

"I'm sorry," Roget whispered. "It's not my aim to disturb you. I am old now—and dying. It is important to me to tell you this—to clarify my own mind, if no more. . . ."

"Gautier, for God's sake," Pietro said harshly. "Let him speak."

"I—I came back to Languedoc. And there I hired scholars to translate for me the Word of God. I read it, and then I understood how much more nearly right were the Albi than we! We have erected temples in the name of a man who entered the temple not above thrice in His life, and then to dispute with the doctors and scourge out the thieves! We have overladen them with gold and silver in the name of Our Lord who despised wealth, held neither lands nor gold. We have built up a system of ritual, beautiful and pagan in the name of Him who taught us to go into our closets and pray unseen of man. . . ."

"Uncle Roget," Gautier almost wept. "Have care for your soul! This is no time for blasphemy. . . ."

"I know, I know. That is always the answer, isn't it? But there are those among us who must question—who are born to question. No matter. We doubters are born before our time, because men are not ready for us. There has never been, nor I doubt ever will be, a miracle which intelligent, dispassionate inquiry could not easily discredit; but when will intelligence and tolerance be allowed to operate in this world? Men need their miracles, their saints' bones, their splinters of the true cross—of which now there are so many as to reforest the world. . . ."

Gautier turned his back. There was in his face, Pietro saw, both fear and struggle. Against these things his good, simple heart had scant defenses.

"They need them because life in our times is so ugly and terrible. Force reigns with bloody hand. The good and gentle have no chance against the strong . . . No wonder they clutch at straws: the illusions of hysterical shepherd children, the ravings of men and women, who if they spoke thus of aught save God would be caged, lest they harm themselves and others. We—we proved that. We made an image of the Virgin, humped of back and with one eye—so ugly as to frighten children. Of it we claimed many miracles, hoping to show our friends their folly when we revealed our hoax. . . ."[7]

"It didn't work," Pietro said.

"No. They refused to believe us when we said we had carved it, that it had not been cast up from the sea; and when we explained how we had done the spurious miracles, they told us of others beyond our ken that our self-made Lady had done! Life is too hard—they want to escape it by the easy route: unquestioning belief in whatever nonsense is most comforting; by the roseate paths of hope, rather than the stony trails of truth. . . ."

He lay back upon the straw smiling. Pietro could see the strength ebbing out of him. For a moment he was tempted to point out to this formidable skeptic the miracle they had all been witnessing: the complete victory of human will over the weakness of the flesh. Bleeding, dying, Roget of Saint Marcel had spoken with strength and authority of those things closest to his heart. He had, while speaking of them, been able to dominate pain, forget weakness, the rod of his will standing erect as steel amid the broken, bloody rags of his flesh. But he had spoken now, and the strength went out of him.

It was a long time before he slept. At once Pietro hovered above him, washing and binding his wounds, while Gautier watched, his young face troubled.

"I—I promised him, Pietro," he muttered.

"I didn't," Pietro snapped.

Roget stirred once or twice while he worked. Groaned. But he was too weak now to awaken fully.

They sat beside Baron Roget in the darkness broken only by the flickering light of the lantern Gautier had brought from the house. They didn't talk. The cleavage between their two minds was too great, and by now both of them knew it. They sat there watching the wounded man. They tried to stay awake. But they had been up since before dawn, fighting throughout the day. They had had no food and little water.

For a time the pangs of hunger kept them awake. Then Gautier went out to his horse and came back with a loaf and a piece of cheese from his saddlebag. Pietro purloined a flagon of wine from the house. But so disturbed was he by all the pillage of the day, that he left a coin twenty times the value of the wine to pay for it.

They tried to give Baron Roget some of the wine. But they couldn't awaken him. When they tried to pour some of it down his throat it only choked him.

The wine curled warmly in their bellies. The vapors of it rose to their heads. They sat there yawning, blinking, fighting sleep. It was a hopeless fight.

Some time during the night, while the young warriors slept, Baron Roget of Saint Marcel woke in great pain but in his right mind. He found that all his wounds had been bandaged.

He tore off the bandages.

They had stuck to the wounds, and when they came free there was a great rush of blood.

Roget looked at the two of them sleeping there. He smiled.

"Oh God," he whispered, "I commend them to Thee, that Thou mayst bless them and keep them all the days of their lives. . . ."

Then he lay back upon the bloody straw. He lived, sane and conscious, until the sun came up and died with the great blaze of it lighting his eyes.

Pietro and Gautier buried him, using the farmer's spade. They put a little wooden cross above his grave. Upon it Pietro carved:

"Here lies a brave knight and a gallant gentleman, whom God, Who comprehends mercy—will receive."

They dared not put his name, or the place of his birth, lest the crusaders desecrate his grave.

Pietro looked at Gautier.

"Well, My Lord?" he whispered.

"Back to Montrose!" Gautier growled. "If Simon of Montfort requires further service of us, let him seek us there. But by heaven, let him come armed!"

Chapter Six

When Gautier of Montrose and the Lady Simone, his bride of six months, rode up to the small castle of Petit Mur, they saw Pietro even before they reached the walls.

He was in the lists, mounted and armed. He was alone and from the other end of the tourney grounds a whole mob of knights and men at arms rode down upon him.

"God and Montrose!" Gautier roared and leaped from his palfrey. One of his sergeants held the stirrup of his great warhorse for him to mount. Then Gautier thundered toward the melee.

But, when he was close, he pulled up his destrier. Pietro's weapons were of wood; and those of his opponents were blunted and padded.

God's death! Gautier swore. What's he up to now?

It was, he saw now, only a practice joust. But even so a little fellow like Pietro could get himself seriously hurt against one big knight, and here he was taking on five or six.

Pietro sat there upon his black stallion. He was frowning with concentration. Now! he thought, and flew toward his opponents. He didn't even have a lance.

When they came together in the middle of the list, Gautier saw a curious thing. Pietro flung himself over sidewise, so that none of him was visible above the saddle. Then, to Gautier's consternation, he rolled out of the saddle into a somersault like an acrobat and landed on his feet. Then the horses were upon him.

He didn't run. He danced in and out amid all those flying hooves, and each time he cracked the animals across the forelegs or hindlegs, as the occasion presented, with a wooden ax. The ax had been smeared with some sticky substance so that each time it left a mark. Pietro laughed gaily as the big knights milled around, getting in each other's way, trying to strike his nimble form with their mock weapons. Now he drew his wooden sword, which had a ball of the sticky stuff on its tip, and poked the horses in their bellies in high glee.

Gautier and his bride rode over to the canopy under which Antoinette sat. She had her small daughter with her. The child —the Saints be praised!—was tiny and dark, like Pietro. The whole countryside marvelled over the fancied likeness. She had been born on a bitter winter's day early in 1213. She was now more than a year old, for the spring of 1214 was near its close.

"What the devil is Pietro doing?" Gautier demanded, without waiting even to greet his sister.

"Practicing," Toinette smiled. "It's a theory of his. He's been at it for almost a year; but this is the first time he's put it to test against skilled knights. . . ."

"Isn't it awfully dangerous?" Simone breathed.

Toinette shook her head.

"Not at all. I've seen him do this dozens of times against the squires and sergeants and never get a scratch."

"Just what is his theory?" Gautier asked, never taking his eyes off Pietro's wild dance.

"Pietro's small. He weighs from one hundred thirty-five to one hundred forty pounds—never more. He contends that for him to joust against Norman knights, big as they are, is suicide. So he's figured out a way to beat them. Speed, he says, instead of strength. Horseflesh instead of armor. Bring down the horse, and you've got the man. . . ."

"God's Eyes!" Gautier roared. "Look!"

Pietro brought his wooden ax across the forelegs of a destrier so hard that the horse stumbled to his knees, pitching his rider head first onto the earth. The man lay there, dazed. Then he struggled to get up. Instantly Pietro was upon him, hammering his helmet with the wooden ax. All the others pulled up and sat in their saddles roaring with laughter.

"I surrender!" the fallen knight cried. "God's death, Sire Pietro—have done! You're killing me!"

Pietro stopped and helped his fallen foeman to his feet. Then they all remounted and rode toward the palisades.

"Note well your mounts' legs." Pietro laughed. "Had my ax been of steel, all six of you by now would have been stretched out lifeless upon the earth. . . ."

"It's a most unknightly way of fighting," Sire Toulon said, rubbing his head, "still. . . ."

"Consider," Pietro said. "Were I to engage you in a tourney, Sire Toulon, your first lance would lift me from the saddle. In a tourney, a man of my size hasn't the faintest chance. This way, I do have—I take great risks, remember. All I ask is some opportunity for victory. . . ."

The knights got down and saluted the ladies. When they looked at the lines of soft pitch that Pietro had left on their steeds' legs, they stopped smiling, became thoughtful.

"Sire Pietro," Baron Toulon said, "I think we'd better ask of you a favor. Out of respect to the knightly order, to which you belong, you'd better keep these new tactics a secret. . . ."

"Why so?" Pietro said.

"The warhorse is the very root of our power. Don't you see that villeins and serfs could use this method of yours against us?"

"Scarcely that." Pietro smiled. "It requires both great speed and great skill—and what villein have you ever seen who could move faster than an ox?"

They took some comfort from that.

There was no necessity of presenting them to Gautier, for all of them had known him before Pietro. As for his lady, every knight present had been a guest at Gautier's wedding at Montrose.

As they rode the short distance to the little castle, Pietro looked at Gautier. He needed only once glance. Gautier was happy. Brimming over with happiness. As for the Lady Simone

—every time she looked at her tall husband, her eyes glowed with adoration.

Pietro could not help glancing just once at his own wife's face. God and His Mother! he thought. Yet—after two years!

A maidservant carried little Aleinor—as usual. Since her birth Pietro had yet to see Antoinette take her daughter into her arms. He had had to get a stout peasant wench from the village to serve as wet nurse, though Toinette had had plenty of milk.

"I cannot," she had said in that cold, careful voice of hers, "bear for it to touch me."

It. For the first time, this past month, she had stopped referring to the child as "it." And then only because Pietro had spoken to her about the matter with some sharpness. . . .

The tables had been laid in the garden, and though today was no great feast but merely a casual gathering of neighbors, Pietro's cooks outdid themselves. All his villeins worked a great deal harder for him than they would have for any other lord. He was so kind to them.

"In two years," they marvelled, "he has not yet struck one of us! And he listens most kindly to all our troubles and complaints. . . ."

When old Jacques, because of sickness, had not been able to produce his rent, Pietro excused him. When that ignorant oaf, Pierre, seeking like malcontents everywhere to take advantage of what he considered his master's softness, had refused his côrvée of labor, Pietro had merely put him off the fief—whereupon, witless and masterless, with neither the courage nor the intelligence to turn brigand, Pierre had nearly starved. He'd come back and begged Pietro's mercy. And Pietro had taken him back, without either a harsh word or a blow.

And when poor Aiglentine found herself with child by a passing low jongleur who called himself Grosboeuf—what his true name was the good God only knew—Pietro obtained a good husband for her, the son of a merchant of the town; and people said no few livres passed between them on account of this peasant girl.

Naturally such unbelievable behavior had brought his people

to a state of near worship. Nothing was too good for Sire Pietro in their eyes.

At the table Antoinette was chatting easily and pleasantly with Baron Toulon, and Sire Peronne. Many a knight hereabouts, Pietro knew, envied him his fair lady.

If they only knew, Pietro thought, if they only knew. . . .

Most men by now would have come to hate Antoinette. But Pietro, was not like most men of his time. His dominant emotion toward his wife was pity.

True, there were a couple of other matters that influenced his relationship toward Toinette. He looked across the table at the stately Count de Harvengt and flushed. Count Geoffroi was such a good man. A very gentle noble and a Christian.

Dear God, Pietro thought, for that sin my soul will be eternally damned. . . .

But what did a man do about a sin he couldn't give up? He didn't love Yvette. He hated everything about his relationship with her. Its furtiveness. The shame he felt at betraying so good and kindly a man. He could not have borne being married to Yvette and he knew it. She was simply a fine and spirited animal with a wonderful body. Such a body. Soft curving, long-limbed with small hands whose caresses goaded a man beyond madness.

But no mind. The few times that they had met socially and he had had to talk with her had been disasters. A man had to talk to his wife occasionally. Pietro wondered how so intelligent a man as Count Geoffroi stood it.

With little Martine, daughter of a local merchant whose business kept him often away from home, it was better. Martine was plump and warm and soft, but she lacked Yvette's devastating passion. Not that she was cold. She was just—Pietro searched for the word—gentle.

The way Yvette was, Pietro guessed with an insight that outstripped the science of his times, was a kind of a sickness. In the throes of passion her lovely face became—ugly. Her lust devoured her and there was no tenderness in her, nor any love.

She, Pietro realized miserably, uses me, in the same fashion that I use her. We serve each other—she to burn out of me the fires that Toinette lights but will not quench, and I to make up for her husband's years and impotency. . . .

"You're very silent, good brother," Simone said.

"I know," Pietro said. "Sometimes it's hard for me to think in French."

"What language do you think in, then?" Gautier's bride demanded.

"Arabic, usually—or Sicilian, or the two mixed. They were the tongues of my childhood. . . ."

Simone stared at him wonderingly. But, sensing his mood, she did not press him to talk.

What he was doing was sin. Mortal sin. Yet, it kept him from something not to be endured. He was a Sicilian with all the hot blood of Italy in him. Sooner or later, had it not been for this adulterous business of Yvette and of poor, gentle Martine, he would have been forced by his natural desires to try to alter the relationship between him and Toinette. One look at the unhealed hurt just behind her eyes and he knew how ugly that would have been.

Better the moral ugliness of these sins of his. . . .

He became aware at last that the faces of all the knights at his table were very serious.

"Yes," Gautier was saying, "I'm afraid it does mean—war. Ever since our great King took the Chateau Gaillard from John of England in 1204, that wicked monarch has been smoldering with rage. . . ."

"He's waited a long time," Count de Harvengt said. "That was all of ten years ago. . . ."

"He dared not strike before," Gautier said. "But now the situation is changed. Our King supported young Frederick against John's nephew, Otto, in Germany. So now John Lackland can count on the support of all the Welfs. Frederick's holding his own—I hear—even growing stronger. But if that half English swine could crush the main bulwark supporting Frederick—our good King Philip—the Ghibellines of Germany would dissolve overnight. King John has other allies, too. We took Anjou and Normandy from him, but his agents have been busy. The Counts of Flanders and Boulogne have scant love for our King anyhow; but King John's hirelings have been spending money like water in Flanders and Germany. The Dukes of Brabant have declared for John. Limburg, Count of Holland, is mobilizing. And I had word but yesterday that the Earl of Salisbury was gathering thousands of Flemish mercenaries. As for Otto, he'll be able to bring so many Saxons that you might as well try to count the sands of the ocean. . . ."

The knights sat there, looking at each other. There was despair in their faces. What chance had France against such a host? Many of her best fighters were still in Languedoc, fighting the stubborn heretics.

Toinette leaned across the table.

"If war comes, My Lord," she whispered, "will you have to go?"

"Yes," Pietro said and searched her eyes. Yes, yes, he thought, I'll have to go. Mayhap I'll even be killed and you'll be rid of me. As much as he hated fighting and killing, he was glad suddenly of this war.

It was an honorable war, with the destinies of great nations at stake. It would be fought between great and honorable knights, who respected the rules of warfare. Prisoners would be ransomed. The wounded would be tended. The dead would be given honorable burial. Not like Languedoc—not like that bloody ravishment of a fair and helpless land with a cruelty that was a sickness and no mercy shown. . . .

But there was no joy in Antoinette's face. Her brown eyes were troubled. She looked as any other wife would have upon learning of possible danger to her lord.

Dear Mary's Son, I thank Thee! Pietro exulted. If it takes threat of war to make her look to me, then bring on the war, I say!

"We must talk of this," Antoinette whispered. "Later . . ."

"Very well," Pietro said.

"Any day now," Gautier sighed, "the King's man will come with a 'brief of summons.' You know, My Lords, how dearly I love a fight. But now, I must confess, I find myself strangely loath to go. . . ."

"Hardly strange, Sire Gautier," Count Geoffroi said. "I, too, must leave a young wife who is very dear to me; though I've often thought that to marry one so young at my age, was veritable folly. . . ."

Near Pietro, Sire Garnier, a young knight, covered his face with his hand suddenly, to stifle his laughter.

Pietro looked at him. How much, or how little did he know? Above all things Pietro wanted no open scandal. He'd have to question Garnier. Though how to even go about it, he didn't know. It was plaguedly difficult to inquire into such matters without revealing your own guilt. But if the story were abroad, he'd best know it.

Count Geoffroi stood up and proposed a parting toast to Sire Pietro. That was another thing. Since he had come into possession of Petit Mur, all the neighboring nobles simply assumed he was a knight. To keep up the deception, he had been forced to make a coat of arms for himself. It was bright blue on a red field and had mystic symbols written in the beautiful flowing script of the Saracens. "Al Saffah," the script read, though he never translated it for anyone, preferring to preserve the mystery. "Al Saffah—the Shedder of Blood."

For so, when God granted him to return to Sicily, he would become. The blood of the Siniscolas. It was for them only that he had so schooled himself in war. . . .

Pietro walked with his guests to the stables. But as young Garnier prepared to mount, Pietro detained him.

"A word with you, fair Garnier," he whispered.

"Of course, Sire Pietro," Garnier smiled. "I am at your service." He was a very pleasant knight—and very handsome, too, Pietro saw.

Lacking other means, Pietro struck directly.

"Why did you smile when His Lordship spoke of the Lady Yvette?" he asked, calmly enough.

"Oh, that!" Garnier laughed; "all the world knows that scandal. Scarcely a night passes, after that good, but ancient warrior has fallen asleep, that the so very generous Yvette does not depart the castle to meet some knight or another. . . ."

"Do you," Pietro asked, keeping his voice steady by an effort, "know the name of this knight?"

"This knight?" Garnier hooted. "Good Lord! Those knights! I could name you five, if I cared to. . . ."

"And you, Sire Garnier," Pietro's smile was perfectly steady, "are doubtless among them?"

"That no—not now. I'll confess I was—up until three weeks ago. But I have a certain amount of fastidiousness about me. I have never consorted with the women of a house of joy, for fear of what legacy my predecessor may have left me. Why should I take the risk of the same thing even if the lady is possessed of a great name? When I discovered, in a chance chat with two friends, that I had been sharing her favors with them—and others—I bade her a most tender adieu. . . ."

"Thank you, Sire Garnier," Pietro whispered.

"Don't mention it. You are indeed fortunate in your Lady. She is an angel above all reproach. . . ."

Watching him go, Pietro felt sick. He was hurt in his most vulnerable spot: his pride. He had romanticized even that base affair with Yvette, dreaming poetry into it; making songs for her, which he had sung to her right often in their favorite rendezvous.

Their rendezvous. His and how many others? He was sick to the pit of his stomach with disgust and shame. With—with jealousy. What had been between himself and Yvette was an ugliness, and he had hated it. But now that he had to give it up, he didn't want to. There were too many memories. Hardly, now that he considered it, good memories. They were all so—so physical. Body glued to body on a hot summer's night with the sweat of what had resembled mortal combat more than love, lying in the lassitude of complete exhaustion—except that Yvette's exhaustion was never complete—and he had known with a reluctance approaching fear that in a moment or two those devilish hands. . . .

"God, Thou Son of Saint Mary!" he swore.

He'd go no more to her. Not tonight. Not again—ever.

He had an appointment with her this very night. Well, then, let her wait.

But—how long would she wait, before summoning another?

All right—then—he'd go. But only to hurl his bitter denunciations upon her head. Her lovely head. Her so very lovely head.

Fool! he half wept. Fool, fool, fool!

In his turmoil he forgot completely that Antoinette wanted to speak with him. He went to his chamber and changed his clothing, and rode out from the castle before it was even dark. He flung himself down upon the grass near the edge of the great wood. He had a long wait. He lay there, chewing fiercely upon a blade of grass while the light spilled slowly out of the sky. On the rim of the world a star glimmered palely. The blue of the sky deepened into purple, into black. There were many stars and a thin, bright crescent of a moon.

He heard her palfrey. Doubtless, after the exertion of today's mock tourney Count Harvengt had retired early. He stood up.

She raced up to where he stood and flung herself down. He caught her in his arms. Then he released her. Stood back.

"Darling," she whispered. "Darling, darling, darling. . . ."

"You—you street woman!" he spat at her. He had intended using the shorter, uglier word. But seeing her face in the moonlight, he couldn't. He knew how ridiculous it sounded.

Yvette looked at him. Then very slowly, she tilted back her head and laughed aloud.

"Poor Pietro!" she whispered. "I have hurt him—I have hurt his poor little pride!"

"You—you—" he almost wept.

"Not that," she laughed. "Such women get paid. I don't. Say rather, fair Pietro, that I am generous. A great lady distributing largesse out of the kindness of her heart. And my heart, Love, is very kind. . . ."

"Don't," Pietro said. "Don't call me—Love!"

"But you are my love," she whispered, coming closer. "My little dark love with all the fire of Italy in his veins. . . ."

Pietro fell back a step.

"There must be," he said, "a word for women like you. . . ."

"Oh, there are!" Yvette said. "Many. And you have used them all. 'Breath of my life. Moon of my delight. Sweet falconess whose talons rip apart my soul. . . .' "

"Stop it!"

"You were very poetic, my Pietro. May I console you a little?

Then I'll tell you this: you, my inexhaustible darling, are the best of them all!"

He didn't answer. He couldn't.

Yvette came closer.

"Now," she whispered, "let's forget all this nonsense. We're here, and that's all that matters. What I have done on other nights with others concerns only those other nights and those others. Tonight is ours, Pietro. Let's make the best of it."

He was strangling. He was beyond speech.

Her arms came up. Her long fingers played in his thick curling hair. Her mouth found his mouth, moving on it, working, the soft, outward-turned underflesh of lip and tonguetip hotly, wetly, clinging; the adhesion broken in momentary, devilishly expert play, caught again, slow, moving his flesh to alien womansflesh, seared so that there was no longer any point of junction.

There were hammers at his temples. Drums.

He tore free of her. Inside of him a legion of devils danced and howled. He drew his arm back, far back, held it there.

"You're going to hit me?" Yvette whispered. "Go on, Pietro! That, at least, you've never done. . . ."

He let his hand fall to his side. Lamely.

Yvette threw her head back and laughed. It was clear laughter. Damnable laughter. It bubbled up out of her throat like spring water. Silvery. Sweet. It went on and on.

"You—" she gasped. "You're so funny, Pietro! So very funny. . . ."

He half turned. Her laughter beat about his ears. He started back toward his palfrey, half running. But something touched his arm. Lightly.

"Wait, my husband," Antoinette whispered.

The rage drained out of him. He was cold. Icy cold. He shivered.

"My Lady of Harvengt," Antoinette said quietly, "it's best that you go back to your husband. Come, Pietro. . . ."

Pietro went. The shame inside him was the worst, the most terrible, the ugliest thing in the world.

Antoinette didn't say anything. All the way home she rode

without saying anything. Her face in the moonlight was sweet and serene.

Pietro couldn't stand it. No woman on earth, he thought, could witness that and not. . . .

But Antoinette was no other woman on earth. She was herself.

She could.

"Good night, my husband," she said, and turned toward the little chamber where she had slept these last two years.

"Toinette!" Pietro said. "Toinette—by God's own love—"

"We'll talk of it later," she said. "When I've had time to think. . . ."

She must have thought of it long and carefully. For throughout those last two weeks of June, she spoke only with calm cheerfulness of the casual matters of everyday living. She talked often to Simone, for Gautier and his bride prolonged their stay.

Pietro tried hard to be at ease. He took Gautier out to the armory and showed him the new weapons he had designed for himself. The armorer had made them, under dire protest. Looking at them, Gautier agreed with him.

The helmet was light—too light, Gautier swore, though inside it was well padded. The hauberk was a vest, no more. It had no sleeves and came only a little below Pietro's waist, leaving his arms and legs free of mail. And the shield was a little round target, stout enough, to be sure, but so small as to cover only part of Pietro's chest.

The offensive weapons were made to the same scale: a surprisingly heavy little ax, with an edge honed to a sharpness that could be used for shaving. Pietro proved this by hacking off a three days' growth of beard with it. And a sword that was exactly like every other sword except that it was so short that it almost seemed a dagger, and so light that when Gautier hefted it he couldn't feel its weight at all.

"My weapons, Gautier!" Pietro explained. "Don't you see? Weight me down with those the size you bear and I can scarcely move. The only thing I have is quickness—agility. I'll make these toys count, believe me. . . ."

"You," Gautier groaned, "will be slain the first hour that you do battle."

Pietro looked over to where Antoinette and Simone sat. Simone was holding little Aleinor.

"That," he whispered, "might not be too ill, Gautier. . ."

The next morning the King's messenger came.

Pietro heard the blare of his trumpet and went down to let him in.

"The King," the messenger bellowed, "bids you ride with every man of yours even every lad who can stride a horse or trudge with a spear! Know you that Otto of Germany hath invaded France! He stands now at Valenciennes, with a host like unto the locusts that stripped Egypt in the days of old. The King hath need of you, come!"

Pietro saw Antoinette's eyes widen. Perhaps now, he thought, even now, she can forgive me. . . .

But she said no word.

Pietro and Gautier made their preparations. They summoned the good Abbot of Fontdubois, and confessed their sins. Then they wrote out their wills and gave them to him, witnessed by his hand, to keep at the abbey. Gautier arranged to be buried at the church at Montrose, should he die in battle; Pietro, who had not thought of such a fate, now made similar arrangements —his body should lie here at Petit Mur, in hallowed ground; and five hundred livres were provided for perpetual masses for his soul.

It was a solemn time. Hearing these grim arrangements, Simone wept.

But Antoinette was dry-eyed. Yet her great dark eyes never left her husband's face.

It was very hot now that July was here. Pietro couldn't sleep. He was riding tomorrow to war—not a minor expedition against heretics poorly armed and overmatched. The German knights were the biggest men and the most formidable fighters in Christendom. It helped not at all to reflect that if his side won, Frederick would become in truth as well as in name, Emperor of the Roman Empire. . . .

He sat by the window, gazing out at the night. It was very

late; but he had no hope of sleeping. What he had done was perhaps beyond forgiveness; but now that he faced death itself, it seemed to him that she could find it in her heart to say those few gentle words. Words that meant so much to him now.

He got up tiredly and stripped off his clothes. He lay down upon the great bed and stared at the ceiling. The same ceiling he had stared at, so many nights—alone.

He wasn't sure that he heard it at first. He lay there, straining his ears. It came again and now he was sure. The whisper of bare feet over the floor.

She came in very quietly and sat down on the edge of the bed.

"My Lord—" she called to him, quietly. "Are you asleep?"

"No, Toinette," Pietro said.

She had been to bed, and now she was very nice to look at. The moonlight came in the window and spilled silver all over her. Very nice. She slept, as was the custom, without clothing.

"Listen," she whispered. "What I have to say is very hard, my husband. Don't look at me. Just turn your head, and listen. . . ."

Pietro turned his head.

"I've tried so hard to learn to love you," she said. "You—and my child. I—I've failed. I prayed to Our Lady—to God, Himself—nothing helped. What is in me is a kind of death. . . ."

Pietro lay unmoving.

"I talked to the abbot. I've always had a religious vocation. He bade me try to fulfill my vows to you. Then, if I could not, an—an annulment could be possible. I could join one of the Sisterhoods. I want to, Pietro—so much! It would be so peaceful in the cloister, with the matins and evensong, and prayers throughout the day. . . ."

Pietro groaned.

"I," he said bitterly, "will not stand in your way."

"Simone has promised to take the child and rear her as her own. It would be so much better for little Aleinor. . . ."

Pietro said nothing.

"I was sure you'd understand. I'm still sure. Only—God help me!—what I'm no longer sure of is—whether I could leave you—now. . . ."

Pietro turned and looked at her.

"Yes, yes!" she wept. "Look at me! I want you to, now—for Pietro, my Pietro, I've cried myself to sleep every night since I found out about—her!"

Pietro rose, his arms outstretched. They closed around her, quickly. Too quickly.

"Wait!" she wailed. "I'm not yet ready for—please, Pietro, please!"

He drew her down. Found her mouth in the darkness. Then he felt the shudders go through her. Her flesh, so warm to the touch a moment before, was icy now, roughened with cold.

"Pietro," she sobbed. "By God's love—Oh, Pietro, let me go, let go, let me go. . . ."

He turned her loose. She staggered from the bed. She bent over and was very quietly and completely sick upon the floor. . . .

Pietro lay upon one elbow watching her. When the terrible spasms of retching had ceased, he lifted up his eyes toward heaven.

"Dear God," he prayed. "Let this battle to which I ride tomorrow—be the last battle of my life. . . ."

She came back to the bed and knelt down beside it. She put up her soft hands and stroked his hair.

"You see, my darling," she whispered, "I am not for you. I tried—honestly I tried—but I couldn't help it. I love you, Pietro. But my love is not of this world. You will be free of me now. There will be another maid, gentle and fair, who will bring you happiness. . . ."

"Like—Yvette?" Pietro said cruelly.

"No. I—I drove you to that. You're a man. You couldn't be expected to live like a monk—I have forgotten that now—forgiven it. And don't pray to die in this battle; I've prayed that you live and find happiness. And God will hear my prayer—for I am very close to Him, now. . . ."

First in the morning, when the abbot came to bless the departing knights assembled at Petit Mur, which of all the castles had the most central location, Pietro and Antoinette were closeted with him for above an hour. When they came out, certain things had been sworn to, certain documents signed. These still must be considered by a council of bishops, but Georges,

Abbot of Fontdubois, was certain that they would agree. He knew truth when it was spoken, being a wise man.

Then Pietro rode away to war. At the top of the rise, he turned and looked back at the lovely little castle of Petit Mur. He would never see it again. Of that he was certain.

Pietro and Gautier being veterans of past wars and much wandering, traveled light. They had but two sumpter mules, and two retainers between them. On the road to Peronne, they had cause to be glad of their frugality.

It was hot. All the roads leading toward Peronne, the point of assembly named by the King, were choked. From all over France, the hosts gathered. And in that most feudal of all feudal lands, their gathering made unmatched pageantry.

Every hour new banners poured in upon the town. The very heavens throbbed with the drum beats, the blasts of horns, trumpets, tabors. Sitting tall on their palfreys, with their war-horses at their right hands, the great barons came. Behind them the slow-stirred wall of dust blotted out the ends of their mule trains. They came with silken tents, multicolored. With coffers of their finest clothing. Their jewels. Many extra sets of matched arms and armor. Wine. Foods. Jesters and jongleurs for their amusement. Their falcons and hounds for sport. . . .

Pietro stared at them. It was hard to believe that these men were about the serious business of defending their native land. Still the endless, miles long mule trains clopped into the city.

And behind them the peddlers, thousands of them, with all sorts of charms and amulets against wounds and death. With silks and laces for my lords' fair ladies. Then the jongleurs twanging their lutes and chanting. The mountebanks, the jugglers, and still another army of that nefarious sisterhood without which, apparently, no war could be fought. A soldier needed consolation before riding out to death.

"God's Death!" Pietro swore. "Do they think they ride to a tourney?"

Gautier shrugged.

"Many will die," he said. "Would you forbid them one last brave show, Pietro?"

"No," Pietro said. "Forgive me my ill mood, Sire Gautier. . . ."

Gautier put out a mailed hand and let it rest upon Pietro's shoulder.

"I understand," he said quietly. "But know this, Pietro. To me you're still a brother. A well loved brother. And much lies before you. I don't like to see you ride out to battle in this mood. Turn the page, Pietro! The new lies blank for the writing. What will you write upon it? Glorious deeds, I think, and a new love worthy of you. Advancement. . . . Turn the page, Pietro!" Gautier concluded.

The waiting was bad. Food began to run short largely because there were so many useless mouths to be fed. And, as in every summer campaign in history, men started dying like flies from dysentery. The water was undrinkable after a week. In the town the smells were so bad that Gautier and Pietro camped five miles away from it.

They were glad when the orders came to march, on July twenty-fifth. As his father's representative Gautier had a seat at the Royal Council Tent. He didn't say anything; but he listened well. No one knew what the Welf was up to. The French knights hoped to engage him in the plain near Cambrai; but certain old heads swore he'd slip past and head straight for Paris.

On the twenty-sixth, they camped at Tournai, on the edge of Flanders. No one slept that night. The scouts had brought the news that the Germans were advancing upon Bouvines—a scant nine miles away.

Pietro sharpened his weapons and oiled his light mail. This battle was not of his choosing. Tomorrow he was going to ride forth and risk his life for a foreign land. . . .

But a land that had treated him well and dealt with him justly. Where he had found friends; where, but for a quirk of fate, he might have been content to live and die, and bring up his sons to be Frenchmen.

And beyond that, the fate of Frederick hung in the balance here. If Pietro's stars were ill, they were the same stars under which Frederick had been born. He was linked to Frederick. If at Bouvines the Emperor's life took a turn for the better, did it not follow that his own. . . .

He looked out into the grey dawn, smiling. The strange feeling stirring inside his heart was hope.

Early as it was, the camp was already astir. They had to get to Bouvines first. They had to cross over the Marque River, and get those marshes on their flank. Then Otto couldn't surprise them. At the same time, if his hosts veered toward Paris, the French could deal him a killing blow. . . .

Pietro rode along, silently cursing the heat. Even a snail could have made better speed. It was the mule trains that slowed them down. From five in the morning until above noon they crawled through the heat and the dust, and at that, only the infantry and the mules had crossed the bridge over the Marque when Bishop Garin, of the Knights Hospitaler, those bravest of priestly warriors, came back from his reconnoitering.

Pietro and Gautier were sitting on the grass near the King. Their being there was not without guile—at least on Pietro's part. If the chance came to do anything of note—what better place to do it than before the eye of the King?

The Bishop flung himself down from the saddle.

"Good news, My Lord!" he laughed. "The Germans will fight. The knights are in panoply and behind them march the infantry!"

King Philip stood up.

"God save us," he whispered.

Pietro knew what he meant. The footsoldiers were across and most of the supplies, but the knights and mounted men at arms were still on this side of the river. The Germans must be delighted. They could ride down the French Foot at will, and destroy their baggage.

Gautier stood up.

"Come," he said quietly. "We mount the high horse, Pietro!"

To mount the high horse was to show yourself in full panoply of weapons, tall in the stirrups, terrible in your pride. But Pietro didn't feel like that. Nor, curiously, did he feel afraid. He was very calm as he mounted. He'd ride with Gautier, charge with him; but what happened didn't seem to matter.

Philip Augustus saw them start out.

"But two?" he murmured. "Mark well those knights, My Lord Garin—it's upon such that France depends. . . ."

"The tall one is Gautier of Montrose," Bishop Garin said. "The other I don't know. . . ."

But seeing them moving off, certain sergeants of Champagne fell in behind them. No knights. Just Pietro and Gautier and the sergeants. One gently born lad and all the rest the sons of varlets and villeins, and in their mailed fists—the course of Empire, the history of Europe.

"Lace helmets!" Gautier ordered. He didn't shout. It was one of those times when shouting is out of place, when a whisper falls like a drumcrash. "Ready?" he said.

The men nodded.

"Charge! For God, Saint Denis, and for France! Charge!"

Afterwards, Pietro never could remember how it was. Not all of it. Only the fragments. The ropes of beastmuscle under his thighs, knotting, loosing, knotting, hoofhammering, clods blasted out of the ground and Amir's black mane flying. On the bridge now, the timbers reverberating, the whole bridge shaking, the waters of the Marque green beneath them, then down and across and upon earth again, the trees, the rolling fields blurring out of shape with the speed, the lance gripped hard, feeling his palm sweating against the wood, hoping that it wouldn't slip. Then—the Germans.

Big men on big horses. Sitting there, waiting, while Pietro and Gautier and twenty sergeants charged an army.

The shock when they hit. The sound that tore the sky open, and let in the din of metal smashing metal, horse-scream and gasp of wounded men. They recoiled, and Pietro was laughing, his white teeth flashing in his dark face.

It had worked! Part of his new tactics had worked. That business of rolling sidewise along the horse's flank so that he presented no target and the German's lance had whistled upon emptiness, the force of the missed blow throwing him off balance so badly that Pietro had caught him squarely in the middle unprotected by his shield and lifted him from the high saddle on lance point, his mail pierced, dying.

They fell back before the thousands. They and the fifteen

sergeants that were left now. Then again charging. For God. For Saint Denis. For France. Again. So many times that Pietro lost count. Until his arms ached from swinging that deadly little ax that cut through helmets like a knife through soft cheese.

He took wounds. Scratches mostly. His agility saved him. Gautier's strength.

But it could only end one way. Eleven sergeants now. And all of them wounded. Gautier bleeding, but roaring like a lion still: "For God and for Montrose! A Saint Denis, Le Bon Dieu, La Belle France!"

Then suddenly it was quiet. Pietro slumped in his saddle in utter weariness, lóoking dully at the Germans, outnumbering them a thousand and more to one, who had reined in their destriers and sat there staring stupidly at this handful that they could have crushed in one more charge.

This handful. Gautier and Pietro and the sergeants of Champagne, who, looking backward over their shoulders now, could see that the whole army of France was across the Marque now, their standards fluttering in the light breeze and the sun gleaming on their armor.

This handful who had just saved France.

Bishop Garin rode up to them.

"The King commands," he said, "that all of you join his bodyguard! He would not lose sight of you!"

Gautier looked at Pietro and grinned.

"Your new page, boy!" he said. "And by God, we've just begun to write!"

They rode over to where the King's great oriflamme, that mighty scarlet banner of samite, danced in the breeze. And the greatest cavaliers of France broke ranks to receive them.

"For this work, our thanks," Philip Augustus said quietly. "After the battle you will learn the greatness of a King's gratitude! Now—join us. There is work yet to be done. . . ."

Again the waiting. The priests moving up and down the ranks hearing the confessions. The muttered *meas culpas*. The horses shying, dancing with nervousness, and the men sitting there, sweating, under a brazen sun.

Hot. Like a foretaste of hell. The flies. Beastsmell and mansmell. And across from them, Otto's hosts, waiting.

For an hour—just out of bowshot. On the right, facing the forces under Counts Ponthieu and Dreux were the Earl of Salisbury's mercenaries and the men of the traitor Boulogne. To their left the lines of Flemish horsemen stretched out of sight, with only the knights of Champagne and Burgundy to oppose them.

And in the center under the great scarlet oriflamme, the King.

Directly across, Pietro could see the German center. There was a great press of Flemish and Germany infantry and behind the foot, the Emperor's chosen knights. It was easy to see Otto. He was the biggest man in the line. He sat on his warhorse beside his standard, which, oddly, was not borne by a standard bearer but was mounted on a tall car drawn by four horses.

Pietro gazed at the great silken dragon of white and green, flying upon the pole capped with a golden eagle. That beast must fall. God willed it.

He felt good. This day his stars were going to be uncrossed. After this hour he'd no longer be destiny's fool, but his own man and a master. He knew it with an absolute certainty that had nothing to do with logic.

Before them, their own foot shivered with fear. Pietro felt sorry for the infantry. They bore the brunt of every battle and did most of the dying. Usually his good armor and fighting skill assured a knight of nothing more serious than a few wounds. But the town levies were ridden down and hacked to pieces without mercy.

Pietro could hear the King now, praying:

"Lord God," Philip prayed aloud, "I am but a man; but I am also a King. Thine it is to guard the King. Thou wilt lose nothing thereby. Wherever Thou wouldst go, I will follow Thee!"

The heat. The flies. The muted clangor of arms.

Behind the King, the royal chaplain, William the Breton, and another clerk lifted up their voices:

"Blessed be the Lord my strength," they sang. "Who teacheth my hands to war and my fingers to fight!"

Bishop Garin rode the lines.

"Extend yourselves!" he roared. "You want the Germans to outflank you? You there! Have you not shield enough that you hide behind another knight?"

Two thousand French knights. Five thousand sergeants. Five and twenty thousand foot.

Thirty thousand German, Flemish and English foot. Fifteen hundred knights. Six thousand sergeants.

Two lines, a mile and a half long, facing each other across fields fair and pleasant and smooth as any lists for the jousting.

Then the right flank of sergeants charged the Flemings.

The Flemings beat them back with ease, crying: "Think on your ladies!" as though this were nothing more than a tourney. Then the Burgundian and Champagnois knights joined in and the Flemings had a hard time keeping the field.

In the center—nothing. Just the waiting.

Then it came.

The whole German center surged forward at once. White fire of spearpoints, helmets, hauberks, dazzling in the sunlight. The ground shaking under their feet and all the horns crying. The infantry marching with measured step, their bass-voiced "Hoch! Hoch!" rolling down upon the French center like thunder.

The French infantry broke. They threw away their weapons and ran.

"Open the ranks!" Gautier cried, "and let the villeins through!"

The lines opened and the levies from the communes fled through.

Pietro put out his hand to Gautier. They clasped hands. Then all the French knights charged. All along that mile-long line. They cut through the German infantry without effort, and met the shock of the Teutons' counter charge.

Pietro didn't see Gautier any more. He was too busy. The little ax was priceless. With it he could do what he had never been able to do with a sword. Each time a German knight engaged him, Pietro was able sooner or later to break the neck of his steed with it and send the giant Teuton crashing to the earth. There the footmen finished him.

He kept looking for Gautier, but he didn't see him. What he

did see caused his blood to turn to ice in his veins. Sire Wado de Montigny was tossing the great oriflamme up and down in distress and everywhere the cries broke out: "The King! The King!"

Pietro spurred Amir toward the melee. The Flemish pikemen had caught King Philip alone and one of them had hooked his halberd in the chain mail around the King's throat and dragged him from his horse. Pietro was there almost as soon as the King struck the ground. He was there because he had deliberately followed Philip throughout the entire battle.

And now his self-imposed training served him well. He rolled out of the saddle and landed on his feet amid the Flemings, and the little ax cut the shaft of the halberd in half with one blow, and the arm off the footman who held it with the next. In two minutes Pietro had made a circle about the King. Never had the Flemings seen such ax work. Pietro charged their pikes on foot, smashing them wherever they threatened the King; and Philip had his good sword out and he and Pietro and Wado were the three of them an army against the more than fifty Flemish footmen, until Sir Peter Tristen came riding down at the head of a party of French knights, and dismounting, lifted the King upon his own horse. The rest of the knights cut the Flemings to ribbons. Not one of them escaped.[1]

But when Pietro got back upon Amir, he was bleeding from a dozen pike thrusts. None of them were deep or very bad, but all together they were enough. He was reeling in the saddle, hanging on to the pommel, his bloody ax dangling from its cord, breath gone, dazed, hurt; but when Philip Augustus ordered another charge he charged with them.

It was all bits and snatches after that. He saw Otto go down and his Saxons get him up again, bringing him another horse though it cost them three hundred men to do it. But once mounted, Otto whirled in the saddle and ran. Like a sheep. Like a whipped cur. He didn't stop until he reached Valenciennes.

That did it. The Flemings and the Netherlanders fled in droves. But the German knights fought until the last.

After a time only the traitor Reginald of Boulogne to whom

defeat meant only death by torture held out. It took the whole French army to crush him finally.

By then, Pietro was past caring. He reeled out of the saddle and the King's standard bearer, Wado, caught him as he fell. On that day Pietro could do no wrong. He even succumbed to his wounds and his fatigue in full sight of the King.

They laid him upon the ground in front of the royal tent, and the King's own leech dressed his wounds. He was working upon Pietro's slight form when Gautier thundered up, leaped from the saddle and clasped Pietro in his arms.

"The boy's your friend, Sire Gautier?" the King asked.

"More—my friend and almost brother—who has saved my life countless times, My Lord," Gautier whispered, his eyes upon the leech. "He—won't die?"

"Hardly. His wounds are slight—and gained with great honor, defending our King."

"Perhaps, Sire Gautier," Philip said, "you could suggest a suitable reward since this boy took those wounds afoot against fifty, defending our person?"

"Aye, My Lord," Gautier said, standing up, "that I can. Knight him! He's baseborn, but he's had gentle nurture and he yearns after knighthood with all his heart and soul. To one of his station, rank is dearly bought. But I think, My Lord, that Pietro has this day paid the price. . . ."

"Pietro—an odd name," the King said.

"Italian, My Lord—attached many years to that Frederick of Sicily whom Your Majesty has just made Emperor in fact!"

The King smiled.

"When he has recovered sufficiently, let him be brought before me. But now you'd better take him to your tent."

Three days later, Pietro di Donati, son of a blacksmith and a villein, knelt before the King of France and took the buffet of honor.

"Rise Sire Pietro of Petit Mur," the King said. "Honor God, your King, and all Ladies—and from this day forth, let no man question your rank!"

No man would. Pietro knew that. He had been knighted by the greatest King of Christendom. But he felt no triumph. He was Lord of a castle to which he could not return. He had in truth no home, and only the ransom of those German knights his own squire had thoughtfully bound as Pietro maimed their horses for treasure.

His life was before him now—an open book. But the pages were blank.

What now could he write upon them?

Chapter Seven

PIETRO LOOKED DOWN from his window at the crooked streets of Aix la Chapelle and sighed. He had been in Germany nine months now, sent at his own request by Philip to Frederick with certain tokens of the great victory at Bouvines. Nine months—quite long enough—to Pietro's way of thinking. Not that it had been bad in Germany. For one thing, Frederick had knighted him all over again. The Emperor had been human enough to show a slight distaste at the news of Pietro's knighting at the hands of the King of France. Thereupon, yesterday, the day after his own coronation, he had done it over again, knighting Pietro for services to the crown before all the assembled German princes. And he had given Pietro a magnificent suit of armor, and jeweled weapons, which Pietro had no intention of using, for his own, battle-scarred though they were, suited him much better.

For another, his life in Germany was compounded of almost boring ease and constant pleasures. There were many fetes and banquets. The hunting here excelled anything that Italy could offer. Never had he seen boars half the size of those that the Schwartzwald afforded. And there was no lack of game birds for hawking. . . .

But Pietro was little more than twenty years old. And he was homesick for Sicily. There were hungers in him. After Toinette, his heart had need of healing. He thought more and more often of Iolanthe, and even occasionally of Elaine. He remembered that she was as beautiful as an angel. And as cruel as death itself. Sometimes at night, he dreamed of Yvette, and found his coarse pillow wet with tears. There must be in this world some happiness in store for him. Into twenty years of living, he had crowded a lifetime of pain.

The day before yesterday, at the coronation, he had taken the cross of a crusader from Frederick's own hand. But that must wait until Frederick himself was ready to sail. Time hung heavy upon Pietro's hands. He wanted to see Sicily again. Sicily and the wild Ancona March.

Ancona before Sicily. Roccablanca—the loved, the hated. The towers of Hellemark. Then Castellmare—Palermo—home.

He'd been gone a long time. A very long time. He was tired and his mind was scarred with bitterness. His body was scarred in many places with wounds. When it rained, they ached. At twenty, his mind was an old man's mind, full of the crabbed wisdom of books and the bitter teaching of life. He'd been a bridegroom innocent of his wife's body. He'd given his name to a daughter not his. He'd fought battles against people whom he admired with the awed admiration that the worldly often have for the pure. He'd fought other battles against the enemies of his King and his adopted nation.

He'd won glory and knighthood. He was no longer only a serf's son. Men called him "My Lord." He had longed for that glory and that position all his life, and now that he had them they were nothing and less than nothing and the sunlight of the long days ahead had a grey in it.

At twenty there were wrinkles at the corners of his eyes and the hair above his temples was turning white. For that was what he had never had—his youth.

When he twanged his lute, only sad songs came from it. He sang often now in the wild Arabic triads, which to Western ears sounded but little like music. His sadness was the sadness of the desert. Of emptiness. Of loneliness.

He had always been a handsome lad. As a boy, his beauty had been soft, almost girlish. As a man, he was something more than handsome: he was striking. His dark eyes looked out from beneath heavy brows, brooding. His wide, firm mouth always held a hint of pain at its corners. He was thin, too thin, but he was strong and wiry. He was very quiet and most people who knew him had never seen him smile.

Women looked into his dark face and wondered about that sorrow, that loss. And about their comforting him. . . .

But Pietro didn't even notice. He was preoccupied with a dream, haunted by memory. And in the slow July days washing with light the ancient town of crooked cobbled streets and houses whose upper stories were built bigger than their lower ones to avoid the tax so that all the streets were shaded, the dreams and the memories grew intolerably within him. He was choked with them. Bursting.

So he sought out the Emperor Frederick. He put the matter baldly.

"Sire," he said, "I want to go back to Sicily. It's been many years and I have almost a sickness to see Palermo again. It's fair here; but it is not Sicily. There is only one Sicily, my Lord. . . ." Frederick looked past him out into space. Pietro could see the hunger in those blue eyes.

"Aye," Frederick whispered. "There is only one Sicily—the one true counterfeit of Paradise upon earth. Would God I were there now!"

"You will come back, Sire."

"Yes—but when? These princelings with their eternal bickerings! Every toll road, every ford is a matter of state. Every quarrel with a vassal—every privilege of the church. God's eyes, but I'm sick of it all!"

"And when you do come back, Sire, you must leave again for the Holy Land," Pietro reminded him.

"Don't remind me of that! That will be arranged . . . So you want to go back eh?"

"Yes, Sire," Pietro said.

It was no longer strange to say "Sire" to the twenty year old Emperor. Like Pietro, Frederick looked older than his years. Those who had called him the Apulian Boy, now, looking at his reddish blond hair, remembered his grandfather, Frederick Barbarossa—redbearded Frederick the First, asleep now in the Kaiserhof, with his red beard growing through the stones of the mountain.

"Go," Frederick said. "And when I come, you will get that Barony—remember?"

Pietro rode the next day with five mules and three retainers. The German journey took him some weeks. It led him past all the quiet old towns whose names were bass music: Aix, Koblenz, Frankfurt, Wurzburg, Nürnberg, München, Innsbruck—then upward into the mountains through the Brenner Pass. It was very cool and quiet there. The snows lay on the peaks like a benediction. There is, Pietro thought, something about mountains that cleanses a man's heart. . . .

Slowclopping, quiet. At night the campfire sculpturing the momentary shapes of dreams. Then down again through the morning mists. And below him now—Italy.

In the North, after he had left the mountains it was very flat. There were the plains and the fields and the grains bowing before the wind. A very different kind of country from Ancona, even more different from Sicily. But his heart sang, looking at it. Somehow, even this north country had the feel of home.

He was driven now. He begrudged himself the necessary stops for rest, for food. He forced his retainers to stay in the saddle long after dark; he had them up when dawn was only a promise in the eastern sky.

But his route slanted ever more eastward, toward the Adriatic. That wasn't a good thing. He knew that. Sicily lay off the toe of Italy. This easterly route was taking him miles and days of weary journeying out of his way. Only Ancona lay on the Adriatic shore. Only Roccablanca rose frowning out of the mists a few miles inland in earshot of seahawk's scream and surf thunder. Roccablanca. That monument to his sorrows. Where Isaac had died of torture. From whence the men at arms had streamed out against Rezzi and done his father to death. To which Wolfgang of Rogliano had borne Iolanthe, delivering her up to the arms of the burly Enzio. . . .

Io. That was it. Io—the need, the drive, the hunger. Wife of the bearded Enzio, now. Mother, perhaps, of his sons. . . .

Even to think that bred a sickness in Pietro. It couldn't be. There must be some way, somehow, to unravel the web of disaster. Some means of restoring the lost, the loved.

As he neared Roccablanca, he was lashed with memories. Every stick, every stone, every clump of marsh belabored his heart. Here they had ridden when they fled the castle. Here they had turned, here doubled back upon the trail.

He turned his mount from the path, riding for a time away from Roccablanca until he came to the place that he always called in his mind in the sweet Sicilian phrase: "the place of the nightingales."

Here. Dear God—here.

It tore at him. It ripped him apart inside. It was daytime now but the place hadn't changed. It was still the place of the nightingales, of poplar spears lancing the night, of a big moon. Of the soft grasses of the wild fiercetender whisperings of the bodies' devouring unspeakable ecstatic agonies, of the smells of love.

He cried. Without shame.

Then the other place that put the ache back in his wounds. The place where he had been hacked down to bitter defeat and given life only by the gallantry of Gautier. Where Io flesh now of his flesh blood of his blood so lately fused to him flesh to flesh seared soul with soul commingled had been torn from him so that the place where she had been was left forever ripped open and in the night listening he could almost hear the slow seeping of his blood.

When he remounted his face was still. It was like granite. As hard. As unmovable. What was in his mind led downward out of life. But first—Io. If afterward he died, he had added the costs, balanced the accounts and he and life were quits.

So be it, he thought, and turned his horse's head toward the half rebuilt town of Rezzi.

He found lodging in an inn, run by a townsman who had once worked in the employ of Isaac and Abraham ben Yehuda. The innkeeper, Ruffio, remembered him.

"It's widely believed hereabouts that you are dead, Messer Pietro," he said. "In fact, it's not a good idea for you to linger. Should my lords of Siniscola discover that you live. . . ."

"I will cease to live," Pietro finished for him, drily. "But so, good Ruffio, will they."

"You are but one man," Ruffio said worriedly, "and these varlets of yours would be of little help in a fight. I tell you, Messer Pietro—"

"Sire Pietro," Rainaldo, one of Pietro's squires, corrected him. "Don't you know how to address a knight properly, fat son of swinish parents?"

"A knight?" Ruffio said wonderingly. "How can that be? Messer Pietro's father was a villein and. . . ."

"Messer Pietro, as you call him," Rainaldo said, "was knighted on the field of battle by the King of France, himself; and again at Aix by the Emperor Frederick for services to the crown. Now shape that tongue of yours to more respectful accents before you part company with it!"

"Your pardon, My Lord," Ruffio whispered, and what was in his voice now was a curious thing. Wonder, yes. But more than that. Something—something like joy. What had happened to Pietro di Donati came to the baseborn innkeeper in the shape of hope. A serf's son knighted. A crack in the walls. One more crack, because there were others. He, Ruffio had wiggled his fat bulk through one such crack. He wasn't tied to the land any longer. He owned his inn. Nobles visited here. He was expected to be humble in their presence; but he could be a shade less humble with impunity than any peasant in the fields stinking of animal dung and his own sweat. The walls were beginning to crumble now. In places like Venice, Pisa, Genoa, the sons of serfs were living in palaces. Gold was coming to be increasingly an ample substitute for gentle birth. All over Italy the townsmen were winning charters of privileges and immunities from their liege lords. And in a town a clever man, by engaging in commerce, could pile up treasure. Until at last he could dress better than a lord. Until he could buy an education for his sons and often—very often now—the younger sons of his lord, himself, as husbands for his daughters. It was very easy for an imaginative man like Ruffio to enjoy Pietro's triumph with the keenest of vicarious pleasure. . . .

"It doesn't matter, Ruffio," Pietro said. "Don't concern yourself. It's a wonder to me that you're alive yourself, considering what happened to Rezzi. . . ."

"Oh, many escaped," Ruffio said. "Chiefly those who had enough tarens laid by to buy their lives. The good Jew, Abraham, my former master, was among them. . . ."

Pietro clapped a hand upon Ruffio's shoulder. Here, indeed

was news. Abraham was alive. Pietro was very fond of Abraham ben Yehuda. He had had many lessons in the practical workings of the world of trade and commerce at his feet. Of course, Abraham was no scholar as Isaac had been; but his hard-headed business sense had contributed much to the success of Isaac's establishment.

"Where is he now?" Pietro demanded. "Does he prosper?"

"In Sicily, My Lord. There, men say, he has taken over Isaac's affairs and made them flourish beyond any of Isaac's dreams. Of the two, I think Abraham was much the smarter. He will be pleased to know that you live. . . ."

"As I am that he escaped," Pietro said. "More news, good Ruffio. Tell me—how fares—the Lady Iolanthe. . . ."

"I've been waiting for that one, My Lord," Ruffio grinned. "It was common knowledge hereabouts that the lady eloped with you. Every baseborn churl for miles around was delighted to his soul. Naturally it got back to my lords of Siniscola—and the bad blood between them and the Roglianos that it caused. . . ."

"But what of the lady?" Pietro whispered.

"She is well—as well as any lady can be who hates her husband with total passion. Many say that that accounts for the fact that there has been no child. . . ."

Pietro's dark eyes rested upon Ruffio's fat face. There was the beginning of a glow in them. No child. Without that bond to tie her to Enzio, there existed almost limitless possibilities. . . . He studied Ruffio carefully.

"Have you," he said, "any dealings with anyone inside the castle?"

Ruffio looked worried. Then he shook his head.

"No, Milord," he said. "And if I did, you must comprehend the danger of a townsman's meddling in the affairs of the gentlefolk. . . ."

"I do understand it," Pietro said. "But my emissary would have no part in any scheme of mine. He would merely be called upon to deliver a gift to—my lady. . . ."

Ruffio thought about that one.

"Jacobo, the wineseller," he said finally, "has many dealings with Roccablanca. My Lord Enzio is a great one for the cup. It's said that his winebibbing is only exceeded by his lust for gold. . . ."

"A greedy swine, eh?" Pietro mused. "There is, perhaps, even a possibility in that . . ."

"Yes, My Lord. Sire Enzio was responsible for letting Abraham escape. Count Alessandro would never have freed a Jew—since he hates all men of that persuasion with all his heart. But Sire Enzio's hatred cools easily at the sight of gold. . . ."

"Good," Pietro said. "Ruffio, have the goodness to get me some ink and parchment and a goodly supply of quills. . . ."

"The ink I can manage," Ruffio said. "And, as for quills, I need only to pluck a few from the tails of mine own geese. But parchment is another matter. It's hard to come by and hellishly expensive when you do find it. . . ."

Pietro put his hand to his belt and lifted out a purse.

"Send a lad out," he said, "and buy me a fair sheet—well scraped, soft and free of blemish. . . ."

"As you wish, My Lord," Ruffio said, and took the purse, bowing grandly. It pleased him to do Pietro honor. Another man might have resented and envied the sudden rise of Donati's son. But not Ruffio. He had done some rising himself, and in his heart the hope existed of doing yet more. Envy, Pietro reflected, was the disease of hopelessness. . . .

The sheet that Ruffio's youngest son brought was far too large for Pietro's purposes. He sat down before a table and cut a small square out of it. Ruffio stood beside him, busily engaged in cutting points on the end of the goosequills and then splitting those points to carry the ink well. Ruffio could read and write. He had acquired these precious accomplishments since he had bought his freedom from his liege lord.

Pietro sat before the tiny square of parchment, frowning. He knew well what he wanted to say; but what puzzled him was which language to say it in. Io knew Latin; but then so did Enzio. The vulgar tongue likewise could doubtless be read by both of them. Pietro cursed the distaste that had caused him to learn almost no German during his stay in that land. Io spoke and read the language of her fathers fluently and Enzio comprehended no word of it. As for the other tongues that Pietro's linguistic curiosity had caused him to master, neither Io or Enzio knew any of them.

He was reduced, then, to writing in a language that Enzio could read. That increased the danger many times and made it painfully necessary for the message to be delivered secretly.

Still, it had to be done. He bent over the little parchment, and began writing in his beautiful minuscule, the sweet Tuscan flowing from his pen in music and poetry, so that reading over his shoulder Ruffio sighed:

"Ay! How lovely that is! It would melt the heart of a stone image, My Lord. . . ."

"You will forget these words, Ruffio," Pietro said gravely.

"I have forgotten them already, My Lord," Ruffio said.

There remained the mechanics of getting the letter to Io. Pietro got up and walked the few paces to the shop of Jacobo, the wineseller.

"A flagon of your best," he said.

One look at his dress, and Jacobo was flying toward his cellar. He was back in an instant with a stone flagon, bedewed with the cold.

"Just taste it, My Lord!" be begged; "One sup and My Lord will swear that even in paradise the angels don't enjoy such nectar! Let me get you a cup, and. . . ."

"There's no need of that," Pietro said. "I don't mean to drink any of it. It's a present for a lady. And I want you to deliver it to her. You, Jacobo, not one of your hirelings. You understand me?"

"Yes, My Lord," Jacobo whispered.

"Good. This is for Lady Iolanthe of Siniscola. It is my wish that you place it in her hands personally—not in the hands of any of her maids. And with it, give her this scroll which I'm tying to the neck of the flagon. If she deigns to answer, bring me word at the Sign of the Golden Heron—there will be a purse in it for you above the price of the wine."

"And death in it for me, if Sire Enzio—"

"Silence!" Pietro snapped. "You have delivered flagons many times to Roccablanca. Why now should Enzio question you?"

"But," Jacobo wailed, "if he does, My Lord? What then will I say to him?"

"That the wine was ordered by Milady. She sometimes does order wine of you, doesn't she?"

"Right often, My Lord." Jacobo brightened. There was, after all little reason why Enzio of Siniscola should question him. And if this rich young lordling should receive a pleasing answer, who could gauge the weight of the purse he might throw his messenger?

"Good," Pietro said. "Off with you, then. And thinking about the purse you'll get upon your return should lend some speed to your feet. I shall be waiting for you. . . ."

It was already late evening, and Ruffio was turning a goose on the spit over the fireplace for their supper. Rainaldo and Waldo, Pietro's squires, devoured the goose, washing it down with many a draught of Ruffio's good wine; but Pietro found that the well prepared fowl choked him. He couldn't get it down. His stomach revolted at the very thought of food.

They sat a little apart from the others in Ruffio's public room. Ruffio had given them his best table, but it was so far from the door that Pietro had to crane his neck to see out. Each time he did so, his frown deepened. It was already dark, and there was no sign of Jacobo.

God, Thou Son of Saint Mary! Pietro thought. What the devil is keeping him?

He had scarcely formed the thought when the door opened. Quietly. Too quietly. He stood up.

Elaine of Siniscola leaned against the doorpost looking at him.

Pietro felt something moving inside his body. Something like pain. Like joy.

She had changed. She seemed taller. The last time he had seen her, wrapped in furs, with the streamers of her breath pluming about her face upon that bitter day, there had been in her eyes. . . .

Confusion. Compounded with fear into—into hate.

That had lessened. But it was there still, some of it. And he could see it flare up again as she looked at him.

Strange. And the strangest part about it is, he thought, that this hatred breeds no answering hate. That, were it not for Io, I could love this arrogant witch. This sorceress blessed with beauty that blinds me, that brands me hip and brow and thigh until I am unmanned before her and dare not, cannot speak. . . .

"This," she said in that clear, sweet voice of hers, "I had to see for myself. . . ."

"What?" Pietro breathed. "What must you see for yourself, My Lady?"

"The cause of my cousin's confusion. I was with her when your messenger came. I guessed it must be you, Messire Pietro. I made excuses to leave, which wasn't hard as she so obviously wanted me to. . . ."

"And now that you've seen me?" Pietro said.

"I beg of you to go. Now—without seeing her. My cousin Io is very dear to me—despite all our quarreling. And Sire Enzio returns this night, together with my husband, may the Saints preserve him . . . What can you bring her, except further trouble? Or yourself—except death?"

"That," Pietro said flatly, "should please you, My Lady. . . ."

Elaine shook her head.

"No," she said. "I am ashamed that I allowed a baseborn churl to so trouble me. I care not now if you go on living. In fact, I want you to, since it is my obligation to protect the lives of animals and the inferior orders. . . ."

Pietro stiffened. Seeing his face, Rainaldo came to his side.

"Must you stand for this, My Lord?" he said.

Pietro sighed. The stiffness went out of him.

"Yes, Rainaldo," he said. "I must. . . ."

"My husband, Ricardo," Elaine said, "has chided me more than once because I lack patience with Io's madness. But no matter. We waste time, Messire Pietro. I beg of you—please go."

"And if I refuse?"

"Upon your own head be it. You leave me no choice but to acquaint Sire Enzio of your presence—and its possible consequences. . . ."

"Upon my head, then," Pietro smiled, "be it. I have no intention of leaving before seeing Io. My Io, who was snatched from my arms by that soulless brigandry you great ones call gentleness. . . ."

Elaine half turned.

"You," she said, "have earned your death."

"Perhaps," Pietro said. "Remember me to your Lord. I hope he fares well. . . ."

She whirled.

"He," she said flatly, "is dying. What justice is there in this universe, that Ricardo should die and things like you should live!"

"I—I'm sorry, My Lady," Pietro said.

"Don't be. He does not need your sorrow. Nor I—though I must watch him wasting away over the years of a sickness unknown to the wisest leech alive. Enzio took him to take the waters at Campagna—which have certain curative powers. They return tonight—Dear God! why am I telling *you* these things?"

"There is a certain relief in talking," Pietro said, "even to a baseborn churl. . . ."

She looked at him.

"You won't go?" she said.

"No," Pietro told her.

She opened her mouth to speak, to say—

But Jacob flew through the doorway, his face pale with fright, and knelt at Pietro's feet.

"The purse, My Lord," he gasped. "For this night have I earned it, truly! I only hope I live to spend the half—or even the quarter. . . ."

Pietro threw him a purse heavy with silver. Jacobo snatched it up, and turning, looked straight into Elaine's face.

"Oh, my God!" he moaned. Then he ran out of the common room as though all the hounds of hell were pursuing him.

"A queer churl," Rainaldo said. "You'd think that the devil himself was hard on his heels. . . ."

"Not the devil," Pietro said grimly, "but perhaps his son." Then he loosened his dagger in its sheath and stood there, waiting.

Elaine stared at him. Whatever she was about to say, he never knew. For both of them heard, at the same instant, the clatter of hoofbeats on the cobblestones outside. They came to a stop. Then they danced again, briefly, as the rider dismounted. One horse. One rider. Certainly not Enzio then. He would have come with twenty men-at-arms, with their blades already drawn. One horse.

Pietro's gaze swept over Elaine's face. Mother of God, no. It couldn't be. Folly was one thing; but if his guess was right, this went beyond folly. Only one word could describe it. Suicide.

His hand came away from the hilt of his dagger. He stood, frozen.

He had—in that long moment that Iolanthe stood in the doorway staring at him, oblivious to Elaine, not seeing her, nor Waldo nor Rainaldo nor Ruffio nor even the casual hangers-on in the public room, they, and all other men alive on the face of earth being nonexistent for her, unliving, veiled out of being by the intentness of the concentration by which she created anew his image out of love and loss and longing—one moment of bitter clarity in which he knew how seldom the realization of a man's dreams fits the pattern of their conception. . . .

He compared her with Elaine. She won, hands down. Against that icy perfection, this vital, square cut face, not beautiful, but living. Against that cold, taut-held confusion, this blinding clarity, this joy that leaped and blazed behind those grey eyes, warming him, consuming him.

Then she was coming toward him. Running.

Her mouth on his had a quality distorted out of memory. It smothered him, working. Hotwet, clinging. Tart. Fierce, demanding. Wild. But now—no tenderness.

Like Yvette's, he thought suddenly, and was astonished that he could shape that thought. She drew away from him a little so that her hands clung to him still and her eyes were naked. This, he thought wildly, painfully, this is an ugliness and I, oh God, I. . . .

"Where is your room?" she said simply.

"Above," Pietro whispered.

"Come," she said.

Pietro turned, aware that every eye in that room was upon them, and the sickness in him was ugly and terrible, clutching with cold tentacles about his heart.

Elaine took a step forward. The motion was indescribably graceful. Like a dancer's. But her face was twisted. Almost ugly.

"You—you whore!" she said.

Io looked at her. The grey eyes were gentle.

"Whore?" she said. "What woman is not, sweet cousin? We are all of us paid for the rental of our bodies in one coin or another. And mine, I think, is the honorable mintage—the one God intended. Great joy—the clean love of the man who loves me. Not castles and lands and the cojoining of fiefs arranged by our fathers for commercial advantage. To submit to that is prostitution. The fief of Siniscola must embrace all holdings upon its borders. And for that great and noble reason I had to be sold to Enzio and you to Ricardo. You say you love your husband. Then why, my cousin, this bitterness? Is it that you envy me the courage of my sins—or do you perhaps covet this fair and pleasant knight of sweet visage, tender heart, and body strong and unrotted by pustulant loathfulness born of his indulgences?"

It was then that Elaine slapped her. Hard across the mouth.

Pietro caught her wrists. The sickness inside him was black bile and nausea, the thing he had dreamed of for so long was reduced to this: a tavern brawl between two women whose high birth and great station in no wise prevented their behaving with precisely the same female felinity of any tavern wench, or proving the essential democracy of fine bitchery.

"You needn't hold me, love," Io laughed. "Her blow but proves my words. I'm sorry for you, Elaine. I have no shame of Pietro—as you have of your dalliance with Andrea. That childish dalliance that lacks the will or the strength to grow into actual sin, which all men respect more than mere folly. . . ."

Elaine hung there. Io's words struck her, tore into her with visible impact. Then she whirled, and ran from the inn.

"Come," Io said again.

But Ruffio barred the way.

"My Lady," he said, "forgive me. But I have a great desire to die in my own bed from the weakness of old age. My Lord, your husband, would burn this inn within the hour with my fat carcass chained in the midst of the pyre, if I were to consent to—this— For God's love, My Lady, take your fair and pleasant knight and go—elsewhere. For already have I forfeited half my earnings for furnishing merely the place for this folly. . . ."

"Ruffio's right, Io," Pietro said.

"Come then," Io whispered, and turned toward the doorway.

Pietro went with her, and stood outside in the darkness, while the stable boy brought his horse.

But only for a moment. For she caught him to her again, and clung her body to his, not mouth to mouth merely but breast and trunk and thigh slowmoving so that when the hoofclopping sounded around the side of the inn, he reeled away from her lip-bruised, limbscalded, and along all the network of his veins the pounding of savage drums. . . .

"Our place, Pietro," her mouth brushed his ear. "Our place—where the nightingales were and the poplars—remember? We'll be safe there—Oh, darling, darling—it's been so long!"

Pietro didn't say anything. He couldn't. His thoughts inside his mind beat one upon the other in broken rhythms, patternless and wild. This. Not Io—this. This ugliness. This passion without tenderness this nakedness with all the unlovely parts of nakedness showing this thing compounded out of hatred out of revenge against Enzio instead of love for me love killed tenderness dead this nakedness of desire and I have no alternative. . . .

I have loved this woman. Then, that other time, our coming together was beautiful and natural and right because what we had was a thing of total loveliness of our minds our dreams of our souls' music so that what we wanted was that not even the walls of flesh could separate us any longer that our need of belonging to each other be fulfilled that there be no longer two lovers but one commingled blood and breath and flesh and fire and spirit a new thing upon the earth a new entity—us. . . .

They rode very fast through the darkness. There was no moon. Clouds hid the stars. But they found the place. And as Pietro swung down from the horse, the clouds broke and a thin crescent of a moon came up over the hills and he could see her.

Inside his chest he felt something tearing. This face this good face loved remembered looking up at his with that terrible hunger in the eyes that need that was more than the body's simple cravings much more that was seeking searching through this beyond the merely physical for—

For comfort. For assuaging.

He felt like crying. What had been done to her to leave her

like this? What had destroyed that serenity, even that mastery of life she had had? She had changed. She was still fair—almost beautiful. But she had changed.

Then her mouth was on his. Somewhere within him the shutters dropped across the rational part of his mind.

She was tearing at him with her fingers. At his clothing.

They destroyed each other. Utterly. But it was not the good destruction of before. It was like death like tortured dying and the instant before life jetted out of him leaving that terrible emptiness that reeled into night into death he heard her scream. Just once. Terribly.

He came back slowly. He was torn back into life by taloned fingers. He was drawn into breath by a mouth a little swollen and tasting salt. Of tears. Of blood.

There was time now for tenderness.

They had not lost that, not entirely. They were beginning to find it again. They could kiss now with mouths that were gentle. And when passion came back again, it was clean.

They rode back into Rezzi in the grey light of morning. They had even reached the fork where one road swung away toward Roccablanca and the other toward Hellemark when Enzio and his sergeants fell upon them.

Pietro killed two of them before he was taken. And he knew with black and absolute certainty that he was alive because Enzio had ordered them not to kill him. That would have been too quick. Too gentle.

Enzio sat upon his great horse, his white teeth flashing amid the darkness of his beard.

"You fought well, Messire Pietro," he said. "I have a great fondness for brave men . . ." He stopped, smiling. "Sometimes they are disappointing though. Often they don't die nearly as well as they fight. . . ."

Pietro said nothing.

"Take him to the castle," Enzio said pleasantly. "But handle him most gently. We must conserve his strength. . . ."

Iolanthe found her voice.

"Enzio," she said, "for God's love . . . Don't . . . Please Enzio . . .

I'll do anything you say from now on for the rest of my life I'll do anything . . . Enzio!"

Enzio didn't answer her. He rode toward her with his even, perfectly white teeth showing in that smile that was almost a feature of his face. He didn't hurry. He rode very slowly. And he never stopped smiling.

Pietro saw his mailed hand go back, far back, then he swung it open-palmed across her face so that the noise it made striking was like a small explosion.

Io was a big girl. But the blow knocked her from the saddle, so that she lay face down upon the earth, crying.

Enzio got down. He knelt down above her, so that one knee pressed into the small of her back, and caught the fingers of his right hand into her hair. Then he ground her face into the dirt slowly.

"Sup your dirt, whore," he said pleasantly. "It's your natural food, isn't it?"

"My Lord of Siniscola," Pietro said, his voice very low, tight, rage-strained, ugly. "You are a dog and a son of a dog. A man who abuses a woman should be hanged like a felon. But I beg of you, release my hands and give me a sword. Let this be between the two of us. Afterwards, even if I win, your sergeants can deal with me. But have the decency to fight!"

Enzio got up, slowly. He was still smiling.

"Decency?" he laughed. "You speak of decency, Messire Pietro? What honor lies in my slaying a serf's son? My father would disown me if I crossed blades with a whoreson churl. Sorry I cannot accommodate you; because oddly enough you've displayed rare skill. . . ."

Pietro looking at Io. She was trying to get the dirt out of her eyes, her nostrils. The little stones had made scratches all over her face. She was bleeding.

"Sire Enzio," Pietro got out, "At another time I would not have told you this, because it ill becomes a man to boast of his honors. But I was knighted at Bouvines by King Philip of France, and again at Aix la Chapelle by your own liege lord, the Emperor Frederick, for services to the crown. Believe me, you can fight me without dishonor. . . ."

He saw Io looking at him now, and her eyes were glowing. Suddenly, singularly, she was lovely. With her face caked with blood and dirt, she was lovely. How little, Pietro thought suddenly, is beauty a thing of the flesh merely!

There was sudden craft in Enzio's eyes.

"Nor yet will I fight you," he laughed. "That might displease My Lord the Emperor—were I to kill you, say—since you're so great a favorite of his . . . No, Messire—forgive me, My Lord—Sire Pietro; perhaps it would be better if I entertained you as an honored guest, for some ten years, perhaps, until he has forgotten your existence . . . Of course, if during or after that time, some unfortunate mishap were to befall you . . ." He whirled, facing his men.

"Enough of this nonsense," he cried. "Let us be off!"

To Pietro's great surprise, it was not to Roccablanca that they rode, but to Hellemark. Before they reached it, Io managed to ride close to him.

"Why Hellemark?" Pietro said.

"It's his, now," Io whispered.

Enzio looked back at them.

"How romantic!" he laughed. "Chat your fill, my doves! Soon there will be an end of all chatting. . . ."

"His?" Pietro said. "But your father—your brothers. . . ."

"Dead. Of poison, almost certainly. They perished in a single week, raving mad, and the leech that Count Siniscola so kindly sent to their aid prattled of demonic possession!"

Pietro looked at her.

"I'm sorry," he said. "Your father was a good man, and Hans likewise. And Mark and Wolfgang were more influenced than sinning. . . ."

"I have more to weep over now—than them," Io whispered. "Pietro, Pietro—oh my love—I—"

She couldn't finish.

"Don't grieve for me," Pietro said.

"Grieve? When it is I who have slain you? Grieve—I shall tear heavens apart with my screaming, drown the whole world in tears and go out of this life in truth madder than my brothers! Grieve! For you? For you, my Pietro, for whom I would gladly die over weeks by even the most fiendish means that unspeakable beast, my husband, can invent—Oh my love, my lost love. I shall not survive you by an hour!"

"No, Io," Pietro whispered. "I'm alive yet and dungeons have been escaped in the past. . . ."

"Escaped? Have you ever seen that pit beneath Hellemark?"

"Yes," Pietro said, and the hope was gone from his voice.

It was very dark in the dungeon. Somewhere, near at hand, Pietro could hear the dripping of water. The floor was slimy. It was so cold that he shivered constantly. He had been there for three days and three nights, now. He knew that because of the number of times he had been fed. The food was coarse and plain, but good. Enzio had no intention of weakening him.

The strange thing was that Enzio had not commenced the tortures at once. Did he really fear incurring Frederick's displeasure? But Pietro knew better than that. There was no earthly way, should he by some miracle return to Italy this very hour, by which Frederick could discover what had happened to Pietro.

No. What stayed Enzio's hand could only be something else. Something ugly.

He was thinking about that when he heard the noises above his head. He stiffened and the sweat appeared on his forehead despite the cold. He had faced death many times now. But not like this. Not helpless and alone. Not this kind of a death. He had seen men die under torture and he knew that there was a point beyond which the bravest man alive will scream and beg for mercy. He wasn't the bravest man alive. He was afraid now. Horribly, sickeningly afraid.

He didn't want to die. He didn't want to leave Io helpless in the hands of that brute. He wanted to live long enough to right many matters that had needed righting for so many years. After that, he might be willing to die. He didn't know.

But the noises at the trapdoor weren't very loud. Enzio and his executioners would have made much more noise than that. There was something furtive about them, something secretive —frightened.

He heard the noise of the great key in the lock. Then the trapdoor was lifted quietly and a ladder came down. Pietro waited. From above, the light of a torch flooded the opening. Then there was the billow of skirts gathered high, and the sheen of slim white legs.

"Io!" Pietro gasped.

"Quiet!" she said; then: "Giulio, for God's love, throw us down the torch!"

The bearded face of the turnkey appeared in the opening above them. Then he tossed the torch down. Pietro caught it, deftly.

He stood there, looking at Io.

She came up to him, and pressed her mouth to his. Achingly. Endlessly.

Pietro tore free of her.

"Io, by God's love—" he got out.

She was crying.

"So little time," she wept, "and I have to waste it with explanations. . . ."

"Where is he?" Pietro demanded. "My God, Io, I don't want you killed too—tell me. . . ."

She laid a soft hand over his mouth.

"Gone," she said, "to Perugia. He has a woman there. Would God he had one in every city in Italy!"

Pietro stared at her. This didn't make sense. None of it did.

She was smiling now, but the tears didn't stop. She took the torch from him and stuck the end of it in a chink in the wall.

"You won't die!" she whispered. "Oh, my love, my love, you won't die! He's going to release you!"

Pietro stepped back and stared at her.

"At what price, Io?" Pietro said.

"I—I reminded him that Isaac had left you a fortune in Sicily. You knew that, didn't you?"

"No," Pietro said.

"Abraham told us, before Enzio released him. He thought, perhaps, that Enzio was holding you prisoner. So now, Enzio has dispatched messengers to Abraham for your ransom. It—it will beggar you, Pietro—but you'll be free!"

But there was something more. Even by torchlight, Pietro could see that. Enzio was a greedy beast, but how much greed did it take for a man as proud as any Siniscola to accept cuckoldry?

"And the rest?" he said quietly.

"What rest?" Io said, but her eyes leaped.

"The rest of the price," Pietro said.

It was no good to lie to him, and Io knew it.

"Is already paid in part," she whispered, "and will be fully paid—after you are free. . . ."

"What is it, Io?" Pietro said.

"Pietro, please!"

"What is it?" Pietro said.

Io put up her hands and pulled her pelisson, her *bliaut,* and her *chainse,* down from her shoulders, so that her body was bare to the waist. Then she turned her back.

"This was the first part," she whispered. "But of this there will be no more, my love. . . ."

Pietro clung to the wall, deathsick and fainting.

"The sweet blue eyes of God!" he got out.

"Don't be troubled," Io said. "It was a small price to pay for your life. And he won't do it again, or—"

Pietro came erect again. Io had said more than she intended to. One word more. "Or—"

"Or what?" he whispered.

"Pietro, Pietro don't make me tell you that . . . For God's love, Pietro please. . . ."

"Not even for God's love. Tell me, Io. . . ."

"The rest of the price is," Io wept, "that I cease practicing the arts by which I have denied him—a son. . . ."

Pietro stared at her.

"And you thought," he whispered, "that I would accept life at such a price?"

"No. I thought I could keep from telling you. But the choice is beyond you now, my love. The messengers ride for Sicily. And I have given my word . . . Oh, my love, my love, I have so little time with you! Already you have wasted the half—please, my Pietro, I want you so— While he is gone each night for an hour Giulio will let me in— You must not, you can not cheat me with your talk of prices and honor! I don't understand those things—I only know I hurt from wanting you so that my body screams inside itself for need of you and you stand there and torture me thus!"

Pietro put out his arms and drew her to him gently.

"But if Giulio has the key," he said, "why can't I. . . ."

"Only of this cell," Io said. "There are still all the doors and the gates and towers and the drawbridge and the arbalists and the men at arms . . . If I even took you above out of that chamber that tops this pit, you'd die within minutes . . . Pietro, no more talking, for God's love please!"

I will be free, Pietro thought. When Frederick comes. A Baron, too. Then Hellemark will see a siege that never has been equaled before in all the life of man and I will drag him behind my horse's tail twenty times around the moat and tear him asunder with his limbs fastened to four wild horses!

His arms about her tightened.

She almost suppressed her cry.

Pietro released her at once.

"No, Io," he said. "What we have done cannot be done with your back in ribbons . . . Tomorrow, the day after. . . ."

"God's eyes!" Io swore, and threw herself into his arms.

"Io," Pietro gasped.

"It will hurt," she whispered. "It will be bad, very bad, but that pain I can bear. The other I cannot bear, will not bear. Oh my love, don't you see that it's only the choice between the greater pain and the lesser and the lesser is nothing and less than nothing while of the greater I am dying? Pietro, thou fool, thou sweet and tender fool whom I love, I want, I need, Pietro!"

It was bad. Very bad. She cried.

It was terrible. And lovely. And perfect.

They had, out of the two months of Pietro's imprisonment, twenty such nights.

On the twenty-first, Io crept into the dungeon with death in her eyes.

Pietro stood there staring at her in the flickering light of the torch.

"He—he's back," she whispered. "Oh, Pietro—Pietro. . . ."

He held her, stroking her shoulders.

"Tell me, Io," he said gently.

"Abraham is dead! He was very old and the imprisonment and the journey were too much for him . . . And in Sicily there is no one—no one with sufficient authority to dare—pay your ransom —Your inheritance is locked in the Emperor's own coffers . . . Enzio is wild with rage . . . Oh, Pietro my dearest. . . ."

Her voice drowned in tears.

"Then," Pietro licked dry lips, "it will be tonight?"

"I—I don't know! He's exhausted from the ride and—" She stopped, looked at him. "Here," she said, almost calmly—"take this. . . ."

He knew without looking at it, what it was. A dagger. He knew why she had given it to him.

"Tonight—or tomorrow night," she whispered. "What does it matter? You'll die. But he mustn't win, Pietro—he mustn't! I can almost see his face now when he finds he has been cheated of his tortures—and of me. . . ."

"Of you?" Pietro said.

"Yes, yes! You don't think you can leave me? We've been separated too much in this life . . . I think now they can never separate us again. . . ."

She put up her hands quickly and drew her *bliaut* apart so that one white breast showed.

"I'll be first," she whispered. "Just one hard stroke—it won't even hurt much and it'll be over very quickly and after that you can put yourself out of reach of Enzio and his torturers for they are very skilled, Pietro, believe me, very, they could wring screams from the throat of a graven image. . . ."

"No," Pietro said.

She stared at him.

"Are you afraid?" she whispered.

"No. Yes—but not in the way you mean. I don't want to die. I don't want you to. And it seems to me that there must be a way out of this thing. . . ."

"Believe me, Pietro," Io said. "There isn't."

Pietro searched her face in the light of the torch.

"Tell me," he said. "Has Enzio other prisoners?"

Wonderingly Io shook her head.

"Then," Pietro exulted, "the other cell is unoccupied!"

"Yes, but Pietro—I—I don't see. . . ."

"Nor will he! Come, get Giulio down here. Of all the coinages of earth, time is the one we have the least of!"

He waited while she climbed the ladder, and after a moment Giulio came down into the cell.

"My Lord?" he muttered.

"You have it in your power to save us," Pietro said. "There is, I admit, some risk in it. But this risk is not very great. I think you love the Lady Io enough to take it. Am I right?"

Io had come back down the ladder and stood beside them before he'd finished speaking.

Giulio looked at her.

"Giulio, please!" she wept.

"Well—" Giulio got out, staring at her tears, "My Lord Enzio is a hard man and no mistake . . . If he was to—"

"But he won't!" Pietro snapped. "Look, Giulio, the beauty of my plan is that you won't know anything about it. I'm going to fetch you a buffet across your head and take away your keys. Or you strike yourself, if you prefer—hard enough to draw a little blood. Enzio will think you were overpowered—"

"But," Giulio said practically, "I got no keys for any gate leading out of the castle. You'll still be trapped. . . ."

"Let me attend to that," Pietro said.

Io came up and laid a gentle hand on Giulio's arm.

"Please, Giulio," she begged.

"Well—all right," Giulio said. "But take care you don't crack my skull!"

Pietro came up at once, the stone in his hands.

"Turn your head a little," he said.

Giulio did so, fearfully.

Pietro brought the stone down all at once and very hard so that the guard, powerful as he was, collapsed, his limbs loosening, and the whole of him striking the floor like a sack of meal.

"Pietro!" Iolanthe said.

"Sorry," Pietro laughed. "I'll explain later—come!"

They raced up the ladder and across the floor of the chamber above, the chamber that was merely a hallway and served no other purpose but to lead to and conceal the entrances to the two cells.

"But, Pietro—" Io wailed.

"Listen, Io. I cannot escape by the gates or the walls. We both know that. But I can hide until the false trail Enzio will be following leads him and his sergeants so far from Hellemark that. . . ."

"Where can you hide that he will not find you? Enzio knows Hellemark like the palm of his own hand. . . ."

Pietro smiled at her.

"Where," he said, "he will not even think to look for me. Tell me, love, where is the last place on earth an escaped prisoner would go?"

Io stared at him.

"Into—into the other cell! Of course! And I—"

"You'll dangle a rope over a remote spot of the walls. Then, while they're beating the brush, seeking me, I shall scale down another rope of my own—and take you with me. By the time they give up the search, we'll be half way to Sicily . . . Come!"

He kissed her just once, hard, before he climbed down the ladder into the deeper, darker of the two cells. There were tears on her face, but half of joy. Of hope.

The waiting was bad. Very bad. There was no light, and he had no way of telling the time. He didn't know whether Enzio had left the castle or not. He was sick with anxiety. With fear.

But he had to chance it finally. The first thing he saw when he pushed open the trapdoor was that the torches were lit. He had waited long enough. It was night.

He reached the walls in the rear of the castle without difficulty, for Hellemark was home to him, too, well remembered. He guessed Enzio must have taken nearly every available man with him, for even the back towers had been left unguarded. Here where he was, the moat was very deep, and beyond it, the hill upon which Hellemark stood slanted away into almost a precipice. It was the most difficult spot from which to launch an attack against the castle. Even in times of war, it was but lightly guarded.

But Io was not there. And there was no rope. She had promised to leave one there, but there was none.

He was standing there, shaking with fatigue, with hunger, with the very bad emotions that rose up in him unbidden when he saw the man coming toward him. He had the dagger out and was crouching, ready to spring, when he saw that the man had a rope coiled about his shoulders.

It was Giulio. When he came closer, Pietro could see that his head was bandaged. Pietro came out of the shadow.

"Giulio!" he called, quietly.

The big man turned.

"My Lord?" he whispered. Then: "Yes, it's you, whom both Saints and Demons must preserve! Here is your rope. Take one end of it quickly, and down with you! I am a fool, God knows, to take this further risk. . . ."

"But My Lady!" Pietro whispered. "Where is she? She said. . . ."

"My Lord Enzio insisted that she go with them on the hunt for you. That was the very barbarity of cruelty, methinks. He said that he would not think of having her miss such fine sport. . . ."

"Dear God!" Pietro said.

"Before they left," Giulio said, "My Lady had a word with me. She gave me this fat purse to give you to speed your journey—and this message: 'Tell him,' said she, 'to go—and when he has come into his fortune to ride against his enemies and take back what has always been his own—but to be not—not foolishly impatient and to wait until he can ride under a forest of spears in overwhelming force . . . I have waited so long,' said she, 'that another two or three years of waiting will not destroy me . . . But his failure—and his death would unseat my reason and send me unshriven into hell by mine own hand. . . .' "

He paused, staring at Pietro.

"She said also—to give you her love. . . ."

"The sweet blue eyes of God!" Pietro wept.

"Take the rope, My Lord," Guilio said.

Pietro took it. There was nothing else he could do. As he swung downward toward the stagnant, vile smelling moat, he remembered exactly and precisely and in complete detail those twenty nights. He had the sick feeling that they were going to have to last him a lifetime.

And that that lifetime, remembering them, would be purest hell.

It was easy at first. Too easy. That should have warned him. He knew better than to go into Rezzi. He would have to strike out southward over the wild country between Hellemark and Rocca d'Aquilino, and try to obtain a mount in one of the small towns beyond Ricardo's castle. Ricardo of Siniscola would perhaps give him one, for he bore Pietro no hatred but gratitude rather, born of that day on which Pietro had aided Iolanthe in saving Rocca d'Aquilino from Andrea's attack.

But Elaine was there now—married to Ricardo. Mistress of Rocca d'Aquilino. And it was she, Pietro reflected bitterly, who had brought Enzio down upon his head.

That, no. He could count upon thirty miles at the least of weary walking before he could risk trying to buy a horse. He had ample money. The purse Io had sent him would buy a herd of horses. It would buy him everything he needed—except happiness, except peace.

He was in the underbrush of the great forest where the nobles of Roccablanca, Hellemark, and Rocca d'Aquilino had always hunted when he heard the winding of hunting horns. The baying of hounds. They were close, very close. He saw them almost as soon as he heard them.

Enzio, riding at the head of his sergeants. Io at his side. With—with death in her eyes. Death and hell.

Pietro whirled away from the trail. His eyes were blinded with his own tears. He ran wildly, without caution, so that the sound of his passage was loud under the trees.

He could hear the hounds behind him now, setting up their deep-voiced baying. He was lost and he knew it and that was death itself baying upon his trail. But he kept on running, breath gone, blind, until he crashed through the underbrush full into the arms of a party of huntsmen.

They were, he saw, when he could see again, dressed in the

green and gold livery of Rocca d'Aquilino. And their leader, sitting there upon her dappled grey palfrey, was the Lady Elaine.

He made her a slow, mocking bow.

"A man cannot escape his fate, can he?" he said. "I doubt not that my Lord Enzio will reward you greatly for this. . . ."

She did not answer him. She just sat there.

"They say the prayers of the dying are specially potent," Pietro went on, resting there quietly without struggling in the grip of two burly hunters; "I shall remember you in my prayers—that is while your good cousin leaves me a tongue with which to pray. . . ."

She stared at him.

"Why," she whispered. "Why would you pray for me, Messire Pietro?"

"That God and Our Lady grant you a heart to match your beauty," Pietro said.

The hounds were closer now. He could hear them give tongue, bellowing against the earth.

"For your beauty is without peer and a gift from God. I think that you profane it, Lady Elaine—by pride, by cruelty, by hate. I think that you will lose it finally—and that part of its loss will be caused by remembering that you gave over to torture a man who never harmed you—only because he dared do what he could not help doing—loving the sweetest and best lady who ever drew breath . . . Now wind your horns and call him!"

"Ruggiero, Rodolfo!" Elaine said suddenly, clearly. "Take him to that little declivity we just passed and cover him with branches. And take him up—carry him so that his feet do not touch the earth and leave a scent for the hounds. . . ."

Pietro stared at her, his dark eyes widening in his face.

"Off with you!" she said. "Hurry!"

There is, Pietro thought suddenly, a God in heaven after all —Whose ways are inscrutable, Whose judgments unsearchable, and Whose instruments are sometimes past all believing!

Then the hunters lifted him aloft, and bore him away.

He had only the shortest wait. After some twenty minutes, when they lifted the branches and the leaves from his prone form, she was there beside the pit, watching them.

"Take him up behind you, Rodolfo," she said. "It's best that we reach home as soon as possible. . . ."

Then she rode away to the head of the line before he could even mumble his thanks.

At Rocca d'Aquilino, there was more time.

Pietro stood before her, acutely conscious of his torn and muddy garments and his two months' growth of black beard. Of those things and of the confusion in his mind.

"My thanks, gracious Lady," he said. "Yet I must presume more upon your generosity and ask of you—why? In the few times I have met you, you have never deigned to utter a civil word—yet now you've saved my life. You lied gloriously to Enzio, hid me, brought me here—I—I find myself confused. . . ."

She looked at him and her eyes were troubled.

"I would tell you," she said, "if I knew myself. Call it an impulse—call it madness. I gave you into Enzio's hands before—then I remembered his cruelty and repented of my act. I—I've repented of so many things, Messire Pietro—of my pride, of my own cruelty, since God has seen fit to deal me my punishment here upon earth. . . ."

Pietro waited.

"Io was right. I envied her great love. I did not envy her you—though you are, as she said, very fair—no, it was the love itself I envied. For I had so great a love, and I have lost it—through my husband's careless folly. He was wounded in a tourney. The wound healed over—and festered all beneath. The leeches say he will not last the year. . . ."

"I'm sorry, My Lady," Pietro whispered.

"I know. I believe you are. You have the imagination and the heart to grieve for others' losses. No matter. Come inside. My seneschal will give you fresh clothes, and a horse to speed your journey. . . ."

But he did not go that night. He did not because Elaine of Siniscola asked him to stay. She took him by the hand and led him to Ricardo's chamber. Her husband was asleep—or unconscious.

"Look," Elaine said.

Pietro stared down at the one Siniscola who had been both

noble and fine, seeing him reduced to mere bones under the yellowish, taut skin, his eyes sunken into cavernous hollows, his lips drawn back over his teeth in a horribly macabre grin; and he wondered once more, as many a man has done before and since, at the workings of a God, of providence, of fate that struck down thus in such bad, ugly, insufferable ways the noble and the good while leaving to their joyful rapine the brutal, the cruel, the unjust; and the hope that was in him that his own misfortunes could be, would be righted, quailed before this emaciated bundle of dying flesh that had been once a man living, dreaming, hoping on the face of earth. . . .

When he turned to Elaine, he saw that she was crying.

He could not comfort her, being himself comfortless. He could only understand her now, comprehend at last the dark compulsions that had driven her to lash out at Io, at him, at all the visible happiness about her that tortured her by contrast, by exclusion.

He said, wordlessly, a prayer for Ricardo's soul.

Tired as he was, Pietro could not sleep that night. So it was that he heard, half in a dream the soft scuffling outside his door. He got up, taking down the sword from over the mantel, and opened it.

Elaine was struggling in the arms of a man. Pietro could not see his face, nor hers. It was too dark for that. He could discern merely, formless and wild, the fierce locked struggle of their two forms, hear Elaine crying:

"Let me go, let me go, let me go! He is not yet dead, and you'd dishonor him thus!"

"But you love me," the man growled, "Me—not that rotting corpse!"

"I'm no longer sure of that!" Elaine said, and Pietro put out his hand and seized the man's shoulder in the darkness.

"Let her go," he said quietly, and flung the intruder out and away from her.

He heard the rasp the man's sword made as it left the scabbard. Then he thrust out at once, hard, hearing the blades clang against one another, seeing the sparks they made, then his point went home, deflected a little by the other's parry but not enough, so that it pierced the sword arm and he heard, after only the smallest interval, the clatter of his unseen opponent's sword as it struck the floor.

Elaine screamed just once—a bleak sound, shrill and formless; then there was no other sound save their breathing.

The man turned and ran down the long hallway. Pietro took a step after him but she caught his arm and clung to him.

"Let him go!" she wept. "For God's love, Messire Pietro—let him go!"

"Who was it?" Pietro demanded.

"My cousin, Andrea," she sobbed. "Though that concerns you not—and I think that you have killed him!"

"No," Pietro said. "It was only a scratch—though I'm sorry I could not see to do better."

He could feel her eyes on him in the darkness.

"You will leave this house at the first light of morning," she said flatly. "Your horse will be ready. You will leave—and never come back."

Pietro looked at her. He couldn't see her face. He was sorry he could not. It might have told him something—helped him understand.

"Very well," he said. "I will leave—and trouble Milady no more with unwanted intrusions. . . ."

When he rode away that next morning, she was up to bid him Godspeed. But her eyes were veiled. As he galloped through the portcullis he knew that he would never know with any degree of certainty the extent of her duplicity—the extent of her betrayal of Ricardo. Or—for that was what all betrayals amounted to finally—of herself.

The thing that surprised Pietro most was that he cared. He didn't know why. He was in love with Io, he had lost her, he must embark upon the perilous task of winning her again. But there was pain in his heart when he thought about that unlovely struggle in the blackness of the hallway.

It would be a long time yet before Pietro knew his own heart.

Chapter Eight

THOSE FOUR YEARS between April 1216, when Pietro finally arrived in Palermo, and September 1220, by which time Frederick finally crossed the Alps into Italy, were one of the bad times in Pietro's life. The way that they were bad was very simple: Pietro was constantly and completely blocked at every turn from doing anything whatsoever about Iolanthe. He spent the first six months in fruitless efforts to gain possession of the great fortune, amounting to some millions of tarens, that Isaac had left him. He should have known better. Frederick's stewards on the Island had not the slightest intention of letting so much money, or even any part thereof, pass out of the Emperor's coffers without a direct order from Frederick, himself.

Pietro wrote Frederick, but it took three to five months for a letter to pass from Sicily to Germany—if it got there at all—and Frederick did not bother to answer at once. When Pietro finally got his reply, it stated simply that he would attend to the matter personally upon his arrival. It did, however, contain one thing of great value: it acknowledged Pietro's claim to his inheritance.

Upon that simple acknowledgment, penned above Frederick's signature, and bearing the Imperial Seal, Pietro was able to live for four years. He was able to borrow sums of money from the banking houses, who would gladly have let him have much more, seeking thus to win Frederick's favor. But Pietro hated debt. He contented himself with sums just large enough to keep himself and Waldo and Rainaldo, his retainers—frugally. In any case, no one would have lent him money enough to hire the two or three hundred mercenaries he needed to attack Hellemark, which was all he wanted money for. So there was nothing for him to do but wait.

For Frederick to come. For something to happen. Anything that might change things. That might even give him hope.

By the Spring of 1219, he couldn't stand it any longer. Out of pure desperation, he took to the saddle and rode northward to Rezzi, accompanied by Waldo and Rainaldo.

The innkeeper, Ruffio, stared at him with unconcealed awe, admiration and not a little fear.

"My Lord has nerves of iron!" he said. "To return to this place—and accompanied by only two men at arms! Are you tired of living, Sire Pietro?"

"I," Pietro said, "am not tired of living. Break out a flagon, good Ruffio. Then from you I would have news. . . ."

Ruffio set out a flagon.

"What would My Lord know?" he whispered.

"Everything," Pietro said. There was, in the very back of his mind, a wild, formless, excuse for a plan. Somehow he would slip into Hellemark. Somehow he would bring Io out again. Then the two of them would ride. . . .

"Sire Enzio," Ruffio was saying, "is plaguedly unpopular. Many knights have left his service. His villeins, as you might expect, are constantly on the point of revolt, so badly does he treat them. With the peasants being in the state of mind they are, the crops have been miserable. . . ."

"And Count Alessandro?" Pietro said. Strange, he mused, that I should ask after him—that I should postpone asking the one thing I rode these weary leagues to ask, but no matter . . . "Count Alessandro," he said again, "tell me of him. . . ."

"Count Alessandro is in Rome, trying to mend the evidences of his treachery before the Emperor arrives. Only Andrea is at Roccablanca, and his reason for being there does him no credit. Since my Lord Ricardo, rest his soul, died at Rocca d'Aquilino these three years ago, wagging tongues have persistently linked the names of Andrea and my Lady Elaine. That, they say, is the reason that Andrea lingered behind instead of going to Rome. They say, further, swine that they are, that this connection—began long before Sire Ricardo's death. . . ."

Pietro was surprised again at the bitter stab his memory brought him. Elaine's behavior, her morals or lack of them, were no concern of his. Yet, recalling that struggle in the night-locked hall he felt again like—like a lover betrayed. Like a cuckold.

"Why," he said, forcing his voice to remain calm, "does he not marry the lady, then—since she is now a widow?"

"He can't," Ruffio said. "Didn't you know they are first cousins? That's well within the forbidden degrees of kinship. His Holiness recently forbade the nuptials of a couple who were four degrees removed. It's a wise law, for else all the great families would turn to near incest to keep their holdings within the family bounds. . . ."

Pietro looked at Ruffio's fat, kindly face. There was no help for it now. He had to ask him—the thing he had ridden so far to find out, the final, slender prop for all his hopes. . . .

"How fares—the Lady Io?" he whispered.

"Well—" Ruffio said, and stopped. "My Lord," he said at last, "I know not how to tell you this—"

Pietro stood up. Stared at him.

"There—there is a child now, Sire Pietro," Ruffio said. "A son. And my lady is wondrously happy. They say she sings all day long. . . ."

Pietro could feel his limbs loosening under him. He put out his hand to steady himself. Then very slowly, he sat down.

I could do it still, he thought. Slip into Hellemark—slay Enzio, take Io as my wife. Mother of God! How have the deepest instincts of womankind cursed me! Io is no Antoinette. She is woman, all woman, and can love this child of her womb though it was begotten of the man she despises. . . .

Still, I could do it. Kill Enzio and spend the remainder of my days with his face looking at me out of the face of a child! Living with the daily, hourly reminder that the sweet flesh that was now my flesh had been clasped in hot and close surrender to the sweating body of that beast . . . I think I would be incapable of her.

I think it would breed a sickness in me like Toinette's sickness so that her fair flesh would smell of corruption and befoulment and I would retch at her kiss . . . God, God! What manner of tender fool am I?

"I'm sorry, My Lord," Ruffio said. His round face was troubled.

Pietro took a silver coin from his belt and flung it on the table.

"Don't be," he said. "You've just saved a life—perhaps even my life. Come lads."

He did not go back to Sicily. Instead, because everyone was now convinced that Frederick must soon appear in Italy, Pietro rode with his men toward Venice. But he did one more thing he had not planned.

He paid a call upon the Lady Elaine.

To his surprise she greeted him kindly.

She was dressed in the white of widowhood and the color became her. Her face was grave and still, and the hatred had gone out of her eyes. There was peace in them now. Acceptance.

Still, she troubled him. In her white weeds, her beauty in the dark halls of the castle was like a cry. There was no warmth in her gaze when she looked at him. There was nothing in her gaze. Not even interest. Still, she troubled him.

Why, he realized suddenly, I could love this woman. I'm mad. Even to think that is madness. I've grown too lonely. After Io—after losing Io—these fantasies come too easily—fantasies? No. Since the first day I saw her, this Elaine has troubled me. There is something of Circe in her—if she hated me it would be better. Anything is better than this—this disinterest. She buries me alive beneath mountains of cool unconcern . . . I must leave this place. One more day in this castle of dark enchantments and I shall lose my soul. . . .

But he stayed for three full days. He went with her to the grave of Ricardo, and knelt a little behind her as she prayed. He sat at meat with her and she talked to him with grave courtesy. Often she fell into long silences which he was careful not to break. At those times, she seemed to have forgotten he was there.

As he rode toward Venice once more, the bleakness of his heart was a divided pain. His loss of Io was a terrible thing, too bitter to be borne. But he could bear thinking of Elaine, so he did.

She had been kind and gentle and polite toward him. Too polite. Her courtesy had been a kind of self discipline. She was teaching herself the graciousness of a great lady who is always gentle and kind toward inferiors. Especially toward inferiors. She did not know, or at least had not deigned to mention, the advancement of his station. To her, he was still a superior kind of serf.

That hurt. He was not even sure why it hurt, but it did. It rankled in his heart like a thorn. He did not love Elaine of Siniscola, though her beauty delighted him. He did not love any woman—except the one woman now finally and completely and eternally lost to him.

But Elaine had pricked his pride. He found himself, during that long ride to Venice, devising schemes by which to humble her. And all of them, oddly, ended one way, with that cold and distant beauty stretching out her white arms to him, offering her love. Which was pure fantasy and he knew it.

Three weeks later, he reached Venice.

The year he spent there was another of the bad times. He consoled himself with drinking and gaming—with transient lights o' love. Afterwards he could not remember their faces, nor their names. And they were actually no consolation at all. More than once he pushed a disappointed maid from his quarters—a fair purse in her hands, to reward her for something that had not occurred—for unaccountably sudden revulsions would rise up in him and he hated himself with a sick hate that nothing could cure.

Then, late in 1220, Frederick was at Verona, at long last on Italian soil. Pietro rode out to join him. He rode in borrowed splendor, accompanied by twenty men at arms lent him by the great Venetian banking house which had subsidized his stay in that city. The night of his arrival he and Frederick talked until dawn, not as Emperor and subject, but as old friends. Learning that Frederick still had precious little money, Pietro offered him a loan of one million tarens from his inheritance once they reached Sicily.

"Would you buy me, Pietro?" Frederick smiled. "That isn't necessary. My life itself is in your debt. Of course, I'll take the tarens. I have to. But whether you had offered them to me or not, you would have got your Barony. . . ."

"How go things in Rome, Sire?" Pietro said.

"Better. Since Innocent's death[1] I have a much milder man to deal with. Honorius is my idea of a good Holy Father. Of course, he's trying valiantly to follow in Innocent's footsteps and demand everything that wily old soldier of God tried to get out of me; but he simply hasn't the strength of character to withstand me. . . .

"Herman of Salza, the Grand Master of my Teutonic Knights is in Rome now, preparing everything. He advises that the Pope's disposed to accept my trick of reuniting Sicily with the Empire by having my son Henry crowned king of it. It's a *fait accompli*, anyhow. That was a good one! I swore on every pig's knuckle that serves the old scoundrels for saint's relics in the Empire that I would never reunite Sicily with the Empire—*in my name!* They didn't pay attention to that little phrase, Pietro—and there I had them by the backs of their tonsures! What does it matter if Henry is king, since he is but eight years old and I must perforce rule as his guardian? What think you of that, Pietro?"

Pietro smiled.

"Only," he said, "that I pray God I never lose your favor, Sire. Else you would arrange a deceit by which I would be ushered into hell without even the devil's by your leave."

Frederick threw back his head and roared with laughter.

"How well you know me, Pietro!" he said.

"That's because I know myself, Sire. We were born in the same town, Iesi, on the same hour of the same day. My mother's labor was brought on by watching the pangs of that noble and saintly queen giving you life. . . ."

Frederick stared at him.

"Can you prove that, Pietro?" he demanded.

Pietro was more than a little astonished at the Emperor's tone.

"Of course, Sire. Your Majesty needs only to ask any of the older townspeople of Iesi. For that matter, my birthday and the circumstances surrounding it are recorded in the priestly canons of the church there. The good fathers thought it something to marvel over, and recorded the date of my birth as well as that of my baptism. I think I'm Iesi's only son who has his birthdate recorded instead of merely his baptismal one. . . ."

Frederick was staring at Pietro now and his face was pale.

"That," he said harshly, "accounts for the feeling I've had about you almost from the day we met. You're not to ride abroad, Pietro—unless accompanied by some of my sergeants as well as your own retinue. . . ."

"Why so, Sire?" Pietro asked wonderingly.

"Don't you see! The same day, the same place, the same hour, under the influence of the same stars! That makes you my alter ego—any fate that befalls you is very likely to overtake me upon the split of the same instant! By guarding your life, Pietro, my soul's brother, I guard my own!"

Pietro found it hard not to smile. This mighty king, this most brilliant of all Europeans, this man who spoke seven tongues and wrote nine, who already had the bulk of the world's known science at his fingertips, was a prey to the most abysmal of superstitions. Yet a moment later his keen brain was awake, racing. My soul's brother, Frederick had called him. What was a barony in comparison to that? If Frederick II was the greatest king of Christendom, he, Pietro di Donati, was now the second most powerful man in Europe—immune to fear and loss of favor, above the reach of the most powerful lords in Italy, no one of whom would Frederick now permit to harm a single hair of his head. . . .

"I shudder now," Frederick was saying, "when I think of the dangers you've undergone. Why else on earth should we have been confronted each in his turn by that same boar? And the dangers that have imperiled me have been paralleled in your life. Tell me, Pietro—have you ever been imprisoned and held for ransom?"

"Yes, Sire," Pietro said.

"As I was held by Diepold of Schweinspeunt! That's the last link. All else I know of you. What were the circumstances surrounding this?"

Pietro told him.

"You should be wed," Frederick said when he had finished. "I have a son and that breaks the pattern. . . ."

"Men say," Pietro smiled, "that you have two sons, Sire."

"True. There is my natural son Enzio, born of a great German lady. Strange that he should have the same name as your bitterest enemy. You see that, Pietro? Always a connection! In names, in events—you must be wed!"

"Why, My Lord?"

"Because unless you have sons, an ill fate may befall mine. Yet, I cannot violate my oaths and take away another man's wife to give to you, however much you may love her. . . ."

"I—I don't want her any longer, Sire," Pietro whispered.

"Good—but why? Has your love cooled so fast?"

"No. But there is a child. Even were she widowed through natural causes, think you I could daily bear the sight of the living image of the man I hate? Yet, I could not harm a child. Your Majesty will comprehend that love is greedy, jealous. A reminder of physical intimacy with him I loathe would be like a brand upon her forehead. . . ."

"I see. Then I will find you a maid."

Pietro stared at the Emperor. Frederick was perfectly capable of doing just that and Pietro knew it. That towering, overwhelming arrogance would think nothing of taking some unknown maid by the hand and saying with total calm, never dreaming that anyone might object, "Pietro, behold your bride."

And the maid would be fair. Frederick had wonderful taste in womanflesh. But she would still be a gift—an object incapable of stirring into life a heart dead to all but—

He did not complete the thought. It wasn't true any longer. It hadn't been in a long time.

"I know just what type you'd like," Frederick chuckled. "The same type that pleases me. A tall, willowy blonde—who looks like so much ice, but with all the fires of hell beneath that snow! Oh, yes—Pietro—we're the Goatstar's children. Capricorn rules us—Saturn was in ascendancy when we were born. We saturnine ones are all alike: towering ambitions, devilish cunning, but undone by our lusts. Now, let me think. . . ."

"Sire," Pietro said quickly. "If it pleases you, I can suggest a maid. No, not a maid—a young widow . . . But I beg your Majesty's indulgence that you do not press the matter until I have come into possession of my barony. She is the proudest lady alive. Each time I have seen her, she has openly, or covertly scorned me, always on the score of my humble birth. Yet, I think now that her scorn is lessening. . . ."

"Her name?" Frederick growled.

"Can't I," Pietro said, "keep that one little secret a while—even from you, My Lord?"

"No!" Frederick thundered. "Everything you do concerns me, Pietro. This matter must be completed in some haste. Come now, her name."

Pietro looked away from him, his dark eyes brooding.

"Her name," he whispered, "is Elaine—Elaine of Siniscola. . . ."

"Of Siniscola!" Frederick said.

"Yes, Sire. She is a cousin of that house. Like yourself, Sire, she is half German—and very fair. In a curious way, I have loved her nearly all my life. I say curious, for perhaps I have not loved her at all. Can a man—a rational man—love a maid he has seen but five times in his whole life? A maid, who, additionally, scorned him with the bitterest words on three of those five occasions. . . ."

"And the other two?" Frederick said.

"Upon one," Pietro whispered, "she saved my life—because she repented of having betrayed me into the hands of her cousin. And the last time, a year ago, she seated me at her table like an honored guest, spoke fair words to me, and bade me godspeed upon my journey. . . ."

"She has come to love you," Frederick said at once. "That's very clear."

"No, Sire. Her courtesy was too cool, too disinterested. A woman does not look upon a man she loves as Elaine looked upon me then. . . ."

"Yet you think you love this daughter of your enemies?"

"I don't know, Sire," Pietro said honestly. "Put it this way: of all the maids on earth except the one now lost to me, I believe I could come to love Elaine. . . ."

"Why?" Frederick said.

"Because never since I've known Io have I been shaken in my devotion to her—except by this same Elaine. It may be merely her beauty. For she is, Sire, most wondrously fair. It may be that curious quirk in the minds of men that forever seeks the unattainable—I don't know. I think maybe that she would be wrong for me. I am almost sure she would be. Yet I have dreamed of her for countless nights—even—even, Sire, before I lost my Lady Iolanthe. . . ."

"You," Frederick growled, "have used one wrong word for her. Nothing that Frederick of Hohenstaufen desires for a subject and a friend is—unattainable."

"Please, Sire," Pietro said. "Do not command her to wed me. If you do that, all the ground I've won—all the little kindly feelings I may have built up in her heart will be blown away like autumn leaves before a sudden storm. Love cannot be commanded. It's a delicate thing, My Lord. You could force her to wed me; but by the same token, you'd force her also to hate me. I don't want the mere possession of a woman's body, Sire. That can be purchased in ten thousand brothels through the length of Italy. What I want is to see her eyes kindle at the sight of me—watch them grow soft with tenderness at my touch . . . I want her love, Sire. . . ."

"As you will," Frederick said.

The journey down the length of Italy was slow, for they had to bear the welcome of many towns. Pietro noticed that Frederick confirmed the rights of the towns—but only those rights and privileges that they had already enjoyed under the Empire. Not one word did he say concerning Sicily. Genoa, Pisa, and Venice needed, above all things, to have confirmation of their loading and shipping and harbor rights on the Island, which was the place of departure for all the longer sea voyages. But Frederick told even the loyal Genoese that under no circumstances would concessions be made in Sicily before his arrival there.

They rode leisurely across the Apennines, travelling by the Via Flaminia. And, as they neared Rome, the Pope's emissary met them.

The Pope, he declared to Frederick, was anxious to be assured that the Empire had no claims at all upon Sicily, that Sicily was to continue exclusively as the hereditary possession of the Queen-Mother Constance. His Holiness would like a promise from Frederick that he'd install no foreign officials in the Twin Kingdom and even employ a separate seal.

Frederick laughingly agreed to all this. What difference did it make after all about the legal phraseology, when Sicily was his in fact?

On November twenty-second, Frederick rode with his Queen, and his retinue down from the Monte Mario along the Via Triumphalis into Rome. Pietro rode directly behind the royal pair, an indication of the Emperor's favor that the jealous Barons did not fail to note. The procession halted at a little bridge outside the city where Frederick confirmed the rights and privileges of the Romans.

Then the procession surged on, banners flying, the drums rolling a solemn, muted march, the bronze and silver horns sounding, too; but not loudly, for this was a sacred hour—not to be blasphemed with noise and shouting. At the Porta Collina, near the baths of Diocletian, the clergy met him and did him homage. The priests fell into triple lines at the head of the procession, and led it toward Saint Peter's, with uplifted crucifixes, the swing of censers and the deep-voiced chant of a solemn mass.

It was intensely moving: the barefoot priests moving slowly ahead, chanting, the drums still now, the horns mute; just the chant of the priests and the slow clipclopping of the horses' hooves on the stones and the tinkle of the coins as Frederick's chamberlains scattered largesse to the crowd. Even the people scrambling for the coins fought each other in silence. Then came the *praefectus urbi* bearing the sword before his face and after that the Emperor and his Queen.

Pietro wondered how Frederick was going to behave during certain of the ceremonies. His grandfather, that Barbarossa for whom he was named, had created weeks of turmoil by refusing to hold the Pope's stirrup for the prelate to mount, a symbolical act signifying the submission of the worldly to the spiritual authority; and both Barbarossa and Otto had refused the usual largesse that Frederick's chamberlains were scattering so lavishly abroad. As a result, Pietro knew, Barbarossa had had to be crowned in secret, and pitched battles had accompanied Otto's coronation. . . .

But Frederick was an unknown quantity. He might refuse the humiliating parts of the ceremony with scorn, or he might simply ignore their implications, counting such petty matters beneath him.

They had reached the square before Saint Peter's now, and once more the guard was changed: Roman Senators strode with great dignity on the King's right hand to take his horse at the steps of the church.

As Frederick and Constance dismounted, a solemn procession filed out of the sacristy of Saint Peter. His Holiness, Pope Honorius, was in the center on the topmost step, with the cardinals on his right and the cardinal-deacons on his left. Below him on the other stairs, the lower clergy arranged themselves.

Slowly Frederick mounted, and all the people held their breath. Everyone knew the story of Barbarossa, and this was Barbarossa's grandson. But Frederick flung himself down with almost theatrical grace before the Pope, and kissed not one, but both of his golden slippers.

Pietro smiled. He wondered if others had noticed what he saw in Frederick's submission. Probably not; few others knew the Emperor as well as he. That quality of mocking exaggeration that said: I care not for this trifle—not even thus can you humiliate me. For in the end I shall triumph and whose horse was held by whom and whose feet kissed will be nothing and less than nothing upon the scroll of my days. . . .

Honorius raised him up graciously, embraced him, and kissed his cheek. And Frederick gave the Pope the required tribute in gold.

Then the whole procession, with retinues of King and Pope now combined, moved toward the Chapel of Santa Maria in Turribus.

Kneeling there in the first row of pews, Pietro heard Frederick's voice clearly:

"I swear before Our Lord and the Holy Virgin, to be forever the defender of His Holiness, the Pope, and the one, true, blessed, everlasting Church of Christ, in every hour of weal and woe, unto the very end of my days."

How much or how little of that did Frederick mean? Pietro

couldn't be sure. His voice sounded utterly sincere. But Frederick was a consummate actor . . . So great a mime, indeed, Pietro mused, that often he convinces himself. . . .

The Pope had mounted the steps of the altar to pray, but Frederick remained behind to be received into the brotherhood of the Canons of Saint Peter. It was the belief of the Popes that an emperor could not remain entirely a layman: having such power over men as he did, it seemed to them fitting that that power be consecrated, at least in part, to the glory of God. So Frederick, like his predecessors, had to submit to being anointed on the arm and between the shoulder blades with consecrated oil, and received into the Canons as a lay brother. Even this was a diminution. Before Innocent's time, the emperors had been made full bishops; but Innocent reduced their status while exalting his own. . . .

Every step in the rest of the coronation ceremonies, from now on, was like a dance: beautifully ordered and precise. Frederick, clad once more in the Imperial robes, striding through the silver gate into St. Peter's, the cardinals meeting him there with chant and prayer; halting now before Peter's tomb to do reverence, anointed by a cardinal before St. Maurice's.

Confession at the altar of Peter, and upon his cheek now Honorius' kiss of peace. The retinue swirling out like the members of a troupe, falling into ordered arrangement; the Pope rehearsing the prayer. . . .

Pietro watched it all in wonder and awe, forcing himself to remember mankind's genius for hypnotizing itself with show and ceremony. Still, it was a thing for a man to remember, this crowning of Frederick of Hohenstaufen finally in Rome. . . .

The smell of incense and the chanting of the cardinals, and Frederick advancing now, seeming almost godlike in his robes and bearing. He knelt before the Pope. He was crowned with mitre. With crown. . . .

Then taking the sword from the hand of Honorius he brandished it three times to show that he was now *miles Beati Petri*—a captain in defense of the Vicar of God.

Only then was he given at last—after long, long last, so many years since his childhood and his father's death, twenty-three long years since he had become in truth an uncrowned Emperor at the age of three—the sceptre and the Imperial orb.

Pietro wondered how he felt now, checked so long by this same Papacy from the receiving of his rightful heritage, honored of the prelates now, hearing the thunderous chorus: "To Frederick ever glorious, of the Romans the unconquered Emperor, be life and victory!"

Triumph? Or impatience? Or—like Pietro himself the emptiness of the fulfillment that comes too late?

They crowned the Queen after that. In the High Mass that followed, Frederick laid aside crown and mantle, and administered as Honorius' helper, as a subdeacon of the Most High God. . . .

Outside in the sunshine, Frederick held the stirrup for the Pope to mount, and then led His Holiness' horse a few paces, again going beyond the requirements of the ceremony.

He will not extend himself over trifles, Pietro thought; but when the issues are really joined, then will he be terrible. . . .

The issues were soon joined. Frederick's first act upon entering Apulia was to issue a *Demanium* in which it was declared that all grants, gifts, donations, privileges, confirmation of titles in the thirty years since the death of William II, the last Norman king, were null and void. Every German noble in Italy was reduced overnight to beggary; most Norman knights suffered the same fate, and many Italians—including all who held fiefs of Otto, the Welf.

As, for instance, the Counts of Siniscola. And Sire Pietro di Donati of Petit Mur, whose inheritance fell within that fated span.

Nothing hastened Frederick's hand. He let even Pietro, his friend, suffer for ten full days before restoring to him Isaac's legacy. It amounted to a full four million tarens—reduced now to three by Pietro's so-called loan to the crown. So-called, because Pietro knew he'd never ask repayment of Frederick. And Frederick would never be troubled by the trifle of repaying a loan. . . .

Pietro sat at a long table with his quill ever busy, listing the lands, castles, holdings, submitted to the crown. Most of these Frederick directed him to return at once, with the proviso that they could be recalled at any time the realm had need of them.

Most of the nobles submitted peacefully. Many did not. The Count of Ajello; the brother of that Diepold of Schweinspeunt who held Cajazzo and Allifae; the Count of Sora, the lesser nobles who held castles at Naples, Gaeta, Aversa, Foggia. Most formidable of all, the Count of Molise. Only a little less terrible, Count Alessandro of Siniscola and his sons.

Using the forces of the barons who, overawed by witnessing his coronation at Rome, had submitted to him, Frederick smashed them one by one. And to Sire Pietro di Donati, he assigned one of the hardest tasks of all—the sieges of Hellemark and Roccablanca.

Pietro did not want to attack Hellemark—not now. Roccablanca, of course, was another matter. But the Emperor's command was law.

When Pietro rode out he had more than a thousand knights behind him, as well as some hundreds of sergeants, and infantry.

First Hellemark, for which he had in his saddle bag grants assigning it to him and his heirs forever, signed by Frederick himself.

Studying the situation, Pietro was troubled. He didn't want to use catapults and mangonels against it. What assurance had he that one stone misdirected might not. . . .

No, it would have meant a long series of feints, and the use of sows and rams. A *bellfroi*, perhaps. Skill.

He drew up his men around the walls and cut off every avenue of escape. In a month he could starve Hellemark into submission; but that meant starving Io—starving the child.

But I hate that child, he told himself. It was no good. He couldn't. The child was Io's—of her flesh, and breath, and spirit. Of her fire. Her tenderness. Cursed with the black strain of Siniscola—true. Half beast—yet half angel. He couldn't. He was still destiny's fool—a tender fool who could not war upon the woman he loved, nor her child.

So he spent three whole nights in sleepless planning. Thereafter he sent forces charging out again and again, charging and falling back hastily, making a brave show of force, making mighty noises with sow and ram, and *bellfroi*; while secretly from afar his engineers tunneled under the walls, shoring them up with timbers soaked in oil, the whole cave under the wall being then filled with oil-soaked fagots and set afire.

Enzio was occupied with his defenses against the battering rams, against the sows. He wondered why no single stone had been hurled from any engine into the bailey. That troubled him. It had sinister implications.

He had at most five days to be troubled. On the morning of the fifth, the engineers applied the torch. At dusk, a great stretch of the wall crashed into rubble with a great roar. Pietro rode through the gap at the head of his men. In twenty minutes, it was over. Enzio's men at arms had been too surprised to put up much of a fight.

Then, to the astonishment of his men, he allowed Enzio of Siniscola to depart in peace. Io was not in the castle. At the first news of the coming attack, Enzio had sent her and the child to Roccablanca for safekeeping.

Pietro was glad of that. He didn't want to see Iolanthe now. Least of all did he want to see that child.

But he couldn't deprive that child's father of life. Not now. To do so would be to force upon himself a relationship now grown repugnant. He loved Io still; but he couldn't become step-father to Enzio's child. He couldn't face living with the reminder of a former intimacy with the man he hated playing about his feet. He had the wrong kind of a stomach for that. The wrong nerves.

He demanded of Enzio not one copper in ransom.

And after his foe had gone, in full sight of the men he had led into battle with more bravery than any lion, the young, newly made Baron Pietro of Hellemark, sat down upon a stone—and wept.

The next day, he set his engineers to repairing the walls. Under the one weak place where the sappers had dug their deadly tunnel, directed by Pietro out of his intimate knowledge of Hellemark, they piled stones down to bedrock itself; when the new wall rose, it could never be sapped again.

Then he sat down with his leaders and plotted his strategy.

"I have no wish to take Roccablanca," he said. "I merely want to make them surrender it to the Emperor. In the bargain, for personal reasons, I wish to kill as many Siniscolas as possible, sparing only my Lord Enzio out of the respect I bear his lady—that she be not widowed . . . Now here is how we will do it. . . ."

The next days were spent in feverish preparation. Each fifth man at arms was issued five arbalists. These men were placed in a well camouflaged trench before the walls. With each man were two helpers, who had no other duty but to wind the winches of the crossbows and pass a newly cocked weapon to the bowsman as soon as he had discharged his piece. Thus did Pietro overcome the handicap of the crossbow's slow rate of fire. After a few days' practice, his men could send an endless stream of quarrels whining through the air, so that any charging knight would be picked off long before he reached the trench.

Then, with great art, he and his engineers transplanted a row of living hedges, and behind that another, and after that a third; but every hedge of the high hedgerows concealed a lance, angled just high enough to rip open the belly of a charging horse.

Upon the walls, mounted winch-wound bows converged their fire of arrows each larger than a knight's lance, upon this spot. Mangonels with casks of Greek fire. Trenchbuts with mighty stones.

The men looked with awed admiration at these mighty defenses. Still—had not the Emperor commanded their lord, the young Baron to subdue Roccablanca? That could scarcely be done with defensive engines. . . .

Pietro smiled.

"You are aware, gentlemen," he said, "that no mightier fortress exists in these parts than Roccablanca. It can be taken—but only after terrible losses. You—all of you down to the last foot-soldier—have served me well. I don't propose to sacrifice a single life, needlessly.

"Hellemark was easy, because I knew its weakness—but Roccablanca which I know as well, has no single weakness—not one. It is a masterpiece of the builder's cunning . . . Now listen well. Some of you know that the lords of Siniscola have committed terrible crimes against my house and against my friends. I have one desire that has torn my heart since I was but fourteen years of age—to slay every man of that blood who now draws breath.

"Roccablanca interests me not at all. I have no wish to capture it. In fact, His August Majesty, our Emperor has need of it—intact. Behind those walls, my lords of Siniscola can do much more harm to us than we can do them. It would require a siege of half a year to starve them out. And, against the thickest walls in Ancona, our rams, our sows would be like fleas tickling an elephant. . . ."

"I see My Lord's drift," Waldo laughed. "Make them come to us, eh? Then below, in that lovely pit of hell we have fashioned, muddy the very earth with their blood!"

"Yes," Pietro said, "but without joy, my Waldo. I have not your German capacity for enjoying slaughter. As executioners merely, dispensing justice long overdue . . . One thing more. My Lord Enzio is not to be slain. That is an order—under any and all conditions his life is to be spared."

"That, begging My Lord's pardon," Rainaldo said, "I don't see. Of all the Siniscolas, it seems to me he has offended Milord most grievously. Anyone with half an eye could see that the lady loves you, My Lord—not him. . . ."

"Silence!" Pietro thundered. "Look you, good Rainaldo, the lady is very dear to me. I won't deny that. But she is his wife in God's sight, and the mother of his son. I don't wish her widowed. . . ."

"But, Milord," Rainaldo grinned, "she need not remain a widow. . . ."

I, Pietro thought, have been too good to them. They abuse my kindness and discipline suffers. Yet I cannot be otherwise. They are men, and loyal to me. . . .

"And the child, Rainaldo?" he said quietly.

Rainaldo was a Sicilian, with some of the poetry of that land in him, some of its sensitivity.

"I see," he mused. "To My Lord the lady who loves him so is like a lost wife—and the child, like another man's bastard, is it not so? My Lord is a Sicilian, and so am I. These things, I understand. Forgive me, my presumption, My Lord. . . ."

Pietro smiled at him, sadly.

"With your permission, good Rainaldo," he said, "we'll now leave my personal affairs and turn to military matters. Now, the whole thing hinges upon our getting the Siniscolas to leave the protection of those walls and attack us here. They are not fools, but men of great cunning. We, then, must be more cunning: listen. . . ."

If Count Alessandro had taken the additional precaution of putting sentries outside the walls and the moats, he might have discovered a part of Pietro's plan. For, in the dead of night, an archer crept close to Roccablanca's walls, hiding himself in a pit which he and three others dug on the edge of the moat. The others crept back, and left him there.

But Count Alessandro had supreme confidence in his walls. He had no inkling of the bowman crouching there with a quiver full of blunted arrows having on their ends, instead of sharp arrowheads, balls of sticky pitch.

Inside of Roccablanca, Io fed her child that morning. He was more than four years old. And just to look at him usually made her glad all over. But not today. Today the long awaited attack might come. Strange that Pietro had not attacked before now. Was that on her account? Yet, he must attack. He was under the Emperor's orders to subdue the rebellious nobles of this district. Last night she had learned that only the Siniscolas held out now. After the fall of Hellemark, the lesser suzerains had quickly dispatched messages to Pietro and to Frederick indicating their willingness to do homage. . . .

She had almost finished with the bowl of gruel, which little Hans—a name upon which they had compromised, since never would she name him after one of the Siniscolas, nor dared she give him the name that with all her heart she desired to—had spat out almost as fast as she had got it into him. He was a nervous child, thin and wiry. He was darkly beautiful, which delighted her. Still. . . .

It was then that she heard the first stone crash against the walls.

She screamed for a servant, and gave little Hans to her. He howled; but for the first time in his four years of life, his mother paid not the slightest attention.

She dashed through all the corridors, and up the narrow spiral of stairs until she came out on the outer wall. She saw Enzio there with his father and his brothers.

"Are they mad?" Count Alessandro said.

She saw what he meant. Pietro, with all his knights behind him in full array, was charging wildly toward the walls.

It didn't make sense. To take a castle, you tried to batter the walls down with rams, or cut through them under the protection of an iron-roofed sow, or climb over them with scaling ladders, or swarm across them from the platform of that tower on rollers called a *bellfroi*. Or you sapped under them as Pietro had done at Hellemark. Pietro was no fool. He knew these things. Then why in the name of high heaven was he charging uselessly as though he opposed other knights upon the field of battle?

She could hear the quarrels whine from the crossbows. She didn't want to look; but she couldn't help it. So it was that she saw directly beneath her, the hidden archer rise from his pit and aim his bow full at Pietro.

She screamed. Her voice was like a knife with jagged edges going through silk. The men of Siniscola heard her.

"You fool!" Enzio roared. "Get below where you belong!"

"Pietro!" she screamed again. "For God's love—Pietro!"

He couldn't hear her. She saw the archer's fingers come away from the string. The arrow leaped out, the trajectory of its bright feathers clear in the sunlight. Down below the scene boiled suddenly into confusion.

She saw, at the last moment that she could still see, Pietro going backward in the saddle, the bright shaft standing straight out from his bosom.

She heard through the roaring darkness that crashed down upon her from every direction at once, the voice of Count Alessandro crying exultantly: "A hundred tarens to that archer!"

Then, she heard nothing more.

She was aware slowly that she was moving, being carried. It was the speed and abruptness of the motion that had restored her. The jolting. Enzio's face cleared out of the blur above her. It had a curious expression: terrible hurt, commingled with hate and savage joy. . . .

Why, she realized suddenly, he loves me! This thing—this creature they married me to—has tears in its eyes!

She had no time to analyze her reaction to this discovery. For immediately she remembered its cause. Something formed inside her, black and terrible. Something shapeless. Insane. It had claws though. It ripped her. There was nothing inside her now but blood. And pain. The worst the most terrible the most unspeakably unbearable pain in the world.

He's dead, she thought. Dead.

Then she saw Enzio looking at her. Without knowing it, she had spoken aloud.

"Yes!" Enzio said. "He's dead! May all the fiends in hell have much pleasure of his soul!"

She didn't answer him. Her eyes moved slowly away from his face. Down his body. Without intent—without conscious intent. Then they widened. There were pinpoints of fire in their pupils.

At Enzio's belt swung a dagger with a blade of the finest steel.

She moved so suddenly that the blade had risen in a glittering arc before he saw it. Then she swung it downward. He dropped her, tore at her wrist as she went down. He was too late; but not entirely too late. He ruined her aim. The blade slanted diagonally in above her left breast, with such force that its point reappeared under her left armpit.

Enzio stood there, staring at her foolishly, watching the first tiny droplets gather, combine . . . the slow trickle start.

She lay there, smiling at him.

"Draw it out, Enzio," she whispered. "It—it hurts so. . . ."

He put his hand to the hilt and pulled. It was lodged very firmly. He had to put his other hand against her shoulder. When it came free finally, there was a great rush of blood.

"Be good to Hans," Io whispered.

Then she fainted.

He picked her up and ran into the bedchamber. Her women bandaged the wound. The leech came and seared it with irons. Enzio did nothing. He had tortured men to death with his own hands. He had ridden home wounded from battle, reeling in the saddle, his armor stained with his own blood. He was a Siniscola and not without courage. But he was sick now. Sick unto death. He cried noisily—like a whipped child.

So it was that Count Siniscola's eldest son took no part in the attack upon Hellemark.

At evening, a handful of knights rode back to Roccablanca. A handful, out of all the hundreds that had ridden out in wild pursuit when the men of Hellemark, bearing with them the body of their Baron, had fled the field.

Andrea, Count Alessandro's youngest son—his father's image and handsomest of the Siniscolas, came into the bedroom where Iolanthe lay. He came very slowly, trailing blood from a dozen minor wounds. He stood there looking at his brother. He tried to speak. He could not. His lips moved, shaping words; but nothing came out of them—no sounds at all.

Enzio stared at him, dumbly. Then he saw his eyes. He leaped to his feet, gripped his young brother by both arms, hard.

"Tell me!" he got out, "by God's love, Andrea—tell me!"

"Tricked . . ." Andrea mumbled. "He was there, leading them —not a mark upon him. He held in his hand an arrow—its head a mass of shapeless pitch—tricked!"

"That archer," Enzio whispered, "his man, planted there by him, so that we might be drawn beyond the walls . . . And father threw that villain a hundred tarens!"

Andrea slumped into a chair.

"That," he said very quietly, so quietly that Enzio had to strain his ears to hear him, "will never concern—our father—again, my brother. . . ."

Enzio stared at him, his face working. The question he could find no voice for, leaped into his eyes.

Slowly Andrea nodded.

"And Ippolito," he whispered, "and—Ludovico. . . . We Siniscolas have been beaten by an upstart—a serf's son . . . God, God, God! How we were slaughtered! Like sheep—like pigs—in all my life, Enzio, I've seen so many fair knights. . . ."

Io stirred. Groaned.

"What ails her?" Andrea whispered. "You—you didn't . . . ?"

"No. She thought him dead—and found my dagger. Andrea, by God's love, I conjure you! She must never know—that he lives. . . ."

Andrea laughed, cruelly.

"So abject, my brother? So willing to do anything at all to retain your soiled, second-hand goods?"

Enzio got to his feet. Then he stopped, mumbling to himself.

"Too many dead," he whispered. "Far too many—let us not quarrel, Andrea. . . ."

"No," Andrea said. "We cannot, can we—how that villein's bastard would laugh if the last two Siniscolas alive slew each other." He got up from the chair and strode about, forgetting his wounds.

"He beat us, Enzio, because he was a serf. Because his mind worked in dirty, unknightly ways . . . like having shifts of foot to reload the crossbows and pass them to the archers, so that instead of riding the clumsy arbalisters down as usual, there was not one second that we weren't under fire. Like fixing lances aslant under the hedgerows so that when our bravest knights charged behind father and Ippolito and Ludovico and me in spite of the quarrels, our horses impaled themselves so that in one minute there was a mound of thrashing, screaming horseflesh piled up ten deep; and those behind, unable to check their mounts, crashed into it and from the walls and from that trench the quarrels whined, then the catapults started sending down bolts as big as spears that pinned horses to the ground and the trenchbuts rained boulders down until whole parts of the earth were covered with entrails of beast and man; and last of all they released the mangonels with casks of Greek fire. . . ."

He stopped. He passed the tip of his tongue over his lips. Looked at Io, then again at his brother.

"We fled then—those of us who were still alive. But he—may hellfire consume his soul—had thought even of that. From the edge of the wood he came—riding at the head of a party of horsemen three times greater than ours. Oh, damn him! Damn him! I shall never forgive what he did next . . ."

"What?" Enzio whispered.

"He lifted up his hand and commanded that two thirds of his party fall back; and came out and fought us man to man with not one man greater in number than we! I could bear being beaten by overwhelming numbers, but he charged them on pain of death to stay out of it—He fought me. . . ."

Enzio waited.

"You know how small he is? He was like a serpent, everywhere at once while I hacked air and panted, he sat there laughing, giving me always the point of a sword like a child's toy, never missing, that point flickering in, stabbing, stabbing, until the world reeled, and then he brought a little broadaxe he carried down the back of Demon's neck and the poor beast went down and I with him . . . Three of my knights came to me and he killed one of them—Francesco, I think—the others got me up. But it was over then. Only that handful you saw, came back with me—and that, Enzio, by his leave—by his gracious leave—that child of the dungheap, standing there and permitting us graciously to go without ransom and without pursuit—speaking fair words, bearing himself so like a knight—it's that I cannot forgive!"

"He gave me leave to go once without ransom," Enzio whispered. "I cannot understand him—my life alone stood between him and his possession of Io—and he would not take it. . . ."

"He has a serpent's mind," Andrea said slowly. "There are other tortures than those of the flesh. And how subtly does he know to use them! Putting our nobility to shame by acting more lordly than any lord—heaping coals of fire upon our souls with graciousness. . . ."

"You must have those wounds looked to," Enzio said.

"So I must," Andrea whispered. But he made no move to go.

In the morning a servant awakened the brothers.

"My Lords!" he cried. "Come to the walls, as God lives, I beg you—come!"

Drugged with sleep and fatigue they followed him, and there they saw it.

A procession of monks from the abbey—bearing tapers. The deep-voiced chanting of the requiem mass. The Abbot himself going before, holding aloft the crucifix praying. And there—with two monks before and two after each one—three biers, borne on the shoulders of knights. Bareheaded knights, without weapons. And upon the biers the still forms, covered over with the banners of the noble house of Siniscola. . . .

"Cause the gates to be opened," Enzio whispered.

They went down into the bailey. The procession filed in. A monk stepped forward, passed Enzio a scroll. Enzio read it, gave it to Andrea.

"From His Lordship, Pietro, by God's Grace, and by Eternal

Grant of His Puissant Majesty, Frederick II, Emperor of the Romans; Baron Rogliano, done by his own hand at Castle Hellemark, this Twentieth Day of December, Anno Domini 1220,

"To the Lords of Siniscola, greetings:

"I return you the bodies of your brothers and your father, that you may give them Christian burial. They sinned grievously in their lives, but of that, let the good God be the judge. They gave unto my father and my guardian death by torture; unto them I rendered knightly death in the field—without undue pain, and with full honors.

"Yet now, I repent me even of that, for it seems to me that vengeance is a thing of God not of men. I have therefore instructed His Grace the Abbot that perpetual masses be said for their souls, the expense of which I have undertaken.

"Now, touching Castle Roccablanca, I am, as you know, under orders from His Majesty to force you to surrender it. Since you lack both the men and the means to further defend it, I suggest that you surrender it within the week to his Grace, the Abbot, whom I have empowered to receive it in the name of the Emperor.

"I have no interest in Roccablanca. I have no desire to set foot within its walls. I obey, simply, the orders of my Liege Lord. Therefore, I suggest to you that you present yourself to him at his temporary headquarters at Foggia and throw yourself upon His mercy. You may do this with security, as I have already written him asking clemency for you, in view of the fate that has already befallen your house. In the past, His Majesty has, without notable exception, paid gracious heed to my humble requests.

"Should you not comply with this within five days, I shall, regrettably, be forced to attack.

Signed,

Pietro, Baron Rogliano"

"Dear God!" Andrea whispered.

On the fifth day thereafter, they surrendered Roccablanca to the Abbot. There was nothing else they could do. The Abbot in his turn, granted them leave to remain in the castle until the Lady Iolanthe was well enough to travel.

At Foggia, in early Spring of 1221, Frederick refused to renew the grant to Roccablanca, sending instead a garrison of his own to fortify it. Then, almost as an afterthought, he granted them a small fief near Loreto not twenty miles from Iesi, remarking as he did so, that they owed this indulgence to the intercession of the new Baron Rogliano.

Thus did Pietro di Donati have his revenge.

Chapter Nine

WHAT HAD LAIN between him and the House of Siniscola was far from finished. Pietro knew that. Waldo and Rainaldo, his knights, were loud in their complaints that leaving any man of that blood alive was folly. It was. But Pietro had had enough of bloodshed. There were degrees, limits beyond which he could not go. He had drawn their talons. It would be years before they built up sufficient power to attack him openly. And the fanatical loyalty of his men was protection enough against assassins and poisoners.

He had, during that season of Christmas, ample time for thinking. He sat before the great log fire in the hall at Hellemark, with Waldo and Rainaldo. But he did not talk to them. On the wall were bright tapestries—only a few, just those that had been woven by Iolanthe's hand. And in the fire the memories shaped themselves in momentary pictures made of flame.

There were things a man could do, and things he could not. A man could win victories; take terrible vengeance upon his foes. A man could become knight and baron, lord over men and lands, powerful and respected.

But man could win no victories over himself. He could not fill the emptiness in his heart. Or subdue his memories.

Just twenty miles away at a small castle that the Siniscolas had held, Rocca d'Aquilino, a woman sat. A young woman, some twenty-three years of age. All the countryside sang her beauty; priest and vassal alike urged her to wed. All reports that had come to Pietro, Baron Rogliano, confirmed the vivid memories that he had of her. Elaine of Siniscola seemed lovely to other eyes besides his own.

Yet, he had not seen her. It required only a slight effort of the will, for him to rise and ride those twenty miles. Bearing gifts, perhaps; taking his lute to sing her songs of love and tenderness.

But he could not make that effort. He was bound here before this fire in sullen idleness, gazing upon tapestries of gold that loved, lost hands had made. Lost. Bound indissolubly now to Enzio by a tie so close that God alone held the breaking of it.

Pietro, Baron Rogliano. He formed the title in his mind, mockingly. How that would have delighted him once. Now it was nothing. Words scrawled upon the wind. Honors written with a reed upon the surface of the water.

In thirty years, the House of Rogliano had changed blood four times. First there had been the Italian Roglianos, bearers by right of birth of that proud name. They had died. By natural causes some of them; but the rest by the sword of the valiant Orri of Grostete a Norman knight, follower of the last Norman King of Sicily—the maternal grandfather of Frederick, William II. Then Rudolph of Brandenburg, Io's father, had in his turn put the Norman to the sword to become by blood and conquest the second foreigner to hold the fief and the name Rogliano. Then Enzio of Siniscola, by poison and craft had taken Hellemark and the fief, though in fact he had never become Baron Rogliano, being unable during Frederick's absence to obtain the grant, holding it therefore, without confirmation.

Now at last Rogliano was once more an Italian fief. But held by a bachelor. A man without sons. A man who sat listlessly before the fire and would not go wooing.

How can I? Pietro told himself. How can a man sing and mouth tender words when his heart is dead? I could praise her beauty, for she is fair; but she'd see in an instant how little enthusiasm I had for beauty or for her. Women are never fools in such matters. It is said that she has no desire to wed again, having had such happiness with that Ricardo, that she cannot bear to leave the memory of him. I can understand that. It's a feeling that I share.

My happiness with Io was but bits and snatches, but it was—happiness. . . .

I owe it to the fief and to my Lord Frederick to wed. But I need more time. A year perhaps to heal my heart of these fresh wounds which ripped open the very scars of the old ones. That is the one thing I have never had in all my life—time that was really my own. Before, time was waiting, hoping that life would open up to me. It was a tyrannical master, never my servant. Now when I have become a Lord, and achieved my wealth, my honors, and know finally that Io is lost to me, time is emptiness . . . It is so now, but there is in it now the quality of acceptance in which the hurt grows dull, the wounds flesh themselves again with scars—tender and sore, yes, but better than the ache and the bleeding. . . .

He heard Manfred, his seneschal, coming up behind him. Pietro did not turn.

"Yes, Manfred?" he said tiredly.

"A courier of His Majesty," Manfred whispered, with ill suppressed excitement. "He won't give his message to anyone but you, My Lord."

"Send him in," Pietro said and rose. He had little curiosity about this message, for he was almost sure he knew what it contained. He had dispatched a message in great haste—sending it by carrier pigeon, a method that Isaac had learned from the Arabs, and that the Emperor himself had now adopted, receiving from Pietro a goodly supply of the valuable birds. This message that Pietro had sent, contained merely the news that he held Hellemark and that Roccablanca had been surrendered. He had, too, in a previous message, advised Frederick that the Siniscolas would probably appear before him to ask clemency, and interceded for them—largely for Io's sake.

The Emperor's message, he was sure, would only acknowledge all this, and perhaps give some small further instructions. He was not even surprised that Frederick had sent a special courier. (The Emperor could not in any case have replied by pigeon post, because there had been no birds domiciled at Hellemark for the long period necessary for their homing instincts to become accustomed to it.) Besides, the use of pigeons while unbelievably fast, limited the length of the message, as the birds could carry no great weight of parchment; and Frederick was accustomed to expressing his ideas and his commands in some detail. . . .

He took the scroll of parchment from the courier and broke the imperial seals. As he expected, it expressed Frederick's pleasure at Pietro's rapid accomplishment of the task he had asked for, and consented to Pietro's request that Enzio be given some means of supporting his wife and his child.

But the rest of it was a shock. Frederick wrote:

"The Queen complains that Prince Henry has been fretful of late and not in the very best of health. We are aware that you do not share Our fixed belief that the stars control the destinies of men. Still it seems to us [Frederick, Pietro understood, spoke only of himself. The 'We' was only the Royal plural, designed to honor the throne; it did not include the Queen. Frederick, Pietro knew well, and smiled over that knowledge, was incapable of even entertaining the idea that a woman's head could contain anything worthy of note. In this, as in many other things, he was pure Oriental] that it is an unjustified risk that you continue to break the pattern of our star-linked lives. We sent for the records of the church at Iesi. They confirm your statements in every detail. We commanded brought before us, certain elderly citizens of the town—eyewitnesses of the events surrounding our birth—and yours. Ah, Pietro, what a marvel that was! As you said, we almost *caused* you to be born upon that day. . . .

"We are therefore impatient at your delays. The matters at hand being settled, we command you, therefore, to seek out the lady of your choice—we have been informed that she lives nearby at Rocca d'Aquilino—and lay siege to her heart.

"Should she prove overly reluctant We shall be forced to take a hand in the matter. In Our new laws, handed down at Capua, no subject can wed without Our consent. This we give unto you willingly. Further, if the matter is not accomplished to our satisfaction by February Last, we shall deem it fitting to hand down to the lady a royal command.

"Once you are wed, we shall send you a horoscope upon which

will be indicated the best days and hours for consummation in order to insure the conception of a male heir.[1]

"Our thanks and our blessing.

Signed,

Fredericus,

Rex et Imperator

Foggia, December 1220."

The last day of February. A little more than two months. Pietro stood there, holding the letter, his eyes dark and brooding. Then he sighed.

"Good seneschal," he said, "See that this knight is fed and courteously entertained. I shall dispatch an answer to—this by him on the morrow."

His gaze strayed to the walls, where in gold and scarlet, the deeds of the vanished house of Brandenburg were displayed.

"And Manfred," he added, "send one of the maids to me. . . ."

When the girl came she found Pietro once more sitting by the fire.

"My Lord?" she murmured.

"Maria," Pietro said, "take down those tapestries from the walls. They have become a sickness before my eyes. . . ."

Then he leaned forward, staring into the fire.

It was cold, that next day, and driving rain sent down needles of ice. Pietro, and his twenty men at arms were bundled in cloaks and furs. Two of them led mules, laden with costly gifts. Under his cloak, Pietro was magnificently clad. He wore no mail, but instead a suit of red velvet, as dark as wine or old blood, embroidered with goldthread and encrusted with rubies. Inside his riding boots his velvet shoes were stiff with golden ornaments. About his throat was a great golden chain, bearing on a pendant the newly set coat of arms for his house, in enameled gold.

That Elaine would receive him, he had no doubt. The rules of everyday courtesy demanded that a nobleman or woman give shelter in her castle to passing knights who came in peace. Beyond that, he was worried. It was a strange feeling to ride out to seek the hand of a woman who had never bothered to hide her distaste for him and whose hand he was seeking with none of the customary motives. . . .

Great barons, it was true, seldom married for love. But their reasons were usually sound and sensible: to combine great fiefs, to bring into their coffers the wealth of a widowed lady.

But Elaine's holdings were negligible, and would constitute more of a burden than an advantage. She was poor, which didn't concern Pietro—because his own wealth was impressive, and becoming greater all the time.

If he loved her, that would be a different matter. But his heart was a burnt out ember, incapable of love. He was being driven into this loveless match at the commands of the Emperor, commands founded upon a towering nonsensical superstition unworthy of so great a man. That was the only chink in Frederick's armor; his one blind spot. Already the Emperor was commanding his Cistercian monks to commence scientific experiments that would put Sicilian agriculture years ahead of that in the rest of Europe. There were treatises upon scientific animal breeding—some from the Emperor's own hand—that would improve beef cattle and sheepbreeding immeasurably. Frederick tried everything. He knew the ways of birds, his savants could, with amazing accuracy, predict the weather. They were even experimenting upon ways to control it. He talked of founding a secular university, staffed with lawyers and Saracen scientists, which would have a free hand to explore all the avenues of truth, unhampered by religion or priestly control. He granted pensions to mathematicians and geometers, and everywhere his keen mind was pushing back the darkness of ignorance and superstition—except here. He believed that the stars controlled men. He would not set foot upon a new project until his seers had cast horoscopes determining if the time were propitious. Because of that, Pietro must beget a son, to preserve the pattern that the Emperor believed existed between them. Because of that, he must wed this woman who perhaps hated him—this woman possibly incapable of opening her heart to love. . . .

They rode slowly because the weather was terrible. Even the fur-lined cloaks could not keep out all of the chill. They had started long before dawn, but it took them until almost nightfall to make the ride to Rocca d'Aquilino. The mud was a curse. The horses had to pick their way, and could make but little speed.

When they reached the castle, the torches were already lit upon the walls. But the guards at the gate were friendly. After years of service under the amiable Ricardo, whom all his neighbors loved, they had all but lost their suspiciousness toward the rest of mankind. Pietro was glad of that. After the most casual inspection had revealed the fact that his retinue rode without armor, and was armed only with daggers, the sergeant at arms sent word to his lady without even bothering to ask Pietro's name.

Her answer was immediate and gracious. The gates were opened wide, and the Lady Elaine, herself, greeted Pietro at the door of the little *palais*. She was dressed, still, in the white of widowhood. She was small and well formed and willow slender.

And beautiful.

It was then, at that moment, that he stepped into the light of the hallway and she saw his face.

He saw her stiffen. She was pale to begin with; but now she was white. Death white. She stood there a long moment, looking at him.

"You!" she whispered. The word shuddered up from the depths of an unutterable loathing. Pietro stared at her.

"Courtesy forbids me," she said, "to turn you out upon such a night. Yet I can only request of you that you quit my house as early as possible tomorrow. I—I have had many sorrows. But none so great as being asked to entertain—the murderer of my kindred!"

Pietro took a backward step. Of all the possible contingencies he had turned over in his mind, this one had never occurred to him. This simplest, most logical one of all: that this great lady of Italy's proudest blood would react so to the deaths of the relatives she had always held in high esteem.

Yet, oddly, he found himself intrigued by the challenge. There were arms enough and mail enough in some of the mule borne coffers for his twenty knights to take this castle in five minutes of fighting. Elaine had no men-at-arms to speak of. Only Frederick's presence in Italy, and the love her neighbors bore her had prevented her possessions—and her person—from being taken by force long ago.

She could not make him go—he began the thought; but then he changed it. She could. Of all the things on earth that Pietro was incapable of, warring upon a woman headed the list. He felt, suddenly, almost happy. This command of the Emperor's was going to be precious easy to obey. He'd always despised doll-like women. One of Io's chief charms had been her fire. . . .

God! In five minutes, how many of his highflown denials had vanished! What manner of man or fool was he that this rebuff should heat his blood like wine?

He bowed to her, deeply.

"As My Lady wills," he said. "My men and I will quit Rocca d'Aquilino within the hour. But first, I crave of My Lady a boon: that she see that my knights are fed, and the animals fed and watered. It's a long ride back to Hellemark. . . ."

She thawed a little. But only a little.

"You need not ride tonight," she said. "You may stay and sup your fill. Only do not request of me that I honor you by my presence at the table. . . ."

"I will not ask it. But I will ask one thing more: that My Lady consent to hear from my lips the story of my warfare with her kindred. Even a felon is given the right to speak before he is hanged. My Lady would condemn me without knowing one word of my history. . . ."

"I know enough," she said. "It was you who began all the trouble in the first place, by kidnapping and ravishing my cousin Iolanthe many years ago. . . ."

"You believe that?" Pietro said incredulously.

"No," she said. "I don't. I know Io. Enzio was a fool to marry her. She was of a great house, but that neither made her a lady, nor prevented her from having the morals of a dairymaid!"

Pietro's face tightened.

"Were you a man, My Lady," he whispered, "I would slay you for those words."

"Don't let that bother you. There is enough Siniscola blood on your hands to make your scruple over my sex a trifle. . . ."

Pietro shook his head. This was going badly. He looked around him. His knights had been led into the banquet hall by her seneschal. He put out his hands suddenly and took her wrists.

"Sit down," he said harshly. "To this you will listen whether you will or not. I have suffered enough at the hands of the Siniscolas. In return I have dealt with them honorably—far beyond their deserving . . . You remember the siege of Rezzi?"

"Yes," she whispered.

"After that siege, your uncle, Count Alessandro, hanged my father to an olive tree, after having tortured him in ways that sicken my stomach to think about, much less describe to you. On top of that he took gold of my guardian to spare my father's life, kept the gold, hanged my guardian upside down from the parapet of Roccablanca after having ripped open his belly. And Enzio took me, after you, My Lady, had told him of my whereabouts, and cast me into a dungeon, from which I escaped finally, only because of your change of heart . . . You remember that?"

"Yes," she said. "And now I weep at my folly in aiding you!"

"No matter," Pietro said. "In exchange for these and other such fair courtesies, I fought your kindred upon the field of battle, at my Emperor's express command, since they would not submit their grant to him for his examination. I slew them—true. But in knightly fashion, exposing my body to their swords. I could have captured them, tortured them—but I have not in me the capacity to descend to the depths of bestiality so characteristic of your kindred's house. . . .

"I gave them honor in their deaths, sending their bodies under escort of monks to Roccablanca for burial. I spared Andrea's life, released him from capture. I spared Enzio, not once, but twice. And because I am in some ways, a Christian, I provided with the abbot for perpetual masses to be said for their souls.

"Additionally, I begged of my liege lord, the Emperor, that Enzio and Andrea be given a fief to compensate them in some measure for their disasters—disasters brought upon themselves by their stubbornness, of which I was but the instrument. . . ."

Elaine stared at him. Her mouth was a tight line across her face.

"You expect me to believe all this?" she said.

"Why not," Pietro answered. "Since every word of it—is true."

"As true," Elaine said tartly, "as the fact that you made a cuckold of my cousin Enzio with his lady?"

"As true as that," Pietro said. "As true as the other fact that Io and I had given each other solemn pledges of eternal love since our childhood. As true as that she was snatched from my arms by force and wedded against her will and bowed in tears to that beast! You were at the wedding. You saw how overjoyed she was at becoming your cousin's wife."

Elaine looked away from him.

"Yes," she whispered. "I saw that—and I pitied her. But, My Lord—how mad has the world become that I must call a villein's son—My Lord!—she could not have wed you, since you were not gently born. . . ."

"No great house was in the beginning. Every barony in Italy is the former abode of brigands who fortified a height and robbed all who passed by, who accepted the allegiance of lesser brigands, and with their swords' edges hacked their patents of nobility from the flesh of living men. It will not always be so, My Lady—the time will come when men will know that goodness of heart and greatness of soul are the only true tests of nobility—not the wild accident of birth. . . ."

"And these, of course, you have?" Elaine said bitterly.

"No," Pietro said, and looked away from her. "If I had had these things I could have forgiven your cousins for their crimes against my kindred and my friends. I could have obeyed the teachings of Mary's gentle son. I had it not in me to forgive. I was choked with hate—of which I repent me greatly!"

"Why?" Elaine whispered.

"Because of you, My Lady. I am a lonely man. I have become reconciled to my loss of Io—who, despite your harsh words, is a great lady, of high honor. You see, for many years—since that day you first turned your back upon me for staring at you, the same day my poor Io's murdered brothers were knighted—I have held a dream of you unbidden in my heart. It was a bright dream. Each time that I have seen you it has grown brighter. Not even your scorn of me, your bitter words, could shake it. You are the loveliest maid I've ever known. And I—God help me—have cherished that loveliness.

"Into my days have been crowded many sorrows. I am tired of grief, sick of loneliness. I want to spend the rest of my days in peace, with sons about me, growing tall in honor. Besides, it is my Emperor's wish that I be wed. . . ."

Elaine stared at him incredulously.

"You thought," she whispered, "that I would marry—*you?*"

"Yes, My Lady," Pietro said.

Elaine stood up. Stared at him.

"Know you, Sire Pietro," she said, "that had you never lifted sword against my kindred, my answer would be the same. Immortal God! that a woman should be so helpless before such insult! Now that my husband no longer lives, I am expected to consort with stableboys—smelling of sweat and horse's dung. . . ."

Pietro stood up. He looked at her a long time, and very clearly.

"I see I am mistaken," he said quietly. "It was my intent to marry a great lady, that my sons be brought up—as I was—in an atmosphere of gentility. But they would be scarcely benefited, would they, by exposure to a shrewish mind, and expressions unseemly even from the tongue of a fishwife. . . ."

"Go!" she screamed at him. "I can't endure the sight of you any longer!"

"I shall give myself the great pleasure of quitting your sight, presently," Pietro said. "But first I would leave with you a challenge. A brave knight never refuses a challenge, nor—a brave knight's lady. And your husband, I have heard, was both a brave knight and an honorable one—the only Siniscola in history who can claim that last distinction. . . ."

She stood there, looking at him.

"Now, here is my challenge. I bid milady investigate by any means at her disposal what happened to the townspeople of Rezzi: why they revolted in the first place, and what fate they suffered after being vanquished. Further, if milady dares, let her discover if she will the fates of Liepold of Brandenburg, Io's uncle, of the gentle lady Brigarde, her mother; and more lately, of her father, and her brothers. Summon before you, milady, Count Alessandro's leech—ply him with questions; but do not put him to torture. Give him assurances of immunity beforehand, a purse of gold afterwards so that you know that he speaks truth and that no lies have been wrung from him. I know how my father and my guardian died, but milady will not believe even the truth, when she hears it from my lips. I bid her, therefore, seek it from the mouths of men and women she knows and trusts —and then if she can find it in her heart still to hate me, I can do no more. . . ."

It was still in the great hall after Pietro had gone. Elaine sat before the fire, and stared into it.

He lied of course, she told herself; he lied, he lied, he lied!

Strange that I have to tell myself that so many times. Serf's son, baseborn peasant (with manners like a prince's, and a face wondrously gentle and sad—good God!—am I mad?), part of a villein's litter—standing there making such accusations against gentle men . . . My uncle Alessandro never—

But there came into her mind a memory of a peasant woman, who in great distress had clung to Count Alessandro's stirrups, begging the life of a peasant boy about to be hanged for poaching. She was seeing again in the fire, her uncle's face twisted almost out of recognition with rage as he rose in his saddle and slashed the woman across the face and back and arms and shoulders with his whip, his arm rising against the blue sky and falling and the lash biting into the woman's filthy smock, cutting through it, bringing blood; and the woman clinging to the stirrups moaning and Count Alessandro slashing at her and she still clinging until at last he spurred his destrier and the great beast bounded off, dragging the woman a full twenty yards until she dropped at last face downward into the dirt and lay there weeping.

And the next day the Count had hanged her son.

Oh God, oh God, Elaine wept, why did I have to think of that? I had pushed it out of my mind, I had forgotten it—it and the faces of the lads with bellies caved in from hunger, swinging by their necks above the moat of Roccablanca. Paying with their lives for a rabbit taken. For a small and furry beast, this punishment for God's creatures—for men with immortal souls. . . .

I won't look into the matter! I won't! I won't!

Why not? If he lied, it will but prove it.

And if—he did not lie?

She didn't want to think about that. The consequences were too horrible.

Pietro had put into her mind a thought that had never existed there before: In God's truth, of what account was gentility of birth, if it were not accompanied by gentility of behavior? She was a great lady, but there was more than a little truth in his accusation that she had acted like a fishwife. It reminded her of one of the things that her mother, the gentle Lady Hilda of Saxony, had said: "The nobles have an obligation to behave nobly—and the greater the difference in class between them and the person with whom they have dealings, the greater the obligations of gentility. . . ."

So few people shared that belief. No one she knew thought it his duty to extend his chivalry toward peasants and serfs. Of course, she had always been kind to them; but beyond that rather impersonal kindness—displayed more often and to greater degree to a pet animal—had she ever really dealt—nobly—with them?

Her cheeks burned suddenly with shame. It came to her that Pietro of Hellemark had had much the better of the exchange. Even in anger he had descended to no real discourtesy—except perhaps when he took her wrists. She looked at them. They were white and unmarked. His touch had been firm, but gentle.

I should wash them! she said suddenly, savagely. I should wash away the touch of filthy peasant paws!

There came into her mind suddenly a surprisingly vivid memory of the look of Pietro's hands: slim, long-fingered, with nails cut square, and clean. The hands of a knight. Of—of a prince. . . .

I am mad, she thought; but her mind went on about its uncontrolled work of remembering with feminine exactness every detail of his dress and his appearance. She had had suitors before. Many of them from within one month of Ricardo's death. But none of them had disturbed her even slightly.

But this peasant did. This serf's son masquerading as knight, as baron.

So perfect a masquerade. All the fair courtesies offered with greater ease and naturalness than any man had offered them before. The compliments paid her beauty in artful, lovely speech, the fair Tuscan rippling from his tongue without a trace of peasant coarseness or violation of syntax. . . .

Rudolfo, her seneschal, came into the hall. He was frowning a little.

"It is strange they left so soon, My Lady," he said. "Never have I met more gentle knights. His Lordship bade me give you these, my Lady. . . ."

He bowed and placed a small casket in her hands. When she opened it, the stones within threw the light back in a hard, multi-colored blaze. They were beautiful. Utterly beautiful.

Elaine was a woman. She could not resist the temptation to take a few of them up and let them trickle back into the casket like greenfire and whiteblaze and blooddrops. Then she slammed the cover shut.

"By accepting them, Rudolfo, you have earned yourself a long and thankless ride. For, tomorrow you must return these to My Lord of Hellemark," she said.

Rudolfo stared at her.

"Begging My Lady's pardon," he said. "All of us—all My Lady's people who love her with all our hearts, are agreed that she has mourned enough. Truly one so young and so exceeding fair should wed again—surely this house should not perish for want of sons. . . ."

"Are you," Elaine said drily, "suggesting that I wed—him?"

"I don't know, My Lady. His knights told me he seeks your hand. It's too early to rightly judge, but I must say that in all my days I have not met a more fair and courteous young knight. . . ."

"I thank you for your interest." Elaine sighed. "Now leave me —no! Rudolfo, do you know that leech, Arturo, who served my late Uncle Count Alessandro?"

Rudolfo's face changed at the mention of that name.

"Yes, My Lady," he said.

Elaine studied his face.

"Why did you grimace, Rudolfo," she whispered, "when I mentioned my uncle?"

"Grimaced? I? My Lady must not think. . . ."

"Don't be afraid, Rudolfo," Elaine said. "There are things I must know—certain questions that have been raised by My Lord of Hellemark—" (Strange how easy it was becoming to use that phrase now, how simply, readily the words My Lord came. . . .)

She looked Rudolfo full in the face.

"Why did you grimace, Rudolfo?" she said.

"I—I'm but a poor and landless knight, My Lady," Rudolfo begged. "Please, My Lady—men have lost their lives by expressing opinions not pleasant to the ear of the gentlefolk who asked them. . . ."

"Rudolfo, you have my pledge that no harm will befall you if you speak freely. Do you require of me that I swear upon the hair of Saint Anne that is embedded in my crucifix? If so, go and fetch it."

"My Lady's word is assurance enough," Rudolfo whispered. "What would my gracious Lady know?"

"Why my dead uncle's name could bring such an expression to your face. That's all. Pietro of Hellemark slew my uncle. He seeks my forgiveness and claims justification. What say you to that?"

"Forgive me, My Lady," Rudolfo said; "but any man alive who slew your uncle has both justification and the blessing of the entire fief. Know you what the peasants called him?"

"No," Elaine whispered.

"Count Satan. I don't doubt that Satan himself was flattered. Remember My Lady, that you asked me, and gave me leave to speak freely."

"Nor do I withdraw it. Tell me more. Do you know aught of the siege of Rezzi?"

"Yes, My Lady. There had been three years of crop failures in a row. The peasants were starving. They begged your uncle for succor. He—he beat them. Finally they could stand no more the sight of their children dying in their mothers' arms. They revolted. Count Alessandro slaughtered them like sheep. Those who escaped fled into Rezzi, where one Donati—a blond giant of a man utterly without fear and of great nobility, being, people say, a natural son of Baron Orri of Grostete, the former Baron Rogliano—fought off your uncle for weeks.

"The town fell, of course. Then occurred things of such cruelty that my brother Nicolo, who fought in the siege, fled your uncle's service rather than take part in them. Men impaled upon stakes, crucified upside down, dragged to death by wild horses—drawn and quartered. . . ."

"No more, good Rudolfo," Elaine whispered. "By God's love—no more!"

"You asked me, My Lady," Rudolfo said.

"So I did. Rudolfo, in the morning take back to Baron Pietro his gift. Then summon me Arturo, the leech from Iesi. Bring me, too, whatever knights who have spent above fifteen years in my uncle's service. I want to question them, too. . . ."

"Might I ask why, My Lady?"

"Pietro, Baron Rogliano, is the son of that Donati you spoke of. He was baseborn. But from your words, I see that there is perhaps reason for the ease with which he bears himself in his new role. Baron Orri was a great knight. Tell me, Rudolfo—is it true then that my Uncle had this Donati killed?"

Rudolfo stared at her wonderingly.

"*He* led the revolt, My Lady. Enzio, Ippolito, Ludovico and Andrea tormented him with their own hands—him alone they did not commit to the regular executioners. Which poor Donati had cause to regret, for your cousins, My Lady, were much more expert at torture than any executioner. It took Donati four hours longer to die than any other man. . . ."

"God!" Elaine whispered.

"I'm sorry, My Lady," Rudolfo said.

So it was that Rainaldo, Pietro's man, returned from Iesi a few days later in high glee.

"You've won, My Lord!" he laughed. "She is making those inquiries! She has summoned Arturo, that murderous leech to appear before her. Several ancient knights of Count Siniscola have been called, too. I would wager my good horse, Belacon, that in a few days My Lord will receive a letter begging him to come to her. . . ."

"I wouldn't be too sure about that, Rainaldo. After all, she returned my gift. . . ."

"But that, My Lord," Rainaldo said, "was before she knew the truth. . . ."

January came to a close. The mountains above Hellemark were white with winter snows. But from Rocca d'Aquilino—no word. No word at all.

I should forget it, Pietro thought. I could tell the Emperor I will wed any other maid he deems suitable. She has proof and it moves her not. She knows now that I was right, and still she hates me. . . .

It came to him then, that justice was seldom a thing that carried much weight in the human mind. The presentation of proof of the wrongness of people loved, might inspire only greater fury. What indeed was more terrible than to have the beliefs you'd cherished for your entire lifetime—in the nobility, kindness, honor of those you loved—smashed in an instant? With what could he replace her pride in being a Siniscola?

With love? With tenderness?

Which she might not accept. Which in truth, he might not have truly to give.

I could love her because she is fair because there is fire in her and greatness I could try to bring her happiness to make her forget, I who cannot myself forget, whose heart is lined all over with the scars of old wounds and whose memory is filled with the memory of Io . . . Dear God! If finally I should marry her, will I still in the night in the dark and secret places of my soul awake crying for the loved the lost the forever lost the unforgotten?

In the morning, he mounted his horse, and rode alone and unescorted to Rocca d'Aquilino. Rudolfo greeted him at the gate with a broad grin.

"We have waited a long time for you to return, My Lord," he whispered. "I'm glad of the chance to tell you, that all of us—all her people are on your side. We have been urging that our Lady send for you. . . ."

"Which," Pietro said, as he swung down from the saddle, "she did not do."

"She is confused, My Lord. The discovery of her cousins' villainy has been a great shock to her. She weeps often, and is much troubled. Now, if My Lord will deal gently with her, and have much patience. . . ."

"How, Sire Rudolfo," Pietro said, "do you even know that she will receive me?"

"Truthfully, I don't," Rudolfo said. "But I think she will. She is a very gentle lady, and upon yesterday, the abbot visited her. From him she had the story of the perpetual masses you ordered for the souls of men who had wrought you every evil—and the knightly courtesies you offered their remains . . . She wept a long time, but, I think, less bitterly. . . ."

"Then go and announce me, Sire Rudolfo," Pietro said.

She did not come down and greet him as before, but Rudolfo ushered him into her chamber. She looked at him a long time, before she said:

"Greetings, My Lord Rogliano." Then she turned away her eyes.

Pietro said nothing. He sat there studying her profile by the firelight. It was the loveliest he had ever seen. And the saddest.

"If," he whispered finally, "my presence grieves you, I will go. . . ."

She didn't answer him.

He stood, put out his hand to take his cloak.

"Don't go," Elaine said quietly.

Pietro sank once more into the chair.

Still no word. She seemed to be struggling with herself. He could not help her.

"Of all men on earth, My Lord," she said at last, "you have caused me the greatest grief. First—by destroying my cousins. And secondly by destroying them over again—in my heart. . . ."

"I'm sorry, My Lady," Pietro said.

"Don't be. What fault is it of yours? You could have done them no harm had they been blameless. I made the inquiries you suggested. I tried not to. I wasn't going to—but I stumbled upon some information here in my own house that gave color to the things you said. After that I had in honor to find out. . . ."

"And?" Pietro said.

"I discovered that you had uttered not one syllable of untruth. That they killed your father, and the Jew—by fiendish tortures. That God Himself could not forgive what they did to the people of Rezzi. Iolanthe's uncle. Her mother—indirectly. Her father and her brothers almost certainly—by poison. I had that leech hanged. I'm sorry, but then I'm a Siniscola, too—and I made you no promises. . . ."

Pietro stared at her. He felt cold suddenly.

"When I look at you, My Lord—I wonder. Are you really kind—or the most subtle fiend who ever drew breath? You refrained from torture. You held back more than half of your superior forces and fought them man to man. You released Enzio—though to slay him would have certainly given you Io. You released Andrea. You spent a small fortune for masses for my cousins' souls—gave them every honor in their deaths . . . This seems to me to go beyond kindness. . . ."

"Then what was it, My Lady?"

"I don't know. What goes on inside that head of yours, Sire Pietro? You're not mad. Old soldiers told me that the way you fought was a masterpiece of purest cunning. That you outgeneraled, outthought, outfought my cousins at every turn. Perhaps, then, you discovered the one way to outdo them in cruelty, too. . . ."

Pietro's eyes were dark with wonder. He anticipated her thought. Was she wrong? He wasn't sure.

"They would have died of torture without whimpering. The Siniscolas were the bravest men alive and the proudest. Dying, they would have defeated you by their courage. But you didn't give them that chance, did you? Instead, you honored them, heaped knightly courtesies upon them, forced them to receive from a serf's son, the subtlest of all defeats—the cruelest of all tortures—that of being outdone in chivalry by one whom they had despised, that of being taught a lesson in noblesse oblige—by one who had no true claim to nobility. . . ."

Pietro sat there, waiting.

"The Holy Writ alone explains it fully. The second mile, the turned cheek. And after that, the true, the barbaric reason, killing the pride in a man: 'For, by so doing, you heap coals of fire upon his head!' But My Lord, My Lord, why must you heap them, too—upon my heart?"

She bowed her head, and wept stormily.

Pietro came over to her and took her, very gently, in his arms.

She did not shrink away from him, or struggle to be released. She put her face against his *bliaut* and sobbed like a child. A lost child, frightened of the dark.

He tilted her head back with his hand and found her mouth. She did not struggle even against that. But her lips were like ice. As unresponsive as death itself. Slowly she quieted.

"I don't know," Pietro whispered, still holding her in his arms, "if you are right or wrong about that. I don't know myself why I behaved as I did. The reasons I do things are often unclear to me. It's only now that I am clear about one thing—I can come to love you, if you'll let me. You could make me forget Io, and find peace. . . ."

She looked up at him, studying his face.

"You," she whispered, "you—you held me in your arms. You kissed me . . . An hour ago, I would have died before I permitted that. I can believe that you don't know your own mind—for now I don't know my own thoughts either . . . I should hate you, and I don't. I should despise you as being of peasant blood. And yet I cannot even think of that—or believe it when I see you . . . You're as fair as any prince, as courteous—and I—and I—Oh, God—I'm afraid!"

"That you may come to love me?" Pietro whispered.

"Yes," she whimpered. "Oh, yes, yes, yes!"

"Don't be afraid," Pietro said gently. "I think that you would never regret it. It's only in your mind that you dishonor yourself by wedding me; men care no longer how or where or to whom I was born. . . ."

She lay quietly against his shoulder.

"They say," she murmured, "that you were knighted by the King of France, for saving his life in battle. And afterwards by the Emperor Frederick himself, for services to the crown. Is that true?"

"Yes," Pietro said. "But in this, as in all other things, you need not take my word for it."

"You wouldn't lie," she said tiredly. "You could not hold Hellemark without the Emperor's consent. You're a Baron now, and your sons will be Barons after you, and after a time no man will think to question their nobility. . . ."

"Which is precisely," Pietro said drily, "how all nobility came into being. . . ."

"I know. Now leave me till tomorrow. It grows late, and I want to think. . . ."

"Will you," Pietro said, "give me your answer tomorrow?"

"Hardly. It requires more thinking than that. A month maybe —or two. In the meantime, you are always welcome here. That way, perhaps, I shall accustom myself to the sight of you. . . ."

Pietro kissed her once more. She stiffened, but that was all. She didn't draw away, or turn aside her face.

A month, Pietro thought. Or two. A race with time before Frederick's impatience could spoil things.

God help me if he will not wait, Pietro mused, and followed the servant toward the chamber they had prepared for him.

Chapter Ten

WHAT WAS BETWEEN them now, was a quiet thing. Quiet, and pale, and unsubstantial as water. Ever shifting. Sometimes it seemed to Pietro that there was warmth in her voice when she greeted him; at other times there was a sudden, frightening upsurge of revulsion. But every time she flared up at him, calling him "stableboy," "upstart peasant," "churlish knave," she would beg his pardon most humbly upon his next visit. The first time it had happened, Pietro had stayed away from her. Whereupon she had sent for him, sending him a charmingly worded missive in her own hand, full of misspellings, childish expressions, and awkward constructions.

Pietro was almost sure she loved him now. But she would not surrender to that love. She fought it with all her strength. And her strength, Pietro learned, was great.

February, 1221, had but days more to last. Pietro hoped with all his heart that the Emperor would not interfere. Frederick was very busy. At his coronation, he had taken the cross again from the hand of Cardinal Hugo of Ostia[1] and promised to sail for the Holy Land in August, 1221. That, Pietro knew, was a promise quite impossible for him to keep. There remained the matter of the Count of Molise, who held out stubbornly. Additionally, Frederick meant to remove all the Saracens from the Island of Sicily. The ramifications of the things he was trying to do were staggering: Little by little, never bothering to conceal his aims, he was creating a monolithic state. Roccablanca was staffed by his garrisons now, as was every other castle he had captured. Pietro, himself, had been informed, that while the Emperor was willing to await his convenience, within the next two years, Frederick expected him to surrender Hellemark and build himself a pleasant manor house upon his fief. The fief was his; but castles and other fortifications could only belong to the Emperor. It meant the end of feudalism in Italy. Pietro was not sorry to see it go. With his engineers, he drew up the plan for a villa so lovely that, out of pride, he submitted a copy to Frederick.

Frederick's response was immediate, and characteristic:

"We," he wrote, "have had your plan copied, and the copies distributed to all the nobles who have surrendered their castles. To us, it seems a masterpiece of the builder's art. We have informed our subjects that we will permit deviations from this plan, but only in minor details, so eminently does it suit us. When you have completed it, you will inform us of that fact; for, if the pressure of the affairs of state do not hold us, we will pay you a visit, and inspect it personally.

"We command you additionally, to draw up for us a plan of a fortress-castle to be built at Foggia. It must be invulnerable to attack, and yet must contain within the fair comforts that you have indicated for your villa. . . .

"We note, with some displeasure that you say nothing of whether or not you have wed the Lady Elaine. We wish to remind you that but little remains of the time we allotted you for the accomplishment of this matter. . . ."

There was more, but Pietro scarcely read it. He swore long and feelingly. Once more had his pride betrayed him. He should have known to let well enough alone. He didn't want his fine villa duplicated up and down the length of Italy; and he certainly did not want Frederick interfering in his affair with Elaine. Yet, he was powerless to prevent it.

He toyed with the idea of informing Elaine that Frederick might take a hand. But he knew with painful exactness what her reaction would be: all the gains he had made, all the slow, quiet progress in gaining her confidence, even her liking, would be swept away in an instant, before this—this which she could only regard as a naked display of force.

He, therefore, occupied himself for some days with the plans for the castle at Foggia. Frederick had left Foggia; he was no longer in Apulia at all; but in Calabria, the toe of the Italian boot. Pietro knew that there was no need for haste, that it would be years before Frederick could commence to build a castle at Foggia; but the plan gave himself something to do—it kept his mind from being overly tormented with worry.

He was still working upon the rough sketch, consulting with his engineers over the details, when, on the afternoon of the second of March, Manfred, his seneschal came to him almost speechless with astonishment.

"My Lord!" he gasped. "My Lord!"

"You've said 'My Lord' twice," Pietro said drily. "Out with it, man—what ails you?"

"Below! In the bailey—my lady! And with a great retinue, too! I let them in—I knew you wouldn't want her kept waiting—"

"The sweet blue eyes of God!" Pietro swore.

"The Abbot's with her! Before God, my Lord, it looks for all the world like a wedding party! Her maids bear flowers—gathered God knows where in this inclement season . . . Surely my Lord did not forget . . . ?"

"Don't be an ass, Manfred. How could I forget my own wedding day? The Lady has yet to give her consent. . . ."

He strode down the stairs and out into the bailey. Elaine was seated on a white palfrey, gorgeously arrayed. There were flowers in her hair, and that gown . . . God's sainted mother!—was unmistakably a wedding gown . . .

Pietro put up his arms and helped her down. He stared at her, his dark eyes wide with astonishment.

"I have come to wed you, My Lord," Elaine said. Her voice had splinters of ice in it.

"But—" Pietro whispered; "but. . . ."

"Surely," Elaine said clearly, "My Lord has not the temerity to disobey the commands of His Majesty, Frederick, Emperor of the Romans!"

Pietro was strangling. He could not breathe. God, Thou Son

of Saint Mary! he thought. Why wouldst Thou not prevent this!

"I will write him," he said rapidly. "I will beseech him to lift this command. . . ."

Elaine's blue eyes were wide and clear, filled with that devastatingly sweet poison of womanhood.

"Why?" she said. "Does my Lord no longer wish to marry me?"

"Yes, I want to. Yes, oh, God, yes! Only—Elaine—I wanted you to come to me of your own free will, not by any king's command. . . ."

"It doesn't matter now," she said sweetly. Too sweetly. Her voice had something in it that he remembered, a tone he had heard once. But he couldn't remember. . . .

"Let us not keep His Lordship, the Abbot waiting," she said. "The sooner the Emperor's commands are obeyed, the better, I am told. . . ."

He remembered the tone now. When she had said of Arturo, the leech: "I had him hanged . . ." her voice had sounded like this. He was cold all over.

"Then," he said quietly, "let my maids conduct your party to your chambers. I must have time to dress. And Manfred, too, needs time to prepare fitting entertainment. This is all rather unexpected, you know. . . ."

"Is it?" Elaine said suddenly. Her voice was naked, now—with the sudden, dazzling nakedness of a blade drawn half from its sheath in the full blaze of the sun.

Again, Pietro wept inside his heart, again I must be wed to a maid who loves me not and this time it is worse than before . . . Antoinette did not hate me wanted indeed to love me tried to but this one hates me with a hatred cold as death and as merciless . . . I was winning little by little I was destroying that hate —but now, Oh Sweet Infant Babe of Mary!—now. . . .

When he came down again to the little chapel, he was attired not in the bright array of a bridegroom, but in somber black. His clothes were of samite and velvet, and were encrusted with black pearls. Even his thumb ring had a stone of jet set into it, and his hat had plumes of midnight hue circling round about the brim.

Elaine stared at him in some astonishment, but she said nothing.

The ceremony was mercifully brief. Even the Abbot sensed that something was dreadfully amiss.

They sat upon a dais before the banquet table. Neither of them ate anything or looked at each other or smiled or held hands. Manfred was in actual tears over the inadequacy of the repast. In actuality, he had done wonders upon so short a notice; but he had planned for weeks now, a fete putting all other wedding fetes in Italy to shame. But this feast was no better, and in some regards not so good as a holiday fete in honor of some saint. Some of the food was not done; others, particularly the pastries, were burnt.

He had managed to summon jugglers from the village. But there was no great jongleur there to move the women to tears with their songs of tender love and loss.

There was wine in plenty and an abundance of food. But the whole thing had somehow the aspect of mourning guests sitting around a bier and breaking, reluctantly, the funeral meats. . . .

Wedding feasts often went on for days. But this one did not. At nightfall, the hastily summoned guests began to leave. And disgracefully early, the matrons prepared Elaine for bed, and the lesser nobles clad Pietro in a dressing gown of silk, and led him to the great canopied bed. It was the barbaric custom for those in attendance to wait within in the bed chamber until the groom put his head through the curtains and announced that the marriage had been consummated. Great matrons of the house or related to it, might demand and get proofs of virginity. But in the case of the marriage of a widow, these customs, Pietro thanked God, did not apply.

The Abbot, after having blessed the nuptial couch, had beaten a hasty retreat. From the sounds outside the drawn curtains, Pietro was aware that the others were leaving, too.

He lay very still. His body was as cold as ice. Far away from him on the other side of the bed, Elaine was as rigid as a statue of marble. He could not even hear her breathe.

He made no move to touch her—to draw near her.

Then in the darkness, in the silence, he became aware that she was crying.

"Don't," he whispered. "Please, Elaine, don't cry. . . ."

"You couldn't wait," she sobbed. "You couldn't have patience . . . You were winning, Pietro—day by day I was coming closer to actual love for you; but now. . . ."

"Now?" Pietro said.

"Marriages are made in heaven, aren't they My Lord? All, but ours. Our marriage, good My Lord—was made in the deepest pit of hell!"

"Elaine," Pietro said. "I did not write the Emperor. Believe me. I prayed nightly that he would not interfere. . . ."

"Then—he knew of this, from the first?"

"Nearly a year ago, he commanded me to wed. I begged him for time, knowing his impatience. I knew, and sickened at the thought—that my Lord Frederick, would think nothing of selecting some unknown maid and saying: 'Good Pietro, behold your bride!' So I told him of you—that since my childhood I had dreamed of you. I asked him to permit me to see you again—preferring in all ways to wed a maid I could come to love, of whom I had tender memories—than some stranger. . . ."

Elaine was silent.

"Please," Pietro whispered, "is this not understandable? In what way does it do you less than honor?"

Elaine stopped crying. She was very still now.

"Why?" she whispered, "did His Majesty wish you to wed?"

"Because," Pietro said sadly, "Frederick and I were born the same hour of the same day in the same place. Our lives have been linked from childhood. There have been many strange parallels between the events of his life and my own. The Emperor, being superstitious, believes these parallels must be preserved. He has sons—and I have not. He fears for the safety of his sons, unless I, too, obey the dictates of our common stars. . . ."

Elaine laughed suddenly. Startlingly.

"Yet," she said, "by this very command, he has made the parallel impossible of fulfillment—at least with me. . . ."

Pietro stared at her in the darkness.

"You will never have sons of me, My Lord. Go to your serving women and beget of them sons of the same base blood as their father's! But if ever you should touch me with desire, I shall kill you. Failing that, I shall kill myself—for as God lives, never shall I mother child of swinish peasant blood!"

Pietro felt the little flames of anger running along his veins. His face felt hot. He put up his hands and drew the curtains so he could see her. The angry clamor of his blood stopped. Then it started again. But not in rage. No longer in anger.

Her attendants, as was the custom, had taken her silken robe from her as she entered the bed. His gentlemen in waiting had done the same for him.

She made no effort to cover herself from his gaze. She mocked him with her eyes.

"How," Pietro got out, his voice hoarse, strained, "does My lady propose to prevent me?"

"With this," she said, and drew the Saracen blade from beneath the pillow.

Pietro stared at the dagger.

He looked away from her. He sat very still, staring at the torches flaming on the walls.

"My Lord," she mocked, "is a brave and noble knight. Surely he is not afraid of this small blade in a woman's feeble hands?"

He could feel inside the envelope of his flesh, the tensing of his sinews. The stopping of his blood. His breath. When he whirled, the motion was incredibly swift.

She cried out, just once. The hands that held her wrists, that pinned them against the bed, were slim, graceful. But strong.

She looked up into his eyes.

"There is a difference," she whispered, "is there not, My Lord?—between marriage—and ravishment. . . ."

Pietro did not answer her. He bent toward her, slowly.

Her head thrashed like a frenzied thing. Turning right, then left, then right again upon the slim column of her neck. Moving as though it had an independent life of its own amid the bright cloud of her hair.

But he found her mouth.

It was ice. Death.

Yet, there was that hunger in him. That need for her.

He kissed her mouth, cherishing it with his own. Slowly. Tenderly. Taking all the time in the world about it. Knowing that her hatred for him was neither unmixed nor pure. That she was a woman who had been loved. Who had loved.

That in such a one, the body's hungers were known hungers. Well remembered. The ice was thin. The blood warmed by memory.

Yet, when the thaw set in; it came so swiftly that it startled him.

He felt her lips opening under his like the petals of some great flower exotic and sweet, then they flamed quite suddenly on his, reaching, searching, clinging, until all the drums in his veins rolled in one prolonged gigantic thunder.

He drew back. Released her wrists.

"My Lady," he whispered, "still has her Saracen blade. . . ."

She lay there, staring at him. Her pupils were so wide they hid the irises of her eyes, only a thin circle of blue showing around the blackness. Her mouth was sullen, stormy.

"Oh, damn you!" she wept. "May all the fiends in hell destroy your soul!"

Then her arms swept up and her hands locked behind his head. He heard, far off and faint, the clatter that the dagger made, when it struck the floor.

Their marriage, Elaine had said was made in the deepest pit of hell. She was right. It took him less than two months to find that out.

Two months of sullen silence, watching her across the table. Two months of seeing her grow daily thinner, picking at her food.

The flareups were almost a relief. The screaming, face-twisted bursts of rage. The names she called him. New ones every time the tight held reins of her emotions broke. Uglier now. Actually obscene. Until he wondered how she knew such things. From what lips she had heard them.

Hatred was one thing. Love was another.

Twins, perhaps. Joined by a bond like a strip of living flesh.

He had thought the day after their marriage, that there would be nothing more between them. That if he had need of her, the easing of that need would be close to actual rapine. The change that next morning had been so sudden. Complete. Devastating.

She had surrendered and she hated that surrender, she hated herself for surrendering.

No more, he thought. I have no stomach for force against her. Any son of mine must be bastard born. . . .

So he had gone into the small chamber and slept that night. Or tried to.

The next three nights as well.

On the fourth, there had been the first of her outbursts. She had screamed at him, telling him how she hated him, swearing that he smelled of the stable, of the barnyard, of the peasant's hut. That she would die before she'd give birth to any child of his. . . .

He listened in silence. His dark eyes brooded over her face. Then, sighing, he had gotten up and gone into the little chamber. Through the open door he could hear her crying.

An hour later, she came into the little chamber and crept whimpering, into his bed.

He was very gentle with her.

She was gentle, too. Even tender. She put her mouth against his ear and cried and begged his forgiveness.

The next day she stormed at him again.

When there were no bursts of screeching rage, she would not come to him. The rage, he learned, being nothing if not intelligent, though hurled at his defenseless head, were directed actually at herself. At the duality of her nature. When the wanting, when the need for him became too strong, when it tortured her like a brand within the flesh, she would seek the release of tormenting him in turn. Except that it never worked like that; except that lashing at him with words only whipped the desire up into a thing past bearing.

And in the night, the whimpering. The whisper of her bare feet upon the floor, coming toward where he lay waiting, knowing how to wait. The abjectness of her surrender. . . .

He could not have borne it, except for her tenderness. But she was never wild like Yvette had always been, like, in fact, Io had sometimes been. She was always very gentle, melting into love. Even the explosion of passion's release, relief was a soft explosion. But very thorough. Very complete.

But in the morning, the sullen, sick hatred was back in her eyes.

There was a pattern in the destiny of man. A pendulum swing. A balance. The secret is, Pietro told himself, to want the right things, to discover what is needful for the soul's health, the spirit's growth, and seek after those things. But therein lies the problem. The things I've needed have never been the simple things, the obvious things, that the world flaunts before a man's eyes each hour of his life.

Honors, nobility, wealth. I have them all, and in the seeking for them I am undone. Honors in a world without honor, where the length a man's sword can reach is the measure of his nobility, the blood upon his hands proof of his right to rule. I have piled up gold and treasure which can buy nothing in this world that ever really mattered: neither peace of heart, of health of soul, or the respect of men of good will. . . .

He went over to his great chest, and opened it; there among the clothes long packed away was a little cross of white. The crusader's cross. He held it in his hand, looking at it.

The attack against Egypt had been going on since 1217, and nothing had come of it. In August, Frederick had promised to sail. He couldn't keep that promise, Pietro knew. The hounds of time dogged his heels here at home. Pietro even knew the Emperor's intent: To send Herman of Salza with five hundred knights in token of his willingness to aid.

Egypt. That far away land under the blue skies. What might a man find there? Peace, perhaps, death perhaps. An end to terrible hungers and black doubts . . . (An end to looking into eyes filled with loathing, an end to hateful words and shrill screeching, an end even to love that was the twin of hatred, an end. . . .)

It was flight. He knew that. He cared less than nothing whether Saracen or Jew or Christian held the Holy Sepulcher. He doubted mildly and without much interest whether after so many centuries men knew whose sepulcher it was or whether it were holy; and his wiry mind pictured the disgust in Jesus' face over the blood shed in His Name. He was very honest. He knew that he was running away. He even examined dispassionately the seductive notion of death upon the field—far away. He had no fear of dying; but he hated the thought of dying in defeat, of having been vanquished by life. What he needed was time. Time to put his life in order, to make decisions, to discover what out of life was true and beautiful and meaningful and worth the having.

He was running away, but he would come back. With the greatness of soul he needed to bring about peace between Elaine and himself; with the peace of heart and mind to wait and be patient and cherish her into love untroubled by doubts and fears and irrational hatred.

And she, too, would have time. He hoped she had love enough for him to surmount her difficulties; that quiet and alone she would lose her shame over the compulsions that drove her into his arms, come, indeed, to accept them as natural and right, sanctioned of God and man; that in time all the sickness her world had bred in her, all the sad, artificial divisions that men had erected between themselves and other men, equally the children of God, barriers built to bolster up vanities so unreal they could be supported by no other method—would vanish like the morning mists before the sun of truth. That she would come to accept truth, even to love it.

He told her of his decision in the morning.

She sat very still, looking at him. She didn't say anything for a very long time, and when she did speak, what she said surprised him.

"Don't go, My Lord," she whispered. "By God's love, and that I bear you—don't. . . ."

He took both her hands and held them, looking at her.

"I must go," he said. "Nothing will ever be right between us, if I stay. . . ."

"Then go!" she flared. "But upon your own head be whatever happens in your absence!"

He looked at her a long time, and his eyes were very clear.

"Upon my head be it," he said.

For the few supplies he needed to purchase for the journey, he went not to nearby Rezzi, but to Iesi, where he and the Emperor Frederick had been born, although it was further away, telling himself that the larger town, never having suffered destruction by siege and fire, would be more likely to afford the medicines and traveling garments he needed.

But Rezzi would have done as well, for his needs were few. He knew that. What he didn't know was why he chose to go to Iesi. He felt somehow, in some shadowy part of his being, that it would be good to see Iesi again, to walk over the stones of the streets where he had first toddled, see once more the house in which he was born.

Being a practical man as well as a dreamer, he made his purchases first. Then he returned to the square and stood there, looking toward the spot where he imagined the Empress Constance's tent had been erected, trying by some dim instinct to stand exactly upon the place where Donati, his father, had stood upon that long lost day.

He stayed there a long time, looking across the sunwashed square. People passed through it, before his eyes, but he didn't see them. His eyes were veiled out of life, turned inward upon the mysteries of memory—no, not memory, for the drama that he was staging in the dark recesses of his mind had had its being, living, before memory had a seat in him. Yet he saw it with dazzling brilliance: the tent, the banners against the sky, the kneeling midwives, busy. . . .

"Yes," the voice at his side said quietly, "It was here, wasn't it, My Lord, that both our troubles began. . . ."

He turned and looked into Iolanthe's grey eyes. Without thinking about it, without being conscious of the gesture or even of where he was, he put out his arms.

But Io shrank away from him.

"No, Pietro," she said. "Sorry—I forgot. No, Sire Pietro, Baron Rogliano. I am honored; but—no."

Her voice had an edge to it. It trembled a little.

Pietro stared at her.

Her chin was tilted back, and her grey eyes studied his face.

"My—felicitations," she whispered, "good My Lord—upon your—marriage. I hope you will have—every—every happiness!"

Then she whirled away from him.

He put out his hand and caught her shoulder. She stopped, but she did not turn.

"Io, please!" he said. He could feel her shoulder shaking, beneath his hand.

"I—I have lost you," she wept. "I think now that I lost you that day my late brothers were knighted, the first day you saw her! You've always loved her, haven't you, Pietro?" She spun back to face him, the tears on her cheeks bright in that wash of sun. "Tell me, haven't you?"

"No," Pietro said.

"You lie! I was always second best. The easily available one, the one that crept into your arms, let you do what you willed—no, not that—not that entirely—for I willed it too. I was always the aggressor, wasn't I? Your sweet, unpurchased whore, your little bitch thing panting after you, while you dreamed of *her!* Fool! Fool! Fool!"

"Io, by God's love. . . ."

"I never dreamed it would come to this," she said, and her voice quieted. "I thought you'd come back, and snatch me from the arms of that black-bearded beast—as I was snatched from yours. And when you did come, you came as gloriously as I thought; but you gave him his life—his miserable life—and you turned your face from me! Why, Pietro, why? Was it she—even then?"

"No," Pietro said. "I came back long before that, Io. But when I reached Rezzi—they told me of—the child. . . ."

"The child?" Io whispered, and one hand crept to her throat. "The child?"

"Yes," Pietro groaned. "I couldn't kill a child, Io—nor face a lifetime of seeing his face staring at me out of its eyes."

"The child," Io said. "Oh, my God!"

"It was only after that I turned to her. I was commanded to wed by the Emperor Frederick, himself. And the extent of my guilt is simply this: that I chose to marry her, whom I admired and respected—not loved, Io—not ever loved—rather than some stranger that he would have foisted upon me. . . ."

"Better a stranger," Io said, "a thousand times better a stranger. She was always cruel towards you. But that I cannot reproach you with, for now she has proved that her cruelty was what I always thought—her efforts to deny the way you moved her. She is not enough alive to put aside the meaningless trappings of this world: name, honors, rank, family—as I could, loving you."

She looked away from him across the square.

"And now you have those honors," she whispered; "and she has you. But she has not what I have—that is the only happiness I have left. More than a happiness—a kind of glory. . . ."

"What is it that you have?" Pietro said.

Io shook her head.

"No. I can't tell you now. The time I should have told you is past. Now to tell you would solve nothing. It would only make matters worse. Perhaps a day will come when I can tell you. That's my only hope now—that such a day will come. . . ."

She smiled at him suddenly, brightly.

"But I must thank you, My Lord," she said, "for by this wedding you have given me some measure of freedom. I can go abroad from the castle, as I please, because Enzio believes you safely out of the way. . . ."

Pietro looked at her sadly.

"I am safely out of the way," he said. "Next week I sail for the Holy Land."

"Oh, Pietro, no!" she whispered, and flung herself into his arms.

"You see," she wept, "I have no shame. I'm still yours, Pietro. Only death can stop that. . . ."

Yes, Pietro thought bitterly, only death. . . .

He joined the Grand Master of the Teutonic Knights at Brindisi, the day before they set sail. He didn't tell Frederick. He didn't need to. A crusader's vow was the holiest, the most sacred in all Christendom. It was a vow taken before God, and no temporal power, not even the Emperor himself, could force a man to violate it.

Herman of Salza welcomed him aboard with grave courtesy. He knew how dear this slim Italian was to his Lord.

They sailed with the tide. They were more than a day at sea, when Rainaldo, rearranging his master's gear, found the note. He brought it to Pietro at once. It was very simple, and very short:

"I love you," it read. "I have, I think, from the first night of our marriage. I've tried to deny that love—to fight against it. But nothing availed. Nothing—except this—your own stubborn folly in leaving me. Had you had patience, I would have won out over my griefs and my fears. I would have become always and in all ways as tender as I sometimes was with you. But you fled the struggle. You left me helpless and alone. I am a Siniscola. Knowing the pride and the cruelty of that house, you will believe me, My Lord, when I say: You shall never see me again—alive. . . ."

It was signed, simply, "Elaine."

He was sick. But there was no turning back now. On the entire voyage to Egypt, he kept away from his fellows, scarcely touched food, sat enwrapped in purest melancholy.

He comforted himself with the thought that she could not do it. The instinct to cling to life was strong. Elaine had borne great sorrow in her life: the loss of Ricardo, whom she had adored, the deaths of her cousins, the loss of her fortune. She had survived them all, had come to something very like peace.

Why then, could she not survive this—especially since he was almost certain to return to her? It would, he told himself, all work out for the best. By the time he came back, Elaine would have had time to evaluate him—to find the basis upon which the balance of their life together could be built—like a strong fortress upon a high hill. . . .

While they were still out of sight of the shores of Egypt, they saw the other galleys crawling over the surface of the sea. There were many of them and the banner flying from their mastheads was strange to Pietro.

He questioned one of the knights about it.

"The Duke of Bavaria, My Lord," the knight said, ruefully.

"That means we're not going to have any time to rest or see the sights at all—not if I know the Cardinal. . . ."

"The Cardinal?" Pietro said.

"Cardinal Pelagius, the Pope's legate. John of Brienne, King of Jerusalem, is supposed to be in command, with the Duke of Austria and King Andrew of Hungary as his seconds; but it doesn't work like that at all. Everything old Pelagius says, goes. He's the real firebrand. And what he says carries all the more weight because he personally doesn't know what fear means. He's always yards ahead of every charge, holding up the cross and crying us on. . . ."

"Another warlike churchman, eh?" Pietro mused. "What do you think of such men, Sire?"

The young knight considered the question.

"It seems to me they belie their teachings, My Lord. I prefer another kind—like that wonderful monk Francis, who was with us in '18 and '19. Men tell many marvels of him: that the birds would come to his hand and that he would talk to them and they could understand him. I don't know about those things. I only know he had the face of a saint—gentle and sad and eyes that looked through you into your soul. I have seen the cruelest warrior grow gentle in his presence; I've seen men who had not wept since childhood kneel weeping at his feet. . . ."

"You're speaking of Francis of Assisi, aren't you?" Pietro said. "I've heard many wonders of him. It was even said he converted the Sultan. . . ."

"No," the young knight said. "Were that true, we wouldn't be at war now, My Lord. But he certainly tried. And that is one marvel of his that I saw. He walked barefooted and alone, through the entire Saracen army, alone—save for one interpreter —and no one lifted sword against him. Some say that they thought the finger of Allah was on him—which is to say that he was mad; but they treated him courteously. And the Sultan, al Kamil, listened to his sermon, then sent him back with an armed guard to our camp, under a flag of truce. . . .

"It was we who lost him, not they. For when we took Damietta, our men behaved in their usual fashion, that is to say, like beasts and butchers, which so sorrowed his gentle heart that he left us, and went home . . ." The young knight, looked out over the waters toward where the Bavarian galleys were crawling like great spiders, their oars moving stroke upon stroke with precision. "I," he whispered, "have never slain a prisoner since. . . ."

They saw the grey-brown of Egypt rising out of the sea before them early the next day. Shortly after noon they landed, being greeted at the shore by Cardinal Pelagius, himself, who conducted a mass upon the spot and blessed their coming.

Pietro could hear the exultation in his voice as he said:

"Now with this aid of yours, sent us by the Hand of God, Himself, we will destroy them! Tomorrow, we march upon Cairo!"

Pietro left the place where Waldo, Rainaldo, and others of his men were setting up his tent. He wandered about among the armies, listening to the talk. Messengers had already gone out to John of Brienne and the Syrian Lords, telling them of the planned attack. But the men were not without their fears, for even should the King of Jerusalem, and the Lords of Syria come in time, Malik al Kamil would still be able to bring into the field three times their number. He had the armies of Damascus, Hamah and Baalbek at his disposal, any one of which was greater than their own.

There was much grumbling, too, over Cardinal Pelagius' impetuosity. His recklessness, the soldiers swore, had cost them more casualties than any other factor in the campaign.

And everywhere, Pietro was asked the same thing:

"When is the Emperor Frederick coming? If he were here we'd have this over with and would be homeward bound within the month. . . ."

Pietro had no answer for that one. He had overheard Herman of Salza saying to the leaders: "My Lord will sail in August. . . ."

But that was a lie. Whether or not Herman believed it was unimportant; the simple fact remained that with the Count of Molise still unsubdued, the rebellious Saracens raiding from the hills about Palermo, treachery and intrigue growing up like well watered plants under a summer sun, Frederick couldn't leave Sicily.

What must be done would have to be done without Frederick.

But he didn't have the heart to tell them that. All he could answer was: "Soon, I hope. . . ."

The next evening John of Brienne and the Syrian Lords arrived by sea from Acre, and the preparations were complete.

The stars were low over the palm trees, and the wind blew in from the sea up the Delta. Pietro could hear the whispering of the Nile waters, one branch of which passed some yards before his tent. It was very quiet and the sky was a nightshade blue unlike any other sky he'd ever seen. It was cool and well watered and there were trees and grasses and rich earth underfoot. Beyond the beaches there was no sand. None of the desert country he had expected to see. There were camels laden with the army's gear; but beyond that it might as well have been Sicily.

He sat very still and looked up at the stars. Inside the tent Waldo and Rainaldo were already snoring. Tomorrow they were going to march up the Nile toward Cairo. Tomorrow Pietro was going to ride into battle once more. He had fought so many battles. He was twenty-six years old and he had been fighting since he was fourteen. He was very tired of fighting. In a curious way, he felt very old—that his life was over. He had never gone into battle without feeling afraid; but tonight he not only felt no fear; he felt nothing at all. He had a complete and numbing indifference to what happened to him.

Then he remembered Elaine. Some of that numbness left him. He remembered her face twisted with rage, her voice screaming at him, and, quite suddenly it didn't matter any more. He had lost Io, and nothing would take the place of that memory, but his memories of Elaine were more recent, more detailed. He could feel his body loosening, thinking of her. If, so far, there was nothing of the spirit between them, what there was between them was very fine. He had that keen Italianate appreciation for woman's flesh. He knew that Elaine's talent for love was a rare thing, subtle and complete and fine—oh, absolutely fine.

If they had had nothing else, they had had that. His mind was occupied suddenly with details: the longcool feel of her against him in the darkness, the delicate warmth of her mouth, opening under his clinging, the slender, snowy, ever so slightly curving look of her, like an alabaster statue brought startlingly into life by the wisps of whitegold down and palest flecks of pink like the buds of unearthly flowers peeping from the snow. . . .

Pietro was cold suddenly. He was shaking. The numbness was all gone and the desire to live was upon him, holding him hard in his grip. He was afraid the way he had been afraid before every battle he had engaged in, and he was glad of it. There was something comforting about that fear. It was the first normal emotion he had felt since his marriage.

He was still thinking about Elaine when he fell asleep.

There was no battle the next day. They rode up the banks of the Nile, and toward nightfall a group of Saracens, carrying the white flag of truce, met them. They had with them an *Ifranji,* a Frank, as they called all Europeans, to serve as an interpreter. Pietro recognized this man as one of the hundreds of Venetians whose trade with the Moslems was so profitable that they had sabotaged every crusade they could. He didn't like the looks of this man.

When the Venetian began to speak, Pietro interrupted him suddenly, and put the question directly to the Amir who led the group.

"Thou, oh Lord of the armies," he said, "and shadow of God's shadow upon earth,[2] will speak directly to us in thine own tongue. For I much mislike the looks of this son of Shaitan thou hast brought with thee!"

Cardinal Pelagius stared at him in astonishment. Most of the Syrian Lords now spoke Arabic, some of them well; but few of them could have managed the high rhetoric Pietro had just used. Unfortunately for the King of Jerusalem and the Syrian Lords, they had learned their Arabic from servants and slaves, with many small violations of the rules that governed the richest and most intricate tongue on earth. What was worse, they knew few of the formulae of courtesy.

"Let us make camp," the Cardinal said, "and you, young Lord, will serve us as interpreter—for truly you seem master of this heathen tongue. . . ."

An hour later, they sat around the campfire.

The Amir, or General, made a speech. What it came down to was very simple: Jerusalem for Damietta. The knights roared out a cheer when Pietro came at last to that phrase. They had had enough of fighting. Those of them who had lived for years in the newly won Christian states of Syria, knew that they could never conquer the Saracens. There were those among them who knew, as Pietro did, that the crusades were only the last of the barbarian conquests—an attack of an inferior civilization upon one vastly superior to it in almost every regard. . . .

But the warlike Cardinal was on his feet, waving his arms about. He roared out his denials, his refusal as the representative of the Vicar of Christ, to accept any compromise. So great was his anger that Pietro had to slow him down several times in order to get his thunderous oratory into Arabic phrases having anything like an acceptable degree of courtesy.

The Amir's speech of farewell was short and to the point: The Conquering King, Malik al Kamil, Allah's Caliph, had magnanimously made this offer to spare them further loss of life. Now, regrettably, they had left God's Shadow Upon Earth no other choice but to crush them. . . .

"Widows will weep," the Amir said, "in the *hareems* of Frankistan;[3] sons will go fatherless, and lay their curse by the Ninety and Nine Sacred Names of God upon the men so mad as to persist in such stubborn folly. For thou knowest that our soldiers are like the sands of the desert, that clouds of arrows from our archers will darken the sun; that our horsemen are the wind's own sons, as swift, and as terrible, that our *Naffatun*[4] will drench thee with flames out of the bowels of hell. Our King is great, and gracious. Accept his terms—or the deaths of pariah dogs!"

Every soldier there agreed with him. But they were powerless against the one man who could lay upon them interdict and excommunication, threaten the only thing they held in greater terror than their lives—the fate of their immortal souls.

The attack began the next day.

Pietro saw from the first, that it could only end one way. The armor of the Europeans was somewhat superior to that worn by the Saracens; but the Moslem knights had, because of this very fact, greater mobility. In their light armor, mounted on their small, wonderfully beautiful horses, the Arabic *Fursan,* or cavalry, could ride rings around the powerful warhorses of the crusaders. If you could hit one with your lance, it was easy to lift a Saracen out of his saddle; but the Saracens were seldom so obliging as to charge straight at you, European fashion. Instead, they circled, depending upon the incredible speed of their little horses, coming at you from the side, the back, from all sides at once, so that nearly every crusading knight was nearly always surrounded and had to hack his way out with his sword.

Their infantry, the *harbīyah,* were better armed, and better disciplined than the European foot; the *ramīyah* or archers, used the crossbow but little. Instead they depended usually upon a short, double-curving bow that seemed to have twice or three times the power of the puny European longbow. For the first time in all the battles he had witnessed, Pietro saw men knocked from the saddle by the arrows of archers. Of course the arbalist was more powerful, and the Arabs had adopted and modified it; but they preferred their own short bows with their rapid rate of fire.

On the face of it, the German, Hungarian, Italian and French knights had the better of it in that first battle. They killed many more of the Saracen forces than they lost themselves. But the Saracens could replace their losses; from an hundred cities they could draw fresh swarms of well armed men.

June went out to the ugly clangor of arms. Throughout July they fought ceaselessly. Only they weren't winning any more. There were too many wounded, too many dead. They couldn't win a battle now. They could only make their defeats as costly to al Kamil as possible.

Pietro thought often of Elaine. But sadly now. Every day that Cardinal Pelagius, by the sheer force of his will, kept John of Jerusalem and Andrew of Hungary from ordering the retreat that the military situation demanded, his chances and the chances of all the others of seeing wives and children again grew pitifully slimmer. "Widows will weep in the *hareems* of Frankistan," the Amir had said. And if there were in truth no *hareems* in the Frankish lands, there would be widows in God's plenty to weep. . . .

On the twenty-second of July, the Nile began its annual rise.

Anyone could see now that they must retreat. Their camp lay in the narrow triangle of the Ashmoun Branch, and it was on low ground there. They would have to strike their tents and move on in considerable haste. Anyone could see that. That is, anyone but Cardinal Pelagius.

"God," he thundered, "is on our side! We will prevail!"

The trouble is, Pietro thought bitterly, that nobody seems to have notified God.

He looked at the water creeping up under the edges of the tents. He thought about Elaine and he was bitter.

In his bitterness he was moved to more than his wry witticism about sending God proper notification of their plight. He was forced into doing some thinking about Crusades, past, present, and future. He knew their history intimately, from the lips of living men who had served in the later ones, from the chronicles of the earlier. In every case, the Saracens had had much the better of it; even in defeat they had been victorious. No Saracen leader had ever disgraced himself, no Saracen army had behaved to the conquered like the soldiers of the gentle Christ. From the very first, when they had left their homes to "take back the Holy Places from the unclean hands of infidels," they in the first of the Crusades had marched out by the light of the pyres in which screamed the helpless Jews that they had murdered in their homelands as an earnest of their intent. And when these gentle Christians had won at last, they flocked to the Church of the Holy Sepulcher, and embraced each other and wept, thanking the merciful God for their victory. But they marched to the Church through streets choked with the bodies of their victims; on the corners they had to circle the carefully piled stacks of severed heads and hands, stepping over the bodies of infants whose heads had been smashed against posts. . . .

They had been whipped into battle frenzy by the sight of the "Holy Lance" that had pierced the side of Jesus, and the sudden appearance, clad in white, of the three Holy Martyrs, St. Maurice, St. Theodore, and St. George. Only the Holy Lance had to be withdrawn from the standards after three days, a proven fraud, the Holy Martyrs were found to be young knights specially dressed for the occasion, and the monk Peter Bartholomew, who had conceived the whole idea of such divine intervention, was forced to perform the "miracle" of walking through fire to vindicate his honesty. But the miracle's effect hadn't lasted through the following day, and Peter had died of his burns.

The second Crusade was defeated wholly, after having pillaged only the towns of the Christian Greeks, instead of the heathen Turks. It, Pietro recalled wryly, had been notable chiefly for the number of prostitutes who had accompanied the armies, and those great ladies like Eleanor of Aquitaine, who insisted upon accompanying their husbands and who amused themselves mightily with handsome stalwarts from the ranks while their husbands quarreled over the rule of cities not yet—and never to be—conquered. . . .

In contrast to these, Pietro mused, let them consider Saladin. In contrast to fraud and brutality, to rapine and fiendish cruelty, to treachery, and adulterous lusts, let them consider Joseph, son of Job.

He repeated the name aloud in Arabic, almost reverently: "al-Malik, al-Nasir, Salah-ed-din, Yusuf ibn Ayyub. King, Defender—Honor of the Faith, Joseph, son of Job." Honor of his faith—of any faith. Who spared the conquered of Jerusalem to a man, gave back to them the ransom they paid him, sent peaches and pears and snow to the stricken Richard, Coeur de Lion, his most relentless foe, a charger for Richard to fight upon when his own horse was slain; who seldom slew, and then only those who had grossly provoked him, offering life even to that Reginald who had taken his own sister prisoner—killing him finally only when he refused Muhammad honor as a prophet of God. . . .

Of the Fourth Crusade, Pietro had had the detailed report of Sire Roget, Gautier's uncle. To torture, murder, rapine, add treachery. Add thievery. Add fratricide. For Constantinople had been the target. The victims, Christians. The motive, greed instead of sanctity.

Now this one. No better than the rest. At Damietta's fall nearly all the outrages of 1099 had been repeated. Except there had been fewer victims for the slaughter. Far less than the seventy thousand Moslems butchered at Jerusalem's first fall. No thousands of Jews to be herded into their synagogues and burnt alive. But enough. And for what?

To the honor of this murderous perversion of the faith of Jesus. To the glory of these priestly ones who could not consider that there are many forms to truth, and God neither so cruel nor so parsimonious as to leave only one road open to His Grace. Who believed their rightness made them executioners; that another's wrongness was sin enough to put his life in jeopardy, to forfeit his immortal soul. Who were, and herein lay the fearsomeness of their power, incapable of distinguishing between what was, and their own opinions. Who held their opinions up as mirrors of the will of God and struck out blindly with the sword's edge at any having the temerity to differ. . . .

Who could, now, condemn any army to death by drowning in confident expectation that God Himself would feed their already overwhelming vanities by performing a miracle in their behalf.

Only, there was no miracle. On July twenty-fourth, the Nile flooded the camp. From the high ground of Mansura the Arabs rained down stones from their engines. Arrows whistled down in clouds upon the tents.

Pietro rode with John of Brienne in that last, suicidal charge. The horses bogged down in the mud, and from the dikes the *ramīyah* swept the crusaders from the saddle with their arrows.

They floundered back to the camp. Below them now they could see al Kamil's galleys. No supplies would reach them now from Acre or Tyre. Nothing would reach them, except death.

There were the sounds of the water, and the whistle of the arrows. Every tent became a pin cushion. A porcupine. From the high ground the engines heaved the great stones, rising ever so slowly in lovely parabolas, hanging almost visibly upon the peak of the arc, then thundering downward to crush a tent and the men within it to ribbons.

Cardinal Pelagius knelt in the water up to his waist and prayed.

"Oh God," he cried, "deliver us, Thy warrior-children who have served Thee well!"

Pietro stared at him. He, too, stood in the cold water up to his knees. He had stopped thinking about anything so inevitable as their deaths or capture and slavery. His mind, as it always did under stress, wandered off into odd tangents.

This man of God has great faith, he thought, and men have always praised that. I have no faith and that is accounted evil; but the world if it is ever saved will be saved by men of goodwill of much thought and of little faith . . . Faith stops thinking, and thought is the root of life without which we become beasts, faith is surrender and dependence and becoming children again, it is refusing to accept the unimaginable variety of truth and the unwillingness to permit another his variant. Faith stops progress, and legitimizes murder. . . .

I could be burnt for such thoughts; instead I shall die by drowning or by the Saracens' arrows because of this man's faith, his very mistaken faith that we have served God well—by murder and pillage . . . I am too much the merchant, too little willing to invest in goods that over the centuries have paid so little dividends . . . Faith has never brought any man deliverance in human history unless it happened to coincide at that moment with the mysterious workings of the will of a very capricious God. And what God permits to happen to a man has ever had so little to do with that man's deserving that the very prophets were moved to the belief that He chastized those whom He loved. . . .

He shook his head, and turned back to his tent. He pushed aside the flap and entered. Waldo, and Rainaldo lay in the muddy water holding their heads above the surface, keeping well away from the walls of the tent which were enough usually to stop the arrows or so break their force that they did little harm.

Pietro stared at them, but he wasn't thinking about them. What he thought was that any civilization built upon, "The substance of things hoped for, the evidence of things unseen," would die of mental and spiritual stagnation; and being what he was, his mind proposed the alternative: The republic of the future, would be built upon the search—by experimentation, by exploration of every practical means—for things hoped for; the proof, the sorting out of the existing unseen from the fantasies created by the wishful mind of man. . . .

When we shall love truth and hate error, but not the holders of error; when we shall have no need to hypnotize ourselves further with censer and ritual and ceremony; when we can gaze upon truth naked and be not blinded; when we can abandon our most cherished beliefs if they prove false, and look not back upon them with sorrow; then shall we be free. . . .

Another arrow whistled through the tent. Pietro laughed.

"Get up!" he said. "Let us not die upon our bellies in the mud. Lift up your heads, my knights, look destiny in the face—and smile. If we must die, cannot we manage it with dignity?"

They got up, shame showing in their faces.

"There is," Pietro said, "in that goatskin, a little wine left. . . ."

In the morning, they started the march back toward Damietta. But they floundered in the ditches. They died by the hundreds. By drowning. By the arrows whistling from the dikes. The stones.

Pietro managed to get his horse free from the mud. On a little rise he could see a group of Saracen cavalry. There were about twenty horsemen. His mind was working very well and very clearly. He knew his choices: to die in the stinking ditches, choked with mud and foul water and silt; or to die on that lonely little hill, alone and surrounded by his foemen. Neither choice was sweet.

He shivered a little, looking at the foul water. He thought about Io and about Elaine. He commended them to God. Then he charged.

But he never reached the horsemen. A small stone from a mangonel crashed against his helmet, denting it. He pitched backward out of the saddle into the yellow flood.

When he opened his eyes, he was lying on the hill. A tall and powerful Shaikh knelt over him, his poinard resting lightly against Pietro's throat.

"Allahu Akbar!" the Shaikh said. "God is great!"

Pietro smiled. To him the choice was an easy one. Living, he might one day win back to Italy, to Elaine again.

"Allahu Akbar," he agreed.

"La ilaha il-Allah!" the Shaikh growled, menacingly. "There is no God but Allah!"

Pietro smiled again.

"Muhammadum rasulu 'llah," he whispered. "And Muhammad is His prophet!"

The knife went away from his throat.

"Rise, oh dog of a Frank," the Shaikh said. "By thy words thou hast earned thy life. . . ."

"Not by my words, oh Shaikh," Pietro said, "but by the words of the merciful and compassionate God."

The Shaikh stared at him. The other Saracen knights looked at him, too, with great curiosity.

"How does it happen that thou, a Frank," the Shaikh demanded, "speaketh so perfectly the tongue of Allah's people?"

"I was taught it in my youth," Pietro said, "in Sicily by the *khojas* and *hadjis*[5] of that land. I learned with the sons of your people to recite the Qûr'an. In the house of my youth, no other tongue was spoken, for though my guardian was one of 'the people of the book,' a Jew, his youth was spent in Moslem Spain. . . ."

"Good!" the Shaikh said. Then he turned to the others. "This one will I keep, for I have much dealings with those Ifranji dogs from Venice. He will guard my accounts and they will not be able to puzzle him with strange twists of speech; for, by Allah, I'm tired of being cheated!"

He turned back to Pietro.

"Thy name?" he demanded.

"Pietro."

"Then Pietro, from this day forth, you shall be my slave. In Islam this is no dishonorable estate, for those who serve their masters well are rewarded with kindness. Do you know anything of shipping and trade?"

"Enough, My Lord," Pietro sighed, "to serve you. . . ."

"Good," the Shaikh said. "In the house of Abu-Bekr Ahmad al Muqtafi, you will find little to regret. . . ."

I, Pietro thought, will have much. . . .

He came with his captors up to Cairo, some days later. His first impression of it was dismal: he saw only the desolate and squalid huts of the poor between the pyramids of Ghizeh and the walls, and the unbelievably dirty Bedouins prowling amid the broken tombs of ancient kings. . . .

But inside the walls, it was better. They passed through the bazaars, piled high with the wealth of all the world. It was a labyrinth, packed wall to narrow wall with buyers and sellers, all haggling over prices as though their very lives depended upon the outcome. Dark roofs shut out the sun over all these alleyways, and within them men lived from day to day amid carpets that would have delighted the heart of any prince, jars of olive oil, chests of spices, fruits, fresh and dried, the carcasses of animals swarming with flies, bolts of silk, samite, taffeta, cottons, linens, and the strange sweet smell of opium.

Jewels glittered under the colored lamps upon the shelves of the jewelers. It seemed to Pietro that one need only to stretch out a hand—then he saw the darkly scowling swordsmen guarding them, fierce tribesmen from Rayi or Marghab. The noises and smells beat about his head. He saw that some of the traders in the markets wore only blue as though it were a uniform. Others had tiny bells about their necks that tinkled as they moved. Pietro saw a white-bearded member of the belled ones go past riding a donkey. To his astonishment, the old man sat backward, mournfully facing the beast's tail.

Curiosity overcame him. He turned to one of his guards.

"By Allah's grace, My Lord," he said. "Would you explain to me some of the many things of which I know nothing? If I am to serve our Lord, the Shaikh, it is best that I learn. . . ."

The young *qā'id,* or captain, looked at him sternly. Then his face relaxed a little.

"Truly Allah hath given thee a fair tongue, oh Frankish dog," he said. "What wouldst thou know?"

"Why, oh Lord *Amir*—"

"I am not an *amir,*" the Captain snapped, "but only a *qā'id,* a commander over an hundred. Abu, over there, is a *khalīfah.* That is, he commands fifty. And Rasul is an *'arif,* having only ten beneath him. Shaikh Ahmad, may Allah bless him, is an *amir*—a commander over ten thousand. Dost understand, oh Frank?"

"Perfectly, my Lord Qā'id," Pietro said. "But there are other things I would know: Who are those people in blue, and those with bells about their necks? Why did the ancient, belled one, ride face to tail upon his ass?"

"Thou hast eyes, Frank," the young captain said. "The belled ones and the ones wearing the blue *shubas,* are both people of the book. Since we acknowledge many of their prophets as forerunners of Muhammad, we permit them both life and liberty, in return for a headtax that is not very great. The wearers of the blue *shubas* are Jews, for whom we have the highest respect, counting them not entirely infidel. The belled ones are Nazarenes, whom once we respected, also, counting their prophet Jesus as one of our greatest prophets, too. But they have lied and cheated, attempted to seize our Holy Places—as thou wert trying—so we have cast upon them burdens: bells to call down upon them the scorn of the faithful, that ridiculous manner of riding to remind them of their lowly estate among us. . . ."

He looked at Pietro, and smiled.

"Perhaps," he said, "if thou servest our Lord Ahmad well, thou wilt escape the bells, and the facing the hindquarters of thy beast. It lies within his power to grant thee that. . . ."

They passed out from the Bazaars into other narrow, crooked streets. Now and again, some dark-clad Shaikh, surrounded by his guard of Negro swordsmen in brilliant scarlet, would salute Shaikh Ahmad gravely, hand touched quickly from breast to forehead, to lips. Once they had to stop while a group of black eunuchs, shapeless with fat, bore past them on litters a group of Circassian slave girls, veiled from head to foot.

They came out upon a square, and there a crier was auctioning off slaves. Shaikh Ahmad signaled for them all to stop.

Pietro looked at the slaves with wonder. There were blondes from Russia, dark-eyed whiteskinned maidens from Spain and Greece, stalwart Mamluks, fierce swordsmen from Turkey, greatly desired and greatly feared; gigantic blacks from the steaming jungles to the South, delicate, sloe-eyed Chinese maidens. . . .

God's eyes! Pietro thought, here might any connoisseur of varied beauty have his fill, any jaded appetite be revived!

The auctioneer caught sight of the great Shaikh.

"Truly," he cried at once, "hast thou come opportunely, o conquering lion of the faith! Not in years have I had so fair a collection to present to thine august eyes. Look thou, My Lord, upon them! This one, perhaps—hath My Lord ever seen limbs of such snowy whiteness, hair like ripened wheat and eyes as blue as the sea of the faithful? Think, o great Amir, o Shaikh most powerful, of these soft and silken arms about thy head! These limbs, sweet and clean and cool for thy caressing, these twin globes of pearl and snow, tipped with tiny roses! Think, o Shaikh Ahmad, of the fierce lion of Muqtafi, the worthy son!—what delights await thee! What fair and pleasant sons, such a one could bear to Allah's glory and thine own!"

But Ahmad shook his head.

"Thou art the serpent's son, o Abdullah," he said pleasantly. "Thy tongue drippeth guile forever. Those northern ones have hearts as snowy as their limbs; there is no warmth within them. Rather would I see that Byzantine maid, who sulketh yonder . . ." He pointed with his jeweled hand.

Abdullah hauled her forward. Pietro's dark eyes widened. It was not her beauty, though she was fair. He had seen fairer maids. Elaine was fairer than this one. No, it was something else, something that eluded him. Then he saw her eyes. They were grey-brown, light almost to the extent of being yellow, and he had the feeling that he had seen eyes like that before. He thought about it, but nothing came. He could not recall a single soul who had had such eyes.

Not one. Then he knew why. No person; but his great hawk, Caesar, had had such eyes; many another gyrfalcon he had since owned. They were so—so fierce. So free of fear. So utterly untamed. The others saw that too.

"By Allah," the young captain whispered. "She hath *saqr*'s eyes! My most noble bird, my *saqr,* Horis—who can sight the small birds a mile beneath him, then plunge like Allah's lance to strike, hath their very twins!"

"Truly she is fair," Shaikh Ahmad murmured. "By what name is she called?"

"Zenobia," Abdullah half whispered. He, Pietro saw, was actually reluctant to make this sale.

The Greek girl's hands were fettered. Of all the female slaves, she was the only one thus bound.

Abdullah licked dry lips with the tip of his tongue.

"My Lord Amir," he said, "thou hast in the past been my patron, and hast befriended me often out of the generosity of the noble heart that Allah gave thee. I beg thee reconsider. I have many other maids—this one, my Lord, is not for thee. . . ."

Pietro could see the Shaikh's dark eyes light. Abdullah could have found no better means to whet his appetite.

"Why so, o son of guile and dark deceits?" he laughed.

"She hath a demon—nay, she is a demon! I tell thee, my Lord—"

He got no further. Zenobia's left hand, moving with incredible stealth, closed over the handle of his poinard. She jerked it from the scabbard, and whirled, slashing.

Abdullah's dark face opened in a great red line from eartip to the point of his chin.

"Aiyeeee!" he screamed.

"Seize her!" Ahmad ordered.

At once his soldiers were upon her. She managed to rip two of them before they subdued her. Ahmad rode close to the platform.

When he was close, despite his more than fifty years, he leaped like a boy upon the platform. He put out his hand and ripped the single garment she wore from her body.

Pietro's breath caught in his throat. To such a one, he thought bitterly, every thousand years the ribald gods give such a form in order to drive men mad. . . .

Ahmad raised two clenched fists to heaven in purest exultation.

"O all wise God!" he laughed; "What cubs shall I have of this lioness! Name thy price, o serpent's son!"

Zenobia lashed out suddenly with both feet, swinging her weight upon the arms of the soldiers who held her. The kicks caught Ahmad unprepared, and toppled him from the platform into the dust.

He came back slowly, and to Pietro's surprise, he was still smiling. When he stood before her once more, he drew back his right hand and smashed it open-palmed across her face, right and left and right, so hard and fast that his handmoving blurred with the speed, and her head pivoted in explosive jerks upon her neck and the tears jetted out of the corners of her eyes from the impact.

When he stopped finally, standing there breathing a little hard and smiling, there were two dark trickles of blood descending from the corners of her mouth, and her face was swollen and red as fire.

"Thy price, o Abdullah," Ahmad said.

Abdullah drew the dirty cloth away from his face. It was already soaked with his blood.

"Two—two thousand dinars,[6] my Lord Shaikh," he whispered.

"Done!" Ahmad said. "Wrap her limbs and her face from prying eyes, and bring her with us."

Abdullah swore very softly under his breath, calling himself a son of a fleabitten, misbegotten camel. He knew now he could have gotten ten thousand.

But they were not yet to reach the palace of Ahmad.

Pietro was dead tired. He reeled in the saddle. He looked with weary pity at the shapeless bundle the soldiers bore between them. He thought he could hear the faint sound of crying. . . .

But, just as they turned into a fair and pleasant street, a cavalcade bore down upon them. Ahead of it a swarm of scarlet-clad, black Sudanis ran barefoot, crying:

"Make way for the conquering lord, the favored of Allah!"

Behind the Negroes came a corps of riders, beating on silver kettledrums, and guards in light armor with cloaks of gold and black, mounted on horses too beautiful to believe. Among them, upon a snowy white mare, with the longest mane and tail Pietro had ever seen sat a tall and pleasant looking man. He wore a black *tarboush*, or long fez, wrapped around with white turban cloth, and his black silk cloak was beautifully embroidered with golden threads. In his girdle was thrust a long scimitar, with a golden hilt crusted with jewels, and the reins and trappings of his mount were covered with golden dinars. . . .

Every man in Ahmad's guard, including the Shaikh, himself, bowed low. Pietro did likewise. Having decided to live, he was not going to get himself killed for a breach of etiquette.

"Thy servant, and the servant of Thy servants!" Ahmad said, "O mighty Caliph, o shadow of God upon earth!"

So, Pietro thought, this is the King! He looked at the Sultan Malik al Kamil, and what he saw pleased him. Here was an intelligent, not unkindly man.

"I thank thee," the Sultan said, "Shaikh Ahmad, and *amir* of my Armies, though as an Ayyubite, I know thou desireth nothing less than my blood. Still, while waiting thy chance, thou hast served me well—and the treason of thy mind shall go unpunished until it becomes treason in fact. . . ."

"O conquering King . . ." Ahmad began.

"Silence!" al Kamil said. "What hast thou in that bundle?"

"Only a slave girl, newly bought, My Lord," Shaikh Ahmad whispered.

"Let me see her," the Sultan said.

Ahmad slowly nodded. The Qā'id drew the cloth down from Zenobia's face.

Even from where he sat, Pietro could see al Kamil's eyes kindle. "Allah," he said, "would bless the donor of such a gift to his watcher upon this earth. . . ."

The Shaikh's face changed, grew ugly. His brows crowded his eyes. Suddenly he put out his hand and snatched up Zenobia's.

"Before Allah," he said loudly, "and in the presence of His Caliph, I take this woman into the bonds of holy matrimony, before these several witnesses, and of this union, only God Himself hath the sundering!"

There was no sound in the street. Now, Pietro thought, we're all going to die. . . .

Then al Kamil's shoulders drooped a little.

"Again hast thou balked me, o Muqtafi," he said. "But the years of my waiting are long, and my patience not yet exhausted. Upon this union, be my blessing. . . ."

He made a gesture with his hand. The kettledrums sounded. The Sudanis took up their cry. The royal cavalcade moved off.

Pietro looked into the faces of Ahmad's followers. They were sick with fear.

I, he thought, have fallen into the lair of tigers.

Then they, too, rode off, down the quiet street.

Chapter Eleven

It was a full year later before Pietro saw the slave girl Zenobia again. He was walking in the garden outside the men's quarters of the palace, when he heard the whistling crack of a whiplash, and after that, a woman's scream.

He started toward the sound, running. He had rounded a clump of tall, tropical shrubbery when he saw her. She lay face down upon the earth. Two great Ethiopian eunuchs lay beside her, pinioning her arms, while a third beat her.

She had received but two stripes. They had not raised welts. They had cut through the tender flesh of her back as cleanly as a knife. The first thing that Pietro saw was the blood.

The big slave lifted the whip again, arching it high above his head. Pietro saw her quiver.

He had his curved dagger out before he even thought about the danger of interfering. And even when he did think he knew he wouldn't stop because of that danger or for any reason upon the face of the earth.

He moved in very quickly in the smooth crouch of the born knife fighter, a thing as natural to a Sicilian as breathing, and the point of the poinard was pressing into the fat of the black's stomach before he could bring the whip down again.

"Another stroke and thou diest!" he shouted. "Thou black and sexless son of a dog! Who ordered this?"

The Negro fell back.

"I ordered it," the voice behind him said.

Pietro whirled. He looked into the face of Harum, al~Muqtafi's eldest son. Harum held a scimitar in his hand.

"Seize him," he said quietly.

Pietro was very good with the Saracen poinard. He was very good with any kind of a blade whatsoever. But you didn't attack an Arab swordsman with a dagger, not even an indifferent swordsman—which Harum was not, being, actually, a past master of his curved, flexible blade. Pietro dropped his arms, and the black seized them, twisting them cruelly behind his back.

Harum stood there looking at him. And now Pietro saw on his right cheek the four parallel furrows that Zenobia's nails had made.

He threw back his head and laughed aloud.

"For these small stripes, o Shaikh's son," he said, "thou wouldst take such vengeance? Or is it the wounds to thy pride that require these blows?"

"Perhaps," Harum said smoothly, "that since the matter amuses thee so much, o Frankish dog, thou wouldst care to take her place?"

Pietro didn't answer him. Then he saw that Zenobia had raised her head and was staring at him. There was something like wonder in her eyes.

"Will My Lord spare her?" Pietro said quietly, "if I do?"

"Yes," Harum said.

"Swear it," Pietro said; "by the ninety and nine names of God!"

"Thus do I swear," Harum laughed, "and by that hundredth which only the camel knoweth!"

"Very well," Pietro said.

"Give me the maid," Harum said. "I will hold her."

"No!" Zenobia said suddenly, "not for me, My Lord. This of the whip is nothing. I can bear it. I cannot permit that thou . . ."

"Silence!" Harum roared. "Proceed with the lashes, Yusuf!"

The two slaves hurled Pietro to the ground and held him there. Yusuf put out one big hand and tore the light silks Pietro wore down to his waist.

It was bad. Even at the first blow Pietro had to clench his teeth to keep from groaning. By the third, he knew that even that wasn't going to do any good. But he managed to keep tight hold on himself. The fourth. The fifth. From somewhere, far off and faint, he could hear Zenobia crying.

"Ye dogs!" she stormed. "See what it is to be a Frank—and a man! See what kindness is—and courage! Oh ye things of slime and total foulness! Ye—"

"What is the cause of this uproar?" the Shaikh al Muqtafi said.

Pietro twisted his head painfully upon his neck. Abu-Bekr Ahmad al Muqtafi stood there glaring at his son, as tall and straight as the Prophet's own lance.

"I will tell thee, o conquering Lord!" Zenobia shrieked. "Look upon thy son's face—see the marks my fingers made when thy treacherous cub attempted to possess what is thine! As for this Frank, he is guiltless of all but trying to save me from being whipped—for which he was made to suffer in my place!"

"This is true, Harum?" al Muqtafi said. Then he leaned close. "Aiyee!" he said, "I see that it is. Release the Frank."

The slaves turned Pietro loose. He got to his feet, and hung there until the palm trees stopped their slow and stately dance before his eyes.

"What wert thou doing," the Shaikh said, "out of the place of the women, Zenobia?"

"He—he commanded them to bring me to his quarters," Zenobia said. "I escaped him and fled. 'Twas here that they captured me . . ."

Al Muqtafi turned to his son.

"Thou whelp," he said coldly, "who thinkest to roar before thy time. Go to thy quarters, I will deal with thee presently."

Harum stood there.

"Go!" al Muqtafi roared.

Harum went.

"Ye dogs of night and foulness," the Shaikh said to the eunuchs, "know that I am master here. I will not punish ye this time, for I know ye feared to disobey him. Now bring the girl and this Frank to my quarters, and summon my physician." They needed the physician. Even after only five stripes, Pietro's back was bad.

Afterwards the Shaikh caused them to be served wine and small cakes.

"I am pleased with thee, Pietro," he said. "After but one year in my service, thou hast cut my losses fully in half. Because of that, and this misfortune which has befallen thee, I am minded to reward thee. First I shall give thee a higher post: from henceforth you will conduct my caravans to the East, and be paid therefor—the hundredth part of all the goods that thou bringest safely back. . . ."

"Thank you, my Lord," Pietro said.

He could almost feel Zenobia's grey-brown eyes upon his face. He glanced at her quickly. So, he thought, those falcon's eyes can soften. Perhaps she is not all wildness and rage. I wonder. . . .

"And since thou hast suffered so in behalf of this maid," the Shaikh smiled, "I will give her to thee. Take her, Pietro—she is thine."

Pietro stared at him wordlessly. He was beyond speech.

"But my Lord—" he got out, "she is thy wife! I know thou marriedst her in the street, upon impulse; but 'twas before Allah's caliph and in the presence of witnesses. Such a match is both legal and binding. . . ."

"I have divorced her, Pietro," al Muqtafi said, "for proving barren. Besides her heathen temper displeases me. Perhaps thou canst gentle her."

Pietro looked at the girl. He remembered that day in the market place. His mind pictured vividly and accurately and in complete detail the vision of her white body bared and dazzling in the hard light of the Egyptian sun. He remembered that. He had been alone and untouched by any woman's hand for more than a year. He was a Sicilian and his blood ran hot in his veins.

But in the next instant he remembered Io in the market place at Iesi. The tears on her face. He thought of Elaine—he had that Sicilian blood with the sun of Palermo in it, but he had, too, a curiously strong sense of good and evil, a dark Italian tendency toward the mortification of his flesh. Ascetic and libertine warred forever in his slender body. Ape and angel.

She was very fair. She was more than merely fair. She had that curious quality of warmth about her so that he had the feeling that if he touched her flesh the touch would burn him. What she had was different from the compulsive hungers that drove women like Yvette—like—be it said, Elaine. This Zenobia, he thought, is a woman, all woman, and that slow voluptuousness in her is a natural thing a clean thing and very fine . . . A man she loved would be destroyed by her but he would die his death of exhaustion praising God for having lived. But I cannot. Elaine would never know, no one would know but I cannot because this would never be a passing thing never casual like the purchase for an hour or a night of a strolling street girl. I am a slave but I am free my mind is and my heart. But having her I would be slave indeed never again freed from the hungers such a one provokes so effortlessly. I would be driven by my lusts a prey to fleshly hungers until all there is of God in me, of decency or right would die in small sacrifices one by one upon the savage altars of my body's needs. . . .

"Well?" Shaikh Ahmad said.

"Please, my Lord," Pietro whispered. "I am not of thy faith. It is forbidden to us to have more than one wife, or even a concubine. I thank thee from my heart for she is most fair, still. . . ."

The grey-brown eyes were enormous now. There was something in them. Something like hurt.

"I won't press you," al Muqtafi said. "Perhaps there is some other maid that you prefer?"

"No," Pietro whispered. "There is no other maid."

He saw, as she left the room with Yusuf, that she spoke rapidly to the great black, and that he nodded slowly. Still, a Shaikh's *hareem* being what it was, her chances of troubling him very much were slight.

But he reckoned without Zenobia. That same night, Yusuf, the chief eunuch came to his quarters.

"My Lord," he said, "the Lady Zenobia wishes a word with thee."

Pietro stared at him.

"Where is she?" he demanded.

"In the garden, outside," Yusuf said.

"You—you brought her out of the *hareem*?" Pietro said wonderingly.

"Yes, My Lord."

"Why, Yusuf? By the Prophet's Own Beard, why?"

"She hath done me a great service, My Lord. There is naught that I can refuse her."

Pietro looked at him, searching the heavy, black face.

"Yet," he said drily, "this afternoon you would have beaten her to death."

"What choice had I, My Lord?" Yusuf said wonderingly. "Had I refused the Lord Harum would have given me a death that not even Shaitan could envy."

"I see. What is this service she has done you, Yusuf?" Pietro said.

"She persuaded the Shaikh to take my small son into his service as a page. And the Shaikh hath treated him most kindly. My woman is dead. The child would have starved."

"*Your* son?" Pietro said; "but Yusuf, how can that be?"

"I was not always an eunuch," Yusuf said sadly. "Which is why I comprehend and have sympathy for—love. . . ."

"Oh, my God!" Pietro said. "Don't you know this folly can cause all of us to die—even you, Yusuf?"

The great black shrugged.

"If that is the will of Allah," he said quietly, "how can we help it?"

"I don't want to die!" Pietro said. "I have a wife. I want to see her again, I—"

"That, too, is in the hands of Allah," Yusuf said. "But have no fear My Lord, I shall stand guard to see that no one comes upon you. She is waiting, My Lord. . . ."

"The sweet blue eyes of God!" Pietro swore. Then he followed Yusuf into the garden.

Zenobia stood there a long time, looking at him, before she spoke.

"I came to thank you," she whispered. "You were kind. It's been so long since anyone was kind to me—especially not at their own expense. Then later—"

"Yes?" Pietro prompted her.

"Then this afternoon, the Shaikh offered me to you as a gift. I was already beginning to get angry. You see, My Lord, if you had accepted that offer it would have destroyed all that went before—the stripes you took in my behalf even . . . But then you hesitated. You turned the matter over in your mind. I could almost hear you thinking. What way, you thought, can I refuse her without hurting her feelings?"

Pietro almost laughed aloud, but he caught himself.

"So?" he said.

"While you were thinking, I watched you. Even earlier I had seen that you were fair. I saw that the day the Shaikh bought me. Of all his followers, only you had a fair and kindly face. You took so long to think it over! Before you were done, my heart was saying: Let him say yes! Please God, let him say yes. . . ."

Pietro took her hand, held it.

"Fair Zenobia," he said gently, "this is folly, and you know it. Because I was kind, you have let your imagination overwhelm you. Think—had you seen me upon the streets of Constantinople, you would not have turned your head to look the second time. I am small and ill favored, and—"

"No! Don't say those things about yourself. You are small, it is true; but so is the hunting leopard. You have a wonderful face, very still and sad, with great dark eyes that brood forever as though you were sorrowing over the wickedness of men. I think now you can see into my soul. Dear Pietro, sweet my Lord—can't you see? All my life since childhood men have wanted me and—and taken me, too—why should I lie?—but brutally, with lust. To them I was a—a thing to be used. But you considered my feelings, I was real to you; a woman living, breathing—with a heart that could feel pain and a mind capable of choosing. You see that, don't you? What that does to me?"

"Yes," Pietro whispered, "I see. . . ."

"They say that I have the eyes of a falcon—wild, hateful, untamed. It's true: I am all of those things. But I could be gentle, Pietro. I could learn that from you. I could learn goodness from you. And I do so want to be good! I want to love you, to cherish you—to do things for you—little things like—fetching you your wine and your dates, your bread and your salt. I could strum the lute for you—and even sing a little; I have a certain small voice that others say is not unpleasing. I could put warm cloths to your head when it aches, and anoint you with fragrant oils. In all my life, no one has ever made me happy. But you could, my Lord. Is it so strange that I want these simple things that most women take as a matter of course, knowing I've never had them?"

Pietro stood there, holding both her hands in his. He could feel a great weight inside his heart. A sadness. She moved him. He understood these things she had said because even as she said them they seemed to him a résumé of his own life. These things, these simple things that were all most men wanted out of life: to have a woman gentle and fair to make his days happy in these quiet, uncomplicated ways. And it was precisely of these that he had been cheated. He had had great honors and fame and wealth which were the coinage that the world prized and, like nearly everything else valued of most men, they had proved to be of base metals and counterfeit.

This would be so easy. Elaine would never know and Io would never know and in what way was the giving and the taking of simple happiness a sin?

His dark eyes brooded over her face.

There was so much in those eyes. So much tenderness. He turned away his face and as he did so, his gaze flickered briefly over the great scimitar that Yusuf carried. That blade could cut through the links of mail as easily as a European blade could hack wood. Yet you could bend it double and it would not break.

I am like that, he thought suddenly, I have often been bent to earth, yet release me and I spring upright again, unbroken. Why? Because like that Saracen blade I have been tempered in the furnace. I have been hammered upon and quenched of the heat within me in the cold baths, then reheated and cooled more slowly (by disappointments, by small disasters, by waiting) until the strength within me is flexible strength, but until now I have complained bitterly of the tempering. . . .

This is very simple very easy and my blood sings within me cries out for me to take this maid, this maid who can only draw out of me the supple strength leaving me brittle so that the next blow (and there will be other blows—doubt it not) will break me. And I can only give to her the happiness that makes the coming sorrow more bitter by contrast. Because men daily betray the words, does not mean that there are no such things as honor, justice, human dignity. We have debased their value by too much usage, by mouthing them to cover the foul multitude of our sins. But they are. And God lives. The vows I took before Him when I took Elaine unto me, are Holy vows, which not even this anguish in my blood this hot swelling of desire can justify breaking. And so—I suffer. God grant it is not in vain. . . .

He tried to tell her what he meant. In Arabic, and then in Greek. But his unpracticed Greek was not equal to the task and the language of the Saracens was shaped upon other concepts of honor and of faith than the stern Christian beliefs. A race who equipped their heaven with fountains spraying wine, and complaisant maidens who renewed their virginity after each time they eased the lust of the Prophet's faithful, had not the words to explain, to make believable the virtues of self denial. A Saracen could be both a mystic and a stoic when he had to be, but he saw no virtue in the things themselves.

When she left him, she was crying and terribly hurt. And he was sick at heart, and full of doubts, with all his high resolutions in tatters about his feet.

He was saved for a time by the fact that al Muqtafi dispatched him almost immediately upon a journey to India. It took him more than two years. When, in 1224, he came back, the very night of his arrival a slave ushered him at once to the baths without letting him enter his quarters. Pietro was too tired even to wonder at this. But when he returned to his chambers he smelled the perfume. She had anointed her body with oil of ambergris and musk. She had painted her mouth with scarlet. Her mouth—and other parts of her body. The effect was startling.

Pietro had been away from home too long now. There were limits to his endurance. And the limits had been passed. That night Pietro knew what the Prophet's paradise was like. And that all Europeans were children. Zenobia was an artist. A very great artist. It was weeks later before he came to reflect painfully upon how she had acquired her diabolical skill.

They were together but rarely. That they were was due to Harum. With all the hundreds of maidens at his disposal, Harum coveted Zenobia still—only because she had balked him, having in this the support of his father.

Pietro was very shortly aware that the maidservant in his quarters was a spy. Even Yusuf advised caution.

What was between Zenobia and him now was a very lovely, fragile thing: a hasty word spoken in the garden while seeming to pass each other by accident, missives left childishly in an empty urn near the women's quarter—now and again, with the aid of black Yusuf—in a rented chamber in the town, a night of stolen bliss.

Then Pietro was off again to Yazdigird and Samarkand, to Damascus and Baghdad.

And in between, the quick, guarded pressure of hand on hand in the night-locked garden, the soft, warm lips pressing his, then breaking, and the sound of slippered feet scurrying away. And in the urns, the scrolls of parchment with the lovely, flowing Arabic script. "O Lord of Lords, more beautiful than the fiery stag upon the mountains! More swift than the leopards bounding after the gazelles . . . My heart, o Pietro, is a gazelle, and hath fainted within me at the sight of thee. O conquering Lord, o noonday sun of my delight, how long, how long?"

How long. Pietro was sick at heart when he thought of that. A certain danger existed in this folly. True enough, Ahmad had offered him the girl. But he had refused her. And now, if he were ever caught taking secretly what he had refused openly, the Shaikh would be honor bound to put him to death.

But beyond that danger was another thing: He had left Elaine to give her time to accept him. He had not contemplated breaking the holiest of all vows. Freethinker that he was, Pietro was not that far beyond his fellows. He loved Elaine. But he was enslaved by Zenobia. He had not known that the voluptuary arts could be carried to such a peak of exquisite refinement. His nights with Zenobia approached something like torture: alone of the women he had known she knew how to keep passion from abating; in the midst of satisfying his clamorous needs, she aroused new ones before the old were stilled. He was hideously ashamed of their few times together. Afterwards he scourged his own body.

This shame rode and bedevilled him night and day. Particularly since the Shaikh was always marveling at his supposed chastity. It was to Ahmad, a thing of endless astonishment and amusement, that his Sāhib al kharāj, that is, his master of finances, which was Pietro's rather imposing title, had thus far refused to take any of the lovely slave girls offered him as his concubine. And when they hinted that perhaps the Ifranji's tastes ran in other directions, Ahmad was able to tell them that Pietro had likewise refused any of the painted and perfumed young *ghilmani,* those well trained and very pretty boys so much affected nowadays by the Arab aristocracy.

"I tell thee, it's a marvel!" Ahmad laughed. "He is a very lion in the chase, having learned as though born among us the control of the hunting leopard. The *saqr,* he knew before, as falconry is not unknown among the Franks. He rides with the best of my *fursān;* I have seen him win a wager of a thousand dinars from the captain of my cavalry in a race between his mare and the Qā'id's. He plays *mall*[1] with my elder sons and beats them, too, driving the ball through the goals as though he and his mare had one body. Yet—he will have no maid. . . ."

Pietro, of course, did not disillusion him.

Pietro's life went on in that curious suspension of living between his journeys. He dallied with Zenobia, walking always a tightrope above disaster. He sat at the feet of the *khojas* and the *hadjis* with the sons of his master, and learned the wisdom of the Qûr'an. He practiced with the curving scimitar, whose blade of marvelous steel was so flexible you could bend it double, yet so well tempered that it could cut through the links of chain mail with ease. The defense against it was the counterstroke, the parry; Europeans with their two-handed, massive blades incapable of bending at all were nearly always bested in a duel with a Saracen swordsman, whose agility and cunning in fence, set at naught the tall Franks' greater strength and smashing blows. He learned Saracen horsemanship, to ride bridleless the exquisite mares, for in this regard, as in many others, Europeans and Saracens were directly opposed, the European holding it unmanly to ride a mare, and the Arab preferring her sensitivity and greater speed, controlling her with the lightest pressure on her thigh. He could now execute the exercise of the lance, in which one horseman pursued another at breakneck speed, hurling a lance at his back. The trick was to turn in your saddle, catch the lance in one hand, and pursue your attacker in turn . . . He dreamed of Elaine. Of Io.

Then, late in 1225, al Muqtafi sent him on the greatest, most perilous of all journeys. On a bleak winter day early in 1229, he was almost in sight of Cairo, on his way back.

He wrapped his burnoose tighter about his face, and hunched forward in the tall saddle his camel bore. Behind him the long line of the caravan stretched out of sight over the dunes. It was flanked on both sides by gaunt Turkoman warriors on beautiful racing dromedaries, their razor edged *yataghans* ready for any Bedouin raider who might sweep over the dunes to attack.

It was going to be good to see Cairo again. He had been away from it for three long years. This, the longest journey that the Shaikh al Muqtafi had yet entrusted him with, had taken him over the roof of the world, through the unbelievably icy mountains of Tibet, and down again into Cathay. Now on this winter day of 1229 he was back again, laden with treasure. Pietro had never ceased to wonder at the extent of the wealth piled up by the wily Ayyubite Shaikh; in one voyage his merchant travelers returned him more goods, slaves, and treasure than a European merchant would have been able to accumulate.

Ahmad had never—and Pietro knew why—let Pietro manage one of the sea voyages that touched on the shores of the Mediterranean. It would have been far too easy for his valued slave to jump ship and buy passage back to Italy on another vessel. His journeys to Yazdigird and Samarkand, to Damascus and Baghdad had all been overland. He had commanded many a caravan on shorter journeys; but never had he been permitted to take the equally profitable voyages to Constantinople or to Cyprus. . . .

Even now he knew he was being watched. Among the Turkomen and Seljuks of his guard who obeyed his commands without a hint of dissent, there were doubtless three or four with direct orders from the Shaikh to prevent any attempt on his part to escape. Pietro, in a curious way, was proud of this fact. It represented concrete accomplishments on his part. He was a slave, yes; but he had his own quarters in Ahmad's palace; he had as gifts from Ahmad, dozens of slaves of his own, trained to anticipate his every whim. Ahmad treated him now like a son—a well loved son.

It would be good to get back to Cairo again. He loved Cairo now, as he had not loved another city since he left Palermo. It is, he mused, as he swayed through that unbelievably uncomfortable gait of the camel—seeing the pyramids now, coming up from the desert's edge, and beyond them the deep green of the trees around the city—as if I've found a second home. . . .

Two hours later, they came at last into the courtyard of the warehouses, having passed through streets filled with Cairo's polyglot throngs. Pietro had looked with delight upon the learned Kadis, sitting sidewise on their donkeys under parasols held by disciples who trotted along beside them, and discoursing on the Qûr'an. He had been pleased to see the fat and pompous merchants in striped *khalats* with heavy purses swinging from their girdles, and the black clad Bedouins of the desert eyeing them and fingering their blades. Holy men sat with shaven heads in the dust, and thrust out their filthy bowls for alms of food; dervishes circled slowly to the somber drumbeats, and hideously crippled beggars thrust out their noisome paws, oblivious to the flies that crusted their eyes and the corners of their mouths. Mamluks in jeweled *khalats* strode along, elbowing from their path the sheepskin clad Turkoman and Kurdish tribesmen, while gigantic eunuchs escorted the litters of veiled beauties of the *hareem* of some Shaikh or Amir. . . .

Late that evening, he lay stretched out naked upon his couch while Abdul, his slave, shaved his body. He had wondered at this custom at first, but after seeing its advantages in cleanliness, coolness, and protection against the insects that even the cleanest man was likely to pick up while in unwelcome contact with the filthy hordes in Cairo's streets, he had become accustomed to it. Afterwards, he lolled in his bath, letting the perfumed waters soak the tiredness from his limbs, sipping orange sherbet and eating little almond cakes, while Abdul brought him up to date on the happenings in Egypt.

He paid but scant attention to Abdul's chatter, lying there in the hot, perfumed water, thinking of other things, when finally it penetrated to his consciousness that Abdul had used the Arabic equivalent of the name Frederick, not once, but twice.

He sat bolt upright in the vast marble bath.

"What say you, Abdul?" he cried. "What is this of Frederick?"

"If my Lord would but harken to his humble servant," Abdul complained, "I would not need so often to repeat myself. The Franks have come again, under the leadership of their Sultan Frederick, to attack our holy places. . . ."

Pietro leaped from the tub.

"Where are they?" he demanded. "At what port have they landed?"

Abdul picked up the huge towels, and proceeded to dry Pietro's slim body.

"At Acre, of course, my Lord. Where else would they land save at that accursed town smelling of pigs and the stink of Frankish sweat?"

Acre. But Acre was on the Syrian Coast, many leagues away. Still, there must be some way that he could slip away, and join Frederick there. He could reach it by sea, if he ever dared board a *felucca*. But that would be the one thing that Shaikh Ahmad would watch. The journey by land was tedious, yet if he were to take Sheba, his racing dromedary, a beast faster than any horse, he might slip through under the pretext of going hunting in the desert. . . .

But almost immediately, Abdul dashed his hopes.

"Our Lord the Caliph al Kamil, hath all his armies drawn up from Nablus to the sea, completely cutting off the approaches to Jerusalem. This Frederick hath not a chance. He hath less than a thousand knights."

Pietro groaned.

"Give me my robes," he said.

Abdul dressed him in his silken garments, winding the turban skillfully about his head and chatting as he worked.

"Still all the world marvels that the Sultan hath not yet attacked this dog of a Frank," Abdul went on. "The Sultan al Muazzam, ruler of Damascus, is dead, and his infant son is powerless to oppose our great ruler. Additionally, our Caliph hath drawn up treaties with Mesopotamia, and hath taken much of the lands of Damascus, including Jerusalem, already. The Frankish Lord can be of no further use to him, though men say that al Kamil did call him to our land to aid us against al Muazzam before the Angel of Death so fortunately took that treacherous Damascene. . . ."

Pietro considered this. A glimmer of light showed under the door of his prison. If there were any kind of alliance, secret or otherwise between Frederick and al Kamil—and knowing Frederick there might well be—some chance existed. . . .

He picked up his silver mounted scimitar and his poinard, and attached them to his girdle. Then he strode toward the salon of his master to make his report. But just before he entered he was halted by the sound of voices: Harum's voice—and his father's.

"I tell thee, father," Harum was saying, "it's the only way! I know the Frank is both dear and valuable to thee, but who else could do it? Consider: The *fedawi* of the Shaikh al Jebal are very skilled in eluding guards, but the sentries about the banquet hall will doubtless be Franks. What excuse could the assassins give to men who speak no Arabic? Don't you see! This Frank of thine, dressed in Frankish garb, smiling and fair. . . ."

"He wouldn't do it," Ahmad growled. "I could not make him, and besides he's too valuable in the post where he now serves. Where could I find me such another?"

"The sacrifice must be made, o my father! The fate of our Holy Places is at stake! What kind of Muslim art thou who putteth private gain above the Prophet's shrines?"

"Thou hast much right, my son," Ahmad sighed. "Forgive me. Tonight after the banquet, the old Shaikh can begin. . . ."

Pietro shrank aside into the shadows and let Harum pass. His brain raced, but his thoughts refused to fit themselves together. He had heard of the Shaikh al Jebal before—but what? Even the words *fedawi*—devoted ones, and *hashshāshīn,* eaters of hashīsh, were familiar to him. Together the words made a pattern: The old man of the mountain, the devoted ones, the eaters of the mind-destroying drug taken from hemp. But what was the pattern? And how did he fit into it? Frankish guards, banquet hall. . . .

He gave it up. He'd have to have more information before he

could solve this riddle. But from the way this thing sounded, he'd better get that information soon.

Shaikh Ahmad received him with an embrace, but he avoided Pietro's eyes. Clearly there was something amiss here.

Pietro spoke rapidly and to the point. The mission had been a success exceeding all their hopes. There were countless bales of yellow Chinese silk now in the warehouses, pieces of carved jade and ivory worth the ransom of a king, and even a delicate, slant-eyed maid or two for his lord's delight. Spices, of course, and lacquered woods and perfumes of extraordinary sweetness. Brass and bronze works, including deep-toned gongs, and the less unusual jewels and golden and silver ornaments. . . .

"Thou hast done well, my son," Ahmad said, but his voice was tight and strained. "Therefore, this night will I honor thee. Tonight will my second son Najmud be wed to Burum, daughter of the Grand Wizir. Though thou art a slave and a Frank, a seat is waiting for thee among my family—and after the banquet, I have plans for thy future which I will discuss with thee. . ."

They were moving very fast, Pietro saw that. But he bowed very low, and saluted his master, touching forehead and lips and heart, saying:

"I am honored, My Lord; and though thy servant is unworthy of this boon, yet will I be present in order to see the union of thy exalted and fortunate son, with the beauteous daughter of the wise and honorable Wizir. . . ."

Then he took his leave. It was now almost night, and as he was crossing the lush garden, just outside the women's quarters, a powerful hand clapped down upon his shoulder. He turned and stared into the grinning face of Yusuf, the giant chief eunuch of the *hareem.*

"There, My Lord," Yusuf nodded, and Pietro saw the little pagoda, built after the Chinese style which decorated one corner of the garden. "She awaits you. Make haste, for in five minutes I must slip her back in. . . ."

"Oh, thou black and ugly panderer!" Pietro growled. "Wouldst have my gullet slit and hers and thine?"

Yusuf laughed.

"Come, My Lord," he said. "She only wishes a word with you. . . ."

Pietro stepped inside the pagoda. It was dark, but he could smell the scents of musk, ambergris, and violet. The scents were all about him, smothering him. Her mouth was sweetspiced, clinging. There was her softness clinging, too, and under that softness, the sinewy feel of her strength, the catlike power of her fingers working slowly, devilishly into the flesh of the back of his neck. He put up his hands and broke her grip.

"Pietro!" she whispered, and her voice broke. "You are in danger—terrible danger oh my love—and I—and I, God help me, I don't know what this danger is!"

"Then how do you know of it?" Pietro growled.

"Zubaydah, the favorite of Harum told me. She taunted me that now at last her Lord would be rid of thee! Beyond that, I know nothing. But oh, My Lord, my sweet—take care!"

"I'll take much care, Zenobia. I, too, have heard of this. I know as little as you do, but I know they plan to employ me in some dangerous mission. Tonight they are going to tell me of it. But I shall outwit them, for Jesus is mightier than the Prophet. . . ."

"Sometimes, my love," Zenobia whispered, "sometimes I doubt —even that . . ."

"Don't," Pietro said, and kissed her. "Sleep well, my love," he said. "Have no fear for me. . . ."

"Sleep!" Zenobia said; "until I learn that you are safe, I shall never sleep again!"

Back at his quarters, Abdul increased his wonder by telling him that he, too, had been commanded to attend this feast along with Pietro. That had some meaning. Slaves of Abdul's lowly rank played no part in the revels of the great.

He stood there, frowning while Abdul dressed him in his *sirwal,* those voluminous trousers of heavy silk. Pietro's were white and embroidered with threads of silver. Then the *guftan,* or short jacket, above a sash of silver cloth, leaving Pietro's chest bare but for a heavy necklace, and over all the *jubbah* or outer mantle, sweeping almost to the floor, white like the rest of his costume, and having seed pearls worked into the embroidery work of silver threads. Abdul carefully fitted the long, dangling ear pendants of great pearls through the small holes pierced through the lobes of Pietro's ears. Then last of all the slave adjusted the black, high peaked hat, the *galensuwah,* and wrapped a spotless, snowy turban of many folds about its high crown. He brought Pietro his rings and additional necklaces, his silver mounted scimitar and matched pair of poinards, and stood back to admire the effect.

"Walk this way, My Lord," he begged, "then turn. . . ."

Pietro did so, though his slippers caused him some difficulty, being so heavily crusted with silver that they hurt his feet.

"Aiyee!" Abdul cried. "Thou art this night a prince and a son of princes, o My Lord!"

"Thank you," Pietro smiled, then he stopped. Abdul was staring past him out the opened door, his face frozen into a mass of terror.

Pietro turned. An old man walked slowly along, flanked by slaves bearing torches. He was a little old man, utterly insignificant in his bearing.

Pietro turned back to his slave. But Abdul had prostrated himself on the floor, and was bumping his head and crying:

"Allah preserve us! O Merciful! O Compassionate! Save us!"

"What ails thee, Abdul?" Pietro demanded.

"That man!" Abdul whispered. "That old man is none other than—" his voice dropped so low that Pietro had to bend toward him in order to hear him—"than the Shaikh al Jebal!"

Pietro stared at the Shaikh's retreating back.

"I have heard that name," he mused, "still I cannot recall. . . ."

"The Old Man of the Mountain!" Abdul whispered. "The leader of the *fedawi* of the *hashshāshīn!* Of those mindless murderers, who kill whomever he wants slain!"

The memory of the things he had heard, long ago, and dismissed as idle gossip flooded back into Pietro's mind. The pieces of the pattern clicked into place, each piece fitting into neat, interlocking dovetails. "This Frank of thine, dressed in Frankish garb, smiling and fair," Harum had said. And Ahmad had commented upon his knowledge of European tongues.

And now, the Shaikh al Jebal. The old Man of the Mountain. The leader of the terrible sect of the Assassins, which word already had come to mean more than merely eaters of hashīsh, which now all over the Saracen world was synonymous with "killers."

Doubtless Frederick and al Kamil feasted together nightly, now. And Frederick was guarded by German and Italian knights. The assassins, of course, the *fedawi,* the devoted ones, those mindless, murderous robots that the Shaikh al Jebal made of normal young men—by what means? Pietro didn't know that. No one did. He knew only that the *fedawi* were like walking dead men; they knew no fear. When they were sent out to kill, they killed, even if they died in the process. They seemed glad to die. But how did they become like that? By what means, by what terrible alchemy did the Shaikh al Jebal rob them of their souls?

He felt sick, just thinking of it; for he knew where he fitted into the pattern. Ahmad was one of those Ayyubite Amirs who hated al Kamil with all their hearts. During that siege of Damietta, they had forced him to flee from the camp at Mansura. Their hatred went back to the day when his brother, the former Sultan of Damascus, had destroyed the walls of Jerusalem in 1220, making of it an open city. This hatred of theirs was all the more poisonous because al Kamil was himself of the Ayyubite line. But however much they wanted to murder Malik al Kamil, and that Frankish dog, Frederick II with him, there remained those German and Italian guards. No ordinary assassin could slip through lines of men who spoke little or no Arabic. But a Frank could. Pietro could . . . dressed once more in European clothes, his beard shaved, smiling and speaking fair words, while in his will-less, mindless soul—controlled from afar by the old Shaikh—reposed only murder.

He loved Frederick like a brother. But it wouldn't be his own heart that spoke. The mind within him wouldn't be his mind. The hand that struck down Sultan and Emperor would be as remorseless, as relentless as the hand of God Himself. . . .

One thing he knew. The ones chosen to become assassins were usually entertained at a banquet. Some time during the night they were given drugged wine. Then they were carried off. When they came back, they were like—that.

He stared out the doorway in the direction that the old Shaikh had gone.

The wine. The drugged wine. If, he thought, I can avoid drinking it, why then. . . .

"Come," he said to Abdul.

Inside the great hall, a two hundred roti candle of ambergris turned night into day; and when the young couple appeared, they were seated upon a divan of gold studded with sapphires, and slaves poured a basket containing a thousand pearls, each greater than a pigeon's egg, over their heads in a milky shower. Other slaves passed balls of musk among the nobles present. Each ball, when opened, contained a script entitling the receiver to an estate, a valued slave, a blooded mare, or a beautiful dancing girl. But the wonder of all wonders was the artificial tree of gold and silver, made in exact imitation of the one that Harum al Raschid had owned, in whose glittering, jeweled branches sang birds of the same metals, with ruby eyes, and sweet twittering voices piped into their mechanical bodies by Allah knew what mysterious means.

The delicacies set before the guests were without number. There were roast fowl, fattened on milk and almonds, served up roasted in a dish of grapes and almonds with a sauce of wine and honey; there were sugared cakes, a dish of slices of fish so small that the guests exclaimed over them. Whereupon the serving slaves proudly informed them that the slices were fishes' tongues, and that each dish of one hundred and fifty tongues had cost their master more than a thousand dirhams. Every form of sherbet, sweetened with sugar, and made of water flavored with the crushed petals of roses, or violets, or with bananas, mulberries, or oranges were served, filled with crushed ice, brought down by swift runners from the mountains of Syria, and packed in heavy layers of straw for its voyage by sea and up the Nile.

Pietro savored all these delicacies, but he was careful not to eat too much so as not to become sleepy, and refused gracefully, on the grounds of religion, the wine that was brought around just before the dancing girls appeared. It was hard to keep alert amid the smell of ambergris and the aloes-woods burning in the censers. But when Ahmad and the other notables started perfuming their beards with rose water, Pietro knew that they were about to settle down to serious drinking, and that all the prohibitions in the Qûr'an against drunkenness would soon be set at naught. Slaves appeared with Khamr, that fragrant date wine, and after that Greek slave girls, with golden crosses about their necks, and clad in garments of silk that seemed more like wisps of vapor than like cloth, came out and danced.[2]

After the dancing, Pietro was conducted to Shaikh Ahmad's *diwan*. Ahmad questioned him at some length about the details of his journey to China, more, Pietro realized, for the benefit of his other guests, than to increase his own knowledge, since he already knew much of far Cathay.

"Is't true," he asked, "that there are men there with heads beneath their shoulders, eyes looking out from their breasts, and mouths opening where sits the navel in the commonality of men?"

"No, my Lord," Pietro said; "it's an old wives' tale. But this I did encounter upon my journey—a tribe of men so lacking in jealousy that they lent to our guards and drivers their wives for the duration of our stay with them . . . It was a wondrous land, far up in the mountains where the snows haunt the earth all year long, and of a chill so fierce that our teeth outpranced My Lord's dancing girls. . . ."

Ahmad's eyes twinkled.

"Sit, my soul's son," he said, indicating a silken cushion at his feet; "and commence thy lying reasons as to why thou didst not avail thyself of a borrowed wife!"

Pietro laughed aloud.

"That I did not is no lie, My Lord," he said, "and for the reason that these Tibetan maids were exceeding short and fat, with faces as flat as earthen platters, and of an equal color. And since, in addition to their ugliness, they greased their bodies with the fat of sheep, and never bathed, they smelt most wondrously vile!"

The guests almost choked with laughter.

"More!" they gasped, wiping the tears from their eyes. "Tell us more!"

"There were in those mountains," Pietro told them, "camels

with two humps instead of one, and more woolly than any sheep. I tried to bring My Lord one back for his menagerie; but it died of the heat on the homeward journey. The leopards among the snows are white, for purposes of hiding, for so hath Allah blessed His creatures—having but the faintest trace of spots. My Turkomen slew several, and I am having the skins dressed and made into a rug for thee, My Lord. . . ."

He talked on, describing every detail of the journey. He told them of the strange ships of the Chinese, with their great sails made of woven matting, and the dragons' faces painted on their bows. He described the hollow tubes the Chinese had, that when charged with a black powder and ignited spoke with voices like thunder and hurled stones for great distances; and how his efforts to obtain some of this powder had been balked. He talked at length about ivory carving, and jade work, and spices, and medicines and magic, and of the wondrous bows of the Mongolian horsemen of the steppes, of which to his own delight, he had been able to obtain samples—together with their whistling arrows and other oddities. . . .

When he was done, many of the guests praised to Shaikh Ahmad the diligence and wisdom of his slave. Hearing their words, al Muqtafi was troubled. He was very fond of Pietro. And Pietro was valuable to him. Yet there was his hatred of al Kamil, and his utter detestation of the treaty that was to be concluded between Frederick and the Caliph tomorrow. The hatred won, but it did not altogether displace his sorrow at what he had to do.

"Thou hast spoken well, my son," he said. "I would reward thee. Tell me what dost thy heart crave?"

Pietro looked at him. If ever there were a time for boldness, it was now.

"Only," he said quietly, "that my Lord give me whatever news he can of the invading Franks."

Every eye among the guests close enough to Pietro to have heard his words, was turned at once upon Shaikh Abu-Bekr Ahmad al Muqtafi's face. He sat there, staring at Pietro for so long that the little pool of silence about them widened to include others of the guests. All over the hall, conversation died.

"Father, no!" Harum said.

Slowly Ahmad smiled.

"And why not, my son?" he said calmly. "Thinkest thou he will recall my words after tonight?"

Pietro could see Harum thinking almost visibly of the drugged wine, of the old Shaikh, of whatever it was that was done to men by his hand to rob them of their souls.

Harum threw back his head and laughed aloud.

"Thou hast much right, o my father!" he said.

"Now will I tell thee, Pietro," Ahmad said, "because thou hast claimed this knowledge as thy reward; but I will speak also because others here have need of this history. . . .

"The Franks came with a tiny force, insufficient to carry an outpost, much less Jerusalem. They encamped outside Acre and sent envoys to our Sultan. In return, our Sultan sent them presents and the Amir Fakhru'd Din to treat with them. Fakhru'd is a great and scholarly gentleman, but somewhat too easily impressed. It seemed that he returned to the Sultan filled with breathless admiration of the Frankish Emperor, Frederick, who, like thyself, o Pietro, hath no need of an interpreter, speaking the language of the children of Allah cleanly and without fault. Fakhru'd was astonished at this Frederick's knowledge of our science, and, also, what seemed to so uncritical a man as the Amir as the Frank's keenness of mind, and largeness of heart. . . .

"Had Fakhru'd Din examined the matter more carefully, he would have seen the cunning of this son of Shaitan. For the Emperor Frederick used the very weakness of his forces as a telling argument, swearing that he hath come to conclude peacefully the differences between our people and thine, and had brought no more than a token force as an earnest of his intent. But Fakhru'd hath not my sources of information: he knew not the great difficulties that prevented Frederick from bringing more men, else would this kindly but childish Amir realize that these talks were designed to delay matters until reinforcements could arrive from the Frankish lands. . . ."

"What were these difficulties, my Lord?" Pietro asked.

"Chiefly that thy Caliph—how is he called? I mean that strange official who heads your Nazarene faith, for I am informed that in

Frankish lands your Sultan is not your Caliph—the two offices, the kingly, and the religious, being separate. . . ."

"True," Pietro said. "Our Caliph is called the Pope, our Sultan, the Emperor; and the two offices are separate which makes for bitter conflict. . . ."

"Your Pope, then, it appears, hates your Emperor with all his heart. He hath sent envoys begging our Sultan not to treat with Frederick. Additionally, he sent a counterfeit of the Emperor, rendered by a most cunning artist, so that it would be easier for al Kamil to recognize him and take him prisoner. Our Sultan hath no distaste for treachery, having dealt in it throughout his life; but he is very pious, so the Prophet's command against making representations of animals or men is kept scrupulously by him. . . .

"With his mighty armies, Sultan al Kamil could crush your Emperor's puny forces in one day. But Fakhru'd Din hath won his admiration and his curiosity concerning your Emperor; besides which—there are many, and this I can say freely, for only those of mine own persuasion were invited to this nuptial feast—who hate worse than death that branch of our own blood line that hath betrayed us in many small betrayals until today our Holy City, Jerusalem—sacred to us as the place of the Prophet's ascent into heaven—lies naked and helpless before any really large and determined enemy.

"Malik al Kamil knows of that hatred. He is tempted therefore, to use these childish tales of Fakhru'd's as an excuse for the greatest treachery that hath ever disgraced a Sultan!"

Pietro was aware that Ahmad was no longer speaking to him, but to the assembled company. There was fire in his eyes. His voice thundered. He had forgotten Pietro completely.

"On tomorrow," Ahmad shouted, "he will conclude a treaty by which our Holy City will be almost entirely given to this Frankish dog, who hath not the strength to take it by force of arms!"

The entire hall broke into a wild uproar. Men stood up, screaming, shaking their fists.

Ahmad spread wide his hands.

"Peace, my brethren," he said quietly. "That matter will be taken care of—forever! Trust me. And now—remember this is a marriage feast. Eat, drink, and be merry—for ye have no cause for fear. Allah reigns still; and his children have both the wisdom and the strength to deal with traitors!"

The guests subsided into murmuring. Shortly thereafter, Pietro saw the sons of Ahmad passing among them, whispering, and they began to take their leave.

Quickly. Too quickly. Tomorrow, by the Christian calendar, Pietro reckoned, would be February 18, 1229. Ahmad had need of haste.

He sat very still on his cushion. When the last of the guests had gone, and the young couple had retired, the Shaikh came down from his divan and smilingly took Pietro's arm.

"Come," he said, "thou and thy slave Abdul. We have planned a reward for thy valor and thy services. Come with me, my son. . . ."

Wordlessly, Pietro followed Ahmad into a smaller hall. There, still another feast had been laid out before them. And at the head of the table, the Shaikh al Jebal sat, looking at them out of his murderous black eyes. The delicacies exceeded those served at the wedding feast. And this time the slave girls danced naked, clad only in ropes of many colored beads.

The girls sat upon their laps, covering their faces with kisses. Pietro laughed, but he did not touch the wine.

In five minutes, Abdul had forgotten his fear of the Shaikh al Jebal. He drank deeply, his small eyes glittering with drunkenness and lust.

Poor devil, Pietro thought. They have him now.

While all the others were watching the singing girl, and listening to her songs of the delights of love, Pietro quickly emptied his tall goblet on the floor beneath the table. Then he made a great show of drinking from it.

"Now art thou wise!" Harum laughed. "Enjoy that cup—for it's the key to such delights as thou hast never dreamed of!"

Pietro watched Abdul. The slave's head nodded, once, twice, three times. Then it crashed down against the table so hard that his goblet and his platter were broken.

Pietro smiled. It had been his intention to feign unconsciousness, and gain thereby an opportunity to escape. But the more he thought about it, the worse that plan seemed. Escape—how? Where could be obtain a camel or a horse? Where could he go, alone and without supplies?

He laughed aloud, suddenly, startlingly. The answer was so simple. He wanted to reach Frederick—and they also wanted him to! Make them send him to Jerusalem. Promise them anything. And once there, cap their cunning with greater cunning, teach them how hard a Sicilian was to outdo in treachery.

But to do that, he must escape the tender mercies of the Shaikh al Jebal. His mind must not be tampered with. He'd need the cunning of a serpent for what he planned to do. . . .

He was aware that they were staring at him, with stupefaction in their faces. He stood up.

"My Lords," he said, "know you that I have a talisman against the action of all drugs and poisons. But I beg of you, give but a moment's heed to my words:

"O conquering lion of the house of Muqtafi, thou knowest well how I was taken. I was sent with others of my friends against Damietta, by that same Emperor Frederick whom thou wouldst like to have me slay. My dearest friends were slain, I was reduced from a Lord in mine own right to a bondsman because he betrayed us, failing to send either the supplies or the reinforcements that he had promised! I lost through him a wife I loved. I tell you, o mighty Shaikh, o Lord most powerful and great, that I will do thy bidding in this matter without the need of drugged wines or the attentions of thy august guest. . . ."

"He lies!" Harum spat. "It's but a trick to escape us and warn them!"

"A trick, my Lords? By the Prophet's beard I speak the truth! Yet, I can comprehend thy doubts. Very well—send me to Jerusalem under guard. Thou hast friends there. Quarter me with them. Give them thy command to slay me if I fail!"

Ahmad studied his face.

"Our friends," he said evenly, "could not touch you once you were inside the palace, where of necessity you would have to perform this task."

Pietro groaned within his heart. Trust Ahmad to put his finger on the pivotal point upon which turned his whole plan. But as always under stress, his brain was racing.

"Thou hast planned, hast thou not, My Lord," he said, "to make of Abdul one of the fedawi? Then send him with me. As my servant he can enter the palace with me. Give him the weapons. Give me none. When he hath become an assassin, he will be impervious to my commands. Then, once inside I can point out to him the Emperor Frederick whom I know well, and hate equally. . . ."

"This makes much sense," Ahmad growled, "save in one point only—why should we take the risk of leaving thy mind uncontrolled? Thy plan is good, but 'twould be safer far to remove all doubts of thee."

"Because then, you wouldst surely fail, My Lord," Pietro said. "I have seen the fedawi, and their faces would betray them instantly to anyone who had known them before. Remember this, the Emperor Frederick knows me well. So does Herman of Salza and several hundred others of the Emperor's knights. At one glance, they would see that something was amiss with me. They would put me to the question, and my befogged brain could not dissemble, or resort to guile. Wouldst rather send me as I am, smiling and keen of eye, than as a walking corpse, whom at best they would think mad and prevent from getting near the Emperor?"

Even Harum's face was puzzled now, but Pietro did not exult. Even if they permitted him his plan the risks were great, hideously great. He would have to throw himself upon Abdul unarmed, and try to take the daggers from him. He'd have to do this by himself and very quickly, for, if he called upon the knights for aid, Abdul would surely kill him before the cry had half left his lips. The assassins were wonderfully skilled at murder. To make it worse, he'd have to wait until they were inside the palace before attempting to disarm his slave. Were he to try it outside in the street, the spies that the Ayyubites had everywhere would cut him down in half a heartbeat. Besides, he wanted, if possible, to save Abdul from being slain. The slave had been very devoted and loyal in his service. Some means might be found to restore the poor devil to his senses. . . .

Ahmad was looking at him. The Shaikh's face was frowning.

"All of this, o Pietro, maketh much sense," he said, "yet one doubt clings in my mind: Why wouldst thou do this thing? The reasons that thou gavest are not sufficient. Thou art a slave, but thy bondage hath been light. Thou hast lost thy wife, but thou couldst have other wives. . . . It is thy lack of real motivation that maketh me doubt thee still. . . ."

Pietro looked at him. I should have known, he thought bitterly, that the reasons that I gave would make but small sense to the Saracen mind. But now, by God's Grace, what other can I give him? What motive would he believe? Then, suddenly, clearly, he had it. The one reason no Saracen would doubt. A man driven by fleshly lusts was always comprehensible to a race who peopled even heaven with *houris*. . . .

"I—I thought, my Lord," Pietro stammered, in well acted hesitation, "that if I served thee well in this, and survived—I might gain thy favor enough to dare ask thee for—for the Lady Zenobia, whom I so foolishly refused when my Lord offered her to me. I have repented of that folly a thousand, thousand times since! But I dared not speak lest my Lord be wroth with me. . ."

Ahmad looked at him, and the ghost of a smile played about his lips.

"Prepare the slave, Abdul, for his journey to Alamut," he said. "Confine the Frank to his quarters under strictest guard until Abdul has been brought back again. We shall adopt thy plan, o Pietro—thou most devious of all Franks. Upon thy return the maid shall be waiting in thy quarters; this maid whom thou couldst have had any time thou wished merely for the asking, and for whom now, thou must pay so high a price!"

Pietro could see the rage in Harum's face. Strange that Ahmad should have denied his eldest son this girl whom he no longer wanted. But then again, considering the matter, perhaps it wasn't strange. Harum feared his father, envied him the continuing vigor that—barring accident, made his own succession to Ahmad's honors and positions a matter of years of patient waiting. The relationship between father and son was strained, sometimes even openly hostile. Ahmad knew Harum. Perhaps he even enjoyed baiting him with this—since to the Shaikh the possession of one slave girl more or less was a matter of little importance.

"I thank thee, my Lord," Pietro said. Then the swordsmen led him away.

Pietro did not see Abdul again. He was sent to Jerusalem by one caravan and Pietro by another. While they waited Frederick's arrival in Jerusalem, they were quartered in different houses. Pietro was much occupied by the things he had to do—always under the watchful eye of his guards. He shaved off his beard, and had his hair cut after the Frankish fashion. His guards brought him an old Jewish tailor. Pietro explained to him with some difficulty how to cut clothes according to the European modes. It took the tailor a long time to get them right. He could see no sense in the tight fitting pantaloons, or the short tunic, or any of the other things that Pietro ordered. But finally, the day before the beginning of Lent, they were ready, and Pietro donned them with some satisfaction.

They were, however, the only cause he had for satisfaction. All else was sadly amiss. Pietro had a certain freedom of movement. He was not imprisoned; he could wander all over the city—under guard. The swordsmen who guarded him did not even prevent him from talking with people. They merely insisted that he always speak Arabic, so that they could listen to his words.

In his weeks of waiting, Pietro had discovered many things, the chief of them being the fact that Frederick had launched this most successful of all the crusades while under the ban of the Church! Even here, the Holy Father's long arm reached out to hinder him; every place he visited was immediately thereafter visited by the Papal Legate and placed under interdict. All good Christians feared to come near him.

Why? No one knew. Without fighting, Frederick the Second had accomplished more than any other crusader in history. He had won Jerusalem with a stroke of the pen, and with it Bethlehem and Nazareth. Al Kamil had ceded him a corridor down to Acre with the castles of Toron and Montfort, so that Christian Pilgrims could come and go to the sea.

On his part, Frederick had left in the hands of the Moslems

that part of Jerusalem embracing the Haram Region, with the Dome of the Rock, and the Al Aksa Mosque, among the holiest spots of the Mohammedan faith; he had pledged protection to the Prophet's faithful visiting those shrines, and to a truce of ten years. During this time, he had pledged that he would allow no crusade to be formed in Europe, and to give no aid to the Christian lords of North Syria against Egypt. As to the matter of rebuilding the walls of Jerusalem, that was a moot point; some saying he had agreed not to rebuild them, others that he had the Sultan's permission to do so. . . .

Then, quite suddenly, all the neatly stitched plans they had made came apart at the seams. All—even Pietro's. And with them went everything he had gambled upon; even—possibly, the chance of saving his own life.

Ahmad sent Najmud, his beloved second son, to warn them. His choice of a messenger spoke volumes. That he should have disturbed Najmud's honeymoon, and dispatched him upon so dangerous an errand clearly showed how important he considered it. Pietro knew why Ahmad hadn't sent Harum. The bitterness between the Shaikh and his eldest son had increased to such an extent that Ahmad didn't dare trust his heir.

So it was that the handsome young Najmud stood before Pietro and his guards and delivered the message that was simply a death sentence:

"My father begs that thou be informed of certain necessary changes in all our plans. He hath been told that al Kamil and the Frankish Sultan travel not together; that, further, thus far they have not seen each other. Therefore, he deems it better that Abdul be dispatched to Nablus; and thou, o Pietro, point out the Lord Frederick to thy guards as he rides into the city tomorrow. . . ."

Pietro was sick. He had depended upon the chance of being only with Abdul inside the banquet hall. Now, instead, he would have to die in the streets of Jerusalem, cut down by the swords of his friends. He didn't sleep that night. He paced the floor of his bedchamber and thought. He knelt and prayed. But in the morning the matter stood exactly where it had the night before. Pietro needed a miracle. And he didn't believe in miracles.

He was there early, with his swordsmen nervously fingering

the edges of their blades, among the crowd that waited the Emperor's arrival. In all the black misery that rose up from his heart, one single gleam of hope shone: Late the night before, Pietro had summoned the old Jewish tailor, sending two of his guards to drag the trembling, pitiful old man from his bed. Pietro had stormed at him in Arabic, swearing that he had made costly errors in the clothes. In a fine excess of rage, he had even struck the old man. As the tailor fell, Pietro caught him, and whispered in Hebrew: "Send thy sons to the Sultan at Nablus! Warn him that the assassins seek his death!"

Then he straightened up shrieking: "Dog and son of a dog, father of unspeakable filth—thou pig of an ancient Jew, get thee hence!"

The guards grinned in real appreciation at his tirade. But just before he shuffled from the room, the tailor gave Pietro a broad wink and a quick smile. By 1229, every Jew left alive in Jerusalem was a practiced conspirator.

Pietro could take comfort from that, and from the fact that al Kamil of all the recent caliphs since Salah-ed-din, had dealt most kindly with the Jews. No Jew wanted the man who had protected their lives and property slain, to be replaced by one of the fanatics who hated them. The tailor had sent his son. Pietro was sure of that.

But, as he stood there waiting by the East Gate, he was sure of nothing else. He could see Frederick's retinue now, from afar off. They wore no armor, because he could see no flash of arms in the sun. But they were brilliantly clad in bright colors, and banners fluttered above them. He could even hear faintly the martial music, and the deep voiced hymns of the German knights and the pilgrims.

Pietro stared around him. In that crowd were bearded Greek priests, with huge silver crosses swinging from their girdles; swarthy Maronites; Jews clad in their blue *shubas*; Moslem *kadis,* wearing the white turbans of the *hadj*; and palmers leaning on their staves. But no one who could help him. No man trained to arms who was not of the camp of his enemies. . . .

No one even, he thought bitterly, with a sword that I might wrest away by surprise and duel with these murderers. The only excuse for a weapon here is that palmer's staff. . . .

His eyes narrowed a little, staring at it. The staff was stout, gnarled. A blow from it, well delivered. . . .

The procession was closer now.

But I'll need time. If I were to point out to them the wrong man as the Emperor . . . But that man would surely die . . . Still, better that, than Frederick. Better some unknown knight, who holds not the destiny of Empire in his hands.

The procession was almost upon them.

"Which?" the Qā'id growled.

But it couldn't be an unknown knight, Pietro realized miserably. Even these Mamluks would realize the difference in the richness of the dress.

Then his eye fell upon Herman of Salza, as bejeweled as any king, more imposing than Frederick, older.

"Him!" he cried, and as they eased out and away from him, he snatched the gnarled staff from the palmer so quickly that that worthy pilgrim fell. But, as he struck the stones, he howled. One of the swordsmen half turned but Pietro brought the knotted staff crashing down upon his head so hard that not even his turban prevented his being felled to the ground. The other three fell upon Pietro.

But by now, Pietro had much skill in fencing, and the staff was longer than any sword. He held them off, parrying their strokes, too busy to get in a telling blow, knowing how it would end; then, seeing, at a nod from the captain, two of them break off from the fight and slink once more toward Herman, he cried out:

"Beware, Herman of Salza! They mean to kill the Emperor!"

Frederick saw the two Saracens pressing the unarmed European. He made a quick gesture with his hand, and five great German knights thundered down upon them. In three minutes it was over: Pietro leaned upon his staff, panting and triumphant without so much as a scratch. All four of the terrible Mamluks were dead in the street, and Frederick, Emperor of the Romans sat upon his mount staring in pure unbelief, into the face of his friend.

"Pietro!" he got out. "I thought you dead!"

Then he leaped down from his horse, and embraced Pietro, kissing him upon both cheeks.

"Again you have saved me!" he said. "I told you our lives are linked. You are my guardian angel. But who are these madmen, you fought?"

"Mamluks," Pietro said tiredly, for the reaction had him now —never until the hour of his death would he be free of his hatred of killing—"sent by the Ayyubites to slay you and the Sultan. . . ."

"Has the Sultan been warned?" Frederick demanded.

Pietro shook his head.

"I don't know, Sire," he whispered. "I tried to get a message through to him; but whether or not it was sent I do not know. . . ."

Frederick turned to a young Syrian knight.

"Ride this hour to Nablus," he ordered, "and acquaint his Majesty with what has happened here, and with the danger confronting him. Spare not thy horse—ride!"

The Syrian was off in a thunder of hooves.

There was no time for questioning now, even for talk. They rode in stately silence to the very courtyard of the Church of the Holy Sepulcher. No bells rang. None of the Christian populace came to greet them. No priests.

Frederick dismounted. Pietro and Herman of Salza followed close behind him. Then they all went into the dark church. The Emperor led the way to the white marble tomb under the cracked dome, and the Greek priests followed him, as though they would prevent him if they dared.

The German knights held tapers in their hands. Frederick knelt before the closed tomb, and all the others knelt with him. Pietro stared at this square of marble, for whose possession so many thousands of men had died. He supposed he should have felt triumph at Frederick's victory, reverence at the resting place of Jesus before His Ascension. He felt exactly nothing. He knelt before a block of stone, and saw a block of stone—nothing more. He was sorry for the emptiness of his heart, but he was himself. One day he would learn contentment with that fact.

Then Frederick got up and went to the altar opposite. There

was a golden crown upon it. But there were no priests, no bishop, no one to officiate, since Gregory had placed his interdict upon every spot upon which Frederick's foot trod.

Slowly the Emperor lifted the crown and placed it on his own head.

"In the Name of the Holy Trinity," he said quietly, "I, Frederick the Second, by Divine Mercy, Emperor of the Romans, forever Augustus, and King of Sicily, announce that I am henceforth King of Jerusalem."

No one moved. No one spoke.

Then Herman of Salza made a brief speech about their obligations to the Emperor and they all left the Sepulcher. . . .

As a mark of his favor, Pietro was quartered with the Emperor and Herman of Salza at the house of the Qā'di Shamsu 'Din. There a great feast was spread before them, and Frederick insisted upon the Moslem amirs attending.

"This day," he told them, "is the beginning in the Holy Land of peace between Moslem and Christian. May it be as lasting here as it has been in Sicily!"

Pietro was consumed with the desire to talk to the Emperor, to question him about Elaine; but there was no chance for that. Immediately after the feast, they began a tour of the city, led by the Qā'di. They passed through the Via Dolorosa to the great wall of the Temple enclosure. Towering above that, they could see the gilt Dome of the Rock.

Pietro thought that Frederick was a little excessive in his praises. But this was diplomacy, at which the Emperor was past master. Pietro had to admit that beauty of the Al Aksa Mosque merited any praise that anyone could offer it. The delicate columns erected by the first crusaders were still in place. Frederick set the example for his knights by removing his shoes as was the custom. Then he climbed the marble *minbar* or pulpit from which the *hadj* taught the faithful.

Pietro saw his face grow red with sudden anger. He dashed down the stairs to the doorway. A Christian priest stood there, holding the Scriptures in his hand, and begging alms of the knights.

Frederick sent him sprawling with one blow, and stood over him roaring:

"You viper! Don't you know that here even we are only the vassals of the Sultan al Kamil? Not one of you is to pass the limits fixed about your churches!"

They returned to the house of Shamsu 'Din that evening, and Frederick climbed the stairs to the roof in order to hear the muezzin call the faithful to prayer. Pietro and Herman went with him, and the three of them stood there a long time, waiting.

Frederick turned to Pietro.

"Go get me the Qā'di," he commanded.

When Shamsu 'Din appeared, Frederick put the question to him directly.

"Your slave forbade them," the Qā'di whispered, "for fear of offending our illustrious guest . . ."

"You were wrong to do that," Frederick said mildly. "There was no need to alter your customs for my sake. Even in my country you could hear the muezzins' call to prayer. And no one forbids them there. . . ."

That night, finally, Pietro had his chance.

"Of course I'll take you back to Italy," Frederick said. "You still must beget sons in order to keep the parallel . . ."

Pietro shook his head. He was beyond speech.

"And Elaine?" he whispered at last.

"She is well, though she misses you sadly. I've visited Hellemark, and she received me most graciously. I even cast about for a new husband for your lady, but she begged me not to. Twice widowed, she said, was enough."

"Thank God!" Pietro said.

Seeing how moved he was, Frederick changed the subject, and began to talk lightly of his own affairs.

But almost at once they were interrupted. A servant of the Qā'di appeared with a messenger pigeon in his hand.

Frederick took the scroll and read it, then passed it to Pietro.

It was from al Kamil. The attempt had been made upon his life, but he had been saved by the warning. The assassin had fled into the desert. He feared that balked at Nablus the *fedawi* would come to Jerusalem to try to kill Frederick. . . .

Frederick looked at Pietro. Pietro shook his head.

"The Sultan is wrong," he said. "Those drugged murderers are beyond so intelligent a thought. I'd wager he'll hide near Nablus, seeking a second chance. . ." He stared keenly at the Emperor.

"My Lord," he said, "May I ask of you a boon?"

Frederick nodded.

"Give me leave to seek this man out. He was once my slave, and a devoted, manly fellow, of whom I had grown fond. I would try to take him alive that some skilled leech might restore him to his senses. . . ."

"Granted!" Frederick said gaily. "What's more, I'll go with you, and take along an hundred knights. I owe the Sultan a favor. Besides I weary of solemnity—a day or two of such sport—good! Go tell Herman to prepare the men. . . ."

After two days, they gave it up. To find a lone man in the desert was like looking for another grain of sand. Then, upon a sudden impulse, Frederick decided to ride into Nablus itself to visit al Kamil. Despite all the correspondence between them, the two rulers had never met.

Pietro was riding slowly, sadly behind Frederick, thinking of poor Abdul, dying by now of hunger, of thirst in that trackless waste, when he saw something odd in the crowds that stood in Nablus' street watching them pass. He had to look again before he saw what it was. A young man, clad entirely in white, with a bright red girdle about his slim belly. Into the girdle were thrust two curving poinards. The man's eyes glittered strangely, in his oddly familiar face.

Pietro's nerves tightened. He broke from the procession. But even when he was close, he wasn't sure.

The man did look like Abdul. But not enough. For one thing, he was clean shaven; and though that was a thing easily accomplished, it didn't account for the extent of the difference. He turned back into line.

White robe. Red sash. Two daggers. Red slippers . . . There was something hellishly familiar in all those details. . . .

Pietro looked again over his shoulder. The young man had

broken from the crowd and was racing toward Frederick's horse, the two daggers ready in his hand.

Pietro whirled his mount, galloping at a diagonal between the Emperor and the assassin. When he was close enough he rolled from the saddle, and landed on his feet, already tugging at his sword. But he couldn't get it out. The borrowed weapon was stuck fast in its scabbard—rusted there. The assassin came on, the two poinards lifted.

Then suddenly, surprisingly, he stopped.

"My Lord," he whimpered. "Pietro—My Lord. . . ."

The flank of the German knight's warhorse thrust Pietro aside. The sword lifted, fell; but Abdul, the now shaven Abdul, his face so changed with whatever madness the Shaikh al Jebal inspired in his followers that Pietro had been unable to recognize his former slave, leaped aside so that the stroke slashed open a part of his neck and shoulder, but failed to kill him.

Pietro got to him first as he fell, covering Abdul's body with his own.

"Please," he begged; "he is drugged, and mad—spare him. . . ."

Frederick, shrugging off those who would restrain him, came up at a gallop. He stood up in the stirrups, staring.

He raised his hand against the knights who came riding up with drawn blades.

"No," he said, "take the Saracen into yonder house and question him. Take him up, Sires!"

Two big German knights lifted Abdul's slight form between them. From the expression on their faces, Pietro had no doubt of the method of questioning they proposed.

"Please, Sire," he said to Frederick, "let me question him. He was once my slave. He will speak to me without the necessity of torture. . . ."

Frederick stared at him.

"You've owned slaves in this land?" he said. "Then you have risen here as you did in Italy—as you would in hell itself, I have no doubt. You have our permission—come. . . ."

They laid Abdul on a diwan. He was bleeding fearfully. He would not live an hour, Pietro could see that.

He knelt beside the diwan.

"Abdul," he called quietly, "Abdul. . . ."

Abdul opened his eyes. His voice, when he spoke, was surprisingly strong.

"Yes, Sahib?" he whispered.

"Why, Abdul? Why would you kill a man who had not harmed you? Whom you had not seen in all your life?"

"Because my master, the Shaikh al Jebal—ordered it . . ." Abdul said.

"On pain of thy death?" Pietro said.

"No—no, Sahib—death, I seek . . . once more to die—to regain Paradise!"

Pietro stared at him.

"Explain this hard saying," he said.

They listened carefully. Abdul weakened fast and talking did not help him. What they had of him was strange. Unbelievable. He had died, he told them, at that banquet that he and Pietro had attended, of poisoned wine. And he had awakened in Paradise. In a place where there were trees the like of which he had never seen before, and fruits of strange and delicate savors. Where the flowers grew larger, brighter than on earth, and the fountains sprayed wine instead of water. Strange birds sang in the trees, and haunting melodies came from everywhere, nowhere, played by an orchestra of Djinns—or angels. . . .

And the gardens had silken tents in them, carpeted with samite, and pools of perfumed water upon which flowers floated. And there were—maidens. The loveliest maidens of all the world, naked and fair, disporting themselves in the pools, or running about the garden in garments made of the mists of moonlight. . . .

He himself had been clad in silks, like a prince. He had eaten of delicacies beyond description. And whenever he had desired one of the maidens, she had come joyfully to his bed. . . .

"I—I never tired," he whispered; "I—I had the strength of ten!"

But he was tired now. He was dying. Happily. With joy. With anticipation.

For, when he had awakened one night and looked around to see which of the maids lay in the crook of his arm, he had found himself alone. In rags. In an unknown street before a filthy hovel. For three days he had starved. On the fourth, he had knelt before passersby, begging to be slain that he might regain Paradise. Then the Shaikh al Jebal had reappeared.

"He offered me Paradise again. If—if—I would slay—whomever he wished—He gave me *hakash* to eat, and strange wine—so that I dreamed—of the trees, of the pools—of those maidens. . . ."

Frederick turned to Pietro.

"Mad," he said.

But one of the Syrian Lords shook his head.

"No, Sire, not mad. He has been taken to Alamut, the Eagle's Nest, and robbed of his soul. Thus does the old Shaikh recruit his murderers. He hires them out to the great lords of this land. They almost never fail, since they have no fear of death, since, indeed, they seek it . . ."[3]

They left Abdul there. His life could not be saved in any event. And if it were, they would have to hang him. He was in no great pain. To let him die after this fashion was a kindness.

They rode along in silence. Pietro was thinking of the fate he had escaped. He was very glad he had escaped it, but he was still curious about the whole thing. Would he have been able to resist the wine, the delicacies, the maidens? He didn't know, but he doubted it profoundly. He had no great opinion of his strength of character.

But Frederick didn't leave him to his thoughts long.

"The matter of your slave interests me," he said. "Though I have been much occupied with weightier things, it has occurred to me that you have a tale to tell, Pietro. How did you come to have slaves? How did you discover the plot against me so well and so cleverly that you were at the right place at the right time to prevent it? And why, by Satan's horns, were you unarmed?"

"Because," Pietro smiled, savoring the moment, "I was a part of the plot against you, Sire. I was to play Iscariot, and point you out to them. . . ."

Frederick stared at him.

"Now, what the devil?" he growled. "This has much need of explanation—tell me!"

Thereupon Pietro told him.

Frederick threw back his head and roared. The other knights stared at him. Speechless, his face streaked with wildly mirthful tears, Frederick beckoned to Herman of Salza.

"Herman, by God's love," he gasped, "listen to this! Tell him, Pietro!"

Pietro repeated the tale.

By the time he had finished this time, Frederick's laughter had subsided.

"Fools," he chuckled, "to try to use for treachery a son of that Island wherein deceit itself was born! Much do I love thee, Pietro. The Sultan, too, must hear this tale. I don't doubt but that he'll reward you richly, as I also intend to, once we reach home. . . ."

"Sire," Pietro said, "in return I beg that you acquaint me with what has passed with you and with Sicily since last I saw you both. . . ."

Frederick frowned. Then he began to talk very quietly. Of his capture and execution of the very Saracens who had sold the stolen children of the children's crusade into slavery. Of his many wars.

He had completed the subjugation of Sicily. The Saracens had been moved to the mainland, and given a town of their own, Lucera, complete with minarets, mosques, and kadis. They had accepted their defeat, and become the most loyal of his subjects. His household servants and the soldiers of his guard were all Moslems.

He had been twice widowed. Constance of Aragon had died in 1222. In 1225 he had married the youthful Isabella of Jerusalem, at the Pope's suggestion, by which means Honorius had tried to bind him to his Crusading oath. And last year Isabella had died in childbirth, but his son Conrad had lived.

He talked of his conversations with Saint Francis of Assisi, dead since 1226, and already canonized in 1228.

"And deservedly so," Frederick said gravely. "He was a true Saint. I tried to tempt him with the loveliest of my Saracen handmaids, and he only smiled and spoke so gently to her in rebuke that she wept. He discoursed upon my soul, and believe me, Pietro, that for four days I was on the verge of repentance. If he had not died, he might have made a godly man of me. . . ."

He sighed. Then he smiled again. He spoke with some pride of the Diet of Cremona, of his founding of the first secular university in Europe, the University of Naples, of his new order, The Teutonic Knights, of his regulation of the exchange of food-stuffs, of new taxes. . . .

"But I had one misfortune—gentle Honorius died two years ago," he said. "Since that time I've had to deal with Gregory IX, that same Cardinal Hugo of Ostia from whom I took the Cross. He is Innocent's image. He plagued me so much, that in the summer of 1227, I assembled my hosts for the Crusade. But pestilence broke out among us—and more than half my forces died. I had put out to sea when I, too, was struck down. When I returned to port, and put myself under the care of my Saracen leeches, His Holiness branded me a liar, said I was not ill, that my preparations were a farce, and excommunicated me!"

He came back to the subject of the crusade. It had delighted the dark humor in him to sail to liberate the Holy Places while still under the Pope's ban. Gregory had forbidden him to sail until the excommunication was lifted. But he had sailed anyway in June, 1228.

"The rest you know," he said; "except perhaps that His Holiness' troops are attacking me now in Sicily. He, who is forbidden by the highest law to condemn or slay, has struck down my troops with the edge of the sword! I shall sail within the next week, and you will go with me. Then we shall show this war-like prelate what war means. . . ."

They had come by now to the tents of al Kamil's camp, which lay on the other side of the town—indeed, some distance beyond it. There the sentries delayed them, to give the Sultan time, they afterwards discovered, to prepare a suitable welcome.

Pietro who knew Eastern potentates, was not surprised at the splendor of the repast that Malik al Kamil spread before them. But the others were. Even Frederick. The Emperor, however, was much too astute to show it. After the feasting, the talk ranged over every topic, conceivable and inconceivable, under the sun. It was a long time before either of these great rulers deigned to mention the recent attempts upon their lives. Thereupon, of course, Pietro had, for the third time, to tell his tale.

Al Kamil smiled at him. It was a slow, thoughtful smile.

"So," he murmured, "al Muqtafi is the root of this tree of evil, eh? That will be attended to. . . ."

"Great Caliph of Allah," Pietro said, "by the merciful and compassionate God, I beg you to be lenient with him. He was kind to me—and he entered into this thing most reluctantly, under the pressure of others. . . ."

The Sultan's eyes were thoughtful.

"I will spare his life," he said finally, "but of his treasure, the greater part will be forfeit. Tell me, Sire Pietro—what was this reward Shaikh Ahmad promised you? We have there, I think, a most interesting point. . . ."

Pietro held back a groan. Not even Frederick had thought to ask him that. It was, he thought, a point better kept hidden. But the Caliph was waiting.

"I asked of him," he whispered, "the slave girl, Zenobia—whom my Lord has cause to remember, for 'twas she that Shaikh Ahmad married before thee rather than deliver her up as thou didst request. . . ."

"Of course!" the Sultan laughed. "She of the *Saqr's* eyes! Thou hadst courage to request such a one of him, Pietro."

"Ahmad hath divorced her, my Lord," Pietro said; "but truly I want not the maid. 'Twas a ruse, merely, to lull Ahmad's suspicions. . . ."

"Ruse or not," al Kamil said clearly, "thou shalt have her! Upon that condition shall Ahmad's life be spared. . . ."

"But, your majesty—" Pietro wailed.

"Silence, Pietro!" Frederick thundered. "Our Royal Host has dealt most graciously with thee!" He turned to the Sultan, and smiled. "Our noble vassal is shy," he chuckled, "but he accepts!"

Pietro looked at Frederick. Clearly the Emperor considered this the best, the most delicious joke in all the world. But then the Emperor didn't have to deal with Elaine, and Pietro did. The worst of it all was that nothing he could say would make the slightest impression upon Frederick. To that half oriental monarch, the idea that a woman's emotions had to be considered in such a case, bordered on the ridiculous. Nor would the plea that the Church forbade polygamy trouble him. What the church forbade had never troubled Frederick in the slightest.

Pietro argued with him about it all the way back to Jerusalem. To his plaintive cry, "What will Elaine think of it, Sire?" the Emperor responded only with great gales of laughter.

"So long a Moslem," he grinned, "and still unable to manage a *hareem*, Pietro?"

I, Pietro thought miserably, will never get any sense into him on this score. I'll have to dispose of Zenobia—as kindly as I can. Even that will take time—too much time. . . .

But even after they were once more at Acre, preparing to sail, Pietro was no nearer a solution to his half comic, half tragic dilemma than before. The only hope he had was that the caravan bringing Zenobia would be somehow delayed until after they had sailed.

Therefore he was consumed with impatience at the delays that followed. But Frederick wouldn't budge until he had loaded his elephant, his giraffe, his blooded mares, with a few stallions to service them; his hunting leopards—and a score of divinely beautiful slave girls, gifts from al Kamil.

The Emperor loaded, too, another gift—from some fair Syrian maid: Frederick of Antioch, another natural son, now but two months of age.

They paid another quick visit to Jerusalem and Frederick amused himself by visiting all the forbidden places of the Moslems. Upon the cupola of the Sakhrah Mosque, he read aloud the inscription:

"Salah-ed-din cleansed this temple of the polytheists."

"But who were the polytheists," Frederick asked, knowing full well what the Saracens meant by that term.

The kadi with much embarrassment explained that the Christians with their three gods in one, were the people that the writing meant.

"And that grille?" Frederick pointed.

"To keep out the sparrows, my Lord. . . ."

"Yet," Frederick laughed, "Allah hath loosed swine among you!"

Pietro gasped. He knew well that the Saracens called all Christians swine. . . .

Some of the Moslems had no great opinion of the Emperor. Of his short stature, one of them sneered, seeing him fair, beardless, small:

"If he were a slave, I wouldn't give two hundred drachmas for him!"

Frederick only laughed and went his way.

As they set out once more for Acre, there came a letter from the Sultan, inclosing a note he had received from the Knights Templar. "Now," they had written, "is your chance to seize this blasphemer of thy Holy Places and Ours!"

Frederick, Pietro knew, would never forget that—nor forgive the Templars. Nor would he forgive Pope Gregory, who had attacked him at home, sent his legate to proclaim interdict upon the very stones of the Via Dolorosa, and finally upon the Holy Sepulcher itself. Men crossed themselves, grew pale and whispered:

"Sancta Maria! What has come upon us? He hath laid the ban upon the Tomb!"

Then on the very morning of their departure, the caravan arrived from Cairo. Frederick was already aboard the galley with the elephant, for the mighty beast pleased him, and the dancing girls, having left Bailian of Ibelin as bailiff to administer his lands until he could send out officials. Pietro was with him, when two eunuchs brought the heavily veiled figure aboard.

"Let me see her!" Frederick roared. But Pietro, could hear the low, muffled sobbing behind that veil.

"Please," Zenobia whispered. "By the Holy Mother, no, Pietro! Do not unveil my face!"

Her voice was strange. It was so changed that he scarcely recognized it.

Frederick was in high good humor, and indulged Zenobia her whim. Pietro took her to his cabin.

"What ails thee, my love?" he said gently.

She moaned. The sound was of pain. Actual, physical pain.

He put out his hand toward that veil. She sprang up shrieking: "No, Pietro! By the love I bear you, no, no, no!"

"Why, Zenobia?" Pietro whispered.

"My face!" she sobbed. "My face—oh, dearest God—my face!"

"Let me see," Pietro got out.

"No—I cannot—I can not watch you—you, o Lord of my very soul—sicken at the sight of the horror I've become. . . ."

Pietro put out his hand and took the veil. His grip was gentle, but firm.

"Don't fear," he began, then very gently, he unwound the veil. It was yards long, but he got it off finally. The ends of it, the part that was inside, was sticky with a fragrant salve—with blood.

Someone had thrown oil of vitriol in her face.

He stood there, trying to speak. He couldn't. He was afraid he was going to retch. He didn't want to do that. He must not hurt her.

She stood there, her eyes big with horror, searching his face. For repulsion. For loathing. For the first hint of rejection.

"Harum?" Pietro whispered.

"Yes."

"May Shaitan torment his soul forever," Pietro swore quietly, terribly, "in the deepest pit of gehenna, in lakes of endless fire. May he feed eternally upon slime and utter foulness and his bowels dissolve within him may he drink brine and blood until his tongue swells and chokes the screams that could in some measure ease his pain. . . ."

Her gaze never wavered from his face.

"But thou, o Lord of my life," she whispered; "canst bear —seeing this . . . ?"

Slowly Pietro smiled. Then he kissed the twisted, hideous, pain-ravaged mouth, holding his body hard against the shudders that rose inside him, against the convulsion in his guts.

It was the kindest thing he'd ever done. And the bravest.

"Cover my face, My Lord," she whispered; "thou needst not look upon it again. For now will I serve thee, all the days of thy life—as thy handmaiden merely, and be glad merely to be near thee—who art so wondrously kind. . . ."

He sat there, holding her hand until at last she slept. And even in sleep the little whimpers of pain came through. They went on and on, until he couldn't bear it any more.

He went up on deck. There was music there, and laughter and dancing, as the hawsers were cast off. The great oars moved, took up their beat. As they pushed off from the quay, men standing in front of the butcher's quarters threw entrails and refuse down upon them.

Pietro stood there, with his back turned toward where Frederick laughed and drank among the Saracen maids. He watched the shore of Syria slipping away behind them.

His body loosened suddenly. He had to grip the rail to keep from falling.

Dear God, he thought.

Then he straightened up and stared defiantly at the sky.

But all he could hear was the white gulls crying, and the muted wash of the sea.

Chapter Twelve

STRANGELY ENOUGH, the voyage from Acre to Brindisi was one of the good times in Pietro's life. The sea was calm; the winds were favorable, though light, and the nights aboard were filled with revelry.

Pietro took little part in the drinking, dancing, and gaming; and none at all in the wenching. His whole time was occupied with taking care of Zenobia. She seemed quite resigned to the total destruction of her beauty. All the old fire he had expected of her was gone out of her now. She was very quiet, very gentle.

Frederick, once he had of Pietro the story, did everything in his royal power to make Zenobia comfortable. He put his personal physician, a wise Saracen trained both at Cordoba and Alexandria, at her disposal. He sent fruits and cakes and wine daily to the little curtained enclosure that served her as a cabin within Pietro's quarters. And he demanded of Pietro a daily report of her progress.

Which, sadly, was slow. The leech, being an honest man, admitted that there was little he could do. He applied the soothing salves, and changed the bandages. The rest, he said, was up to Allah.

Her face, when it healed finally, was much less bad than Pietro had expected. But it was bad enough. The lines of scar tissue crisscrossed it like highroads on a map; and the lower left side, where most of the vitriol had struck her, was so drawn by the burn, that she had, at first, difficulty in closing her mouth. She mastered that again, by slow and painful effort; but her speech remained blurred, thick, difficult to understand like the speech of an idiot child. . . .

Yet the voyage was one of the good times. It was pleasant to be with Zenobia. As soon as she was able she began waiting upon Pietro, doing the small, loving services of bringing him things, fruit, and plumes and parchments and ink for the memoirs of his Saracen adventure which he was writing for the Emperor, sitting at his feet and watching him with her tender eyes. Above the veil she wore even while sleeping, they were lovely, now that the fierceness was gone from them. What was between them now was a very good and gentle thing, absolutely without passion. Zenobia, who had known the passions of many men, could not conceive of the idea that any man could want her now that her beauty was gone; and she was endlessly and touchingly grateful to Pietro for merely being kind to her.

As for Pietro, living in close proximity to Zenobia, he was often reminded that a woman's beauty was not entirely a matter of a lovely face. Veiled, wearing the flowing garments of the *hareem*, Zenobia was still something. She was slender and very graceful. Her figure was very fine.

But he put such thoughts out of his mind. He had now some chance of reestablishing his relationship with Elaine. Before, to have returned accompanied by a slave girl would have been ruinous; but since Zenobia's tragic misfortune, it no longer needed to be. No woman on earth—and least of all Elaine—would consider Zenobia seriously as a rival once she had unveiled her face.

He wondered about Elaine. He remembered all the bad times with her. Then he remembered the good times, too: the time she had saved his life, when she could so easily have delivered him up to Enzio; the times she had come to him in the night with great passion and great tenderness; the way she had whispered: "Don't go, My Lord. . . ."

There is, he decided, no perfect happiness in this world. Perhaps with patience and with time he could make of his marriage an acceptable substitute for—he tried to stop the thought, but it plunged into his mind—for, he phrased it bitterly, the joy I might have had with Io.

Iolanthe, the one bright star in the darkness of my days. The one whole real joyous memory in all my Via Dolorosa. Io who taught me what love was from whom I had a happiness unmatched in heaven whom I loved in a way and to a degree unknown to mortal man. A man's life is seldom what he expects and never what he wants, but I have had that. If I had died at Enzio's hand under torture or been slain in Egypt upon the Crusade or had died trying to save my Lord Frederick my life would have been complete still, for I had had that. I had her love the like of which has been unknown upon earth since the day when the Sons of God came down and consorted with the daughters of man. And having had that love nothing can bow me down, nothing break me to my life's end I shall be able to stop time, hold off death for a little while merely by conjuring up the image of her face. Such a good face. So sweet. So sure. And that love I had of her. That big, fine, titanic passion with no fakery in it, no pretense being of her the way she was uncomplicated unquirked absolutely clean and fine wanting me with her body too because her mind and her heart wanted me and I wanting her in every way in all ways so that there was nothing apart from her and without her life did not exist does not exist and I live on like some disinterred Lazarus called back into life trailing behind me clouded memories of Paradise and yearning to return again. To go back. Only there is no way back. No road.

He bowed his head and Zenobia came up behind him and stroked his forehead very gently with her soft hands. He was glad she was there. It was good not to be alone.

It took them more than two months to crawl—like the big water spiders that galleys always reminded Pietro of—from Syria to Italy. They sighted the shore line late on the evening of June 9, 1229, and hove to until morning.

Pietro did not sleep that night. He couldn't. His mind veered back and forth like a shuttlecock, alternating between elation and despair. How would Elaine receive him? Silently, with contempt. In rage, swearing she'd hoped him dead. With—with joy?

He dared not hope for that. And, as he went ashore that morning of June tenth, he had no idea how long it would be before he could see Elaine again. For in mainland Sicily, Frederick's prospects were blacker than the bottomless pit of Hades.

Some few loyal nobles still clung to him: The Lords of Aquino, Chief Justice Henry of Morra, the Regent Reginald of Spoleto; and the Saracens, since Frederick had generously given them a nostalgic slice of their homeland in the township of Lucera, had come to love the Emperor with all their hearts.

Pietro hated fighting; killing still induced a sickness within. But between him and Hellemark lay the armies of the Pope. Between him and Elaine.

Pietro saw the utter astonishment in the faces of the crowds on the quay when the Imperial Standard was unfurled. He heard the whispers run from man to man:

"It's he! It's he! They lied! He is not dead. The Emperor lives. . . ."

Then in scattered bursts, rolling together, lifting skyward in one long drawn-out roar like thunder:

"Long live our Emperor! Victory to Frederick, Augustus!"

Frederick rode among them smiling, stopping graciously to pat the head of a child held up to him, to give his blessing to men and goodwives and youths and maidens who pressed forward to touch his imperial person.

Although Pietro did not know it, they had already won. Frederick's appearance was enough. Men flocked to his standard, and at the head of a growing army, Frederick II marched upon the armies of the Pope and the Lombard League.

Marched, and that was all, or nearly all. For the most part, the armies of the Holy See failed to make a stand. The terror of Frederick's name was enough. Other factors: horror at the perfidy that had caused the vicar of God to spread false rumors of Frederick's death. Believed, they had won Gregory half-hearted adherents; completely disproved, they proved a two-edged sword that smote the hand which held it. Bad leadership among the Papal forces by men who knew little of war. Bad food. Pay long in arrears. In vain the Papal legates seized the church treasures of Monte Cassino and San Germano to pay the troops.

At the sight of the armor of Frederick's hosts flashing in the sun, they ran like sheep. Like rats.

The rebellious towns of Lombardy fell to the imperial supporters in the North. In four days, two hundred towns declared for him. The last to resist, the town of Sora, was overwhelmed in one wild charge, led by Frederick in person. After its surrender, he burnt it to ashes, ploughed up the streets, and sowed salt, as was done to Carthage of old.

The captured traitors who had hoped for elevation by Frederick's fall, were elevated upon especially lofty gallows. For their treacherous attempt to betray him in Palestine, Frederick seized all the goods and treasures of the Templars in Sicily. This done, he sat down to begin the tedious business of negotiating a truce with Pope Gregory.

And Pietro was free to ride home without having so much as bloodied his sword.

He rode northward toward Hellemark at the head of a retinue of twenty knights, lent to his service by Frederick himself. Squires led his snow white Arabian stallion, and the three equally snowy mares that Frederick had given him in order to establish a line of fine horses on his fief. Another squire led somewhat fearfully, although they were muzzled, two cheetahs, hunting leopards, on the end of long chains.

Pietro and his retinue were all gorgeously arrayed, and the banner of Rogliano floated once more above him in the warm July breeze.

The gatekeeper recognized him at once and opened the gates; his jaw opened wide, staring in speechless astonishment at Zenobia's veiled figure. In the bailey, Manfred, the seneschal, stood talking with Waldo and Rainaldo when Pietro rode in. The two knights had both grown fat with sloth since that day that al Kamil had graciously released all the prisoners taken at Damietta—a gesture that had done Pietro no good since Shaikh Ahmad had already taken him to Cairo by then. . . .

All three of them stood as though transfixed, then they all hurled themselves upon him, kneeling in the dirt, kissing his stirrups and crying.

Pietro dismounted and, raising them up, kissed them gravely

upon their cheeks like equals. He had to blink back his own tears. The love his retainers bore him was a fine and moving thing.

"My Lady?" he whispered.

"Is upstairs in the palais," Manfred said. His glance fell curiously upon Zenobia. "I'll go—"

"No, good Manfred," Pietro said; "I'll go unannounced. . . ."

"My Lord," Rainaldo said, and his gaze, too, swept speculatively over Zenobia's form, "grant us that we may accompany you. I would see her face at the sight of you."

Something in his tone caused Pietro to look at him. A note of something very like bitterness. Mingled with exultation. A man, Pietro thought, might speak thus at the prospect of witnessing the humbling of a hated foe.

But Rainaldo's face was calm, expressionless.

"Very well," Pietro said. Then, in Arabic: "Come, Zenobia."

They tiptoed up the stairs. The door was open, and Pietro stood in it with Zenobia just behind him, staring over his shoulder. Elaine sat in the great chair, sewing. Pietro saw, with a sense of shock, that she had aged; but he saw, too, that the aging had lent graciousness where it had stolen beauty.

"She hath missed thee, My Lord!" Manfred whispered.

But Manfred's whisper was the croak of an old warrior, and it disturbed Elaine. She turned. The hand holding the needle, stopped in midair. Her face paled by slow degrees until it was absolutely colorless. The blue eyes widened in it endlessly as though they would eclipse her face. They were filled with something—something like terror? Pietro didn't know.

She got up very slowly from the chair as he came toward her. She stood there looking at him without moving. Without speaking. Without, he saw, even breathing.

He put out his arms to her.

She didn't move.

"So," she said, and her voice was brittle, "even the Saracens could not rid me of you!"

"Elaine," Pietro whispered.

"I thought you were dead. I'd hoped you were."

Pietro nodded toward his knights.

"Leave us," he said.

Manfred, Waldo, and Rainaldo, went back down the stairs.

"Elaine," Pietro got out, "by God's love. . . ."

But she wasn't looking at him. She stared past him at Zenobia.

"Who is this?" she whispered. "No, don't tell me! You dared do this, my Lord? This upon all the mountains of your sins? To bring your concubine here into my house! Oh, dear God! Why did I not die that night?"

"She," Pietro said tiredly, "is not my concubine. She has never been—else I would not have brought her. . . ."

"You lie!" Elaine spat. "You lie, you lie, you lie! But I'm glad. Because now I can throw into your teeth what otherwise I might have hidden! I have betrayed you, my Lord! Not once but many, many times. And in this only have you the advantage, that I have not brought my lover here to confront you as you have brought your Saracen whore!"

In a little while now, Pietro realized, it is going to hit me. In a very little while. But I'm numb now. I can't think. I can't even feel. . . .

"Andrea?" he whispered.

"What does it matter?" Elaine said. "Him or another or perhaps a score of different men? All that matters is that you and I are even, my husband—even and quits!"

Pietro looked at Zenobia. She was standing there, her eyes flashing back and forth between the two of them. She knew no word of Italian; but she had long since caught the drift of this.

"My Lord," she said, "show her my face. Then I think there will be no further cause for quarreling—over me. . . ."

Her voice, speaking, was sad. The saddest thing, perhaps, in all the world.

Pietro nodded.

"We're not even, Elaine," he said quietly. "Look. . . ."

He lifted the veil.

Elaine took a backward step. The pupils of her eyes dilated until all that there was left of the irises were thin rings of blue. Her hand rose unbidden to her own face, the fingers moving, touching her fair unmarred flesh, as though seeking reassurance.

Pietro let the veil fall.

"Dear God!" Elaine whispered. "Pietro tell me—what happened to her face!"

"Oil of vitriol," Pietro said sadly.

"And you brought her with you—looking like that? Why, Pietro? I'm trying to understand this thing. In the name of God's sweet mother, why?"

"Because this was done to her because of me. I was a captive—later a slave in the employ of a great Shaikh . . ." He went on with his tale, speaking very slowly, very clearly, watching her face, seeing the emotions mirrored there changing, disbelief fading, comprehension showing a little in her eyes, and finally, in spite of herself, pity.

Like everyone else beneath God's sun, Pietro thought slowly, she is not unmixed. She is capable of great evil, but also of great good. She has always been so: Scorning me at the first with bitter words—then saving my life. Calling me the child of the dungheap, marrying me at the Emperor's command, hating me with black hatred and yet loving me wildly, gloriously, tenderly, between. . . .

"I will have the maids prepare a chamber for her," Elaine said. "She can stay here with us as long as—"

She stopped suddenly. Her blue eyes were enormous. He could see the sickness in them. The fear.

"With us," she repeated bitterly. "I said—with us. But there is no longer any—us—is there, My Lord? I have given you grounds to cast me out of your house—even to slay me. There is not now a question concerning this poor maid. The real question is—What does My Lord propose to do—with me?"

Pietro stood there, looking at her. It was characteristic of Elaine that she made no attempt to deny her words, swearing that she had lied out of anger in order to wound him. She was too proud for that, as she was too proud now to do anything but stand there facing him, asking nothing of him, not even mercy.

He could feel the sickness moving inside him now. It was bad. It was very bad and all the complications involved in his relationship with Elaine didn't make it any better. He was married to this woman in the first place because he hadn't been able to marry the one he wanted. He had married at Frederick's command because he dared not mock the savage, childish superstitions that drove that great man. Those being the reasons for his marriage, presumably, he should have felt neither love for Elaine, nor any pain at her betrayal.

But he did. Both love and pain.

I, he thought bitterly, have loved this woman nearly all my life. In spite of Io. Less than Io, of course; but still I have loved her. Singleness of mind and heart are not of the nature of man. The Saracens order these things better with their *hareems* and legalized polygamy. Now, what? She has betrayed me. She has committed adultery, with Andrea, no doubt; perhaps even with others. And for that I must cast her out—even kill her.

Why? Because she has wounded my vanity? We try so hard to deny facts, to avoid seeing people as they are. I was away eight years. God, in that stretch of loneliness a saint would have been brought to bed out of the mere, insistent clangor of the body's needs! Eight years. I am her husband, and must judge her for a sin that I, myself, am guilty of. I have possessed Zenobia—many times. I was ashamed of it. My body bears the marks of the chains with which I scourged myself. But in the words of Our Lord, who am I to cast this first stone?

"Do you," he said gently, "want that it be again—us?"

She didn't move. Or speak. She stood there, swaying a little.

"You," she whispered, "you can forgive—this?"

"If," Pietro said, "you can forgive me for leaving you unguarded from either danger—or temptation—and for mine own sins. . . ."

"Forgive you," she said, "I?"

Then she came forward in one wild rush, and threw herself into his arms.

Behind them, Zenobia turned away her face. She didn't want Pietro to see the tears in her eyes. She needn't have bothered. Pietro had forgotten she was alive.

Those next three years cancelled out for Pietro, Baron Rogliano, half a lifetime of grief. His eyes lost their brooding look. He laughed often, and freely. Having finally received his inheritance from Isaac, he built some two miles from the castle, on high, well drained ground, the villa he had dreamed of. It was of grey stone, with pointed Gothic arches, and tall windows of leaded glass flooded every foot of the interior with light. There were great fireplaces in every room against the winter's cold, and the central court had been transformed into a paradise of flowers. It was roofed over with glass, and there Elaine kept her birds.

Pietro sent to Sicily, even to Africa for new and lovelier species. The birds twittered and sang, and displayed their gorgeous plumage.

Inside the rooms the furniture was carved and gilded, and covered with soft cushions. Pietro had a *diwan* made after the fashion of the Saracens. Tapestries adorned the walls, not on fete days merely, but every day of the year.

Zenobia had made most of the tapestries. She was very skilled at needlework. Her presence at the villa was the one disturbing factor in Pietro's life. True enough, Elaine treated her with rather indifferent kindness, and the servants loved her—never having seen her face. But her life was empty. She tried valiantly to fill that emptiness with her needlework and with learning Italian which she mastered in a year and a half to such an extent that Pietro had to listen hard now to even catch a trace of an accent. The indistinctness that clung to her speech because of her drawn facial muscles, probably hid some of the foreign shadings that might otherwise have colored it. Still, all things being considered, she spoke Tuscan remarkably well.

What disturbed Pietro about her most was her gentleness. Remembering her fire—even the fierceness with which she had lashed out at her tormentors in the marketplace, it seemed to him that she was allowing herself to be defeated by life. He was very kind to her. But as attractive as she was in her new European garments, with her ravaged face concealed, he wasn't even tempted by her. For Zenobia, sitting before the spinning wheel or the loom, or helping Elaine cut flowers in the garden, life had come to a stop. It's a pity, Pietro thought, but there's nothing I can do. . . .

He hunted with his leopards, which struck terror to the hearts of all the serfs; he loosed his falcons after birds. He sang songs of his own composing to Elaine. He was almost happy.

Almost. Except that there were unfathomable things at times in Elaine's eyes. Sometimes, when he turned suddenly, he found her looking at him, her gaze big with terror. With doubt. With questioning. Even with shame. . . .

But she never stormed at him any more. Her lovemaking was ardent. Sometimes, particularly when he returned from the hunt or a journey, she demanded of him more than his tired body was capable of. There was something amiss. Something he couldn't put his finger on. But he didn't let it trouble him too much. Whatever it was, he was quite sure, it existed only in Elaine's mind.

In the evenings, nobles from near and far gathered at Alamut, for Pietro had named his villa after the Old Man of the Mountain's perilous paradise. Knights from Frederick's garrisons at Hellemark and Roccablanca came too, for Pietro had surrendered his castle to the Empire without a qualm.

The nobles, many of whom clung to their cold, drafty, uncomfortable castles, largely because they lay in such places that Frederick had no need of them for fortifications, wondered at the comfort, cleanness and beauty of Pietro's home. But when their wives began to demand one just like it, they answered out of the relentless logic of conservatism:

"But, my dear, it couldn't be defended. What good is its beauty if any envious Lord could burn it about our ears?"

Their ladies could, and probably did, point out to them that under Frederick Second, petty wars between the Barons had entirely ceased; that Italy enjoyed a peace and prosperity unknown since the time of the Caesars.

"But after he dies?" the Barons argued.

"Pray God he never dies!" their ladies said.

With that prayer, Pietro was inclined to agree. He knew Frederick's faults and weaknesses: the lusts that had already produced four bastard princelings, Enzio, Frederick of Antioch, Richard of Theate, and this very spring of 1232, Manfred, by the lovely and talented Bianca Lancia;[1] his towering arrogance and pride; his furious impatience; the smiling hypocrisy that permitted him to burn for heresy, when it suited his devious purposes, men much less heretical in actual fact than he. . .[2]

But his sins, grievous as they were, were like blemishes upon the sun. Frederick advanced science two hundred years beyond his time. He ended feudalism in Italy almost completely. A poet himself, under his favor, the brilliance that Innocent had destroyed in Languedoc flowered again in Sicily—for the first time poems were written, songs were sung in the sweet dialects of Tuscany and the Island. The meanest serf enjoyed his protection; the beasts of the field, the birds of the heavens knew his care. He was, Pietro knew, one of the wisest and greatest men in Europe's history, whose fate it was to have been born before his time. . . .

During 1232 and 1233, Pietro was often away from home. He visited Frederick at Foggia, and took for him diplomatic missives to the Court of France. There he met, once more, Gautier, now Baron Montrose, grown stout with contentment, the father now of three tall sons. They spent many happy hours together talking over old times, and parted with sadness, both of them knowing they would never see each other again.

Upon his return, Pietro noticed at once that the oddness of Elaine's behavior had increased. The change was very slight, so that a less sensitive man would not have noticed it. But Pietro was nothing if not sensitive. He couldn't put his finger on it exactly. She was as devoted as always. As tender.

Perhaps—a shade more so. He had the feeling she was trying to please him. Trying too hard. At night she came to him a little too eagerly. In the morning there was a trace of redness in her eyes as though she had been crying. But he never caught her at it.

Sometimes he felt her great blue eyes upon him, watching every motion he made. If he turned quickly, she dropped her gaze; but not before he caught that expression of—of near terror.

What on earth is she afraid of? he wondered. But he didn't ask. He was a slave to certain aspects of his nature: his sensitiveness, his unwillingness to give hurt.

She will tell me, he thought. It's only some minor matter—like our failure to have a child. . . .

His preoccupation with Elaine's queer behavior prevented him from noticing for a long time that it was shared by other members of the household. By Manfred. By the maidservants. Even by Zenobia.

When finally he did see that, he was greatly troubled. He looked at Waldo and Rainaldo, but they avoided his eyes.

There is, he raged inwardly, something wrong here! What if Andrea. . . .

But that was not to be borne—not even in thought. He had forgiven that before because before he was equally guilty. But he had forgiven it in the silent understanding that there was to be no more of faithlessness—either on her part or on his. And he had stuck to his bargain. Io lived not twenty miles from Alamut, but Pietro had avoided riding any road where they might meet even by chance. He did not trust himself that far.

But, if during his many absences, Andrea had found means to— The dear, sweet, deep blue eyes of God! Forgiveness had to end somewhere. Beyond a certain point it became folly.

His mind was racing. He would get to the root of this. Alone. Without shaming himself by asking aught of others. It would be very simple, really. All he had to do was—

To go to Elaine and tell her that Frederick had summoned him unexpectedly to Foggia.

She stood up at his words. She caught him to her, and her arms were fierce.

"Don't go, Pietro!" she whispered. "Please, Pietro—please!"

For a moment he was tempted to call the whole thing off, to bask in this most convincing demonstration of love and fidelity. But he saw Zenobia looking at them through the doorway. She shook her head slowly, warningly.

He found time for a word with her before he left.

"Look to your lady, My Lord," was all she would say.

He waited until well past midnight to give them every chance. Then he turned back. When he reached the castle, he found Manfred, Waldo, and Rainaldo dressed and fully armed. Rainaldo had both the hunting leopards on a chain.

"You see, ye German swine!" he shrieked at Manfred and Waldo, "My Lord's no fool! A Sicilian can scent treachery at twenty leagues!"

Pietro stared at them.

"Why are you armed?" he whispered.

"We thought you'd come back, My Lord," Manfred said gently. "But if you did not—"

"What then, good Manfred," Pietro got out.

"We, ourselves, were going to avenge you!" Manfred said.

"Come," Pietro whispered.

They said no word. Sheba and Solomon, the leopards, bounded along beside Rainaldo's horse.

Pietro had mounted another horse, the great black stallion, Amir, son of a long line of stallions by that name that he had bred. The other horse was completely blown, poor beast.

He wondered why he thought about those things. Details. He admired the beauty of the leopards, as they ate up the distance with their graceful bounds. Finally he looked at Rainaldo.

"Where go we?" he said.

"Ruffio's," Rainaldo said.

How much of the stupidity of the deceived, he thought bitterly, as they began that ride, is due to their unwillingness to see?

An hour later, they came up to the inn and dismounted.

"Wait here," Pietro said to the others. Then he pushed open the door to the common room.

Ruffio took one look at his face and was reduced to a quivering mass of fear.

"My Lord," he quavered; "I did not know—I—he forced me at sword's point. . . ."

"Have no fear, Ruffio," Pietro said, almost gently. "That you make your money from the sins of others is between you and your God. I will not harm you. Above?"

Ruffio nodded.

Pietro went up the stairs. Ruffio had but one private room. All the others had four or five beds in them.

Pietro put his hand on the latch. He let it rest there a long time. Sweat beaded on the back of it, shining on the little black hairs on his fingers.

He pushed open the door.

There was a candle on the little table by the bed. It had burnt down to within an inch of its total length. But Pietro could see them.

Andrea of Siniscola lay upon his back with his arms behind his head. He was snoring.

Elaine had turned away from him, and drawn the covers up about her so that only one shoulder showed. Her hair was spread over the pillows. Some of it was beneath Andrea's arm. She whimpered a little in her sleep. She sounded like a child crying; like a lost, frightened child.

Pietro looked at them.

He felt sick. Black nausea curled at the bottom of his throat. He had to grip his teeth together to hold it back. He sat down in a chair, looking at them. The drops of sweat formed on his forehead and ran down into his eyes. They felt like ice. Like brine.

Like fire.

He could hear the beating of his own heart.

The sickness inside him sank down and went away and when it came back it wasn't sickness any more. It was pain. It was bad very bad the worst absolutely the worst rising up in him in shattering waves so that he had to grip the arms of the chair to stay on it. He sank his teeth into his lower lip until he brought blood, thinking that this, the real, the physical would bring him back, that the concrete, the actual would somehow exorcise the unendurable the not to be borne the mindshattering. . . .

It was no good. In another moment he was going to scream aloud.

He stood up suddenly, and drew the poinard out of its sheath. Then he caught it by the point and hurled it blindly without taking aim seeing it whirling through the candlelight end over end feeling not hearing the sound it made as it struck the headboard and stood and quivered in the oaken planking.

It had gone through some of Elaine's hair and pinned her to the bed.

She screamed only a little. Almost quietly.

Andrea sat up. He blinked just once. Then his eyes were black with terror.

"Dress yourselves," Pietro said harshly. "When you come out, Andrea—come with a blade."

Then he backed out of the room, closing the door very quietly behind him.

He waited a long time, listening to the sounds in that room. The rustle of clothing. Elaine's sobbing.

Then, suddenly, there was another sound. He heard the crash of broken glass. He threw open the door. Elaine caught at his arms. He threw her off, furiously. She fell to the floor and lay there, crying.

Andrea had taken the whole casement with him as he leaped. Pietro heard the horse dance as he mounted.

"Waldo!" he roared; "Rainaldo! Manfred!"

Then he turned and ran down the stairs. He didn't look back at Elaine, lying there on the floor, crying.

He dashed out into the street. Then he saw it.

Rainaldo had loosed the leopards.

There is no horse on earth as fast as a cheetah. No other beast on earth. Each leap covered twenty feet.

They caught Andrea at the corner.

Pietro saw Sheba rise up, all four paws spread out. Then she was on the horse's neck, her muzzle just behind his ears, working. He saw her head twist, heard from where he stood the sound of the horse's neck breaking. The horse went down.

Andrea fought clear of the falling beast. Sheba and Solomon crouched, the muscles of their haunches twitching, watching him with their great, yellow eyes.

Pietro came up to them and stepped quickly between them and their prey.

"Chain them," he said to Rainaldo.

Rainaldo bent down and slipped the chain onto their collars. Then he straightened up. His mouth came open. Pietro saw it and leaped aside before Rainaldo got his cry out.

He felt something like whitefire go into his left arm. Then Waldo and Manfred were upon Andrea, twisting the poinard out of his hands.

Waldo had his own dagger out, lifted.

"No!" Rainaldo spat. "No, Waldo! Would you give him so sweet a death?"

Waldo lowered the dagger, and smiled grimly. He held the point of it against Andrea's belly while the others bound him.

Then he turned back to his master, and cut away the sleeve from Pietro's arm. It was bad. The blade had pierced the muscles, ripping them. Pietro couldn't lift his arm at all. It bled frightfully.

They worked very quickly, binding it up. Then Rainaldo went into the inn and came back with Elaine.

They rode back to Alamut. No one said anything. There was something unearthly in that quiet, broken only by the slow-clopping of the horses' hooves.

The knights were looking at him. Waiting for him to speak.

Pietro turned toward Elaine. He moved very slowly, favoring his left arm. All the others stood there watching him.

Andrea's face was grey. His eyes were screaming.

But Elaine's face was very still. Calm. There was no more fear in her eyes. No confusion. Her face was very calm and very still and her eyes were clear. She walked over to where the two knights held Andrea. Then, going up on tiptoe, she kissed his mouth. Slowly. Taking all the time in the world about it. Cherishing it with her own.

The grey went out of Andrea's face. He smiled a little.

Elaine turned back to Pietro.

"Both of us, My Lord," she said.

What was inside of him now was a kind of a tearing. Something caught at his guts and pulled them out and apart. He sweated. His mind was racing at furious speed but the patterns it formed didn't make any sense.

Female. It was Sheba not Solomon who led the attack. It is always the she-thing that is the more terrible. If she had asked me I would have spared him but she is all female and very complete and now she has become very simple and uncomplicated and the thing she has is a great thing in a way very fine. Pride. The pride of hers that has always unmanned me. I must break that now I have to break it or I am defeated finished, she cannot win. I have never permitted torture which is a kind of sickness but by all the fires of seven hells I have that sickness now and whatever they can do to him will not be enough not ever enough. . . .

He nodded very slowly.

"And your lady?" Rainaldo said.

Pietro stared at him. Rainaldo had always hated Elaine.

"No," he said, and walked away from them. Then he whirled suddenly, his face furious, working. "Make her watch it!" he said.

There was no dungeon at Alamut. No instruments of torture. Pietro hadn't permitted that. But Rainaldo and the others would improvise.

Pietro watched them leading Elaine and Andrea away. But he didn't go with them. He didn't want to watch it. He couldn't.

All his life he had been very kind and very gentle. But what was inside him now was very great and very terrible. War. A legion of fiends battled the angels of God for his soul. He climbed the stairs very slowly, because he was very weak from loss of blood and shock and fatigue.

He had almost reached his chamber when he heard the first scream. It tore into him. He shook under its impact. He stood on the stair without moving. Then he started on upward, hearing Andrea's hoarse, animal cries, unable to shut his ears to them, feeling them in his own guts. Even slamming the heavy door did no good.

I have always hated this, he thought; I have condemned my Lord Frederick for not being in all ways beyond his own century. It is the greatness of a man that he live beyond his times that he rear himself up tall and proud above ignorance and lust and brutality looking ever toward the day when those things shall be no more and this I thought I had. But I have them not, I am a child of this age and in me is this sickness of cruelty and this very bad kind of pride and hurt vanity and sick hate—God, God will they never have done with him? I cannot bear. . . .

(Her hair pillowing his head her bright hair like silver almost and he sleeping there in contentment and peace the lusts burnt out of him and she crying a little because she had not then lost all shame. Her flesh was so white, so white flesh of my flesh of my known hungers given over to him to him— Oh, scream you beast!—How sweet, how pleasant is the sound!)

No. I did this thing this thing which is not of me. I did it because I was not big enough to admit defeat to surrender when I was beaten, to say to him— Take her and go! But now truly am I betrayed and not by Elaine nor by Andrea for no other soul living upon the face of God's earth can betray a man, he alone can do that. I have done it. I have betrayed myself I Pietro di Donati have permitted a thing to be done that never in my life could I watch without retching God forgive me but what the Siniscolas were I have become!

He tore the door open. He was racing down the stairs when he heard it.

"Pietro!" Elaine screamed. "For God's Love, Pietro!'

He followed the sound. They were in the courtyard. He hung there a moment, staring at that thing that had been Andrea of Siniscola. That burnt, broken, bloody thing that lived still.

"Stop it!" he cried. "Release him!"

They stared at him in wonder, but they didn't argue. When they loosed the chains Andrea fell forward on his face.

Elaine ran to him. She knelt beside him. When she looked up at Pietro here eyes were murderous.

He couldn't face them.

As he turned, he saw Zenobia's veiled face staring down at them from the balcony above.

Andrea lived past morning. Pietro's Saracen leech did all he could. But nothing could save Andrea. Nothing at all.

Not even Pietro's prayers.

He was kneeling before the image of the Virgin when Elaine came into the room. He was not even conscious of the bad pain in his arm where the man who had betrayed him had stabbed him, or the ache in his knees. He had not moved from before that altar in the five full hours it took Andrea of Siniscola to die. His lips moved, mumbling the prayers. He was lost to sight and sound and even when Elaine lifted the dagger to the highest peak of the arc he didn't know it.

But Zenobia did. She came up behind Elaine very quickly moving surely quietly well and caught her wrist just before she could bring that blade whistling downward. It was not until they had both fallen to the floor that Pietro heard them.

He turned slowly. He saw the two women thrashing about on the floor. He started toward them, but he wasn't quick enough. His legs were too stiff from the hours of kneeling. He had lost too much blood.

He saw the blurred tangle of motion stop. One of the women stood up.

Zenobia.

She stood there panting, looking down at Elaine. Pietro followed her gaze. Elaine's blue eyes were open. But they didn't see anything. They would never see anything again. Pietro stared uncomprehendingly at the hilt of his own Saracen poinard protruding from her left breast.

He stood there a long time, staring at it until it dissolved. It and the room and Zenobia and last of all Elaine drifting off very slowly into a thick grey mist and from somewhere far off and very faint he heard Zenobia scream.

When, a full forty-eight hours later, he regained consciousness, they had to tell him about it. How Elaine had tried to kill him. How Zenobia had saved his life.

And Pietro, Baron Rogliano, went so nearly mad of grief that Manfred and Waldo and Rainaldo had to bind him to his bed, and take hourly turns at watching him.

But for Zenobia, he might have gone entirely mad. But she watched beside him, and prayed to God for his recovery.

Which of the two things availed him most, her prayers, or her great love for him, he never knew. But one did.

Perhaps both.

Chapter Thirteen

PIETRO RODE SLOWLY along the banks of the Volturno. He was dressed in hunting green, and a hawk perched upon his wrist. A little way before him, the Emperor rode with Piero della Vigna; and all around Pietro and behind him a gay company of lords and ladies, all of them mounted on the fine Arab horses that Frederick had bred, laughed and sang. Moorish slaves held the brachhounds on their leashes; other Saracens held back the hunting leopards. Before them marched Frederick's orchestra, some twenty Negro boys, clad in the most vivid scarlet and blasting away with horn and drum and cymbal.

Some of the courtiers strummed *qitars* or lutes as they rode; others played the viol, or plucked at the lyre. The sun was going down behind the trees and all the air was filled with light, and music and laughter.

So is it always about him, Pietro thought; one could believe that life for Frederick held no element of sadness. . . .

Looking at him now, chatting so gaily with the Chief Justice of the Empire, it was impossible to remember that this interlude at Capua was taking place in the midst of bitter war with the Pope-supported Lombard League. That, indeed, his own son, his eldest, King Henry, was held in prison by him because of an open revolt against the Crown; that so bitterly did Frederick hold this rebellion against his imperial and fatherly authority, that he had taken away even Henry's name and given it to his youngest son born last year, 1236, to his new Queen, Isabella of England. Henry Secundus, the child was called. But not by Frederick. He made no distinction; to him, the imprisoned Henry had ceased to exist.

A certain distance had grown up between Pietro and the Emperor, now. Piero della Vigna, that most brilliant of all jurists, that stylist without peer in the Latin tongue, appointed *Logothetes*—that is, 'He Who Speaks for the Emperor'—was closer to Frederick in all ways than Pietro. But, Pietro had to admit, this coolness was entirely his own fault. Frederick still treated him with great love. It was that the Emperor had become too much a god to suit Pietro any more. But he was still greatly concerned with Pietro's welfare.

When, for instance, Frederick had learned of the tragedy at Alamut and Pietro's lingering illness, the Emperor had come in person to fetch his friend to Capua. Characteristically, he came in full panoply: Ahead of him rode the Negro boys splitting the skies apart with drum and fife. And with him rode the members of his imperial staff. But what came after caused Pietro's serfs to wonder for the rest of their lives: Costly four-in-hand teams drew mighty wagons laden with treasure; richly caparisoned camels bearing burdens were escorted by uncounted slaves gaudily arrayed in silken tunics and linen gear. Leopards and lynxes, apes and bears, panthers and lions were led on chains by Saracen slaves. Even a giraffe ambled along, his head towering out of sight above the trees. Countless dogs ran in and out through the procession. In cages borne on the shoulders of stalwart blacks were hawks, barn owls, horned owls, eagles, buzzards, every type of falcon, white and colored peacocks, rare Syrian doves, white Indian parakeets crowned with yellow tufts of feathers, African ostriches, and finally, the elephant with his wooden tower upon his back filled with Saracen marksmen and trumpeters.[1]

Pietro had been too sick to be concerned with all this vainglorious display. He knew that Frederick always travelled like that—even on the smallest of journeys. He had gone back with the Emperor to Foggia, and afterwards to Capua. He had been glad to leave Alamut. Zenobia would take care of it. He had the feeling that he never wanted to see that villa, haunted by terrible memories, again, as long as he lived.

Afterwards, Pietro had fought in Frederick's wars, served him as counselor. He had witnessed the Emperor's triumph at Cortenuova. And after that, he had marched in the triumphal parade in which the great cart of Milan, its standard-bearing mast lowered, was drawn through the streets by Frederick's elephant. But what had troubled Pietro was the sight of the Podesta of Milan, Pietro Tiepolo, bound upon his back to that mast, and all the other conquered commanders following the *carroccio*, or standard cart, in chains.

Such barbarism seemed to Pietro unworthy of so great an Emperor. But then Pietro was unusually sensitive about barbarism. He had never forgotten his own surrender to it. Or forgiven himself.

Still, since Frederick set the pattern for the whole Empire, in him it was bad. It ranked with the superstition that had made the Emperor refuse to consummate his marriage with Isabella, sister of Henry III of England, upon their wedding night. He had waited until the middle of the next day, until a certain hour that the seer, Michael Scot, had determined as being propitious, and handed her over to her women with the remark that she was now pregnant with a son. He had, that same day, written an announcement of this fact to her brother, King Henry. And the damnable part about it all, to Pietro, was the fact that she was!

Riding along behind Frederick now, Pietro felt very tired and very old. Not that he was old, really. In that fall of 1237, he was still not quite forty-three years of age. But his life had been full of trouble and strife, so that although he and Frederick were exactly the same age to the day, Pietro's hair was streaked with white, while Frederick had not changed noticeably since his twenty-eighth birthday. He had grown stouter, and his auburn blond hair had thinned—that was all. His youth seemed inexhaustible.

Like Io's, Pietro thought. Pietro had encountered Iolanthe once by chance last year, while riding to the hunt. Enzio was with her, so they couldn't talk. But she was one of those indestructible women, whom sorrow and care refine into something very rare. To Pietro she seemed even more desirable than she had as a girl. Her gaze had swept over him, speaking pure poetry.

Ah, God, he wept, if I had had that constancy!

Enzio's eyes had been murderous.

Back to Capua now. To hairsplitting dialectics. To sweet song and verses, the soft, liquid speech of Sicily. . . .

They clattered through the streets toward the palace. Pietro saw the young nobles, Riccardo Filangieri, Ruggiero di Porcastrella, and Landolfo Caracciolo, glancing up at the windows whose shutters stood ajar.

Once I had such youth, he mused, and heat of blood. . . .

Jacopo Mostacci and Rinaldo d'Aquino were gathering in the falcons now to return them to the royal mews. As Rinaldo took the Emperor's hawk, Frederick asked:

"Still you have not persuaded that brother of thine, Tomas, to give over this religious folly of his and come to me?"

And Rinaldo shook his head sadly.

"No, My Lord," he said; "Tomas is bent upon becoming a monk. . . ."

"Too bad," the Emperor said. "I hear that he is the most brilliant young scholar that Monte Cassino has had in years. Such a mind should not be wasted upon the church. I bid thee keep trying, Rinaldo!"

"I will, Sire," Rinaldo said.[2]

Inside the castle, they sat down to a banquet. As usual Bianca Lancia sat at the Emperor's right hand. He had found the cold English queen but little to his liking. She, Pietro guessed, spent her days in the women's quarters in sad silence with her little son. . . .

He has not known such women as I have, Pietro thought angrily. No one could make a mindless brood mare of my Io—or Elaine. They have souls—God gave them to us as companions, and of all Frederick's bad traits, this is the worst, that no soft and gentle mind influences him at all!

At Bianca's right hand, the notary, Jacopo da Lentino, strummed his lute, and began to sing:

"Madonna, dir vi voglio l'amor m'a preso. . . .

"My Lady, I will tell you how love has taken me. . . ."

And me, Pietro thought bitterly, and left me wounded and alone.

Afterwards Rinaldo d'Aquino stood up and commenced his new song:

"For pure love I go so joyfully
That I have not seen
A man who in joy can equal me. . . ."

There was more, but Pietro wasn't listening any more. He didn't want to hear of love. He had known two great loves in all his life and both had crushed him beneath the weight of sorrow too heavy to be borne. He was on the point of rising from the table when the Emperor clapped his hands and the orchestra of blacks began a gay tune.

At once two Saracen maids of surpassing beauty rolled into the room, balancing themselves with indescribable skill upon two enormous balls. They rolled the balls beneath their feet this way and that, always in perfect time to the music, striking their cymbals, and whirling as though they stood on solid ground. They were clad in the thinnest of silks and their young bodies would have delighted a sculptor's soul.[3]

Pietro sank back, watching them. Then he saw a messenger, booted and spurred, being led into the Emperor's presence. Pietro was on his feet at once. The messenger was Waldo, his own knight.

Frederick listened, frowning. Then he beckoned Pietro to his side.

"Yes, Sire?" Pietro whispered.

"Ill news, Pietro," Frederick growled. "It seems that some of your enemies have had the temerity to attack your villa. The swine! Don't they know we do not permit these petty feudal wars!"

"My Lord," Pietro said, "have I your leave to go?"

"Yes—and take with you a detachment of my soldiers, under the command of Ruggiero di Porcastrella. Mind you, Pietro—you are not to give orders to my troops. For if you do, this becomes personal revenge—and that I will not have. I am sending the imperial forces to punish an offender. You ride with them—that is all."

"Yes, Sire," Pietro said.

Frederick stood up and laid his hand gently upon Pietro's shoulder.

"I hope that you recover your Saracen maid," he said gently; "She deserves better of life than she has had. . . ."

Pietro stared at Waldo.

"Yes, my Lord," Waldo said, "a party—led by Enzio of Siniscola. They—they burnt the villa, killed Rainaldo and Manfred—and took Zenobia with them . . . There wasn't even time to summon the garrisons from Hellemark or Roccablanca. . . ."

Pietro leaned forward, clinging to the table. Then he straightened.

"Come," he said.

Pietro and Waldo and Ruggiero rode out at the head of two hundred mounted men at arms. They did not speak. There was perhaps nothing to be said.

How long, how long, Pietro thought, did that serpent bide his time! I expected for years he would try to send assassins against me because of Andrea. But that he'd dare attack in force I never dreamed. . . .

Strange that my heart is so free of rage. Were it only the villa, I'd let it go unpunished. But Zenobia—God knows what he will work against her. For she, too, is guilty of Siniscola blood. . . .

He felt singularly peaceful as he rode along at the head of that glittering band. His mind was at rest. He was going to do what he had to—but no more. He would save Zenobia, but he would not kill. Enzio was safe from him. Every man now living upon the face of earth was—no matter what crime they might have committed against him. Pietro had grown beyond the need of vengeance. He had been purged of hate. He might die himself, but that finally, was the will of God.

Nothing—not even his love for Io was going to make him betray himself, again; no fire in the flesh, no hate, no fear would force him to blaspheme against the Godhead within him; now finally he was simple and uncomplicated and entirely free. . . .

It was only when they were in sight of Loreto some five days later that he permitted himself to express the thought that lay buried in his heart:

I wonder how Io fares—what she will say to this renewed slaughter. . . .

When he saw the little castle at Loreto, he almost laughed. It was no more than a rough heap of stones, its donjon low and square, its walls crumbling.

The black-eyed Ruggiero set to work with great glee. Here was a siege to his liking. He built three sows, and one great ram, commandeering Enzio's own peasants for the work.

They, Pietro saw, fell to with right good will. So much so that he was moved to question them.

"We, my Lord," a great thewed fellow told him, "will dance with joy around any gibbet upon which you hang Sire Enzio! Never have we been more cruelly treated in all our lives as since the day he took over Rocca Campania. Our former lord beat us, 'twas true. But rarely. Sire Enzio beat us thrice daily, and starved us, and took our daughters and our wives. One boon, my Lord—when you slay him—be not in too much haste. It would please our souls to hear him scream!"

It was over the first day Ruggiero got his ram into position. The walls crumbled within hours under its mighty impact. Pietro was first through the breach himself, a demon, a fiend, knowing no fear, taking wounds without even knowing it, slashing his way across the bailey, until Enzio's forces under a tall young knight led a sally that almost drove him back.

Their charge led them to within feet of where Pietro fought, so that he saw the young knight's face. He stopped still, lowered his waraxe, and hung there, staring into those dark eyes that were his own eyes, into that young face that line for line, feature for feature, coloring, everything, reflected his own face like a mirror. His own face at twenty. And in his heart roared that old exulting cry, that Donati had raised so long ago:

"Behold! (Look you upon him! How tall he is—how fair!) Behold—my son!"

He turned to his sergeants.

"That one," he pointed, "is to be taken alive—at any cost!"

Then Ruggiero's men surged through the breach behind them, and it was over. Pietro's sergeants swarmed over young Hans and bound his arms.

Pietro stood there looking at his son, weeping inside his heart at all the wasted years. I had but to ride twenty miles, he thought, and I would have seen him. Then everything would have been different. Io knew—in the marketplace at Iesi, she all but told me . . . Fool, fool, fool—I could have been spared everything—Elaine, the crusade, Zenobia . . . All those years stolen out of my life. But now—God and His angels—now!

The men of Siniscola surrendered sullenly. Down in the bailey the fighting was over. But Pietro didn't see Enzio. That was queer.

He had started for the stairway when he saw him. The last Siniscola alive was mounted on his warhorse, charging for the gates. He made them, and thundered out into the fields.

Then Iolanthe came out of the donjon. For a long time, Pietro couldn't move, couldn't breathe. Then he raced toward her. But when he was close he saw her stiffen.

He turned.

Out of nowhere, a mob of serfs had risen up. They had seized the reins of Enzio's horse. They were armed with pickaxes, spades, scythes, pruning hooks.

Enzio laid about him mightily, but one of them got a pruning hook about his neck and dragged him down.

"Don't look!" Pietro whispered, and sheltered her in his arms.

Afterwards, in the great hall, he sat holding Iolanthe's hand across the table, hearing her voice, low and sad, telling him of Zenobia.

"He meant to ravish her, I think," Io said, "and in that fashion revenge himself upon you. But when he saw her face, he realized how meaningless the act would be. He thrust her from the chamber, and it was then I saw her face. I was glad. Oh, Pietro, Pietro—I was so glad!"

"Glad?" Pietro said, "of what, Io?"

"That I need no longer torment myself with jealousy. For years I've known of the Saracen slave girl. But, they said, like a Moslem you permitted no other man a glimpse of her face so wondrously fair was she! So when I saw the real reason for that veil, my heart cried out with joy. . . ."

She turned aside her face, but he saw the tears gather in her grey eyes.

"Now do I repent me of that joy," she whispered. "Enzio turned her over to his men—that they might have sport of her—I—I don't know yet where she got that dagger from. . . ."

Pietro stared at her.

"Before they had sport of her?" he whispered.

"Yes," Iolanthe said.

"Thank God for that," Pietro said.

He sat there very quietly holding her hands and looking into her eyes. She was more than forty years of age now, and worn with care and sorrow; but he had never seen a more beautiful woman.

He was still sitting there, like that, when they brought young Hans into the room. Pietro had sent them to fetch his son.

He stood up and put out both his arms to the boy.

Hans stood there, frowning, staring at his father.

"Hans, please!" Io wept.

Hans looked at her. Pietro could see the confusion in his dark eyes. The pain. Then very slowly he came to Pietro's arms.

Pietro kissed him, clasping him hard against his chest. Hans stiffened. Pietro turned him loose, stepped back. Hans whirled on his heel and ran from the hall.

"Oh, my God," Io cried. "I told him long ago—I tried to explain to him . . . I've lived all these years in the hope that someday all of us—you, and I, and Hans. . . ."

Pietro smiled. He turned to her and put his arms about her.

"He's young," he murmured. "Give him time. . . ."

Then, very gently, he kissed away her tears.

APPENDIX

Notes

PROLOGUE—*Part I*

1. The *ius primae noctis,* or *droit du seigneur* was a feudal custom of long standing. It persisted in Russia, for instance, almost until modern times. It must be admitted, however, that in most of Europe, it was very rare for any feudal lord to invoke it; but then an interesting narrative is seldom concerned with the usual. An account of the daily life of a medieval serf would be unbearably dull if it cleaved closely to his routine. Durant, in his *Age of Faith* p. 556, quotes three authorities concerning this barbaric custom. The interested reader might find them rewarding.

PROLOGUE—*Part II*

1. Durant, *Ibid.* p. 714, quotes this story as established fact; but Kantorowicz in his definitive biography—Kantorowicz, Ernst, *Frederick The Second 1194-1250,* translated by E. O. Lorimer, Constable & Co., London, 1931 p. 5, speaks of it as rumor. Rumor or not it has many historical precedents; in Bourbon France, the delivery of a royal child was always a court function, attended by the members of the highest nobility.

   The lineage of Frederick II is interesting. He was the grandson of Frederick Barbarossa, and the son of Henry VI, whom history remembers as the German Emperor who held Richard the Lion Hearted for ransom in a castle at Durnstein on the Danube. On the maternal side, his grandfather was the strange and fascinating Roger II (1130-1154) whom Hitti calls one of the "two baptized sultans of Sicily"; Frederick, himself, being the other. See Hitti, Phillip—*The Arabs: A Short History,* Princeton University Press, 1946 p. 174ff. Roger has the great distinction of having introduced the culture of silk into Europe. He was, of course, a Norman of that great Hautville line founded by Tancred. Frederick's mother, Constance, was half Norman and half Sicilian.

   Thus Frederick gives us history's most convincing demonstration of the triumph of environment over heredity; by blood one half German, one quarter French, and one quarter Italian, he was the most Italianate prince who ever lived. A polylinguist like many Sicilians of his time—he spoke seven languages and wrote nine; he failed even to learn German until he was nearly grown.

CHAPTER ONE

1. In the days of the Hohenstaufen emperors, Sicily was a twin kingdom, including not only the island, but the toe, heel, and part of the calf of the Italian mainland.
2. A taren was a coin minted at Brindisi under the Norman kings. One taren equalled twenty grains of gold. Thirty tarens was one ounce.
3. In his *Deliberatio Super Facto Imperii,* Pope Innocent III advanced these and three other arguments against Frederick's election as Emperor. His real reason was to prevent the union of the German Empire and the Sicilies which would have surrounded the Papal States with secular and possibly hostile Kingdoms. See Kantorowicz, *Ibid.* pp. 19-20.
4. Waiblingen was a Swabian town owned by the Hohenstaufens. From the time that Conrad III of Swabia began the Hohenstaufen dynasty, the princes of Staufen mountain (High Staufen—Hohenstaufen) were opposed by Duke Henry of Bavaria and his Uncle, Welf, or Guelf. When Duke Henry refused to acknowledge the election of Conrad as Holy Roman Emperor, the Hohenstaufens besieged him at Weinberg, and for the first time in history, the battle cries: "Hi Welf!" "Hi Waibling!" rang out. These cries crossed the Alps, and translated into Guelf and Ghibelline, became respectively the names of the supporters of the Papacy and those of the Empire. The fact that Innocent III first supported Otto of Brunswick, a Welf, against Frederick, before Otto betrayed the Papacy probably accounts for the transition; but none of the contemporary accounts gives any convincing explanation of it.
5. Mosheh Maimon, called by Europeans, Maimonides, was the greatest of Jewish scholars. Born in Moorish Spain, he later became court physician to that chivalrous Kurdish-Syrian Sultan Joseph, whom historians to this day with persistent error, insist upon labelling Saladin. (The Sultan had many titles, among which was Salah-al-Din; a partial list of them follows: al-Malik al Nasir al Sultan Salah-al-Din, Yusuf. A rough translation would be: the conquering king, the bountifully religious Sultan, Joseph.) While at the Sultan's court in Cairo, Maimonides wrote the famous Dalalat al-Ha'irin, usually translated as "A Guide To The Perplexed." In it he tried to reconcile Jewish Theology with Moslem Aristotelianism, and thus opened, probably, the conflict between science and religion. For instance, he explained prophetic visions as psychical experiences, a view with which most modern psychiatrists would certainly agree. He also propounded an atomistic theory of creation.

CHAPTER TWO

1. Water wheels of this ancient pattern, consisting of one horizontal wheel, the spokes of which project beyond its rim and engage the spokes of another wheel set vertically in the well, the vertical one having buckets attached to its outer rim to lift the water, the whole rig being turned by a

blindfolded camel, are still in use in Egypt. The author took motion pictures of two of them near Luxor in the spring of 1951.

2. This was necessary, because the bow of the terrible arbalist was not of wood but of spring steel. No man could bend it by his arms' strength alone. Tintoretto's celebrated painting of the attack on Constantinople by the Crusaders in 1204, clearly shows a soldier winding an arbalist into the cocked position with the two handed winch. But Tintoretto obviously knew nothing of the workings of the great crossbow, because his soldier does not have his foot in the anchoring stirrup with which the head of the arbalist was fitted! Without pressing down thus with all his weight, it would be quite impossible to wind one. The steel bow was at once the chief virtue of the medieval crossbow, and its greatest weakness. Once cocked, it could send its quarrel or bolt through a shirt of chain mail with ease. Its bolt would pass entirely through the body of an unarmored man and come out the other side. It probably exceeded in muzzle velocity any firearm up to the age of smokeless powder. But once he had discharged his weapon, a crossbowman was helpless. An arbalist took so long to recock that he could be ridden down and hacked to pieces by the armored knights, before he could fire a second shot. For that reason, the crossbowmen were always protected by men and arms and cavalry.

   Nevertheless, the longbow of that period was seldom used; a puny three foot weapon, its arrows could not even pierce a leather shield, not to mention chain mail. The fine English longbow, five feet of tough yew, with which the English yeoman slaughtered French knights and Genoese crossbowmen alike, firing twelve shots to their one, at Crecy, did not come into use until a century after the close of this story.

   The painting mentioned above can be seen in the Ducal Palace in Venice.

CHAPTER THREE

1. Almost invariably when armor is mentioned, the mental image formed is of the great suits of plate mail with visored helmets which stand in so many museums. Plate armor, however belongs to the fourteenth and fifteenth centuries; its introduction marks the decline of chivalry. Throughout the twelfth and thirteenth centuries, knights wore hauberks—a long sleeved shirt falling below the knees made of double or triple links of fine steel chain, carefully annealed. These hauberks were quite flexible, provided a remarkable amount of protection and were much lighter than the plate mail that replaced them a hundred years later. Witness the fact that a thirteenth century knight was required to be able to leap into the saddle without touching his stirrups, while a fourteenth century knight had to be lifted into the saddle with a winch! A warrior in chain mail, unhorsed, could get to his feet quite easily and fight on; while the walking tank of the next century, once prone, had to remain so until he was killed or some friend or servant lifted him up.

Helmets too differed in the period of this romance from the ones we most often see displayed. The face of a thirteenth century knight was covered, if at all, by a nasal protector—a single strip of metal over his nose. Usually the warrior's face was completely exposed. The thirteenth century helmet was high and conical, and laced to the hood of the hauberk with leather straps.

A third difference was the lance—only ten feet long, and much lighter than the fourteen foot battering rams used by later knights. It was the same diameter throughout its entire length while the later lance belled out just before the place where the horseman gripped it, to prevent it from being driven backward through his fist by the impact.

Hans' reference to polishing his mail reflected a daily duty of a squire. It was a point of pride with a knight that his armor should shine like silver.

2. The political situation in the year 1212 was so complicated as to hopelessly clutter the narrative. Yet an understanding of it is necessary to any clear comprehension of Pietro's situation.

The contenders for the throne had been Philip of Swabia, Frederick's uncle, and a Hohenstaufen of the Waibling/Ghibelline faction; and Otto of Brunswick, a Welf—or Guelf if one prefers the Italian term. Naturally, Innocent III, that most princely of all the Popes, preferred the Welf, in the belief that Otto would not unite Sicily with the Empire, thus surrounding the papacy with secular and hostile states. But the German princes had no use for Otto. He was poor, stupid, and half English—being the nephew of Richard the Lion Hearted, and his brother John Lackland, from whom directly as a result of events related in this romance, the British Barons obtained the Magna Carta—foundation stone of Anglo Saxon liberties. Reluctantly Innocent agreed to the elevation of Philip, but at that moment Otto of Wittelsbach, Count Palatine, murdered Philip for personal reasons.

Weary of civil war, the German princes turned to Otto of Brunswick. The Welf engaged himself to Beatrice, the eleven year old daughter of Philip, in an attempt to sooth the feelings of Waiblings. Innocent, nothing if not a statesman, demanded of Otto and got a free episcopal election in Germany—which no Hohenstaufen, determined as they were to control the Bishops, had ever permitted—the recognition of Sicily as a papal fief, and the cession to the Pope of the March of Ancona, the duchy of Spoleto, and the Matilda inheritance. As a result of these territorial gains, the papacy now cut Italy in half directly across the thickest part of the calf.

In 1209, in Rome, Innocent crowned the Welf as Otto IV, Holy Roman Emperor.

Almost at once, the Apulian Barons, led by Diepold of Schweinspeunt, Count Acerra, induced the stupid Welf to repudiate his promises to the Pope. Diepold had been Frederick's guardian after Markward of Anweiler's death, and recognized the force and genius of the most remarkable young king in all European history. Diepold knew that as long as Frederick was alive and free, ultimately a way would be found to overturn so unintelligent an antagonist as Otto, and with him all those treacherous barons of Apulia and Sicily who had turned against the Hohenstaufen heir. Besides Diepold stood to gain by a Welf victory.

Otto then took back the territories he had ceded to the Pope, made Diepold Duke of Spoleto, and marched to attack Frederick's hopelessly undefended stronghold in the Island of Sicily. Frederick had no army. The Arabs of Sicily were in revolt against him as were the Sicilian Nobles; the fifteen year old king held only his palace in Palermo, and was reduced to keeping a galley readied at Castellmare ready to flee to Africa.

But Otto and his supporters had underestimated one of the greatest, most unchurchly statesmen in history: Innocent III. Innocent sent a letter to the German Bishops beginning: "it repenteth me to have created man . . ." for in a real sense Otto IV was the Pope's creation. He hinted that Otto would soon be excommunicated, and promised to release the Welf's vassals from their oaths of fealty; he made suggestions. The Bishops talked to the secular princes, who had little love for Otto anyway, and the first stirrings of revolt began.

Then the Pope wrote the great Capet, Philip II, "Augustus," King of France. Philip Augustus had reason to fear the nephew of his greatest enemy, King John of England. Otto had a treaty with England—had spent his youth there—had frequently threatened war upon France. Innocent repeated certain threats that Otto had made against France.

Frederick, without knowing it, had powerful backers by the autumn of 1210. So, when Otto invaded the Tuscan Patrimonium, Innocent excommunicated him, releasing his followers from their oath. This bothered Otto not at all. He proceeded to march down Italy, through mainland Sicily—for all the lower part of Italy was part of the Sicilian kingdom in those days—until his hosts stood in Calabria—the very toe of the Italian boot, ready to cross over and seize Frederick—this by September 1211.

But Innocent's diplomacy had won. That very month, the German Princes, influenced by King Philip of France, met at Nuremberg, deposed Otto, and named Frederick King. The Welfs of Germany did Otto his greatest disservice by sending messengers imploring him to return at once. This was the worst thing Otto could have done, but he was too stupid to see it. His one chance lay in seizing the person of Frederick, and either killing him or holding him prisoner—in which event the new election would have become one of history's scraps of paper. There did not exist in September 1211 a force that could have prevented Otto from accomplishing this—except only Otto's own clouded mind, his superstitions and his fears. In panic he turned and fled, crossing the Alps in midwinter, and arrived in Frankfurt in March 1212.

Frederick was free—and Emperor if he could reach Germany without being murdered. And the status of all the Welfs in Italy had changed, as men like Count Alessandro well knew. . . .

3. In 1202, in an effort to unite the Papal fiefs of Aragon and Sicily, Pope Innocent negotiated a betrothal between Frederick, then eight years old, and Sancha, the young sister of King Peter of Aragon. Part of the bargain was for Peter to send Spanish knights to free Frederick from the domination of the Germans under Markward of Anweiler. But the plan failed, and the betrothal was cancelled. Then, like many a fairy tale, the negotiations were resumed, to result in Frederick's being engaged not to the lovely Sancha, but to her much older sister, Constance, widow of the King of Hungary. Constance was ten or more years older than Frederick. The fourteen year old King objected violently, until Constance promised to bring with her five hundred Spanish knights—with whom Frederick knew, he could put down the rebellions that flamed all around him. Constance arrived in August 1209, and the wedding took place. But at the very start of his campaign against the rebellious Sicilian Barons, an epidemic struck down nearly all of the Spanish knights, including Count Alfonso, the Queen's brother. Yet, without their aid, Frederick succeeded in quelling the Barons—at least for the time—and winning back from them at least a part of the crown lands they had seized.
4. Such behavior was not uncommon. Love rarely entered into marriage at all, which was usually arranged by parents and guardians for the sole purpose of uniting important fiefs. As a result, human nature being what it is, every important tale of troubadour or trouvere is of illicit romance. Custom permitted freedom of relationships between men and women that would shock even our sophisticated age: a lady thought nothing of visiting a strange knight, who was a guest at the castle, while clad in a filmy night-robe, and sitting upon his bed chatting with him. If a visitor was of high enough rank, occasionally the wife and daughters of his host joined in removing his clothing and giving him a complete bath. But it must be remembered that these customs were almost entirely free of any sexual connotation. They reflected the idea that much could be permitted high born persons above stooping to dishonorable behavior. And to the credit of medieval man, be it said that such trust was seldom abused.

Of course there were many irregularities—a maid of twelve wedded to a scarred baron of forty in order to connect two great landholdings, should not be too greatly blamed if she turned an attentive eye upon a fair young squire or page near her own age. There are records of husbands and wives who winked at each other's affairs the better to enjoy their own.

Iolanthe's mannerisms and boldness are based upon careful research. In the thirteenth century many a maid took the initiative in affairs of the heart. Custom permitted her, for instance, to declare her love openly for a young knight in a tourney by throwing him a gage—often without even having been formally introduced. Only those wandering singers, the troubadours, trouveres, jongleurs, were really skilled at the arts of love; the average knight was inclined to be bluff, and lacking in finesse, awkward away from the chase and war—no wonder that oftener than not the first suggestion had to come from the desperate maid. . . .

A reader interested in a detailed account of the morals and manners of the thirteenth century should consult William Stern Davis' *Life on a Mediaeval Barony,* Harper and Brothers, 1923, particularly pp. 98-103.

5. The thirteenth century was one of the beardless periods of history—at least among the nobles. There is no accounting for fashion. Anyone with a flair for minor speculation might more profitably concern himself with why in our own history, the colonial fathers were clean shaven and the men of the Civil War period thickly bearded. . . .
6. The Teutonic tribes of the Northern countries, by centuries of conquest and migrations, had made blondeness common among the nobility of most European countries. To the thirteenth century mind it was almost impossible to associate beauty with dark hair or a swarthy complexion. Durant, *The Age of Faith* p. 832 tells how St. Bernard struggled through an entire sermon to reconcile, the "I am black but beautiful," of the Song of Songs with the tastes of his times.

CHAPTER FOUR

1. Education in the early part of the thirteenth century was almost entirely in the hands of the church. University training almost presupposed a religious career. Even the word 'clerk' was used somewhat as we use the expression 'clergy.' But already, throughout Europe and especially in Italy, the secularization of education that was to reach its peak with Frederick's founding of the University of Naples in 1224, had begun.
2. The church attempted to forbid marriage between people of even the seventh degree of kinship, but this proved unworkable, as even godparents were reckoned as kin. The Lateran Council of 1215 made marriages between cousins of the fourth degree invalid; but even this proved difficult, as the great houses of Europe were all too often connected by blood. The church had good reasons: the desire to consolidate family fortunes would have produced a startling degree of inbreeding if it had not been forbidden. See Davis, *Ibid.* p. 101.
3. In 1193, Philip Augustus married Ingeborg of Denmark. As was the case of all—or nearly all royal marriages—this was purely political. The King endured Ingeborg for just one day. Before the year was out, he persuaded a council of French bishops to grant him a divorce. Pope Celestine III would not confirm the decree. In 1196, in open defiance of the church, Philip married Agnes of Meran. But now he had the great Innocent III to contend with. Innocent commanded him to take Ingeborg back. When he refused the mighty Pope placed all France under Interdict. Philip was stubborn, threatened to turn Mohammedan; but the people, after four years in which no mass was said, began to fear for their souls and grumble at the King. Philip reluctantly disposed of his beloved Agnes in 1202, but

kept poor Ingeborg imprisoned under barbarous conditions until 1213, when he recalled her from the castle at Etampes to his royal bed.

4. In the thirteenth century, all over Europe, the church was shaken to its foundations by the discovery through the Crusades, that another great religion existed, which had produced great men like the Sultan Joseph, called Saladin, and the great philosophers, Avicenna and Averroes. Arabic freethinking slowly worked its way through the European masses, and the growth of a delight in logic made the manifest absurdity of many of the church's basic tenets clear to an ever widening part of the general population. In Languedoc, men argued for the idea of a Creator, indifferent since the hour of creation to what happened to his creation (which in the light of twentieth century genocide, and Buchenwald and the Russian slave camps makes much sense!) leaving it to natural law, thus neatly taking care of miracles by showing them to be quite impossible. Lea, *Inquisition in the Middle Ages,* Vol. I, p. 99. At Paris, transubstantiation was denied—Coulton, *Five Centuries,* Vol. I, p. 345. The great skeptic, David of Dinant, who taught philosophy at Paris, even entertained Innocent III with his subtle disputations. He must have been clever, because he was not burned. Lea, *Ibid.,* Vol. II, 319.
5. Abu'l-Fath Umar Khayyami ibn Ibrahim, known to us as Omar Khayyam, was one of the greatest medieval mathematicians and scientists. His *Algebra* made a partial solution of cubic equations, has been called the peak of medieval mathematics. His calendar, calculated in 1074 for the Sultan Malik Shah, was more accurate than ours, though only slightly so —it required a day's correction over a period forty years longer than the time that ours necessitates correction. And of course, Umar was not a tentmaker, any more than an American named Smith is necessarily a blacksmith. As for the Rubaiyat, it seems to have been a casual amusement of the great astronomer; but FitzGerald's paraphrase is held by scholars to be a remarkably accurate rendition of the spirit of the original. Though only 49 of FitzGerald's quatrains can be found in the original, Persian authorities, writing only a century after Umar, speak of him as being a freethinker or an atheist.
6. The Qûr'an. The quotation is from one of the earliest of the Surahs, customarily placed near the end of the book, "The Chapter of the Enwrapped," Verses 1-3; the E. H. Palmer translation from the World's Classic Series, Oxford University Press, 1949 Edition.
7. The reference is, of course, to Saint Dominic, one of the greatest of the thirteenth century's minds, founder of the Dominican Order, and with Saint Francis of Assisi, the first to bring into the Church the idea of voluntary poverty that was winning so many converts for the heretics. It was from the Albigensians that he obtained this idea of a return to primitive Christianity.
8. The rites and practices of the Albigensians are taken from Warner, H. J., *The Albigensian Heresy,* London, 1923, Vol. I, p. 80 ff.
9. Milman, *History of Latin Christianity,* Vol. 5, New York, 1860, p. 242.

10. This quotation, unfortunately, comes from no enemy of the Church, but from the Cistercian Monk, Caesarius of Heisterbach. Both Guizot—*History of France,* Vol. I, p. 507; and Coulton, *Life in the Middle Ages,* Cambridge University Press, 1930, report it. However, Caesarius wrote some twenty years after the siege of Beziers. It is to be hoped that he depended upon erroneous reports, or that his memory failed him.
11. Warner, *Ibid.* Vol. II, p. 67 ff. Readers interested in the first Crusade preached against Christians should consult Funck-Brentano, The *National History of France,* "The Middle Ages" p. 276 ff.; Warner, *Ibid*; and Pierre Belperron's monumental *La Croisade Contre les Albigeois et L'Union du Languedoc à La France* 1202-1249, Librairie Plon, Les petits-fils de Plon et Nourrit, Paris; this is especially valuable for the insight it throws on Simon de Montfort, Earl of Leicester—and his brother Guy.
12. The spelling of Arabic terms in English is rather arbitrary. Arabs write from right to left, and leave out all vowels, except when writing poetry or quotations from the Qûr'an, or the Bible. Hence emir can be spelled quite as correctly amir, and sheikh, shaikh. The author prefers the latter spelling as suggesting how the word is pronounced. There is as little justification for pronouncing it "sheek" as there was in casting the youthful Valentino in the role. The word means literally "old man," and is pronounced like the English verb shake, in "to shake hands. . . ."

CHAPTER FIVE

1. Forks had not yet been invented.
2. Trenchers, originally, were great slices of bread upon which the slices of meat were placed. By the familiar process of extension, the wooden, pewter, or silver platters sometimes placed under them came later to be called trenchers; as—to carry the analogy further—a man with a good appetite came to be called "a great trencherman." The original trenchers of bread were seldom eaten, being saved for the poor and the dogs.
3. William, Archbishop of Paris, was one of the greatest of those military geniuses whom the Church itself so often produced in the thirteenth century. He raised his own army of German Crusaders, and crossed the Tarn into Languedoc, shortly after Simon de Montfort and Guy his brother. Joining them before Saint Marcel, it was entirely due to his skill that that city was finally taken in the summer of 1212. The wars against the Albigensians finally ended in 1229, after thirty years of devastation. With the victory of the Crusaders, the high culture of Languedoc, home of the troubadours, ended. Simon de Montfort, who had taken part in the outrageous crusade against Constantinople in 1204, and was noted for both his chastity and his piety—though not for his mercy or his tolerance—was killed finally at the second siege of Toulouse (1218), by—in one of history's rare instances of poetic justice—a stone fired from a catapult aimed by a group of women.
4. While local priests, all too often, preached hatred, the Popes, themselves, including the mighty Innocent III, and Gregory IX, founder of the Inquisition, have an impeccable record of tolerance for the Jews, and often for

the Saracens. From Gregory I to Innocent IV, most of them found occasion to forbid forced conversions, deny the ancient charge of ritual murder, make restitution for thefts, and forbid mob violence. See Durant, *Ibid.* p. 388, for concise résumé of their efforts in behalf of the Jews.

5. Warner; *Ibid.* Vol. II, Chapter X, p. 68 ff., says merely that the city was taken with all types of atrocities following the victory. It is from Lamb, Harold, *The Crusades*, Doubleday, Doran & Co., Inc., New York, 1931, p. 272 ff., that the details were drawn.
6. All accounts of the disgraceful Fourth Crusade are based upon the masterly reporting of Geoffroi de Villehardouin. If the author be accused of judging this affair from the standpoint of our own day, let it be recalled that Innocent the Third excommunicated the Crusaders from the outset, immediately upon learning of their treacherous attack upon Zara, Catholic Hungary's only outlet to the sea, in 1202; His Holiness then sent them absolution on the condition that they return the booty. They accepted the absolution and kept the booty. Hundreds of honorable men went home rather than take part in such villainy; from this it appears that thirteenth century ethical vision was capable of recognizing piracy even when cloaked with religious zeal. We have the account of the outrages against the religious sisterhoods from the pen of Innocent, himself (see Gibbon, *Decline and Fall,* Vol. VI, p. 171). Even when his overwhelming ambition compelled him to accept the reunion of the Eastern Church with Rome, the Pope continued to bitterly protest against the crimes of his crusaders; but, having accepted one fruit of the conquest, he could not resort to sterner measures. . . .
7. The story of the spurious Virgin is from Lea, H. C., *History of the Inquisition in the Middle Ages,* New York, 1888, Vol. I, p. 103.

CHAPTER SIX

1. The charge of the sergeants of Champagne across the bridge over the Marque is history. It turned the tide of battle by giving the French time to get into position. So, too, is the fact that the Flemish pikemen succeeded in dragging King Philip from his horse. Since thirteenth century battles were fought absolutely without science, no one thought it strange that the commander in chief should dash foolishly off in pursuit of personal glory, outdistancing his own guard. The author hopes to be forgiven for taking advantage of these historical facts for the advancement of his plot. It is rare for facts to be so fortuitously arranged.

   Bouvines was one of the innumerable decisive battles of history. Englishmen and Americans owe to it the foundation of their liberties; for, due to it, and the equally great defeat of King John at Poiteau by the French heir apparent, John's position at home was so weakened that the English barons were able to wrest from him the great Magna Carta.

   The statistics of the battle may prove interesting to students of military tactics. It was claimed that only three French knights were killed. This claim, considering the numbers involved was probably low. One hundred and seventy German and Flemish knights were killed outright; five German counts, twenty-five barons, and one hundred and six lesser knights were taken prisoner and ransomed. But before the reader assumes that medieval battles were all but bloodless, let him remember that the villein infantry were so little considered that their casualties were not even counted. Lightly armed, lacking armor, they were helpless before the charge of mailed cavalry, and would continue to be so until the English longbow would come upon the scene a hundred years later. At Bouvines, as in all battles of the middle ages, they died by the thousands.

CHAPTER EIGHT

1. Innocent III died at Perugia, in July 1216. A little while before he had opened the fourth Lateran Council with the words: "With desire I have desired to eat this passover with you before I suffer." He was fifty-six years of age at his death.

He was one of the greatest men of his age, or of any age. He would have made a magnificent king or emperor, a role to which his talents were better fitted than the headship of the Roman Church. The whole of Frederick's conflict with the Papacy—indeed, the Reformation itself, was born of Innocent's lofty conception of the Church's control over every facet of secular life. One quotation suffices:

"As we cross the threshold of the thirteenth century the dream of world dominion, which had died with an Emperor, springs to life again in the policy of a Pope. We come to Innocent III, the proud Roman patrician and trained canonist, who, reaching the Papal chair at the early age of thirty-seven years and profiting by a temporary eclipse of the Empire, brought the Papacy to the summit of its power. This is the Pope under whose rule the Western Church was imposed upon Constantinople, who dared place England and France under interdict, who launched the most successful of the Spanish Crusades, who exacted from the rulers of England, Aragon, and Portugal the surrender of their respective countries as fiefs to be held of the Holy See, and did not scruple first to excommunicate King John, and then, when the culprit had made an abject submission, to set aside the Magna Carta and to excommunicate the Barons by whom it was supported. It was this energetic ruler who cleared the Germans out of central Italy and Sicily, made himself master of Rome, preserved against dangerous opposition the Sicilian inheritance of his ward, the child Frederick, fomented a terrible civil war in Germany, and then made and unmade emperors on terms most favorable to the Roman Church, and finally crushed out the formidable Albigensian heresy in Southern France, and with it the civilization of a brilliant people. . . ."

Fisher, H. A. L.,
Warden of New College, Oxford—

A History of Europe, Houghton Mifflin Company, Boston, 1939, Chapter XXII, "The Pontificate of Innocent III," p. 265.

CHAPTER NINE

1. It is proof of the curious inconsistencies of human nature, that a skeptic and cynic like Frederick was capable of believing in such thundering nonsense without perceiving the contradiction. The fact remains that he was: Upon his marriage to Isabella of England, sister of Henry III, he refused to consummate the marriage until the hour which the astrologers had indicated as the most favorable for procreation. See Kantorowicz, *Ibid.* p. 407.

CHAPTER TEN

1. Afterwards Pope Gregory IX, and nearly as formidable a Pontiff as Innocent.
2. The Arabic is: Zill Allāh 'ala al-aid. Such extravagant titles applied to the Caliphs were not unusual. But as Pietro was speaking only to the Sultan's representative, he offered the usual flattery by calling the amir (roughly general) the shadow of the Caliph, hence the shadow of God's shadow upon earth.
3. Frankistan—the Land of the Franks—hence to an Arab, all Europe.
4. Naffatun—flame-throwing troops. They used naphtha, hence the name, and were clad in asbestos.
5. The writer has been unable to discover the precise difference between the *khojas* and the *hadjis*. The *hadjis* were almost certainly teachers of religious matters, while the *khojas* may have been teachers of law, science, and other secular matters; but the distinction is uncertain.
6. A dinar was worth roughly $2.40.

CHAPTER ELEVEN

1. Mall is our game of polo, played much as it is today.
2. The wedding feast herein described is taken almost verbatim from the description given in Philip Hitti's *History of the Arabs,* the Princeton University Press, 1946, p. 94 ff. It actually took place in 825, in celebration of the marriage of the son of the Caliph al Mamum to the 18 year old Buran, daughter of his Grand Vizir. Even allowing for the Oriental tendency toward exaggeration, it still must have been magnificent.
3. The story of the Shaikh al Jebal, that is, the Old Man of the Mountain, and his *fedawi* (devoted ones) or *hashāshīn* (eaters of hashīsh, a powerful narcotic whence comes our word assassins because of the murders committed by them) is too well documented to leave much doubt that such an organization existed. Marco Polo refers to them, as does many another medieval writer. See: Kantorowicz, *Ibid.,* p. 193; Durant, *Ibid.,* pp. 309-310; and Marco Polo, *Travels,* Vol. I, p. 24.

CHAPTER TWELVE

1. It is one of the major frustrations of historical research that so little can be discovered about the personal lives of certain great figures. Frederick,

for instance, fathered thirteen children. We know the names of all his sons, legitimate or natural. But of his natural sons only the name of one of their mothers is known, Bianca Lancia, mother of Manfred. Of Frederick's one legitimate daughter, all that is known is that she married the Margrave of Meissen; her name has not come down to us. Of his five illegitimate daughters, we know the name of one; Selvaggia who married the brutal Eccelino da Romano. It is a mark of the position of women in Frederick's Sicily, that we know the names of every one of their quite undistinguished husbands.

2. This, and other blasphemies attributed to Frederick remain unproved. Yet everything about his personality indicates that he was quite capable of them. Their source is the English monk, Matthew Paris, writing during Frederick's lifetime. See: Matthaeous Parisiensis, *Chronica Majora,* J. A. Giles translation, London, 1852, Vol. I, pp. 157-158. See also: Sedgwick, Henry Dwight, *History of Italy in the Thirteenth Century,* Houghton Mifflin Co., Boston, 1912, p. 121 ff.

CHAPTER THIRTEEN

1. This traveling menagerie of Frederick's has fascinated every historian who has written about him. The reader is referred to two of the many comments: Stephenson, Carl, *Mediaeval History,* Europe from the Second to the Sixteenth Century, Revised Edition, Harper and Brothers, New York, 1943, p. 440 ff.; and Kantorowicz, *Ibid.,* 310-311.
2. The Tomas referred to was Rinaldo d'Aquino's younger brother, afterwards Saint Thomas Aquinas, the *doctor angelicus* of medieval Catholicism—and the greatest philosophical mind of his century.
3. The acrobatic Saracen dancing girls and their wonderful balancing act are described in Sedgwick, *Ibid.,* p. 120.

EPILOGUE

In closing these notes, the writer cannot resist the temptation to present two brilliant evaluations of the career of Frederick the Second:

"From the cloud of contemporary detraction, the figure of Frederick II last of the mediaeval emperors, emerges temperamental and challenging, to a point of dazzling eminence. He was fluent in six languages, a lyric poet in the warm Sicilian manner, a munificent patron of architecture, sculpture and learning, a skillful soldier, a statesman of infinite subtlety and resource but also of much careless hardihood. A passionate intellectual eagerness carried him into the fields of philosophy and astrology, of geometry and algebra, of medicine and natural history. He wrote a treatise on hawking, which marks the beginning of experimental science in the West, and travelled in the company of an elephant, dromedaries, and other arresting fauna from the tropics. The traditional inhibitions of his age, so strong in St. Louis, were no fetters for a man who had been nurtured amid the clash of race and creed in Sicily and could use and appreciate the Saracen and the Jew, though to gain political support he would burn a heretic as freely as a Dominican friar. The world marvelled at a prince who talked Arabic with his Saracens, supported a numerous harem, and was so detached from popular prejudices as to challenge the common belief in the ritual murder of children by the Jewish community. Had he not, it was rumoured, written a book entitled, *De Tribus Impostoribus,* in which Moses, Muhammad, and Christ were branded as impostors? There was something uncanny in the prodigious energy of this realist in politics, this exquisite in art, this half-Oriental at once mystical and sceptical, this daring revolutionary in method and opinion. His contemporaries called him the Wonder of the World, and so, despite the lapse of centuries, he remains."

Fisher, H. A. L. *Ibid.,* pp. 278-279.

And:

"Posterity, shocked by his morals, fascinated by his mind, and vaguely appreciating the grandeur of his imperial vision, applied to him again and again the epithets coined by Matthew Paris: *stupor mundi et immutator mirabilis*—"The marvelous transformer and wonder of the world."

Durant, *Ibid.,* p. 725.